A DANCE OF DEVILS

MONGOL MOON BOOK 2

BY
MARK SIBLEY

I0707559

An imprint of Galaxy's Edge Press

The views expressed in this publication are those of the author and do not necessarily reflect the official policy or position of the Department of Defense or the U.S. government. The public release clearance of this publication by the Department of Defense does not imply Department of Defense endorsement or factual accuracy of the material.

Sic Semper Tyrannis

Author's Note

If you've read *Mongol Moon* and you're now here at the beginning of *A Dance of Devils* (The Sequel), I want to thank you for sticking with me for so long. As I said in the Author's Note in the re-released Mongol Moon, I tend to write slowly. Therefore, some things in the real world tend to outpace my story even though this world I've created stands on its own.

Just a few reminders about certain aspects of this story that have changed in the real world. The Queen of England has died and Prince Charles has become King. The Marine Corps got rid of its tanks. Russia invaded Ukraine and COVID hit us. None of these are written into the Mongol Moon world. So, if you like Marines with tanks, they will reside within these pages forever.

There was one other aspect from the real world that changed, quite unexpectedly, after I had written it into the story. The US abandoned Afghanistan and along with it, Bagram Air Base. I chewed on this for some time before making the decision to keep it in the story. The whole episode was so counter to what I believe the US stands for and the loss of our service men and women in the Kabul evacuation. I'm still angry to this day, as many of you are. So, with that said, I did keep Bagram in the story as it's set in time before our pull out. However, I did provide what I believe is a fitting bookend to that episode, to tie it off, so to say.

To close out this brief note for you, even though this story occurs in the near past in my world, there is not a week that goes by and at times several times a day on the news or on social media, that the new "Axis of Evil" or whatever you'd like to call it, is mentioned. Russia, China, Iran, and North Korea are still adversaries of the West and our values. They are more and more acting, I believe, in concert and coordination against us. Whether that be militarily, economically, or financially. You need only dig into the BRICS+ to see this.

While my version of the state of world affairs may not occur as written, I do believe that in the very near future, a version that is just as malevolent will come to pass. In the mean time, sit back, grab your favorite beverage, and dig into one possible versions of what could be. And remember, there's no tacos in the apocalypse. Enjoy!

For Shannon

The love of my life. My best friend. This journey isn't possible
without you.

And for Aynslee, Grant, and Mason

I couldn't be more proud of who you've all grown into. The greatest
joy of my life.

ONE

His hands were sticky with blood.

The blood wasn't his. It was never his. But it was always there. Sometimes a congealed rust color and other times dripping bright red.

Tavis Kinley stood in the dirt street of a small village in Afghanistan on one of their unit's patrols. He was alone this time. On other occasions there were vehicles and villagers here with him, and once in a while his wife, Moira, was right next to him as he tried to explain to her what they were doing here.

A growl sounded from the side of the road, where a dog was tugging at something. He didn't look; he already knew what it was. He looked instead at his hands, which now held his rifle, a C8 SFW 5.56mm, made in Canada by Colt for the British Special Forces—specifically the British Special Boat Service (SBS), the sister service to the famed SAS.

He raised the rifle, sealed his cheek to the stock, and looked through the scope, acquiring his target. He hesitated—as he always did. It was just him, the growling, tugging dog, and the small body the dog was tugging at. No matter who or what else was here, the small boy's body was always here, half eaten by the packs of dogs that roamed the countryside.

He slid his right index finger to the trigger.

Boom!

Tavis opened one eye, then the other. The rusting, baby-blue ceiling of the room pulled him from the dream. It wasn't a nightmare any longer. Not every time, at least. Just a routine of sorts.

He felt a hand on his chest.

"Okay, Tav?" Moira's sleepy voice drifted over him.

His brother, Tanner, had pushed together two cots for him and Moira. It wasn't comfortable, but it was better than the floor in this joke of a stateroom. He noted with some surprise that they weren't rolling this morning. The *Shark* hadn't stopped rolling since they'd left Scotland. But the boat hummed and vibrated, so they were still underway.

"Aye, okay, love. Same dream. Happy New Year."

He stretched his still weak legs. Not long ago he had been in orbit on the International Space Station—before he, Pasha, and Joey had been forced to evacuate. Their rough landing in Kazakhstan was the start of a desperate journey across Asia, then Europe, and now hopefully somewhere south of Bermuda, floating on this rusting, leaking, and squeaking tub his brother called a boat.

"The new year was a week ago," Moira said. "You're addled. Perhaps I could help you put that dream out of your mind." She snuggled her body up next to him and purred like a cat.

"Gross," came the voice of their fifteen-year-old daughter, Maighen. Apparently she was awake on her thin mattress on the floor.

"Shit," Moira said softly.

Tavis gave a low laugh. "Mornin', Meg. How's the seasickness?"

"Mornin', Daddy. Better this morning. Mother." She said the last word flatly.

"This is what I put up with," Moira said. "Wrapped around her pinky, you are, but she's nothin' but snark for me."

Tavis tried to steer the conversation in another direction. "Where're your brothers?"

"Double D are up on deck with Uncle Tanner."

"What did I say about that term, Meg?" Moira snapped.

"You're the two geniuses who named them Dougal and Duncan, not me. This is my hill, and I'll be dyin' on it."

The door opened, and Duncan, one half of the seventeen-year-old twins, stuck his head in. "You awake, Da?"

"Single D," Maighen whispered from the floor.

"Maighen!" Moira barked.

"Shut ya hole, Meg," said Duncan. "Da, Uncle Tanner needs you on deck. He said he wants you to look at something and that we may have a situation. He also said to get your ass up."

Moira snapped again. "Language, Duncan! I swear to Christ, I don't care if the world's at war, you kids will keep your tongues clean, or I'll take 'em out."

"Tell your uncle I'm on the way," Tavis said. Then to his ladies: "You two, cease fire."

As Duncan shut the door, Tavis swung his legs off the edge of the cot. He pulled on pants and a heavy jacket over his white T-shirt, then added his Merrell hiking boots and a tiger-stripe camo bucket hat before grabbing the L1A1 rifle that was propped in the corner. He'd gotten the rifle from Alfie before they'd left Scotland. The weapons were illegal in Great Britain, but the old man and his partner in crime, Owen, had had several weapons of this sort stashed away. Being lawbreakers didn't seem to bother the old fools.

Tavis left the tiny room and navigated the narrow passageway. Their quarters were in the fo'c'sle, in the bow of the *Shark* with the crew quarters. His brother had better quarters, just below the bridge in the squat superstructure aft, but it was his boat, after all. As Tavis emerged onto the deck, his breath curled in the cold January air. The morning sun hit his eyes, and he cursed at his forgotten sunglasses.

The *Shark* was a rear-loading roll-on/roll-off vehicle carrier, smallish by today's standards and Soviet-built in the 1980s. Tanner had acquired her a decade ago and had done a full refit. She had a nice symmetry to her. A wide beam, or width, with the vehicles loaded aft and driven under the high superstructure where the bridge was onto the vehicle deck. There were currently three British Warrior infantry fighting vehicles on the deck, arranged for maximum stability—one under the superstructure and one on either side in front of the superstructure, leaving a large empty area that could easily fit several more. All were fueled and ready to go, though they had no ammunition for their thirty-millimeter cannons.

Tanner and his twins were standing in the open area between the two vehicles. As Tavis joined them, his brother handed him a steaming cup of black coffee.

"'Bout time you were up."

"I'd have more reason if you had creamer for this mud you drink." Tavis sipped the black liquid. It was bitter, but he knew the caffeine would help. He'd been drinking this mud his whole military career. It was standard on deployment, including the several times he was on a submarine for coastal operations in the Gulf or Med.

"Soft is what you've become." Tanner blew cigar smoke at Tavis, but it drifted away on the cold breeze.

"Aye, you're not wrong. Now, why am I up? Sitrep? What's all this now?" Tavis gestured to his twins. Dougal had what looked like controls for a drone in his hands, and they were both focused on an iPad that Duncan held.

"I thought I'd teach the lads here to fly my drone. Got it to help with various situations in dicey parts of the world. Not much use now, but figured the lads would have some fun with it all the same. High-resolution camera on it and other capabilities."

"You woke me up for this?" Tavis said.

"Not precisely, no. There's something in the water I want you to check out with your own eyes. See if we agree. We're in pretty calm seas, which is odd for this time of year, but we are in the Bermuda Triangle, so, stranger things, I 'spose. The water's pretty clear. Dougal has the drone with its camera directly above us, about two hundred feet at altitude."

"We've got company, Da. At least that's what we think," Duncan said, his voice filled with excitement.

"Really? Lemme look." Tavis took the iPad from his son and sat on the deck so he could put his mug of mud down.

"Here. Put this over you to shield the glare of the morning sun." Duncan draped his jacket over Tavis and the iPad. That was better.

"What does that look like to you just to starboard?" Tanner asked.

"I can't really make it out, but… I guess there does seem to be a shadow or something there," Tavis replied.

"Duncan, switch to the thermal camera," Tanner said. "This is where it gets fun."

Duncan must have hit a switch on his controls, because the view on the iPad changed.

"Bloody 'ell!" Tavis said. "That's a sub. Just about periscope depth, though no periscope is up. There's an overall silhouette. I suppose just a tad warmer than the water. That screw churning confirms it."

"Aye."

"What they doin', Da?" the twins asked in unison.

"Duncan, level out the camera, switch back from thermal, and do a full scan of the horizon," Tavis said.

It took Duncan a minute to get it leveled, then he started to rotate the camera.

"Stop!" Tavis said. "Hold it right there. Tanner, get under here and tell me what that looks like."

Tavis and Tanner switched positions.

"Can you zoom the camera right there a bit, Duncan?" Tanner asked.

Duncan once again manipulated the controls.

Tanner gave a low whistle. "Those are two Russian warships. Frigates probably, but I can't fully make 'em out."

Tavis looked at his twins. "You asked me what that sub's doing? It's hiding, lads."

Sammy yelled down from the flybridge. "Captain, air contact to port. Helicopter!"

"Bloody 'ell!" said Tavis. "Duncan, land that drone here on the deck and secure it. Let's go, Tanner."

Tavis followed his brother up the exterior stairs, through a hatch, and up into the bridge. Sammy handed his binoculars to Tanner, Tavis grabbed an extra set from the instrument console, and they both went out on the port flybridge, scanning the area Sammy was pointing at, low on the horizon.

"There it is," Tavis said. "Coming in pretty fast. Looks like an MH60 Knighthawk. Probably American. What's on radar?"

"Sammy, go fire up the radar. We aren't running it full-time, Tav. Only check it every couple of hours so we stay as invisible as possible. That may have been a mistake."

The helicopter approached the *Shark* off the port side, slowed, oriented the cockpit to face the flybridge, and moved sideways to keep speed with the *Shark*. They were only about thirty yards out, spraying salt water everywhere. Tavis relaxed a bit after seeing the US flag on the side of the bird. He also noticed they were carrying two MK-52 torpedoes, one on either side, just underneath the cabin.

The pilot held up two fingers and then pointed repeatedly off to their starboard. Tavis gave a thumbs-up. "Radar up yet?" he yelled back into the bridge.

"It's up! Two surface contacts bearing one-two-zero at just over fifteen nautical miles and closing. One surface contact bearing two-three-zero at ten nautical miles, also closing fast," Sammy yelled back.

Tanner let his binoculars drop to his chest and moved instead to a set of really big binoculars, known as big eyes to some, mounted on a pole on the flybridge. After a moment, he turned back to his brother.

"Two Russian frigates, as I thought, still unsure of class. And Russian for sure, from their masts."

"Not good. That helo is surely from an American ship off the other direction. Helo is using us to hide from the Russians," Tavis said.

Two voices spoke from behind them.

"Fookin' brilliant!"

"Totally wicked!"

Tavis turned to see his twins standing on the port flybridge, staring in awe at the shadowing helicopter. He yelled at them over the rotor noise.

"You two go get your mum and sister and get your life jackets on!"

They went quick, knowing their father's tone.

"Looks like everyone is using my fookin' boat ta fookin' hide," Tanner said.

The noise from the helicopter grew somehow even louder as it lifted and flew directly over them, picking up speed fast. Once it was away from the *Shark*, it began to deploy flares rapidly from both sides of the fuselage.

Sammy shouted another report. "Multiple air contacts moving fast from the Russian ships bearing to the other contact at two-three-zero." His voice rose as he spoke. "Russians are maneuvering now. Change in bearings. More air contacts from the other contact!"

"The other contact is an American ship, Sammy. *This* should be interesting," Tavis said. "Look!"

He pointed aft, where multiple anti-ship missiles from all three ships, some rising high and others skimming the waves, passed each other in the air. Even though the Russians were way out on their starboard, they were firing missiles at the American ship which was sort of on their port but way aft, so all the action was behind them, except for the helo.

A moment later he turned at the sound of an explosion way off the starboard bow. A Russian anti-aircraft missile had been destroyed in the web of flares the helo had laid down behind it as it flew toward the Russians. The helo was just a dot out on the horizon at this point, but Tavis could see it drop both torpedoes as it flew low over the surface of the calm sea. Tavis was getting whiplash by all the action in different directions.

No more than thirty seconds after that, several more explosions rumbled over the water. All from the direction of the American ship.

"Shit! American is hit!"

Then explosions in the other direction. By the time Tavis got his glass to the Russians, there was only one vessel afloat.

"Got damn!" Tanner yelled. "The other one is still in the fight. Still turning, trying to lose those helo torps."

"They should have hit by now. I wonder…" Tavis said as he watched through the glasses. The Russian frigate turned this way and that until it lifted up out of the water so violently the keel broke in half in the air. It was then rocked by a second blast.

"Sammy, what's on radar?" Tanner yelled into the bridge.

"Air contact is the only contact. No surface contacts. No Russian ships and no American ship. That was bloody fast."

"Tanner, get me a wrench or hammer and meet me down on deck," Tavis said. He started down the stairs.

"What ya doin'?"

"I wanna know who's down there in that sub. That last Russian was hit by torpedoes, and not from the helo."

Moments later Tavis was banging Morse code on the side of the *Shark* with a metal hammer. He kept at it until Tanner yelled down from the flybridge. "Submarine on the starboard side! Surfacing!"

At the same moment, the American Knighthawk screamed overhead, heading to where the American ship should have been.

Tavis climbed back up to the flybridge and watched in awe as a submarine surfaced just enough for the conning tower to exit the water, and sailors appeared.

Tavis gestured to the large empty space in front of the vehicles. "That helo doesn't have anywhere to land since there are no other surface contacts. How big's your deck here?"

"It'll be tight," Tanner answered as he came out of the bridge with a bullhorn.

They watched the activity on the top of the smooth conning tower only thirty yards off the starboard beam as someone who could only be the captain with an officer's cover on raised his own bullhorn.

"This is Commander Blackstone, captain of the HMS *Vengeance*. Who are you, and where are you heading?"

"Brits!" Tanner said happily.

"Bollocks," Tavis replied.

"What, Tav? What's wrong? They're British," Tanner said, clearly confused.

"I was on Blackstone's sub during my last deployment. We had a... disagreement."

"What sort of disagreement, Tav?"

"I told him to have sexual relations with a sheep."

"Well, I suppose that was less cordial than he'd be used to," Tanner said, rolling his eyes.

"Tell him who we are and let's get this over with," Tavis said.

"This is Tanner Kinley, captain of the merchant vessel *Shark*. Heading to the Outer Banks for safe harbor." He lowered the bullhorn.

Commander Blackstone's reply didn't sound friendly. "Is that Staff Sergeant Tavis Kinley standing next to you, Captain Kinley?"

Tavis grabbed the bullhorn from his brother and contemplated his words carefully. Blackstone was a rigid, by-the-book sort.

"Top of the mornin' to you, Bobby! Good to see you again. Exciting morning," Tavis said, voice booming across the water.

"If I had known you were on board, I'd have blown you out of the water earlier," Blackstone replied.

Tavis didn't like his use of the word "earlier."

TWO

An scanned the paper map in the flat, somewhat vertical map holder in front of him in the commander's hatch. They were rolling along a side road that paralleled Route 48 in eastern West Virginia, driving west toward Kentucky, and the sun was on its midmorning rise just behind them as they drove, but it provided little warmth to counter the frigid, biting wind that assaulted his face. At least the snow had mostly melted here, at least off the blacktop roads, so they moved at a good speed.

"My ass is asleep. This seat is worthless," An said to no one in particular. The seat in the LAV-25 was even more uncomfortable than his seat in the Abrams.

He and Sergeant Nelson had switched places for this. Nelson was now Alice's commander—Nelson was prior armor and felt comfortable taking charge of the Abrams main battle tank—and An got Nelson's clown car. Sergeant Buford—or Cueball, as the guys had started calling him after dispatching those meth-head clowns on their escape from Kentucky—sat in the gunner's hatch to An's left, his sniper rifle stowed below, his M-4 resting across the hatch. In the back, An had three of his Marines with him, aside from the driver and Buford. He heard loud voices from the passenger compartment, but he couldn't make out what they were saying.

"Hey, Gunny?" came a voice from below.

"What?"

"We in West Virginia now? These my people, Gunny." It was Lance Corporal Francois. They all just called him Frenchie. He was full-on hillbilly and quite excited to be back in his environment. He'd been asking "are we there yet" ever since leaving the Humvee with Sergeant Simmons and Gale Washington at the entrance to Mount Weather a couple hours earlier. Hopefully they would be able to get into the complex, see whoever was in charge, and relay their intel.

That was An's first mission. Complete. Now he was on his own mission.

"Yeah, Frenchie. We're in West Virginia now," An said.

"Nice!" came the reply, and then the singing—badly—of "Country Roads" drifted up from the troop compartment. Of course. The others soon joined in.

An looked over at Buford, who didn't look at him but was smiling.

Then Buford joined in on the chorus.

"Fucking hate you!" An barked. He shook his head and took a long pull from the water bottle he kept close. He was still pretty dehydrated from his rough patch with the flu a few days ago. Many of the people in their little neighborhood had gotten it to one degree or another.

They were doing about thirty-five miles an hour on this two-lane road, which wound around this hill and that. Trees grew right on the edge of the blacktop, then a field would appear, then right back to trees again. They hadn't seen a soul for a good twenty minutes.

Another field appeared, this one with an older man on a horse walking through it. The man waved at An, and An waved back as they moved on past. They didn't stop to talk with people, although they'd need to stop soon to refuel. There were plenty of gas stations, but many were deserted.

"Sergeant," he said to Buford, and pointed.

Buford followed his finger out to a spot in the sky just above the trees. "What is—oh, that's some bullshit. Can a brother ever get away from fucking clowns? Goddamn West Virginia hillbilly mother..."

An laughed, then put on his game face. Clearly there was someone around the next bend in the road, because that red balloon floating above the trees hadn't just popped into existence all on its own.

"Driver! Slow down here. There's some weird shit up ahead."

The LAV slowed to about fifteen miles per hour as they rounded the bend, where the sides opened up into fields and a three-way stop sign. Buford was aiming his M-4, searching for threats, targets, and clowns. The road straightened after the bend. An didn't have to tell the driver to stop.

"What in the farmer's fuck is this shit?" Buford said.

An took in the scene as he pulled his own M-4 up out of the hatch.

Frenchie called up from the troop compartment. "Why y'all badmouthin' my kin? What's goin' on up there?"

"Well, Frenchie," An replied, "there's about a hundred cows, sheep, goats, even a random pig out here. They're blocking the road and all over a field to the right. Get ready."

Buford pointed to the right. "There's the balloon launcher."

"No clowns this time. Just an old dude with some kids," An said.

The old man was out front of an old gas station convenience store, with five young kids all running around him with colored balloons. The old man filled up another one from an air tank, tied it off, and handed it to the only little boy without a balloon.

"Y'all miss a turn or somethin'?" A middle-aged man with an AK-47 cinched up tight to his chest by a sling appeared out of the woods just beside the gas station. A hog walked in front of him.

"Yeah, they lost," a woman said, stepping out of the gas station's swinging glass door, followed by two other women and several men. All were armed in one fashion or another, and all were dressed pretty much as An would expect farmers to be dressed. Boots, jeans, flannel shirts, coats.

An turned to the man with the AK. "How y'all doing?" An didn't think he'd ever said "y'all" before in his life, but for some reason, he wanted to fit in right now. Then he whispered down into the hatch: "Frenchie, get out here and talk to your people for us."

The rear doors of the LAV opened, and Frenchie popped out onto the blacktop as more men walked out of the tree line, all similarly armed. They looked more curious than menacing. As Frenchie walked around the LAV, Buford adjusted his M-4.

"Easy!" The man beside the gas station quickly pointed his AK-47 at Buford.

"Whoa! It's okay. We're no threat," An said. He laid a hand on Buford's right arm, and Buford lowered his M-4 back to where it was.

"Stop!" a raspy but booming voice. An saw the old balloon man was now standing half way between the gas station and the LAV.

"That's Frenchie there," An shouted back. "He's from these parts —or at least West Virginia."

Frenchie walked up to the old man and held out his hand.

"Y'all Marines?" the old man asked, shaking Frenchie's hand.

"Yes, sir! I'm Gunnery Sergeant Nguyen, and these are my Marines."

"I was at Chosin," the old man said.

"Oorah, sir!"

The old man waved dismissively at An's attempt at respect. "Y'all know what's happened? We haven't had any information since the power cut and cars died."

"I'll tell you what we know. Easier if I come down there."

"Well, come on then, Gunny. Anything y'all need?"

"We could use some fuel, if you have any."

"Let's chat, and my boys will fix y'all up with that. Call me Wrench."

Ten minutes later, the Marines were all out stretching their legs, and the LAV was nearly done being topped off with fuel. An and Buford sat in plastic chairs near the balloon-filling air canister, relaying what information they had while the children climbed all over the LAV under the supervision of Frenchie and some of the women, who had to repeatedly tell the kids not to touch stuff. Wrench told them a bit about Korea and how his name was given to him there, where he was a mechanic but always a Marine. Then An filled the old man in on everything they knew about the current situation.

"Fucking' Chicoms!" Wrench spat when An was finished. "And what's your mission in all this, Gunny?"

"A large group of these Russian and Iranian infiltrators hit Fort Knox while I was there on Christmas Eve. Attacked our convoy. We were the only ones that made it out. We're on our way back to find my brother, also a Marine, and one of our neighbors' kids. Going to bring them back with us or die trying."

"Sounds like Marine shit to me. Anything else you need?"

"No, sir. You've been more helpful than we could have hoped for. We may pass back this way. Care if we stop to refuel when we do?"

"We'll be here, Gunny. Doin' just fine, like before 'lectricity died. But just in case, we'll call the Billy in from the hollers yonder. No Chicoms gonna get up in these parts."

"The Billy?" Buford asked.

"Hillbillies, Sergeant. What you see 'round here's just the tip. We're spread out. Here's a red balloon for ya." Wrench inflated another balloon and handed it to Buford.

Buford took it uneasily. "What's this for?"

"To go with y'all's clown car there."

Buford looked at the LAV in confusion.

An laughed. "You didn't even notice, Sergeant. Check the front."

Buford walked back to the LAV and squatted down, looking at the diagonal armor that came up from the bottom to meet the top front armor at a forty-five-degree angle. "What the blueberry fuck! That girl. Who put her up to this shit?"

An and the rest of the Marines laughed their asses off. There on the armor plating was a skeletal face with red eyes, rosy cheeks, orange hair, and a mouth showing rotting teeth in an evil smile. Scrawled beneath were the words *Semper Fi*.

"I hate you all," Buford said.

"Got a problem with clowns, do ya, Sergeant?" Wrench asked.

"I had an incident," Buford replied.

"More than one," said An. "We call him Cueball, sir. For Clown Eradication Unit, but with the letters arranged different." To Buford he added: "You'll have to take it up with Sergeant Simmons when we get back."

"Yep, this the Marine shit I remember," said Wrench. "Does an old Marine good. If y'all need anything on your way back, you come here. We got you."

It was then that a horse and rider appeared at the top of the hill. As he sauntered his mount down to the gas station, An stared, dumbstruck. The man who dismounted was tall, thin, and wore a United States Air Force flight suit. His short red hair was covered by a hat with the rank of captain displayed on it, and the leather holster strapped to the front of his flight suit had what looked like a 1911 in it.

"You lose your ride, sir?" An asked as the man approached.

They shook hands. "It's right where I left it, Sergeant. Name's Voodoo," the captain replied.

"I gotta say, pretty surreal seeing you ride up like that. What's your situation? We're going to Fort Knox to collect a couple folks and bring them back to Northern Virginia."

Voodoo laughed. "It's pretty surreal doing it, Sergeant. I'm with the 75th out of Moody Air Force Base in Georgia. Took a week or so for the crews to get a couple A-10s operational again after the EMP. Mine was one of them. I parked it thataway." He thumbed over his shoulder the way he rode in. "Got a couple of kin collecting jet fuel from the local airstrip. I've got a full combat load. Didn't know what I'd need, so they put a bit of everything on the points. Bombs, Mavericks, rockets, Sidewinders. Just don't have any targets yet."

"Well hopefully we'll be back this way with our people in a day or so. We had some excitement at Knox and then also back in Northern Virginia. I'm sure there's gonna be targets for you. Maybe we'll vector you in for some when we come back through. What brings you this way?"

Voodoo tilted his head toward the old man. "Family."

"He's my grandson," Wrench said. "I don't give him too much grief for joining the Air Force. Hell, Warthog drivers are basically infantry anyway." Voodoo barked a laugh. "It scared the hell out of us when he landed on the road over the hill with no warning. Just appeared like a ghost."

"The Ghost of Appalatcha!" Frenchie blurted out.

"I like it. I like it very much," Voodoo replied. He looked at the LAV and its painted-on mascot. "Nice clown car you got there."

"Shit's never gonna end," Buford muttered, pulling out his Ka-Bar knife to pop the balloon.

"You hold that balloon, Sergeant! Mount up!" An snapped.

Wrench nearly fell over in laughter.

The women got all the kids off the LAV, and An and the rest mounted up.

"We'll be here if you pass this way again," the man with the AK said. He slapped the side of the clown car, then ushered the hogs out of the way.

"Bring targets, Sergeant," Voodoo added. "I've got a lot of hate that needs to be sent."

"Roger that, Captain. Thank you, and good luck." An turned to Buford and said quietly, "And you hold that balloon high and proud until we're out of earshot."

"Shit's not right, Gunny. Some bullshit…"

But despite his grumbling, Buford held the red balloon waving in the breeze as the LAV rolled down the road.

THREE

It was well past full dark when An, Buford, and the clown car rolled slowly along the road into the small valley where An had last seen his brother. They had refueled again an hour east at another abandoned gas station, just to top off in case they needed to hightail it out fast and far; the guys were pretty efficient now at getting directly into the tanks under the stations and siphoning fuel. He was surprised there was any fuel left at this point. The LAV was buttoned up tight as they scanned the road ahead through the night vision and infrared optics in the LAV commander's and gunner's sights. An was filled with a sense of dread and almost sadness, knowing what they'd almost certainly find.

Memories of his father crept back. Not the old, frail, and sick man, but the younger, vibrant, and strong father he remembered as a child. They'd all be together again soon.

As they rounded the bend into the familiar valley, husks of armored vehicles littered the road ahead. They gave off no heat in the infrared. An traversed the turret and his hatch's sights right and left, elevating up the sides of the valley walls thick with trees. Nothing. They were alone.

"Pull up next to the first vehicle and stop," he said. "Dismount. Buford, overwatch."

"Copy," Buford replied as An and the rest of the team exited the LAV.

"Go slow and find the bodies. I know they're here, guys. Use flashlights sparingly. Only to identify."

The team spread out and walked slowly down the road, checking tanks and other LAVs that were burned out. When An got to his former lieutenant's track, he climbed up onto the turret in the moonlight. It was still locked down tight. He looked around the turret until he found the hole where the sabot round had penetrated. He wasn't going to try to get this open. He knew what he'd find.

Jumping down to the pavement, he moved to where he remembered his brother's LAV was. The rear doors were open. There were three bodies in the troop compartment, frozen by the elements. But Bao wasn't one of them.

An went back outside and walked both sides of the road. The ground sank into shallow ditches until it rose into the hills thick with evergreens and leafless trees. "Anyone find him?" he asked.

"Buncha guys over here, but none are your brother, Gunny. Sorry," someone replied. An got the same responses from the others.

Then Frenchie spoke up. "Hey, Gunny, deep boot prints over here. Lead away down the ditch and then up the hill to the left. Maybe I can track these like a deer back home. Bit dark, though. Full moon'll help some."

"Buford, give Frenchie your night-vision scope off your rifle. Let's see where these lead."

Buford unclasped the night-vision scope from his rifle and handed it down to Frenchie, who took it back over to the boot prints. The private walked down into the ditch and then up the side of the hill for a bit. After a few minutes, he came back down to the group.

"Tracks are pretty distinct, Gunny. Look like they lead back toward the fort."

"Do you see any sign of blood or struggle?" An asked. He felt a sudden urgency but kept it out of his voice.

"No, but I did see a handprint like he was scurrying, tryin' to get up the hill. Not gonna see blood with this thing anyway; the indentations and tracks are barely visible as it is. Not gonna lie, Gunny, it's gonna be harder than my wiener in the morning to track these all the way. Since it looks like those tracks are headed back to Knox, I think it'd be easier to just head that way and see if we can catch up with them there. Sorry, Gunny."

"Relax, Frenchie. I get it. Okay, here's the plan. Buford and Frenchie, with me. The rest of you hang here. Shut the LAV down and open the doors like it was part of the ambush and was left here. I want you guys hidden on high ground and not hanging out by our vehicle if a patrol comes by. If they do, they won't give another abandoned LAV a second glace. Don't even know if there's any bad guys around, whoever they are, but heads on swivels. We may need to exfil quick. Get up high on the side of this valley with clear sight to the fort, and I'll do periodic radio comms. Don't know how far these crap Chinesium radios will reach. Copy?"

"We got you, Gunny."

"Gonna be a long walk. We have two to find. My brother and hopefully we can try to get the veterinarian's son, Dallas, as well. I have a feeling this is gonna be a shitshow, so stay frosty."

Frenchie and Buford, now with his M-4 at the ready with his sniper rifle slung on his back, both nodded in the moonlight.

"Okay, Frenchie, you got point. Buford, rear. Let's move."

A couple hours later, the three Marines approached the paved road near the now-empty motor pool lot where they'd started out on Christmas Eve. They hadn't seen any sentries or vehicles yet. He didn't know what to make of that, but he wasn't complaining.

But now that changed. Frenchie held up a fist and stopped. An and Buford gathered near the private on the slope leading up to the road. They all heard the engine at the same time and went as flat as they could on the incline just near the paved road across from the motor pool. The engine came closer, and as An lay there, he looked back and saw a floodlight moving back and forth across the fields they'd just traversed.

"Stay low and still," An said as the vehicle stopped near their position. The spotlight was thankfully on a spot way out in the field, but An was deathly aware of the frozen breath that came out of his mouth each time he exhaled. He turned his head to the side, exhaling slowly parallel to the ground so it was less likely to rise up into the line of the light.

Two doors clicked open. Neither shut. Then two male voices were speaking to each other. It wasn't English. He'd heard it before. Chinese. Had to be. That sealed that deal. These weren't friendlies.

It was then that An heard liquid spattering above him on the incline. He felt little wet droplets hit his face and hands as he realized the two sentries were urinating off the side of the road just above where he, Buford, and Frenchie were hiding.

Motherfucker, he thought. He was being pissed on by the Chinese.

At least he didn't have to worry about his frozen breath being seen; the urine was evaporating all over the rocks and ground where it hit.

Concealed by piss vapor. That was a new one for him.

He stayed still even though he wanted to shoot these two in the face. The spray stopped, and the two got back into the vehicle and drove off.

"Did those motherfuckers piss on us?" Buford whispered.

"Looks like," An said, wiping his face with his uniform sleeve and then his hands on his pant legs.

They slowly rose from their concealment, and with Frenchie scanning for threats with the night-vision scope, they moved silently across the road into the motor pool parking lot.

"Gunny. Bodies," Frenchie whispered.

They poked around, and An lost count of the men on the ground and none looked like his brother. Must be where it started after they'd rolled out that night. The men had just been left here where they'd fallen.

"Gunny, if that was your brother that walked from the valley to here, I don't think he'd stay right here," Buford said.

"Agreed. Okay, let's get to the address that the vet gave us. Maybe we get her kid if he's still there, hiding or something. Find some food, maybe. Frenchie, point. Buford, rear. It's that way."

An pointed in the general direction of where he knew the house would be. It was a colonel's house, which limited it to one of only a couple of streets on base.

In his head, he started humming the chorus to "We Are Never Getting Back Together" by Taylor Swift. He hoped that wasn't his subconscious telling him he wouldn't find his brother.

It took them thirty minutes to slowly navigate the darkened buildings and parking lots crammed with useless vehicles, some civilian, some military. A couple of times they had to stop and drop when headlights and spotlights illuminated the structures near and around them, but finally they came to the more suburban area An had been looking for. He checked the street signs through the night-vision scope, then handed it to Buford, who attached it back on his rifle.

Dixie and Wilson, the signs said. The house was in this collection of single-family homes, about thirty to forty of them on tree-lined streets.

The three Marines moved like ghosts in the shadows the clouds made in front of the bright, full moon, finally reaching the address the vet had given them. They flattened themselves on the side of the house near the back corner.

"I'll go first. Frenchie, you're with me. Buford, look out here," An said.

He crept to the back door, which was a glass slider. He tried it, and it gave. He pushed the heavy door to the left.

Shit. Too dark.

"Hey, night vision," he whispered to Frenchie. The private departed and came back a minute later with the scope from Buford, which he gave to An. An then stuck his head through the opening and scanned right and left. Kitchen and family room. Fireplace. Hallway to the front door and stairs.

He stepped in, followed by the private. An's M-4 was slung tightly to his chest over his chest rig. Frenchie was his security.

They reconned the first floor without encountering anyone. An pointed up the stairs in front of Frenchie's face so he could see his gesture. He got a nod in return. The first step was silent, but the second step creaked loudly. An grimaced and placed his foot on the next step closer to the wall. Less creaky. They continued that way up into the pitch-black hallway, which had four doors. The first was a bathroom. The next was an empty bedroom. As they crept toward the third door, An cocked his head and listened.

Snoring. Lightly.

He took a long breath in and exhaled. It could be the kid, or it could be a Chinese soldier.

He unsnapped the K-Bar knife from its sheath on his chest rig and put his ear to both remaining doors. When he was certain where the snoring was coming from, he opened the other door first. Another empty bedroom. Only then did he turn to the room that was occupied.

He gently pushed down on the door handle and pushed. The door opened without squeaking. A sleeping, snoring body was in the room's double bed, facing away. An walked around in front of the figure and stared at him for a hot minute. A young man, who must have sensed movement, because his eyes opened.

"Don't move," An said. "I won't hurt you. What's your name?"

"Holy shit!"

"Take a breath, son. Didn't mean to scare you. Now, what's your name?"

"Dallas. Who are you?"

"Really? I can't believe we actually found you. Is there anyone else in the house? Or in these other houses?"

"Found me? Who the hell are you? Can I sit up?"

"Yes. I'm An Nguyen, gunnery sergeant, United States Marines. Your mom wanted us to find you. Looks like we did. Where's your dad? Wasn't he the colonel in charge of Armor around here?"

"My mom? Is she okay?"

"She was when we left. Came here to find my brother and you, if we could. Can you confirm that there are Chinese soldiers here? Why are you here in this house alone? Where's your father? Take your time and fill me in before we get outta here." An realized he was asking a lot of disjointed questions.

"My dad died on Christmas Eve," Dallas said. "From what the other sergeant's been telling me, about a thousand Chinese infiltrators attacked the base on Christmas Eve. They overwhelmed the Army and knew where and what to hit right away. Later that night, planes began landing at the airfield with more troops, real soldiers. Over the last week, they've rounded up most everyone and put them in some of the larger buildings and schools. Are you taking me home to my mom? Do you know Layla Washington?"

"Slow down. I'm sorry about your dad, son. I can relate. But this sergeant you mentioned—what's his name?"

Before Dallas could answer, a vehicle's engine broke the silence. Frenchie went to the window to look.

"Humvee out front, Gunny. Like right in front of this fucking house."

An turned to Dallas. "Are you expecting anyone?"

"Yeah, if the sergeant isn't here already, that's probably him getting dropped off. He hangs out with the Chinese commander during the evenings. They drink."

Buford whispered up the stairs. "Guys! Gunny! There's a Humvee out front. Someone's coming in!"

Shit.

"Stay here," An said to the kid. "Frenchie, stay with him."

An went quickly down the stairs, where he met Buford in the front room. An still had the night-vision scope to his right eye, and he saw the knife in Buford's hand, his rifles on the carpet. An took a spot on the wall behind where the door would open, just as it did. A figure came through the doorway and swung the door shut behind him.

"Don't make a sound. You're outnumbered here," An said quietly.

The figure didn't move except to turn his head toward An's voice. An, still looking through the night-vision scope, smiled.

"Bao," he said. "It's me, An."

"An? Holy shit, I just shit myself," said Gunnery Sergeant Bao Nguyen.

An grabbed him in a rough bear hug. "Jesus, it's good to see you alive. Thought I'd find you pushing daisies back at the ambush!"

They separated.

"Easy, man! Walking wounded here. Took shrapnel to the back of my neck and shoulder," Bao said. "Where'd y'all come from? There's Chicoms everywhere."

"Hey Gunnies, dude's walking up to the front door," Buford warned them.

The door opened again, and a dark figure appeared silhouetted in the opening. As the man stepped toward Bao, An pushed the door shut with his foot and put the muzzle of his M-4 in the man's face. Buford did the same.

"Make a sound and you're dead," Bao told the man.

"What is this? I demand an answer! Who are these men, Sergeant?"

"Major, this is where we part ways. It's been fun," Bao said. Then to An: "Let's sit him in the family room and tie him up." Their eyes had adjusted enough to navigate the darkness now.

As Bao and Buford went about that task, An whispered up the stairs for Frenchie to come down with Dallas while he kept an eye on the Humvee out front.

"Bao, who else is in the Humvee?" An asked.

"Just the driver. Has an AK. He's not gonna wait long before he comes in to see what's going on." Bao finished tying the major's hands behind the chair, and Buford, with a roll of duct tape provided by Dallas, ripped off a piece and put it over the man's mouth, ensuring he could still breathe through his nose.

"Buford. Can you take care of the driver? Quietly?" An asked.

"Roger that. I can stick him," Buford replied. His hand went to his knife.

"Nah," said Bao. "Dude out there is squirrelly. The passenger window is down, though. Easy shot if you all have a suppressed weapon.

"Buford does," An said. "Buford, set up here in the hallway from the kitchen to the front door. Frenchie will open the door, you take the shot, shut the door." He handed the night-vision scope back to Buford.

"It's suppressed, not silent," Buford said. "Still gonna make a boom out there. Is there anyone else around?"

"We're pretty far away from the activity," Bao said. "They're over by the airfield, loading the gold onto planes."

"Wait, what? They're stealing the gold from the fort?" Frenchie said.

"Yep. Gold is still gold, man. It's like some Kelly's Heroes shit, but on an industrial scale."

Buford took position in the hallway facing the door with his rifle. It was pretty flat from there out to the Humvee, so he lay prone on the floor.

"Ready, Buford?"

"Ready," Buford replied. An watched Buford go to work as he'd seen many times before. Buford slowed his breathing and put his finger on the trigger as he looked through the night vision optic. Frenchie opened the door a second later and An saw him slowly squeeze the trigger until the rifle recoiled against his shoulder. The driver's head exploded against the driver's-side window.

"Shut the door," Buford said.

Frenchie pushed it shut.

"Okay," An said, "now how about you explain to me what the hell is going on here, Bao? How are you drinking buddies with this guy, and how is it that you're here with Dallas?"

"We got time for this?" Buford asked. "That shot was louder than I'd like."

An ignored the question. "Bao?"

His brother nodded. "I'll make it quick. I escaped the LAV during the ambush. I was hit with shrapnel in the back of the neck and shoulder, not too bad, but I knew it needed attention soon. I used the confusion to make my way back to the fort. The motor pool was… a slaughter."

"We saw."

"Yeah." Bao shook his head. "That's when I found Dallas here. He was looking for his dad, and we found him among the fallen. Dallas brought me back here and patched me up with what he had, but I knew I needed more. So at dawn I stashed my weapons upstairs, and we made our way to the medical center. I had a plan, a stupid plan, but it worked."

"He was great," Dallas chimed in, though his voice sounded flat. The kid probably didn't like having his dad brought up again. An knew the feeling.

"I pretended to be a Vietnamese spy who'd joined the Marines," Bao continued. "Told these two Chicoms—real PLA types, not the infiltrators—that I had information for their commander but needed medical attention first. One communist to another. Isn't that right, Major?" Bao poked the Chinese major in the chest, and the man stared daggers.

"So they got me into the med center. It was only half staffed but operational, with a bunch of wounded Chicoms in there. No Americans. They got me patched up. Then the major here showed up. I explained my spy story to him and started giving him all kinds of information. None of it true, but tons of it. Just pulling shit out my ass. Well, we got to be BFFs and started drinking together, and when he gets liquored up, man, he likes to talk, broken English and all. But he didn't shoot me, which is the only reason he's still alive, and he'll stay that way. Got him to let me keep Dallas here as my gofer while I healed up. Still a work in progress, that." He put a hand to his shoulder. "And then my brother shows up out of the blue. Now you tell me: Do we have any response to this yet? Anyone in charge?"

"Yeah, apparently at Mount Weather. Dropped some of Mom and Dad's neighbors from the International Space Station off there on the way here to get you."

Bao squinted at him.

"Long story," An said. "Oh, by the way, congratulations! You have a healthy baby daughter. Born just after Christmas. Brook refused to name her until I brought you back. I couldn't just let the girl grow up nameless, so here we are."

"Oh damn," Bao said, tears gleaming in his eyes. "Seriously? I'm a dad!"

"For better or worse, yes."

Bao was more emotional than An had ever seen him. In the dim moonlight coming through the glass sliding door, An saw his brother's cheeks were wet. "Okay, well, we *gotta* go in that case. Besides, I need to tell someone in charge what I've learned. There are several divisions of Chinese with armor coming ashore at Baltimore. They're supposed to take and hold the Shenandoah Valley and Central Virginia, to include the Lake Anna nuclear power plant. Mount Weather too. Should also tell them that the Chicoms are stealing all our gold, for what it's worth."

"Then let's get moving. We have the rest of the team and our LAV at the ambush site. My Abrams is back by Mom's house. I don't recommend leaving this guy alive, though." An glanced at the glaring PLA major.

"No, he let me live, so he lives." Bao punched the man directly in the nose, knocking him backward onto the floor, unconscious.

"Maybe we should have done that before talking in front of him," An said.

"When he wakes up, he'll tell them where we're headed," Buford said.

"Then we better head there fast and get there before they catch us. He's our prisoner. I don't kill prisoners. Don't want that on my mind," Bao said.

"But the driver gets to stay on my mind?" Buford said.

"Sorry, man. Driver was a threat. Major isn't. At least not yet. But I won't kill him."

An thought back to the church and that meth-head clown he'd let die instead of keeping the tourniquet on him. *I'd kill him, but not my call*, he thought.

FOUR

Northern Virginia
Sunday Morning

After the lights went out on Christmas Eve, the little isolated cul-de-sac about thirty minutes west of DC got pretty exciting. The Iranian commandos came in the night, pulled to their court by the gunfire that killed two of them. The inhabitants of this cul-de-sac turned out to be very interesting people. Russian spies and Iranian refugees.

The Christmas Eve party was one for the books. Then at the last moment, well about thirty-six hours after the lights went out, Gale Washington's wife, Joey, had miraculously showed up with Marines in tow and one massive tank. Just a day or so prior to that, she'd been the commander of the International Space Station. She was in space when the war started. He really thought he'd lost her. But against all the odds, he had her back.

Gale took a sip of hot coffee from his favorite mug—a wide-mouthed, American-flag mug. He'd gotten used to black coffee, no sugar or creamer now. *The French press is the way to go. It only took a world war to get here.* He stared out the bay window of his living room, watching the morning's activities in the cul-de-sac. There were several Marines working on one of the treads—the Marines called them tracks—on the Abrams main battle tank that sat in the middle of the court. He could hear their muffled cursing through the window as they worked.

There was something wrong with the right track, which was why they hadn't brought the tank with them to Mount Weather yesterday in their failed attempt to make contact with whatever leadership was still functioning. That might have been a good thing. With a tank, they might have let them in, but they didn't and Gale didn't know why. They just said no and told them to leave. Who knows, if they'd have gone sooner, that might've worked as well, but half the cul-de-sac came down with a nasty flu the day after the firefight with the

Iranians. No one went anywhere or felt like it for a week. It was a bad one. Gunnery Sergeant An Nguyen was beside himself but couldn't get out of bed in his mom's house until a couple of days ago. Viruses didn't care about the apocalypse. The flu was the flu. Could've been worse. Ebola and SARS, which popped up from time to time, *would've* been worse. Bio-engineered pandemics were a possibility too. Wouldn't put that past the Chicoms.

Those Marines were really fighting that tread, track, whatever. He leaned forward to get a better look. Yep. Christopher the pug was curled up on the back of the tank above the engine compartment, seemingly oblivious to the goings-on around him. Gale didn't see the Yorkie, Chewie, at the moment, but he was sure she was around. The Marines had adopted her. His neighbor, Floyd, had died falling down his dark stairs right after the lights went out on Christmas Eve. Chewie had been his, but had now enlisted as a furry little Marine.

He thought about Floyd. He missed the old prepper, but what Floyd left in his basement was a treasure trove of food of all kinds. Enough for them to make it through the winter here if they rationed it appropriately. The real treasure was a radio that was stashed in a make-shift faraday cage, which shielded it from the EMP. They'd found it a few days back and Lou worked the dial on it obsessively to find radio traffic. He said it kept his mind off losing Robert, his partner, during the firefight.

What Lou caught was mostly snippets from Ham radio operators far and wide. What was repeated most often was that America and Europe were dark. No power. That and warnings to stay away from cities. Gale figured they were fairly safe here as the only city near them was Washington, DC, and that had been hit with a nuclear bomb. So there were no great hordes of people walking out of the city west toward them. Twenty-three other American cities and military bases had been nuked on Christmas Eve as well. The rest of the news snippets were pretty grim. The Russians were pushing halfway across Europe into Germany, but got stopped butt-cold in Finland.

Elsewhere, it seemed that India had won a short nuclear war with Pakistan, if you could count that winning. Mexico was a horror show with the cartels running everything. Canada was dark as well. There was no word about Japan and the Korean Penisula, but rumors that came through were pretty bleak. Australia and New Zealand were still surviving apparently and no one was messing with Isreal. Apparently, they went all "knives out" and said they'd destroy anyone that attacked them.

The only snippets out of Africa were from South Africa. The ANC was in the process of taking over and re-segregating the country. The atrocities that Lou heard were the worst of anywhere. Gale was looking out the window as he went down the list of really bad stuff that Lou reported from the radio, but he wasn't really seeing anything. He was just lost in thought and trying to figure out how they were going to survive this.

There was a wider neighborhood outside of their cul-de-sac and several grocery stores and pharmacies within a three- to four-mile radius. He was sure those had been picked clean by now. They had the one doctor that patched up their wounded after the firefight. He was on this side of the main road, but they hadn't talked to anyone on the other side of the road yet. They'd have to start building relationships and see who was capable and who was dead weight. That was just a fact of the situation now. They weren't going to survive through this year on just Floyd's food. They'd have to plant food. That was the final treasure Floyd had. Seeds.

If they even made it to planting. Lou said recurring radio traffic warned of Chinese infiltrators and actual Chinese soldiers in the country. He rubbed his face as if it would rub away the mounting problems.

"Whatcha doin'?" A hand snaked its way down his chest from behind, and he nearly jumped out of his skin.

"Jesus!" He tried not to spill what was left of his coffee as Joey laughed out loud.

"Bit jumpy, aren't we?" she said.

"Was deep in thought, watching that pug sleep on the tank and the Marines doing repairs. Scared the shit outta me."

Joey limped around him, sat in the cushiony chair opposite, and looked out the window. "Still pissed about Mount Weather?" she asked.

"Actually, I was thinking about you, and just recovering the last bit from the flu. How's your leg this morning?" He leaned forward and kissed her. As he did, he grabbed the blanket folded neatly on the back of her chair and wrapped it around her. It was all they had for warmth at the moment. There was no electricity. Probably wouldn't be again after the electromagnetic pulse from the nuclear detonation in orbit knocked it out, along with everything modern. They had been sleeping, or had been taking turns sleeping, in Lou and Robert's house. They had the fireplace going around the clock. The neighbors and Marines were taking turns in the family room with the heat. Not all of them, though. The dead didn't need heat. He put that thought away for now.

"I'm here, Gale. That's all that matters. I made it home. Took some doing, but I'm here with you and Layla," she reassured him.

"You smell good," he said.

"Thanks. I came back from outer space for you to sniff me. It's my sole purpose now. To be sniffable."

"Good. So, the hot water was welcome then?"

"Oh, yes. Thank you for doing that. It was wonderful. I've been cold for so long. It was like heaven."

"Yeah, we still have running water from the gravity-fed water towers on the ridge. Also, we filled up all the bathtubs we could find in everyone's house. No hot water, but we moved the metal fire pit into Lou's garage and rigged it with a tarp so the smoke would funnel out so we could heat water for coffee and hygiene purposes."

"Sounds like everyone is adapting. Speaking of Lou, how's he doing? It's sad about Robert."

Lou's partner had died defending his home and the rest of them in the basement when the Iranian commandos attacked that night.

"He's keeping busy with the fire and wood and the kids. He's also still monitoring Floyd's radio like a hawk for any news. And none of that news is good really, but you were there yesterday when he filled us in on the latest. He and Sergeant Simmons were going over firearms with Layla and the rest earlier." Gale pointed across the road to an impromptu firing range set up out of sight.

"Oh? Firearms?" Joey tilted her head and looked out the window.

"It's needed now. They have to know how to shoot and take care of themselves and each other in a pinch. Layla knows what I taught her, but it's not like learning from a Marine and former SEAL."

Lou was a retired Navy SEAL, in his early sixties now, and Simmons was the Marine in charge, now that An had left in search of his brother and Dallas. They'd gone with them yesterday to Mount Weather and continued on from there.

"I know. It's a different world and everything's changed, but knowing that doesn't mean I have to like it. She's still my baby. What else is going on around here, now that I'm up and recovered mostly from my own flu journey?" She changed the subject again.

"Well, Mama and Bibi are in their glory taking care of those little ones you all found. No worse for the wear, it seems. Pasha is recovering really well. He's up and about. Still in pain, but the doctor said he'd make a full recovery. Good as new soon. Bullet was a through and through. Didn't hit anything important. Javad is a different story. He's still touch and go. They've got him on big antibiotics and painkillers. Brook and the baby are doing well."

Brook was Bao's wife, and the baby was born on the night of the attack. Brook had said she wouldn't name her little girl until An brought her husband back, one way or the other.

"Oh, I can't wait to hold that baby now that I'm not contagious!" Joey said, rubbing her hands together.

"Yes, the baby is very cute and cherubic. But I still have to get Javad to Mount Weather, which I did yesterday, but actually get him in to relay what he knows to whoever's in charge now."

They had finally all recovered enough from the flu to take one Humvee with Gale and Simmons, escorted by Gunny Nguyen, Buford, and some Marines in the LAV. The Gunny and LAV had continued on without stopping at Mount Weather. An needed to get his brother back. His Marines were all in support of this decision. Their families were from all over the country, and none close, so this was as much their mission as An's.

"I just don't get it, Joey. Why wouldn't they even want to hear what I had to tell them? It's infuriating. The mountain is where our Continuity of Government is. We're at war, and they don't want intel from the man that planned it all? They're dumber than a box of hair!" He was getting angrier by the second.

"Gale, look, from what you told me, it was probably just operational security protocols, and they didn't know you. Just having Sergeant Simmons with you wasn't gonna do it," she tried to explain.

"Well, we've got to try again. Maybe we could go out there together if Javad can't travel," Gale suggested.

"Dear, I'm a lieutenant commander in the Navy, not the chairman of the joint chiefs. They don't know me, either." She tapped the sewn-on lieutenant commander's insignia on the flight jacket she was wearing. Gale just noticed it. She was in uniform, mostly, with woodland camouflage patterned battle dress uniform, or BDU she called it, pants, and one sturdy hiking boot on the foot of the leg that wasn't broken and in a cast.

"Well, I see you're dressing the part anyway now. You're absolutely known. You're an astronaut, or were, and you have intel from the other side of the planet. You saw flashes on the Indian subcontinent. You know that the Russians are invading Europe. They tried to shoot you down, for fuck's sake," he said, his voice rising again.

"You haven't had much luck lately with the powers-that-be listening to you, have you? Gale, you tried to warn them. They didn't listen. That's on them, not you."

"It's on that idiot three-star Air Force moron, Spenkmeier, that had me transferred from the fusion center. If they'd listened to me then, we would have had a chance to get ahead of this plot. Now look at us… Dennis listened to me, but he's dead now. I blame that fucker for that too." He thought about his old boss for a second, staring out the window.

"I'm sorry, honey. I know he was your friend." Joey took his hand in hers.

"It's funny. Dennis said I had devils dancing in my head. That I had to let them go, but here they all are. All the devils are dancing.

All at once around a big bonfire. I have to help somehow, Joey. We need… some devils of our own.”

Gunshots interrupted their conversation, and they both jumped. Sounded like a lot of firing and then silence.

“I didn't think they'd be doing that this early.” Gale exhaled, letting all his frustration out. “Let's go see what they're getting up to.”

Joey pulled the blanket from around her shoulders, dropping it on the couch and then grabbed the pair of crutches she'd leaned on Gale's chair, and he led her hobbling out the front door.

The sky was overcast and not as cold as it had been as they made their way by the tank and the still-cursing Marines with the big tools fighting the track. Alice was what they called the tank. Alex had painted an angry, skeletal fairy on the turret some days ago. The fairy had a bloody knife in her hand and was standing on a pile of skulls with the words *Sic Semper Tyrannis* written through it. Alex was a scary good artist. She was Layla's best friend and also the coxswain on her crew boat in high school. Layla and Sara were rowers, but Alex was pretty small, so she got to be the coxswain. She also had a loud voice, which worked for being a coxswain. Yelling at her boatmates in Russian was entertaining to watch as well. Gale supposed that rowing and high school were done with at this point. The girl's youth had been robbed.

More gunfire drew them on to the woods behind Floyd's house.

As they approached, snow crunched under their feet. There were the three girls, Layla, Alex, and Sara, along with Val and Nina. Val was in Pasha's care now. He was the grandson of Boris the Wolf. The Russian oligarch who had gotten them out of Kazakhstan, and whose aircraft they'd stolen to get home. Boris probably wasn't happy about that. Nina was Pasha's niece. Her mother, Galina, had been killed by the escaped prisoners that ambushed them on their way here from the airstrip they'd landed at.

Lou and Sergeant Simmons were talking to the kids—well, teenagers. They were all in their mid to late teens. Not kids. Not anymore. Ahmed and two Marines were standing behind the teens and their instructors, watching. Gale recognized the Marines. One was a corporal who was wounded when they arrived that night but seemed to have recovered, mostly. Left arm in a sling with his M-4 rifle slung around his other shoulder. The other one was a lance corporal. Gale couldn't keep these straight. He was the one with the grenade launcher mounted under his rifle, back when they got attacked in the kitchen. He had been knocked unconscious from a grenade tossed at the back door by the Russians in the woods out behind Lou's house that night. He was lucky because the Iranians that came in passed over him, probably thinking he was dead.

Most of us were lucky that night. Mostly.

Ahmed stood a head taller than both. Bald head and full, graying beard. He was Sara's uncle and the childhood friend of Javad, who was still recovering in Lou's basement. Ahmed was a solid ally and friend now. He and Sara were family. They all were.

Simmons yelled, "Fire!"

Gale and Joey quickly covered their ears with their hands. All five of the teens fired three shots at different trees down the slightly sloping woodland. Splinters flew from the hits. They were all shooting AK-47s gathered from the dead Iranian commandos. They all had winter jackets on with web gear and harnesses holding extra magazines.

"How they doin'?" Gale asked Ahmed.

Ahmed smiled. "They're eager to learn. Lou and Simmons know how to teach. Doing well."

"Some real *Red Dawn* shit right here," the corporal said to the lance corporal, and they both grinned.

"Let's hope not, Corporal," Joey said.

"Yes, ma'am! Didn't see you there." The corporal started to salute, seeming a bit confused now that there was an officer in uniform present.

"As you were," Joey said.

"Good morning, Commander," said the lance corporal. "Here are some earplugs for y'all. Your daughter's a natural with a rifle. The short one there, Alex, she's a beast. AK's as big as she is and heavy too."

Joey was still active duty, so she was the ranking officer—well, *only* officer—here. Technically, she was in command of these Marines. She and Gale took the foam earplugs and inserted them into their ears, muffling everything.

"You know I'm standing right here? I can hear you," Alex said flatly.

The two Marines laughed.

"Focus!" Simmons barked at her.

"I'm gonna go get that baby now. I'm sure she's awake," Joey told Gale, and she hobbled away to Lou's house.

Gale watched her go, then turned to Ahmed. "How's Javad?"

"He's a little better this morning, but the doctor says he still can't go on the car ride yet."

Gale wasn't surprised. Javad Shir-Del, now former chief of Iranian intelligence, had taken a good deal of shrapnel in his back while shielding Joey from a grenade. And although he was grateful Javad had jumped in the way, Gale needed him to recover so he could get the old Iranian spy twenty miles west of here, with him, at Mount Weather.

"How are you doing?"

"Still processing what Javad has done. I've known him since we were little. His mother, Bibi, is like my own mother. We are intertwined. Yet I want to stand him against a wall and see him shot."

"Perhaps it will come to that at some point, but not yet," Gale replied.

"Gale! Ahmed! It's Bibi! Help!" Joey yelled from Lou's front door, and they took off running.

FIVE

The Continental Shelf
Sunday Morning

"What did the captain mean when he said 'glassed'?" Moira asked. They were packing up what they had in the small stateroom after another night on the *Shark* heading east toward North Carolina.

"He meant they turned a good portion of Iran into glass. Nuclear weapons gallows humor," Tavis said. "Bobby was captain of a fast-attack sub I was on for a hot minute. He got our team close to some odd places so we could swim in and do some things. My other life. He wasn't really gonna blow us outta the water, dear."

"I figured that out myself. I can't even imagine this, though, Tav. What are we doing?"

She sat on the edge of the bed like the weight of the world was on her shoulders. He sat next to her and put an arm around her waist, and she snuggled her head into his neck and reached up and ran her fingers through his red beard.

"This was the decision we made," he said. "Together. It was safer for us ta be on the *Shark* than home with the possibility of a Russian invasion. Now it's safer ta get on that helicopter than stay on the *Shark*. No matter what occurs, we'll be together. I can't guarantee more than that, love." He was trying, rather poorly, to reassure her of his risk assessment ability.

"All right then. Together. What if we run into that bastard, Boris?"

"Together—we'll deal with him together. I just hope he's found his plane and gone back to Russia and not bothered with Joey and Pasha, but regardless, I owe it to them to do my best to warn them. They're my crew."

Tavis stood and finished packing his duffel, including his prized kukri knife. Tanner had been holding it for him while Tavis was in orbit. It was a gift from a team of Gurkhas his team had trained with—a curved knife about a foot long, thick in the middle, weight forward, with a wicked edge—and had come in handy in Afghanistan. A story he kept from his wife. He grabbed the Iridium satellite phone off the bed along with the charging cord and pocketed those too.

"Will that phone let us talk with Tanner?" Moira asked.

"Aye. I've got his number in the phone, as well as the number for both subs. Nice of Bobby to give 'em to me. Blackstone would like to be under a friendly command structure again, with orders to execute."

"And you think this Mount Weather place is that command?"

"We'll know soon enough. Look, Moira, things are going to go pretty fast once we get over land. One thing at a time. Fuel. Joey. Then they can get to Mount Weather. Then we'll figure the rest out. Boris has a really long lead on us. It weighs on me."

"This was all a long shot," Moira said sadly. "We don't know if they even got home. All we have is her address. At least Pasha's with her."

"Ha! That great Russian bastard's lucky he's got Joey to keep him out of trouble. She'll make sure his shoes are on the correct feet. Let's get this thing movin', lass."

They made their way from their stateroom, down the passageway, through the door to the wide deck beyond. They were greeted by a helicopter that appeared massive on the small deck. Tavis marveled at the skill it took to land the bird at all. The MH-60S Knighthawk's rotors were still but overhung the sides of the *Shark* by a foot or two. It was facing the bow with its tail rotor pointed toward the arched superstructure aft. It was all naval gray. Been a while since he'd been in one of these.

Tavis and Moira walked to the starboard side of the *Shark*, where Tanner was talking with the pilot. The pilot was just what you'd think a naval aviator ought to be—tall, clean-shaven, close-cropped hair, ruggedly handsome. He went by his call sign, Bouncer.

"Lieutenant, we ready to go?" Tavis asked as they approached.

"Roger that, Kinley. Be good to get back over land, to be honest. The sleep and food last night was a good refresher. Your brother was just filling me in on your background. Good to have an operator with us."

"I'm a tad rusty, but I can operate this if needed." Tavis patted the old FAL rifle slung across his chest.

"I'm sure," said Bouncer. "Mrs. Kinley, don't worry at all. We'll get you where you need to be safely. Your husband will keep us safe from the bad guys."

"I'm sure you're right, Lieutenant. Where is your crew?" she asked.

"My chiefs are over on the port side, smoking butts and saying their goodbyes to our shipmates in their own way." Bouncer's co-pilot was a chief warrant officer who went by his call sign, Duck. The other man was a surly senior chief petty officer who handled the helo's weapons and sensors. He went only by Senior Chief.

"I'm sorry for the loss of your shipmates," Tavis said.

"They gave 'em hell. That's all they could have asked for. We searched, but no one was…" He blinked his eyes quickly and shrugged. "You gonna get us to someone in charge so we can get some payback, Kinley?"

"That's the plan. Lejeune to refuel and then north. I assume we're close enough now with the fuel you have left?"

"Roger that. Did the nav with your brother little bit ago. We should be okay with some reserve."

"Then let's go before we lose the day. Tanner, where me minions at?"

"Already aboard." Tanner pointed at the open side door to the helo, and Meg's head popped out.

"Good. You gonna be okay out here?" Tavis asked his brother.

"Aye. I've got me bodyguards." Tanner gestured over his shoulder at the open ocean, where two submarines lurked just under the surface somewhere.

"Roger that. Let's go."

Tavis boarded the helo while Bouncer rounded up his crew. Soon the rotors were gaining speed, doors were closed, minions strapped in. Tanner's crew removed whatever they had against the wheels to keep the helo from rolling.

Moira sat next to Tavis, facing backward. She reached for his hand, and he squeezed hers gently. He prayed the rotors cleared the superstructure aft, but didn't mention this fear to her. Instead he watched his three kids across from them. They were staring out the windows on the sliding doors while the senior chief talked to them in the microphone, expounding upon all the bits and pieces of the helicopter. As gruff and hardened as this man was, he wore kid gloves with Tav's minions.

They lifted off and tilted forward and port a bit, gaining altitude. They'd keep it low in case there were other enemy ships in the area, trying to stay off radar. They were about a hundred miles off the coast of North Carolina and picking up speed. Bouncer said he had more than enough fuel to get to the Outer Banks and turn south down to Lejeune once they were over land.

Camp Lejeune was good for two things. Fuel and information. Hopefully the Marines were still there, but Tavis didn't think they would be. *He* wouldn't be, if he were them.

Twenty minutes later, they could see the coast. They were coming in a bit north of Oregon Inlet. Tavis turned as much as he could to watch the shore through the windshield up front. As they approached, he made out houses on stilts, waves crashing on the beach. They were a couple hundred feet in altitude, and he could also make out small groups of people on the beach. He focused on three men that had stopped whatever they were doing and watched and pointed at the helicopter. All three men had rifles, and there were dogs running around them. One man wore the same hat Tavis did, a tiger-striped boonie, with no jacket, one arm all tattooed up. The man next to him wore what looked like an old Roman centurion helmet, his face obscured but his bushy beard showing. The third man pumped his hands up with the devil's horns, index and pinky fingers in the air, like he was at a Volbeat concert. That was one of Tavis's favorite bands. He supposed he'd never get to see them in concert now.

"What in the blazes?" Moira said over the headphones.

"Looks like the Outer Banks have been secured by a bunch o' goons," Tavis replied.

"Stop touching stuff!" Moira scolded the boys.

"It's okay, ma'am. They're just curious. Can't hurt anything. As long as the big fan is still turning, we're good," the senior chief said.

"Do you see any activity or people, Senior Chief?" Tavis asked.

"Not a soul. It's eerie coming into Lejeune and not seeing any activity. Don't know if I like this. Didn't you serve a while back before you were an astronaut?"

"Yeah. Sergeant in Her Majesty's Special Boat Service. Did things in places."

"Good to hear. When we land, you and me gonna pull security quick, and make sure there's no hostiles before the fam gets off. Copy, Sergeant?"

"Copy, Senior Chief. Although you can just call me Tav or Kinley."

"Bullshit, Sergeant."

"Two minutes," Bouncer announced.

They flew in even lower, and Tavis and the senior chief pointed out landmarks to the twins, who soaked everything in like sponges.

"Welcome to Marine Corps Air Station New River," Bouncer said over the headphones as the helo touched down without a bounce.

The senior chief slid the door open. "Out we go, Sergeant." To the kids he added: "You guys stay here until me and your dad make sure it's safe."

Tavis followed him out onto the concrete tarmac. The chief was armed with an M-4 rifle and Tavis had his fifty-year-old FAL rifle from the Falklands War. They headed toward the buildings before them, rifles at low ready, scanning side to side for threats. Bouncer had landed as close to the buildings as possible and among dozens of other helicopters and Ospreys parked all over the place, hiding their helo in the chaff.

When they got closer to the buildings, Tavis smelled cigar smoke. He and the senior chief looked at each other and then scanned in all directions to track the smell.

"Y'all lost?" a deep voice called from inside a hangar to their right.

They trained their rifles in that direction. "Not lost. Who am I talking to?" the senior chief yelled.

Two older men appeared from the shadows of the hangar and walked out into the afternoon light. Both had cigars in their mouths. One was a tall and skinny black man, the other a bit shorter and much rounder with tanned, leathery skin and a black patch over his left eye. The tall one had a pump shotgun, and the short man looked like he had a 1911 pistol in a cross-chest holster that sat on his rotund stomach. Both wore vintage Marine Corps ball caps and jackets with patches everywhere.

"Y'all Americans?" the round one asked.

"I'm the senior chief on that Knighthawk that just landed. We lost our ship fighting Russians near Bermuda a day or so ago—long story. But yes, I'm an American. Again, who are you all?"

"Goddamn! Good to see some of our boys. I'm Al, and this is my oldest battle buddy, Owen."

"What's Al short for?" Tavis asked.

"Alfred. Why?"

"Fookin' shoot me now. There are more of them. God help me. I'm in some kind of parallel universe here," Tavis said. "I know a pair of gents somewhat like you two back in Scotland. I'm Tavis Kinley. This is Senior Chief. I don't know his name, just Senior Chief."

"And that's all you need to know. Probably the only senior chief left anyway," he said. "You boys know where we can get some fuel for that chopper we just landed?"

"Where ya goin'?" Owen asked.

"Need to refuel to get up to Northern Virginia," Tavis said. "We think there's some command elements at Mount Weather.

Government bunker. By the way, where are the Marines? This place is a ghost town."

"Marine Expeditionary Force headed out north about two days after all the power died. Took everything that would run and every man that could hold a rifle. We're sorta Lejeune security here. Not many left but us old-timers. We ain't goin' nowhere. This's home," Owen said. "That fuel truck out yonder there is full, but engine's dead, with what happened. We can solve that problem for ya, though."

"Sirs, if you all can help us get refueled, we'd be grateful," the senior chief said.

"Hold on." The two men disappeared back into the hangar, and a minute later Tavis heard an engine rumble. Al and Owen came scooting back out of the hangar in a gray aircraft tug.

"We've been tinkering with her for days," Al said. "Just got her back runnin' yesterday. She'll haul that fuel truck to your helo. Jump on." He smiled as big as Tavis had ever seen. Tavis knew that smile. The man was proud they could be of use.

"Here we are, gettin' help from a couple of Elmer Fudds," the senior chief muttered as he and Tavis hopped aboard the tug.

"Heard that, boy," Owen said. "That's *Senior* Fudds to you youngins."

"Don't jack up the Senior Fudds, Senior Chief. They're helping us," Tavis said.

They tooled across the tarmac, weaving in and out of the helicopter husks. That was what they were now—not operational aircraft, just husks. The senior chief waved at Bouncer, who was standing in the sun, holstering his pistol. Bouncer waved back.

"Where did you serve?" Tavis asked the American version of Alfie and Owen.

"Met Owen here when he saved my life in Hue, in 'nam. Haven't been able to get rid of him since," Al replied.

"Wouldn't be able to save shit now. Ya weigh as much as a cow in heat," Owen shot back.

"I'm just well-rounded, ya stick figure."

"But I can bust you in your one good eye hole, ya fat turd."

"Hey! Focus!" the senior chief yelled, rolling his eyes hard.

"It's okay. I'm likely to shoot him before you refuel anyway," Al said.

"Fuckin' Marines," the senior chief muttered.

Owen turned the vehicle around in front of the fuel truck. "Y'all hop out and grab those chains. Hook 'em up under the front there, and we'll tow it over to your chopper." It was clear the Senior Fudds had no intention of getting out of their seats.

A few minutes later, after some cussing and a scraped knuckle, Tavis had everything hooked up, and slowly, with some mechanical complaints, they rolled the fuel truck to the helo, where Bouncer and Duck were waiting to hook up the fuel hose. There was no power to the pump, but they got enough fuel by gravity to get mostly full. Moira and the kids had gotten out and were looking around, pointing at all the aircraft. Bouncer had insisted they get out just in case there was a flame-up with the fuel.

"We've gotten as much as I think we're gonna get," the senior chief said. He disconnected the hose and wrapped it back up on the truck.

Tavis looked at Al and Owen. "Gentlemen, we're in your debt. Thank you."

"Our pleasure. Happy to help out," Al said.

"Hue, you said?" Tavis asked.

"Hue," Owen replied, nodding.

"I'll let whatever command we find up north know that Camp Lejeune is secure."

The two men saluted and watched as everyone reboarded the Knighthawk. Bouncer and Duck started the big fan, and within minutes, they were leaving Marine Corps Air Station New River and its capable security detail behind.

"It's gonna be a little over two hours, barring Murphy's Law. Settle in," Duck said over the headphones.

Tavis gave a thumbs-up, and his mind started to go over scenarios that he knew were useless now. That angry Russian oligarch had a week's time on him. He could only hope Boris had trouble finding Joey and Pasha or, better yet, had died over the Atlantic.

Moira leaned her head on his shoulder. Together again.

The helo heaved, and a bit of nausea crept into his head and stomach. He focused and fought it. All this movement exacerbated the effects of his return to gravity. He tried to sleep, hoping the child didn't visit him again in his dreams.

SIX

Northern Virginia
Sunday, Late Morning

Javad heard quiet conversation as he became more awake. How long had he been asleep this time? He didn't know how many days he'd been lying here since that night. The pain in his back was dull, and he felt the IV stuck into the vein in the back of his left hand as he shifted.

He smelled flowers, and there was a weight on his right hand and arm. He cracked his eyes open and looked down. His daughter, Sara, had her head on his arm.

"I'm here, my girl," he said with a cracking, weak voice.

She raised her head to look at him through red, wet eyes. "Oh, Papa," she whispered and squeezed his hand.

"It's okay, I'm still here." He reached up and wiped a fresh tear from her cheek.

"Papa, Bibi had a heart attack. She's gone," Sara said.

"When?" It was his turn for wet eyes now. A familiar grief rose in his chest.

"Just a little while ago. She passed in her sleep. When she didn't come downstairs this morning, Mama Nguyen went to wake her but couldn't. The doctor said it was probably a heart attack in her sleep. He said she felt no pain. I'm so sorry, Papa." Sara laid her head down on his arm again and sobbed.

Javad's thoughts raced from one memory to the next incoherently. His mother had always been his rock. For him and for others. He wasn't there when she died. He tried to place blame, but it kept falling back on him.

He stroked Sara's long hair, and they both wept for Bibi.

Gale and Joey walked up the stairs from the basement of Lou's house. It was slow going with Joey's crutches. The doctor had looked at her leg and the cast, approved of the work that was done in Kazakhstan over a week ago, and told her it would be about five more weeks until it could come off. Gale supposed she'd be a handful until then. She was pretty irritated by her immobility.

On the main level, there was still plenty of evidence of the night when the commandos attacked. Holes from AK-47 rounds, large and small, littered the walls and furniture. Nearly all the windows had been shattered and were now covered with plywood and/or blankets to keep the cold out.

Sergeant Nelson, Alice's new commander, and Jones, the gunner, were working in the corner near some big music speakers. Standing near the front doorway was Lou, the sixty-something former Navy SEAL, talking to Alex.

"It's not fair," Alex was saying. "She didn't deserve this. She was so sweet, Lou. I'm losing everyone around me."

"You're with me, sweetie," Lou replied. "We're family now. We've got each other. We will go on and walk in their memory. You, me, and Christopher."

"Where *is* the pug?" she asked, looking around.

Gale and Joey had just reached the front door, and Gale spotted the dog on the tank's engine compartment, curled into a pug ball.

"On the tank," he said, pointing to the behemoth that looked completely out of place in the middle of the cul-de-sac.

"Yeah, that pug loves the warm engine compartment," said a voice behind him. Nelson and Jones had walked up, each carrying a large, rectangular, box-like speaker outside. "Thank you for the speakers, sir," he added, speaking to Lou.

"Absolutely! I approve of their new use. I think Robert would love it as well," Lou said.

Gale was now intrigued, and they all followed the Marines over to the tank. On their way they passed Lou's garage, where he'd set up a tarp to funnel the smoke out through the open garage door. Mama and Layla were sitting in plastic chairs, cooking bacon and eggs for everyone in cast-iron skillets. There was still quite a lot of food from everyone's freezers and refrigerators that they'd stashed in coolers with ice and snow. Gale would miss this smell when they ran out, which would be soon if they didn't start to ration it.

"You okay, honey?" Joey asked, hobbling over and reaching out to Layla.

"Yeah. Bacon helps the sadness," the girl replied.

"Food helps everything, Layla," Mama said, schooching eggs around her skillet.

They continued toward the tank, where the other two crewmen, Stewie and Fletch, were sitting in fold-up lawn chairs they'd gotten from Lou's garage. Between them was a table with two red Solo cups, a carton of eggnog, and a bottle of Maker's Mark. Chewie, the little Yorkshire Terrier, was tugging ferociously at the bottom of Fletch's pant leg.

"If it gets much warmer, we're gonna have a problem with those bodies, man," Stewie was saying.

"Ground's too frozen still to bury 'em, though. Gonna have to burn 'em soon, otherwise it's gonna get all death up in here," Fletch responded.

"Guys! Police up that topic!" Lou barked.

Fletch and Stewie stood quickly. When they saw Joey in her uniform, both men saluted smartly.

"As you were and no more of that saluting stuff," she said. "Be careful of that talk around the kids."

Gale glanced at Alex. Her parents were two of the bodies that Fletch and Stewie were talking about. But the girl ignored the exchange. Alex walked to the table, picked up one of the cups, and smelled it. She mumbled something in Russian, grabbed the bottle of whiskey, took a pull, then set it back down and walked back to her house.

"I didn't catch what she said. Was that Russian?" Stewie asked Lou who was attempting to contain his laughter.

"Generally translated, she said eggnog is snot that pussies drink," Lou replied, and the Marines cracked up.

"Where are the other Marines?" Joey asked.

"They're upstairs in my house with Bibi," Lou said. "Going to wrap her in sheets and carry her out to lay with the others."

Which brought the group back to the problem at hand: what to do with the bodies. No one seemed to have an answer.

Joey finally said, "You know, they have a point. We're going to have to come up with a plan for the deceased, and soon. It's been above freezing for a couple of days now. At least when the sun's out."

Gale was about to ask what that plan would entail when the pug suddenly rolled his rotund body up, stood up on the engine compartment, and started barking.

"What's his deal?" Gale asked Lou. Christopher was Lou's dog, after all. He spoke pug.

Lou frowned. "I don't—wait, listen!"

They all fell quiet. A *whump, whump, whump* beat steadily in the air.

"That's a helicopter! Get cover. Stewie, get on your gun," Sergeant Nelson ordered.

Gale didn't know how Stewie got up on the tank and into his position so fast, but he did. The rest all got to the north side of Alice.

"Helicopter!" Pasha bellowed across the court, leading Val and his niece, Nina, from between two houses. He'd unslung his AK-47 and was tracking the incoming helo with the muzzle.

"We can hear it, Pasha!" Joey yelled back.

As the beating rotors neared, Gale was reminded of a scene from a movie. *We're in* Red Dawn, he thought.

"There's a helicopter low and slow to the south!" Simmons shouted as he and two other Marines came out of Lou's front door and aimed their M-4s in that direction.

"Thank you, Sergeant!" Joey yelled.

"Hey, honey?"

"What?" Joey said, watching the helo come in.

"Helicopter," Gale said, pointing south.

"I should have stayed in space!" Joey said with a laugh. She stretched up on her one good foot to look at the helo over the tank's engine compartment. "It's American. Maybe it's from Mount Weather."

"It may be American, but are you sure the people inside are, too, ma'am?" Sergeant Nelson asked.

"Well, they're not shooting at us, so I call that a win," Joey replied.

She hobbled on her crutches out in front of Alice, and as the helo came in over the houses, she waved to indicate it should land up the street in front of the tank. The helo slowly descended and touched down in the street.

Everyone gathered in front of the tank as the rotors slowed to a stop, except for Alex, though she did come back outside and sat on the front stoop. Even Mama and Layla had joined the group.

The doors on both sides of the helicopter opened. "You great Russian bastard!" a voice bellowed from within, and a red-bearded Scotsman hopped out.

"Tav!" Joey yelled. She hobbled over and embraced him.

"That's a long flight from Scotland in a helo," Pasha said to his friend as they gave each other a bear hug. Pasha winced.

"You okay, big man?" Tavis asked Pasha.

"Shot in shoulder. Am okay," he responded.

"It's good to see you all." Others were climbing out behind him, and he introduced them. "You all remember Moira, my wife, and the Kinlets, Duncan, Dougal, and Meg. And these are Bouncer, Duck, and Senior Chief."

Handshakes went all around, and they all told their stories. Joey and Gale relayed the goings-on in the cul-de-sac, Pasha told the story of the landing, Boris's aircraft, and their eventful journey here, and of course they all talked about the Iranians and Russians. Tavis told his story as well, and Pasha's face turned dark when he heard of Boris the Wolf.

"Boris is not a man to let things go, Tav. If you're sure he came here, then he *is* here, somewhere. We need to be diligent in our patrols and security. The Wolf got that name for a reason."

"Aye, he was pissed. Had about a dozen guns with him as well. Armed to the teeth," Tavis said.

"A dozen guns?" Gale asked.

"No. *Guns,*" Tavis said.

"Are you trying to say *goons,* animal breeder?" Pasha asked, his laughter barely contained.

"Aye, *goons!* Ya fooker," Tavis said.

He punched Pasha in the shoulder, and Pasha erupted in a string of Russian. "I was shot there!" he complained.

"Sorry, brother."

Gale was having a hard time understanding the Scottish brogue and the Russian accent. He couldn't imagine being cooped up with these two in outer space. It gave him a newfound respect for his wife.

"Speaking of brothers," Joey said, "I suppose that was your brother's ship coming into Campbeltown as we took off?"

"Aye, it was. It's how we got here. He's still out there off the coast somewhere." Tavis explained the Russian and American warship engagement, and Bouncer picked up where Tavis left off and told his parts of the story.

"We refueled at Camp Lejeune and came here on our way to Mount Weather to see if there's any command authority left," Bouncer finished.

"Mount Weather?" Gale said. "Hey, is that helo a smooth ride?"

"Yeah, pretty much, why?"

"Because if you're going to Mount Weather, do you have room for some passengers? Me and one on a stretcher?"

"Yeah, we can do that easy."

"I know where you're going with this," Sergeant Simmons said. "Go get the fold-up stretcher from the back of the Humvee and get the old man loaded. The corpsman can tag along and monitor him."

People started moving.

Gale turned to his wife. "Joey, you're coming with me this time. We'll bring Javad to them."

"Can I come along as well?" Pasha asked. "Been a while since I flew. Would be good to be in one again."

"You flew helos?" Bouncer asked.

"*Da.* Before I became cosmonaut, I was in the military and did some contracting where I flew Mil-24s."

"Ah, the Hind. You sit up front with me. Duck can ride in the back. Senior Chief, make room for our passengers and a stretcher."

"Roger that," the senior chief said, and went to get things ready.

"I'm going as well," Tavis added. "Got intel that they need to hear."

"Excuse me?" Moira said.

"I know I said we'd be together no matter what," Tavis said to his wife, "but this is critical."

His game face was on, so she just nodded, but the look she gave him made everyone else go on about their business.

"Kids, you take care of your mother, now," Tavis added. "I'll be back in no time. Not like I'm goin' to space this time. Short hop, talk to the powers that be, and short hop back."

"We'll take good care of them, Tavis," Lou reassured him. "They can join the rest of the kids, and we'll just sit and chat while you're gone. Nothing's going to happen while we have Alice here." He patted the front of the tank.

"Settled, then. I'll be back."

Tavis gave Moira and the kids a hug and nodded to Lou. Then he walked to the helo, patting his pockets, pulled out a satellite phone as if to check that it was still there, and then climbed aboard.

Soon all the passengers and crew were aboard, including Javad on his stretcher, with an IV bag hung on a hook made for just that purpose. The engines started up, and Gale and Joey waved to Layla. The senior chief slid the doors shut, and in minutes, they were airborne and climbing, heading away.

Just a short hop, Gale thought, hoping Tavis was right.

✺✺✺

"So, we have more guests and possibly some that are unwanted," Ahmed said to Lou.

"Seems that way," Lou replied. "Hey, Simmons."

The sergeant came over and was joined by the rest of the Marines, while Layla led the Kinley kids over to Alex's house to introduce them. Nina was there already, and Sara was heading from Lou's house to join the gaggle.

"Moira, clearly you know why you've come this far," Lou said. "Incredible that you all did so, just to warn Joey about this Boris fella."

Moira sighed. "My husband's a soldier, first and always. Infuriating as he can be, in his mind he was honor-bound to warn you all. Joey and Pasha were, are, his crew. He couldn't live with himself if he hadn't tried. Obviously, there's always one more mission with him. He'll get a piece of my mind when he's returned. Of that, you can be sure."

"I've no doubt. No doubt at all. In the meantime, we need to up our patrols, just in case Boris and his goons show up. Simmons, square us away on that," Lou said.

It was more of an order than a request.

SEVEN

Major Tang was thankful that he and his crew were now on short missions here in the American interior. He'd spent days on Firey Cross Reef after the strike on the US antenna site in northwest Australia from the South China Sea. Then it was ferrying his two bombers to Panama and on to Gillette, Wyoming, where the PLA had taken up considerable operations out of the Northeast Wyoming Regional Airport. It was from this FOB that the PLA was continuously flying in men, equipment, and most importantly, for him at least, munitions for his missions. Guided bombs, dumb bombs, air-to-surface missiles, and cruise missiles for stand-off punch.

This run was dumb bombs only. They weren't going after key military installations, just hitting a couple of locations where American guerrillas and militias were forming, according to his pre-mission briefing. They'd be back on the ground in Gillette in just over an hour.

It was also just his bomber on this run. Captain Liu, his wingman, was off on another run south of Gillette. They were the only two bombers in the area of operation at the moment, but he was assured that more were coming as soon as they got the Indians under control.

He thought of his wife and three-year-old daughter constantly, and wondered when he'd see them again, if ever. He was a good soldier and just wanted to bring honor to them and his parents. His family lived with his parents in a small fishing village within Magong Harbor on the coast of southeast China.

That brought him to why they were at war in the first place. He'd seen the briefings. Food and land. The central planners had really screwed up the harvests, and the one sure way for them to be run out of power was for a billion people to begin to starve. He supposed that was why the former minister of agriculture was the new prefect in Gillette.

Right after they'd set off the EMPs and killed all the electronics in the US and Europe, the PLA dropped paratroopers into Wyoming and took Gillette's airport. From there, it was just a matter of the continuous transport of men and supplies. They were definitely worried about American citizens, being well armed as they were. However without power, central command's hope was that the majority of Americans would be starving and dead in a matter of weeks or months. That thought actually horrified Tang and he tried to bury it. He didn't like that part one bit.

He put it out of his mind. He didn't have to see it or be part of it. Keeping the militia and counterinsurgents at bay was his job. He focused on that.

The Russians were moving into Europe and Canada, and the PLA would secure most of the US down to the Mexican border. No one wanted to get near that. The stories they were hearing of the border clashes with the US and Mexican militaries fighting each other and the cartels for power down there, with the population caught in the middle, were terrifying.

Focus on your job, he told himself. *Then you'll get to see your family again.*

"We've reached the waypoint to start the run," Tang's co-pilot said.

"Copy," Tang replied. "Stay at five thousand feet and open bomb bay doors. Two minutes to drop." Tang said to his weapons officer, who was in one of the two seats directly behind himself and his co-pilot.

The snow had stopped a couple of days prior but had left two feet on the ground. Nothing moved around the cabin on the side of this small mountain. Tiger Butte, the map called it. Captain Chao sat on the porch with his binoculars and a mug of cold coffee he hadn't touched. It was wicked cold this late in the afternoon with the failing light. His breath was a thick white cloud as he watched the smoke from chimneys drift in the town below them. Earlier there had been children playing in the snow and sledding.

Men on horseback were accumulating in the town. He knew what they were planning, but with the snow, it took time. Letting the town's sheriff go after they'd captured him was a mistake, but Chao wasn't a monster. He was a soldier. They'd agreed not to bother each other for now, but he knew when they had enough men, they'd come back.

He looked at the tractor-trailer with the anti-aircraft missiles on it. Only one of the original three were left. Didn't matter anyway because their fuel had run out for the generator, and the radar was dead. The snow was too deep for them to walk out. It was a matter of time before the fighting started. The world was so small here with all the snow, no sound at all.

His mind drifted to Mei. Still with the minister of agriculture, surely. Safe.

Snow crunching made him turn from the town to four of his soldiers walking up to the front porch. As they came around, he knew something wasn't right.

"Captain, we caught Private Yang with this." The tattooed sergeant handed him a satellite phone like the one he used to communicate with command. The two soldiers behind Yang now made sense. Guards.

He looked at the private closely. Bloody nose and a welt forming over his right eye. They'd roughed him up, and Chao hadn't even heard the commotion. The snow and trees muffled all sound out here.

"What is this, Private?" Chao held the sat phone out, but the private said nothing.

The sergeant spoke, clearly agitated. "We were doing rounds and saw a glow in the trees. We surprised Yang texting a message. To whom we don't know, but it's not command. Read the messages, Captain. It's all in there. Captain Gao shooting Major Feng. Letting the sheriff go back to the town. The missile launches, taking down the American ICBM. Running out of fuel. And then the last one. Requesting extraction soonest."

Chao hit the down button several times to read all the messages. They were short and to the point. Starting when they arrived at the cabin. Whenever Yang could steal away to communicate alone. He then studied the defiant young private. "So. You're a spy. At least Feng was open about what he was. We treated you as part of the team. Any one of my men or me would have given our lives fighting with you, and you spy on us? For who? Who's your boss? Who's on the other end of this?"

Just then, the thunder of jet engines broke the silence. Chao stepped down off the porch, and the two soldiers guarding Yang grabbed his arms and pulled him out of their captain's way. A gray pall had settled over the valley, and he scanned the sky with no luck. The engines came and went, fading into the distance, but the town erupted in massive explosions, six in all, from one end of the once sleepy little town to the other.

Seconds later, the concussions from the bombs passed through Chao. Infuriated, he was about pull out his pistol and shoot Yang in the head, knowing his reports were the cause of the explosions, when another sound crept into the once-quiet valley.

"Sergeant, gather the men quick," Chao ordered as Captain Gao burst through the cabin's front door, followed by the few soldiers that were off-shift, resting by the fire.

"What's going on, Captain?" Gao asked, looking at the burning town below and then at Yang, arms still held by two soldiers.

"Private Yang is a spy, or political plant, in our team," Chao said. "He's communicated with someone about everything we've been doing here. As a result, the town, all the people, including the many children, are probably now dead. Also, we have visitors."

An Mi-171 transport helicopter was landing in the clearing near the tractor-trailer, where the snow was crushed down by their constant patrols. Snow blew violently and stung Chao's face as a squad of armed men in green uniforms took up a perimeter around the helicopter. A tall man with a red beret exited the side door of the chopper and walked toward them.

"State Security," Gao growled.

Chao turned and looked at her and then at Yang, who smiled.

"Captain Chao!" said the man in the red beret, shouting to be heard over the rotor noise. "I am Colonel Vang, Ministry of State Security. You are relieved. You will be debriefed at the base. Please have your men board the helicopter."

"Colonel, I have received no orders from command to abandon our mission here," Chao said. He felt the presence of his sergeant next to him, and laid a hand on the sergeant's rifle, slowly pushing it down.

"Captain Chao, you are relieved, I assure you," Vang said with a sneer. "You have disobeyed direct orders regarding the civilians in the town below, who have now been dealt with."

Down in the valley, where the town used to be, stood the burnt-out husks of destroyed buildings smoking in the late Montana afternoon.

"You will need to answer for that," Vang continued. "Morever, Captain Gao is under arrest for the murder of Major Feng. Shot in the back, I believe, in the course of following the exact orders you disobeyed. Private Yang, take Captain Gao's weapon and place her under guard in the helicopter."

Yang stepped over to Gao, grabbed her pistol from its holster, and gestured to the helicopter.

Chao looked around at his men, their faces illuminated by the helicopter's landing lights reflecting off the snow-covered ground, and shook his head slightly. They were outnumbered and surrounded by these security troops. He knew he'd have to answer for what had happened here. He and Gao. But hoped his men would be needed and thus spared to fight another day without him.

Yang bumped him roughly as he passed with Gao.

"Captain," Vang said, stepping right in front of Chao, "you didn't think you weren't being watched out here, did you? Yang isn't a private. He's a lieutenant, and one of my best men. From the wounds on his face, I'd say we got here just in time."

He held his hand out, and Chao obediently unholstered his pistol and handed it over. Vang then addressed Chao's sergeant.

"You and the rest of this team will be reassigned once we're back on base. Board the helicopter."

The sergeant looked at Chao, who nodded.

"Team! On the helicopter!" The sergeant led Chao's team to the waiting bird as Chao and Vang stood watching.

"Colonel, I take full responsibility for the actions here," Chao said. "My men and Captain Gao are not responsible. I was the commanding officer."

"Captain, you will answer for these crimes. Your men will be treated fairly. Reassigned, as I said. We need all the men we have at hand. However, justice and discipline must be reinforced if we're to be victorious here. Captain Gao will be tried, and justice will be served. Get on the helicopter, Captain."

"Yes, justice must be served," Chao said.

He started toward the helicopter, staring at Yang, who relaxed in the webbed seat facing the rear next to the door. He climbed aboard and took the seat across from Yang, and the colonel stepped past him and sat on the other side of the wide bird. Chao's men were in the back, with Vang's men behind and in front of them, all seated along the sides.

The helo took off, and Vang yelled over the engine noise. "Captain Chao, the door, if you please."

Chao grabbed the handle of the large side door, and it began to slide. At the last moment, he reached out, grabbed Yang's ammo vest, and propelled the traitor from the helicopter, from at least one hundred feet up.

Then he quietly pulled the door shut.

EIGHT

Gale saw the flat farmland rise out of the helo's side door window into a ridge line. The first mountains of the Blue Ridge. Not really mountains, not like the Rockies. These were tiny in comparison, but they rose nonetheless. They'd only be in the air for minutes. It really was a short hop of twenty miles or so. He glanced out the window and saw several buildings ablaze with thick, black smoke rising into the air. That must be Purcelville, one of the many towns out this way. Gale imagined it was like this all over. What he couldn't imagine was what it was like in the cities.

Tavis turned around in his seat, straining to see into the cockpit. Gale saw him realize that Pasha had been flying the helo the entire time. "Jaysus, Mary, and Joseph! You're letting him fly? We'll all be killed. Hasn't flown in years!" He said in his mic that went to everyone that had a helmet or earphones on.

"Flying is not problem. Landing will be interesting," Pasha replied.

Tavis shook his head and looked out his window.

Joey squeezed Gale's hand.

"You're gonna have to use every ounce of command authority you have when we land," Gale told her loudly over the noise of the rotors. "Bouncer, you as well. You both have intelligence to pass on. It'll hopefully get us in where I couldn't."

"Don't worry. I'll put my officer face on," Joey said. "Also, we've got him this time," she added, nodding at Javad.

Javad didn't have a headset on, but he nodded back. The man looked like he was pretty weak still and tired. Gale had explained it all to him, and he was going to be fully cooperative. It was his war, after all.

Gale looked out the window again as they approached the mountain in front of them. They were passing over a golf course with big homes situated along the fairways. He leaned toward the window to get a better look and saw two people pulling golf bags on carts down one of the fairways. They stopped and waved.

"They're playing golf!" Gale said. He couldn't believe it.

"Golfers are fanatics," Tavis replied.

"Landing in thirty seconds," Bouncer announced as the ground came up to meet them. Gale could see low buildings and a Humvee near the landing pad. Armed men stood near it. This was going to go great. He hoped this time he had the key to get in: Javad, the middle-aged Iranian, who had now fallen asleep.

❀❀❀

Javad was jarred from his in-and-out again consciousness by the helo bouncing on the landing pad. He winced at the pain in his upper back and looked around. The man with the red beard was yelling.

"You buckled the landing gear, ya wanker!" Red Beard yelled into his mic. Whatever was said back, Javad couldn't hear; he didn't have earphones.

The rotors of the helo were slowing to a stop. A welcome wind rushed over his face as the doors on both sides slid open. He knew where they were and was actually looking forward to telling all he knew in hopes of making this place safer for Sara, Ahmed, and his mother. Then the realization hit him again. Bibi was gone.

Sadness at the loss of his mother, his rock, nearly overwhelmed him, but he pushed those feelings away into a deep recess in his mind with all the other tragic memories. He'd see her again soon enough. The neighborhood doctor's prognosis for his recovery wasn't good. He'd be with his wife and his sister and mother soon. But first, he would unburden his soul so that he might walk lightly into heaven. Or hell.

The stretcher he was lying on was very uncomfortably shoved out into the cold air. The blanket on his body shielded most of the wind, but his face felt oddly alive. His carriers were the corpsman that he knew and an older soldier or crew member from the helicopter. He saw Gale and his wife, and another crew member and the big

Russian. He was put on the ground as the woman spoke to some other men.

"Yes, tell whoever is in command that Lieutenant Commander Joey Washington needs to brief them. Tell them I've come from the International Space Station to do it, and I have with me the chief of the Iranian Intelligence Agency. This helicopter crew also has vital intel to pass along." She put on an angry affect, but Javad knew it was a command presence.

"Also," Red Beard added, "inform whoever's down there that there's two submarines, one with ballistic missiles, just off the East Coast, and I can contact them via sat phone."

A man with a rifle and a radio relayed this information. Whatever the reply was, it must have been positive. "We just have to wait a few minutes for them to open the blast door," the main said. "We've been ordered to get you all to the main ops center below."

Weary, Javad drifted off.

When he opened his eyes again, he was in the back of a topless vehicle, and they were driving through a brightly lit tunnel. The overhead rock had hundreds of large bolts drilled into it—likely for stability. Then all at once the tunnel was gone and they emptied into a cavernous space, also brightly lit. It may have been another tunnel but if so it was on a far more massive scale. There were buildings in here, some three stories tall.

The vehicle pulled up to one of the buildings, and the corpsman put a hand on Javad's chest as the vehicle stopped abruptly. Everyone got out, and they slid Javad from the back of what he now saw was an open-top Humvee. There were people standing around looking at him. A lot of people.

The man with the radio led the group into the building. Just a normal building, but inside a mountain. Surreal. The crewman and corpsman were carrying him again. They went through two open doors, down a hallway, then turned and entered a glass-enclosed conference room with an operations center beyond the glass. He felt very naked as the people in the operations center all stared.

"Coming through!"

Javad turned his head to see a doctor and nurse enter the room. The doctor was a woman and had a Middle Eastern look to her. Arab or Persian. She reminded Javad of his sister. The corpsman described Javad's wounds, and the doctor inspected the wound in his back. The rest of his issues were secondary and non-life-threatening. As they talked, he noticed the rest of the group had taken seats around a conference table.

"Sir, I'm Dr. Rahimi. How do you feel?"

"I am tired. Pain in my back," Javad replied weakly.

"We're going to give you something that will perk you up so you have energy to talk. I hear you have some information to share when the others get here. After that, we'll get you into surgery and fix you up. Can you tell me your name?"

The nurse attached an intravenous line to the plastic tube already in his arm.

"Javad Shir-Del," he replied.

A voice spoke from the doorway. "Shaitan! Finally, I get to meet the man."

Javad turned his head, and the room fell silent. The newcomer was dressed in blue jeans and a polo shirt. A black belt, tennis shoes. He was tall, with gray hair but a young face, freshly shaven. The man's eyes bored into Javad.

"I do not know you. But that name fits," Javad said. He attempted a laugh, which sent him into a coughing fit that hurt like hell, but he felt more awake.

"I'll give you fifteen minutes," the doctor said, "and then we need to get him to the operating room. We have full hospital facilities here. It has a skeleton staff left over from Christmas Eve. If any of the rest of you have any medical issues, let us know, and we'll get you looked at."

"Javad," said the gray-haired man, "did you know that we knew who you were? That it was, in fact, the CIA that was running you?"

Javad saw Gale lean forward in his seat, staring at him. "I was hopeful. I knew that my Indian contact was running communications up front, and for years I passed whatever I had through him. I assumed my contact on the other end would at least be the Israelis.

Then hopefully my information went on to CIA, but I didn't know for sure. The name—Shaitan. It is the code name for me, yes?"

"It is, and your guess was right. The Israelis passed us everything. In fact, I am—*was* your case officer. You can call me Jack."

"Jack. A pleasure to meet you. What do you do now?" Javad asked, one spy to another. Feeling each other out, before a listening audience.

"Well, due to the EMP and nuclear strikes, a great many of the government personnel and assets have been killed or destroyed. I am the ranking CIA officer here. Therefore, our new president named me acting director of Central Intelligence. I'm the chief spy here now."

"I like the name Shaitan. It fits," Javad said with a smile.

"What does it mean?" Gale asked.

"It has several meanings in Islam," Javad explained. "Generally, it means Maker of Mischief. More specifically, it means Devil."

Gale laughed.

Jack quirked an eyebrow at Gale. "I'm sorry, I don't know you."

"Gale Washington. I worked at the intel fusion center in Reston before all this. My boss said I had too many devils dancing in my head for my own good. I worried about everything. So he's just another devil. Checks out."

"Well, Gale, I wish someone had worried about all of this. Maybe we could have gotten ahead of it," Jack replied.

Joey put her hand on Gale's leg, but the mild restraint didn't work. "I did warn!" Gale snapped. "I briefed the fusion leadership and was told it was nonsense. I was told to focus on more relevant intel by the general in charge of operations. If you were running the Devil here, why didn't you know anything?"

"Alas, I didn't pass the information on to my handler about the attack on Christmas Eve until just prior. They didn't know beforehand. The timing was tight," Javad explained.

"Ten-hut!" bellowed one of the soldiers, and more people filed into the room.

A thin, wiry man stopped in front of Jack. He was balding badly and had a pinched expression behind oversized glasses. His blue uniform jacket had three stars on the shoulders, and his name plate read *Spenkmeier*.

"At ease," he said. "Who are all these people, Acting Director?" The general made the term *Acting Director* somehow unsavory when he said it. Perhaps Jack and the general were at odds here. Javad filed that away.

"You!" Gale and the general said simultaneously, glaring at each other.

"Didn't I order that this man not be granted access?" Spenkmeier growled.

"You're a piece of work," Gale shot back. "We have intel to pass to whoever's in charge here, and I had it when you turned us away before. Now we're here with the source we received it from and more, and you're still being a dick." His voice rose as he walked around the table to stand dangerously close to the general. Everyone rose to their feet too, including Red Beard and the Russian. The room seemed to be getting smaller by the second.

"I bet your intel is as shoddy and inadequate as it was months ago when Dennis allowed you to brief me and my staff," Spenkmeier spat.

"You don't get to say his name. There was not a thing wrong with my briefing except that it included calling you unenlightened in front of your staff—who, by the way, agreed with my data analysis while *you* were too concerned about optics and your career to advance it. Because you're a coward."

Gale's fists clenched and relaxed as he made his speech. Of course, Javad knew who Dennis was and what he had meant to Gale. They had been good friends. The man had died from gunshot wounds just feet from Javad.

Javad scanned the room and saw that none of the group he came in with had their firearms any longer. Probably protocol. He did see that Red Beard had his left hand on the handle of some sort of knife still in its sheath. The man was dead still and staring around the room without moving his head.

Interesting.

"Dennis was—" Spenkmeier started, but Gale's right fist cut him off, connecting with the general's left eye, knocking him to the floor.

The armed soldiers pointed their rifles at Gale and shouted for him to stop. A heartbeat later, Red Beard had unsheathed his knife—a curved kukri blade—and had leapt across the conference table and landed behind one of the soldiers, placing his knife around the front of the startled man's throat.

"Lower your weapons! We're on the same team here," Red Beard yelled as a furious Spenkmeier gathered himself from the floor and started toward Gale, who was now being restrained by the Russian. Joey stepped up to the general.

More and more interesting, Javad thought.

A new voice entered the fray. "Stand down! All of you! Now! What on God's green one is going on in here?"

Javad turned to see who had walked in. The man standing in the doorway wore a dark gray suit, no tie, dull-looking dress shoes, and his gray hair was closely cut. His face was full, though he wasn't overweight. Dark, bloodshot eyes glared around the room, taking in everything.

"Who are you?" Gale asked, still agitated, and it came across.

"I'm the goddamned president of what's left of the United States of America," the man said.

The room went quiet.

"Stand down, Spunkmeier!" the president ordered.

"It's Spenkmeier, Mr. President," the general said quietly.

"I don't give two fucks what it is. Stand down. *Now*. Everyone, take a seat. I don't have time for whatever this shit is. I need information. Whoever you are, remove that knife from my soldier's throat now!"

Red Beard resheathed his kukri, then patted the soldier on his back and walked back to his chair. The show was over.

"Everyone calm now?" the president said. "Who are you all, and why are you here?" And then he caught sight of Joey. "I recognize you."

She snapped to attention. "Lieutenant Commander Joey Washington, sir. Recently from the International Space Station."

"That's it! Holy shit! How'd you get here, Commander?"

"It's a long story, and others have more important intel, but I'll add mine where appropriate. I recognize you as well. Aren't you—*weren't* you the Secretary of Transportation?"

"I was. Only cabinet member to make it here. Everyone else is either unaccounted for or dead. Once we got a justice here, shortly after me, he swore me in and we went to work. Name's James Madison. The mountain here is where our Continuity of Government is supposed to be. Because it was Christmas Eve, there was only a small watch with the normal guards and a few junior officers and contractors, plus some medical staff. And nothing fucking works. Our communications weren't as shielded as they should've been. Generators works and we have food and water forever, but aside from that, we're pretty blind.

"We don't have communications with hardly anyone or anywhere except NORAD in Colorado, and that's sporadic at best. Someone needs to explain to me the term 'survivable communications' at some point. Hell, our comms with them are underground, and they're *still* shitty. They're basically shut down. Took a direct hit by a nuclear weapon. Tried to launch Minutemen III missiles to hit North Korea. We know the EMP that knocked everything out was two North Korean satellites. However, our missiles never reached orbit."

"Your name is James Madison?" the senior chief blurted out once the president stopped talking.

"Yeah, big shoes to fill. Now tell me who the rest of you are."

They went around the table, from the astronauts to the helo crew to Gale, and then all eyes went to Javad.

"I am Javad Shir-Del. Formerly the chief of Iranian Intelligence."

The president gave a low whistle and looked at Jack.

"It's true, sir. But he's also one of our spies. He worked for the US through the Indians and Israelis. Code name is Shaitan."

"The devil," the president replied.

Dr. Rahimi spoke up. "He's wounded, Mr. President. He needs surgery, so we need to make this quick."

The president nodded. "Tell us what you know, Shaitan. Can you explain all this?"

"It started several years ago with the Chinese food crisis," Javad began, and he went on to explain China's intentions as well as those of the Russians, North Koreans, and Iranians. How they had spent two years in Ulaanbaatar in Mongolia planning this. He explained his own involvement and his reasons, as well as his passing of the plan to Indian intelligence just prior to the attack, but that he had only named Iran and North Korea in that intel.

Spenkmeier spoke. "Why wouldn't you pass on Chinese and Russian involvement? The Chinese were obviously the force behind this entire plot and attack."

"Targeted vengeance. The regime in Iran is to blame for the death of my sister, my wife, my father, and now my mother. They are evil. So I became evil to destroy them. If there was a counterattack for this, I wanted it to be fully against Iran. North Korea was secondary." Javad told them why he'd left Iran and ended up here, and how the man he'd been chasing for decades had now ended up a frozen corpse in the dirt ten miles to the east.

"Javad, that's quite the information download. Thank you for that. Now, who else has any relevant information?" Madison asked.

"I have relevant intel that you all should know." The Scottish voice was Red Beard's. During introductions, the man had said his name was Tavis.

"Tell us," said Jack.

Joey cut in. "Excuse me, sir. I think it would make more sense to explain in order."

Madison nodded for her to proceed.

"Just before Tavis, Pasha, and I evacuated the crippled ISS," Joey began, "I saw bright flashes on the Indian subcontinent. It looked like the Indians and Pakis were trading nukes. When we got down in Kazakhstan, we were smuggled by one of Pasha's friends to Saint Petersburg. As we refueled, we heard distant artillery to the east and south of our position. The Russians are mobilized and moving into the rest of Europe. They're dark as well, after North Korea's second satellite took out Europe's power."

"How'd you get here, Commander?" Madison asked.

"We stole a plane from Pasha's friend. We dropped Tavis off in Scotland to find his family and flew to an airstrip south of here."

"Wait, okay, I'm tracking. But if they left you in Scotland, how'd you get here?" Jack asked Tavis.

"My brother has a ship. This is where it gets interesting."

"Oh, now it gets interesting? Proceed," Madison said.

"When we were off the East Coast, we met up with two submarines. The USS *Virginia* and the HMS *Vengeance*. The latter is a ballistic missile sub. I know the captain from a prior life. He relayed that he, along with the French ballistic missile sub *Le Terrible*, had gotten intel from the Israelis via open traffic in the Med. Probably the intel that Javad relayed to the Indians. It was the Iranians and NoKos. So they struck back. Sir, they launched ballistic missiles against Iran, destroying nearly all their military bases with dialed-down yield nuclear warheads. They also hit Tehran. Tehran is gone."

The room went silent, and Javad started to laugh.

***

After Dr. Rahimi got Javad out of the room and to the underground hospital for surgery, the president spoke to the group.

"None of you were expecting to find me here in my new capacity and probably not expecting to be asked your opinions on what the response of the US should be in a third world war. I've got very few trusted advisors here. I wasn't in the military. I'm a politician and probably not a very good one at that. We haven't made very much headway at all here since I arrived about five days ago.

"We've tried using our own satellite phones with the vast phone book of numbers to our bases and sites around the US to no avail. Even if they have them, they have to be turned on to answer. Nothing in the US. We have actually been able to reach our forces in Australia through the Australian military. There's a battalion of Marines there and along with the Aussies, they're planning something, but don't want to speak over satellites about their plans. So there's that for what it's worth.

"We also have the USS *George Washington* strike group in the Pacific Ocean doing its best to hide until we can come up with a response. Raised them two days ago via satellite phone. Our other carriers and strike groups were overwhelmed with hypersonic cruise missile attacks at the beginning. They can't beat China on their own, but maybe we can even the odds somehow for them.

"Everyone in government was at home on Christmas Eve. I live close by, so I walked up here to see if I could help at all and here I am. President after one of the Justices showed up. Now I'm out of what normal options our plans here say we have. None of it works in this very worst of situations with very limited communications. I need whatever help you can provide. You've all done your best to get here. You felt it was your duty. That gets you my respect and my trust. You've come this far. I'm asking you to go a bit further with me. Can you do that?"

"Mr. President, I will serve at your pleasure, sir," Joey said. "I don't know what we can do other than what we've already done, but we'll help with whatever you need."

"Thank you, Commander. You said *we*, but I'd like to hear from the rest of you."

"I'm with her, Mr. President," Gale said.

"I follow Joey, sir," Pasha said.

"Well, I didn't come all this way across the ocean for my crew only to step out now," Tavis said.

"Good. Now let's figure out some sort of response. Who else can we call? The Iranian spy talked about the Chinese landing in Baltimore and their objectives are this place and the Shenandoah."

"What about the West Coast, sir?" Spenkmeier asked.

"Let's leave the West Coast be for the moment. We can't do much about that currently. The fact that they've left Pendleton and Lejeune alone, along with some other bases, is to our advantage. I'm sure the Marines in California are fighting. God, I hope they're fighting. Tavis, you said Lejeune was empty, right?" Madison asked.

"Aye, 'tis," Tavis said.

The president sat back and rubbed his eyes.

"Sir, is it possible for us to deny them Baltimore? Nuclear weapons?" Spenkmeier asked.

"Lookit, even if I had access to nuclear weapons, I wouldn't nuke one of our own cities. The only nukes I could possibly activate are from NORAD and comms are spotty and they might get shot down again. So that's out."

"We do have the Potomac River between us and them. Can we hit the bridges?" Joey offered up.

"Not a bad idea. How can we make this happen? Someone other than the general, please."

Spenkmeier fumed. Tavis thought he detected just a hint of a smile on Gale's face. Then an idea popped into his head.

"Sir," said Tavis, "if the Marines from Lejeune are headed north toward us, and we can somehow drop the bridges... I need a map. Can we get a map in here?"

A minute later a large monitor on the wall behind the president had a regional map of their area on it, and Joey took over and was standing in front of it counting bridges across the Potomac.

"We've got three bridge here close to us. The bridges near DC, well, they won't go near there. I wouldn't. Radiation and the bridges would be down or at least unstable from the blast. If I were them, I'd try to get to these bridges *here*, starting with Point of Rocks and the two upstream toward Harper's Ferry. If we can deny them those bridges, they'd have to cross north into the Shenandoah. If we can somehow contact the Marines, and if they are coming north, we can intercept them in the upper valley, and the Marines can destroy their force."

"Really," said Spenkmeier. "We don't have any forces we can reasonably contact and expect to support this mission. Even if the Lejeune Marines are coming north, we're deaf and blind here with no way to make contact with them."

"Sir—" Joey started.

But Jack cut in. "General, wasn't it you who ignored Mr. Washington's intelligence briefing a couple of months ago that, if you had any sense, you'd have listened to? I think we need to think outside the box here."

"You were just some mid-level case officer until last week, Jack," Spenkmeier shot back.

Madison banged his fist on the table. "Cease fire! Both of you. Listen, Spunkmeier, I think you've done enough. I want different thinking. We need to take risks here, or we're all dead. We don't have reliable comms within the US, but what about OCONUS? We've got troops and assets all over the world."

Tavis was listening to this exchange, wracking his brain. "Deaf and blind" kept coming back to him. *Bingo*. He reached into his lower pant leg pocket and pulled out the Iridium satellite phone, waiting for a lull in the conversation.

"Mr. President," said Jack, "we do have some intermittent comms with OCONUS assets. Commander and Tavis, jump in here to keep me honest. You're both military or former. We have Airborne assets at Bagram." Then he laid out what he was thinking.

Madison nodded. "Go make this happen, Jack. Take Commander Washington and Tavis with you. They can help you relay the targets."

Joey started, surprised. "Sir, I'm only a lieutenant commander in the Navy and was in orbit until a week ago. I don't—"

"It's done. I think we can rustle up a pair of stars for your shoulders. Battlefield commission, General," Madison said.

"I'm Navy, sir."

"Admiral, then. I don't know much about military hierarchy. Go get it done."

"Mr. President, in my experience, if you're fighting deaf and blind, maybe it's a good strategy to make your opponent deaf and blind as well." He laid the satellite phone on the table. "What do ya know of the prime minister's Letters of Last Resort?"

NINE

Mei sat at the desk, which she supposed was hers now. She had a window behind her with a view of the building's parking lot, which was mostly empty. When the EMP hit on Christmas Eve, the Gillette's city hall was closed, and all the workers at home. Just days ago she had been in China at her flat in Beijing. She had no real affinity for that city, but this place seemed like the moon to her. Things had moved so quickly. Her head was still spinning, attempting to digest where she was and what she was doing. She spun in her chair to take in the empty streets outside instead of the skyline of China's capital city. Gillette, a small town of roughly thirty-two thousand people, was situated in northern Wyoming in a valley in the middle of a snowy nowhere.

The call in the middle of the night from the minister was unnerving, to say the least. It came just over a week ago in Beijing. Her orders were to pack a bag, one bag only, of warm clothes and toiletries and meet him at the airport. When she arrived, it wasn't the usual traffic and crowds. There were guards everywhere at new checkpoints. They asked her for her identification and why she was there. Once she told them, they checked a clipboard and waved her through to the next checkpoint further into the airport complex. She was told where to leave her vehicle, and a military car picked her up and drove her to an Air China passenger plane, and she climbed the stairs just behind the front of the cockpit. There wasn't a stewardess but an armed soldier at the door. He checked her identification once again and gestured her inside the first-class cabin.

It was a long and disorienting flight with minimal sleep. As the flight wore on and she was brought fully into the know by sitting in on discussions with the minister and others, if only to take notes for the minister, it became clear that the whole war was about food and their ability to feed the Chinese people. She spent the rest of the flight taking notes and compiling them, still shocked that they hadn't discovered that she was spying for the Canadians. That activity was clearly at an end.

Mei stared out the window, her space heater running full blast, powered by the portable gas generator just outside, with a cord running to a power strip. She relished the warmth. Outside was near zero degrees and dark, the only light coming from the lamp on her desk. It was late evening. Gillette had been chosen, like many of the other forward operating bases, for its relative isolation and proximity to an airport. When her aircraft landed at Northeast Wyoming International Airport late on Christmas Eve, everything was dark except the runway. It was lit by beacons that were placed there by infiltrators. These infiltrators were Chinese nationals that had gained entry to the US weeks or months prior. Some even years prior. They were armed and well-equipped. Most were here on student visas, and many had overstayed their exit dates; none had been found or even searched for, to their knowledge.

She was quite amazed. There were over two thousand of them that secured the airport and the government buildings, setting up checkpoints and roadblocks. They had all driven into the area that day so they'd be there when their vehicles died, although they didn't know that. Over the next several days, thousands of Chinese troops landed via commercial aircraft and PLA military transports, along with armored vehicles and a couple of helicopters. She guessed that's where the portable generators came from as well. Then the bombers and jet fighters arrived.

She heard the exterior door open down the hallway. Then footsteps. The interior door opened, and two people entered. One was a major dressed in the drab green overcoat of the Ministry of Security.

"I am here to see the minister. Where is his office?" the major demanded and gestured for his companion to take a seat in the cubicle across from Mei's desk. Mei was about to inform him that the minister was in a meeting, but his door opened, and a frantic-looking colonel walked out, pausing just enough to look derisively at the two Ministry of Security officers, nod at Mei, and leave the way the Security officers had entered. She filed that look away in her mind. Regular Army and Ministry of Security had no love lost between them.

"Of course, Major. This way." Mei guided him to the opposite end of the small vestibule. She knocked on the door and opened it, sticking her head in.

"Minister, there is a major from State Security here to see you."

"Enter," the minister answered, and Mei opened the door wide to allow the major to proceed past her into the office. She closed the door and returned to her desk. As she sat, she felt an uneasiness and looked across the carpeted walkway to the cubicle. She had forgotten the major's companion.

"Hello, Mei." A slight woman with long black hair leaned forward in her chair and flashed a wide smile. Mei's uneasiness turned to a sense of danger, but she didn't know exactly why. The woman was dressed in a heavy, blue winter coat with a red winter beanie on her head. She pulled black gloves off her hands and set them on the desk, and stared at Mei.

"Do I know you?" Mei asked.

"No. But you may call me Tori. I apologize for the way I'm dressed. I am a captain in the Ministry of State Security. Newly promoted for accomplishing my mission, actually," Tori said and Mei was slightly unnerved by the woman's casual statement and demeanor.

"We are connected, in a way, you and I. You see, Mei, I am a spy," Tori said with another wide, toothy smile.

Mei's heart skipped a beat. Could this woman know about her own spying activities? She hadn't passed anything to her Canadian handler for months. She was careful to a fault. *They can't know.* Mei gathered her wits and proceeded with this odd conversation. She was conscious not to move at all for fear of giving this person across from her a tell of any kind.

"I can't see how we're connected. Tori, was it? Please, enlighten me."

"Ah, but we are, Mei. By one, Captain Chao. Your lover, correct?"

That caught Mei off guard.

"What of him? Do you have news? I know now that he's in this area of operation, but I haven't heard anything. Did something happen to him?" She was genuinely concerned now, and she let it show.

"It seems he'll be here shortly. They're bringing him and his team in via helicopter now. He is okay, Mei. Rest easy. At least for now."

Mei exhaled and relaxed a bit. This woman had her on the defensive. She needed to change that.

She put on a friendly, curious expression. "What mission did you accomplish to get promoted, Tori? If I may ask."

"Of course you may ask. I came to the US a year or so ago to develop contacts in order to gain entry for our surface-to-air missiles and radar systems. Your Captain Chao and his team had the mission of guarding one of these systems some distance north of here. His mission was a complete success. Until it wasn't."

"What do you mean?"

"The major is speaking to your minister about it." Tori waved her hand toward the minister's office door, which opened as if on cue. The major strode out, putting his cap on, and glanced at Mei.

"Let's go. They're landing soon," he said to Tori, who picked up her gloves and stood.

"A pleasure to meet you, Mei. We'll speak again soon, I'm sure." Tori followed the major out the interior door.

"Mei! Come in here," the minister called, and she braced herself for this conversation, whatever it may be.

TEN

Deaf and Blind

Tanner was on the bridge, Sammy beside him at the helm. The seas had picked up this evening. The waves were three to four feet, and the wind whipped spray from their tops. He scanned the horizon with binoculars, but there was nothing about in the late afternoon grayness. They'd turned the radar off as they had the submarines out there gliding beneath, keeping the watch and still hiding. No news was good news, he supposed, but he wondered about his brother and the family. And also about what he ought to do now. He had the *Shark* beneath him and an open sea. Could he be comfortable on land and give this up? Pulling a cigar from his breast pocket, he reached to light it with the torch lighter he always had with him when the infrequent sound of the ship's satellite phone chirped away on the bulkhead behind him and Sammy. Tanner grabbed the handset.

"Tanner Kinley here!" he yelled into the receiver.

"It's Tavis! How copy?"

"Good copy. Are you okay?"

"Roger that. We're all good and safe. Do you have a notepad? I have orders for our friends. Would be easier to call them direct, but unknown when they'd have periscope and comms up to receive, so you're it," Tavis said.

"It's fine. We anticipated that. Hold one." Tanner walked to the plot table, stretching the receiver cord to the limit, and moved the paper maps to the side to reveal the glass top. He grabbed a grease pencil.

"Ready to copy, go," Tanner said, and he began writing quickly, copying what Tavis passed him. After a minute, he stopped writing.

"Did you copy all that? Read back," Tavis ordered his older brother, and Tanner immediately read back what he'd written down.

"Is that accurate?"

"Roger. This needs to happen directly, Tanner."

"Holy shit. Roger that. I'll find our friends below and deliver the message. I'll call when it's done. Over."

"Roger, out."

"What's up, Cap? Tavis?" Sammy asked. He hadn't moved from the helm.

"I need that big wrench. You have the conn."

"Roger, Cap," Sammy replied, and Tanner exited the bridge on the starboard side and took the ladder down toward the stern in the failing light, going by feeling alone. There, where Tavis had left it, was the big wrench, snugged away next to the gunwale. Tanner picked up the heavy metal tool and hammered out a series of clinks on the *Shark*'s steel side. After a minute or so of banging the same sequence out, he set the wrench down. Would be easier to use a hammer, but it was what it was. Climbing the ladder back to the bridge, which was now aglow in red light for night, he watched and waited, not knowing where they'd surface. After several minutes, a red light appeared to port, about two hundred yards out. His radio crackled to life.

"*Shark, Shark*. Request received. This is Blackstone. No contacts that we can see, but let's keep this brief. Ready to copy."

"Captain, this is Kinley. They've reached their objective and made contact with command authority. Here is what Tavis relayed to me…"

Commander Blackstone replaced the microphone in its holder above his head. The bridge was silent, and everyone was looking at him. He contemplated what he just received and what everyone on the bridge had overheard as he'd had it on speaker. He reflexively rubbed his right pant pocket where the prime minister's letter rested, folded in half. It wasn't really a difficult decision, but a heavy one. Again.

"Sonar, Conn. Any contacts?" Blackstone said into the microphone.

"Conn, Sonar. One intermittent surface contact at the edge of our range. Looks like they're heading parallel our heading currently."

"XO, we'll need to move further away from that contact. Make it happen."

"Aye, Captain," the XO replied and gave the orders to the helm.

"XO, go to battle stations missile. Helm, take us down to missile launch depth one-eighty feet." Then he got on the 1MC for the whole ship and repeated the battle stations missile command. The XO then also repeated the command on the ship-wide intercom.

"XO, take these coordinates to Fire Control and advise when ready to launch." He handed his executive officer a slip of paper from his small command desk, and the XO jogged away, ducking through the bulkhead hatch and out of sight.

"Captain, we're at one-eighty feet. Missile launch depth," the helmsman reported.

"Very well. Hold that depth and heading," Blackstone replied and sat in his elevated chair, more of a stool, really, but it wasn't meant for comfort. The XO returned to the bridge.

"Missiles selected and coordinates set, Captain. Here's your missile key." The XO handed him a cylindrical key, then stepped to one side of the bridge, while the XO went to the other side. The console was longer than one man could reach at the same time. He and the XO inserted their missile keys into identical slots in front of them and turned them a quarter turn clockwise. This was the second time in little over a week they'd performed this action.

"Fire control is live, Captain," the XO said.

"Roger that, XO. Fire Control is live. On the 1MC." The XO flipped a switch, and Blackstone grabbed the mic to speak to the crew.

"This is the captain. We've made contact with the new American president. It is on my authority to place the HMS *Vengeance* and her firepower under American command. They have relayed targets for us to prosecute. It is my intent to prosecute these targets with malice and in keeping with the honor and name of our boat, with vengeance for Great Britain, once we've put enough distance between us and the distant surface contact. We should be at enough distance in approximately forty-five minutes." He returned the microphone to its holder above his head.

"Now we wait," he said to no one in particular.

At precisely forty-five minutes of relative quiet on the bridge, Captain Blackstone took the mic from its holder.

"Sonor, Conn. Status on that intermittent contact?"

"Conn, Sonar. Contact is gone. We're showing no contacts, surface or submerged, with the exception of the *Virginia* and the *Shark*."

"Very well, Sonar. XO, stand by for ballistic missile launch. Fire Control, Conn. Missile status?"

"Conn, Fire Control. Missiles ready to launch," came the voice through the speaker.

"Fire Control, Conn, begin sequence and launch ballistic missiles." He handed the mic to the XO, who repeated the command.

"Conn, Fire Control, launching ballistic missiles." The boat shuddered as the first Trident D-5 missile was propelled from its launch tube.

The Russian president was meeting with his command staff in a large conference room adjacent to the massive operations center a mile beneath the Ural Mountains in Central Russia. He was listening to one general after another provide excuses and or outright lies as to why they hadn't yet broken into central Europe. The problem lay with the northern and southern regions. There were enough NATO military assets that weren't impacted by the EMP over Central Europe to provide more resistance than they had planned for.

So far, the only operation that was going okay was the airlift into Dulles Airport near Washington, DC, or what was left of it. They got enough soldiers to push south in order to blunt any American forces heading north from the Marine base at Quantico and the Army base at Fort Eustis. Apparently, they could fight well on the other side of the world, but not on their own doorstep. He'd heard enough.

"Stop! I need a break from——"

The door burst open.

"Mr. President, we've detected submarine ballistic missile launches from the Eastern Atlantic. Also, about an hour ago we intercepted communications in the clear to the Americans at Bagram. They were partially garbled and it took us time, replaying the recording and filtering it to sort out what they were actually saying. We just now assess that it's their intent to send paratroopers from Bagram to blow the bridges that the Chinese need across the Potomac," a very flustered major stated.

"Show me these missiles. Also, Defense Minister, we planned for this contingency. Get our Airborne Corps on this bridge thing. Those bridges are critical for our Chinese friends to get to their objective. Get them moving before we lose the initiative here."

"Mr. President, I put the Airborne Corps on alert several hours ago to take those bridges. I thought it prudent to send them regardless, based on the risk assessment of my staff. I'm sorry if I overstepped, but it looks like we were right to do so," the defense minister explained.

"Da! Initiative! If more generals had that, we'd probably be in France by now. Tell them to go, quickly before they can't." He followed the major out into the operations center, where he and his command staff stood looking at large wall-mounted screens in the front of the room. It was a map of the world, and there were now tracks overlaid on it. Moving quickly. A general called him over to his workstation while the defense minister picked up a phone and began speaking rapidly. The Russian president heard the words *Shagol Air Base* and *31st Guards Air Assault* before his attention was pulled away to more pressing matters.

"Mr. President, we show three tracks. Two missiles are heading over Asia. The third is a depressed shot, which will hit first."

"Depressed?"

"The missile will stay in the atmosphere, sir. It's a short shot."

"Target?"

"The Panama Canal, sir. Should impact any second now."

"The Chinese won't like that. The others?"

"In a couple of minutes, we'll know. Right now, the two missiles are tracking to points above Russia and China. When the warheads separate and begin tracking, we'll know precisely what their targets are."

"Do we have countermeasures? Can we intercept them?"

"There are four A-235 Nudols around Moscow. We were going to engage when within range."

"Do it."

"Yes, Mr. President." The general picked up a phone and gave the weapons-free command to the missile battery commander.

"Sir, the paratroopers have the order. They're on quick standby. Should be in the air directly," the defense minister reported.

"Well, as a preemptive measure, can we hit Bagram?" the president asked.

"We can, sir. I've got ready bombers on standby with nuclear cruise missiles. I'll give the order, and they'll get airborne. That mission will take a few hours."

"Do it. One less thorn in our side," the president said.

"Sir, we're detecting a missile launch near Beijing. They've launched their own anti-missile weapon," another officer said from a terminal in front of the general.

The general nodded and responded to something said on the phone, then hung it up.

"Mr. President, we've launched our missiles against the incoming tracks. Only a few minutes until intercept."

"General! Initial tracks have deployed MIRVs. Five each. There are now ten tracks. Also, the Panama Canal Zone has been hit. Satellite imagery shows direct hit. There is no longer a canal, General," the officer reported.

"Damn. There goes Chinese resupply," the general muttered. He turned to his overly large monitor on his workstation and watched as the multiple independent re-entry vehicles, or MIRVs, separated from each other into their specific tracks. He studied the telemetry closely.

"Mr. President, it looks like one is tracking to Moscow, three of them are not descending, and one is tracking on the Ural Mountains.

That's us. The other missile is fairly similar, three not descending and two on Beijing."

"Chances of intercept? Why aren't some descending?"

"We'll know in a few seconds, Mr. President. However, regardless of the interception of the land-tracking missiles, the others are probably orbital bursts. EMP, sir."

"General! The Moscow-tracked missile has been intercepted successfully!"

Cheers erupted in the operations center, and then the lights flickered. The monitors froze and stopped refreshing.

"Mr. President. At least one EMP has detonated. Hold one," the general said and picked up the phone again, trying different numbers.

"General? How protected are we here? Are we deep enough?"

"We should be, sir. This bunker was designed to take a direct hit and survive. However, regardless of our survivability here, we can no longer see anything. Our communications are out as well. At least the couple of lines I just tried. The Chinese will be dark as well. They've evened the odds with the EMPs, Mr. President."

"Do we have interceptor missiles here to take out the inbound missile targeting us here?" the president asked.

"Sir, we only had so many of them and strategically, Moscow was more critical to protect. We are safe here," he replied.

"We're going to find out, aren't we?" rhe president said, dryly.

The operations center shook violently just then and went dark. The last thing the Russian president heard was rumbling and cracking from above.

Tavis, Joey, and Jack reentered the underground bunker and made their way back to the three-story building and into the conference room. Everyone was anxiously awaiting their report. Tavis went first.

"My brother was able to contact HMS *Vengeance* and passed the target package to Commander Blackstone. They had to move a bit away from a surface contact first, but he observed the launch of three ballistic missiles from the *Vengeance* about fifteen minutes ago."

"Do we know if the missiles did their job?" Madison asked the room.

"Sir, we'll have to wait for some kind of intel. Could be a bit before we know," the acting director of the CIA said. Joey took her turn next since she was the one doing most of the talking on the sat phone.

"We also made contact with the commander at Bagram. He assured me that he has the assets to handle this mission. They should be in the air as soon as he can get the plane loaded and recall the teams from the field. He'd sent most of his soldiers into forward operating bases or at least away from Bagram in case it gets hit," Joey reported.

"Thank you all for getting this done. We've at the very least struck back and I won't lie, it feels good. I realize that we just ordered the death of potentially millions of innocent Russians and Chinese citizens. That's on me," Madison said. "Who wants a drink?"

Tavis and Pasha both raised their hands.

ELEVEN

"Is Private Sanchez whimpering, Corporal Dempsey?"

"I believe he is, First Sergeant."

"Corporal Dempsey, why is the private whimpering in my Humvee when we're in the middle of world war three and trying to be small in these mountains?"

"Private Sanchez, the first sergeant would like to know why you're being a fucking baby in the back seat of his Humvee."

"Corporal, with all due respect to the first sergeant, but we're in a Humvee on a road hanging on the side of the fucking Himalayas or Kush or wherever. It can't even be called a fucking road. There's a thousand-foot drop out my right window, for fuck's sake. And I'm afraid of heights!" Sanchez said as he crossed himself.

"You're a fucking paratrooper, Private!" First Sergeant Sullivan barked.

Sanchez grimaced. "Well, Sully, I don't know if you've noticed, but I don't have a parachute on my back here. If Corporal Driver McDriverFace here fucks up, we're going over the edge! I could get out and walk, and I'd be fine. Parachute at 1200 feet, and I'm fine. Something about being in a vehicle on the side of a mountain, though," Sanchez said as the radio cracked to life.

"Reaper Six. Reaper Six."

They fell silent, waiting for First Lieutenant Rickets to respond.

"Reaper Six Actual, over," Rickets responded from his Humvee at the head of the column.

"Reaper Six, BDOC. Bulldog Actual wants First Platoon to RTB, ASAP. Copy?" The order to return to base was from the Base Defense Operations Center.

"BDOC, Copy. Out," they heard Rickets respond on the net. "Reaper Seven, Six."

"Seven. Go, Six," First Sergeant Sullivan responded.

"Let's back this column up to that wider part we passed a few minutes ago to turn around and RTB."

"Copy, Six."

"So now we're gonna do this road, but backward in twilight? Is that what we're doing?" Sanchez was getting small in the back seat now.

"Easy, Private. Corporal Dempsey here is a real Louisiana coonass. These cajuns are the best at the wheel."

"I'm not cajun, S'arnt," Dempsey replied.

"I'm just gonna shoot myself and end it here," Sanchez muttered.

"Demp, I don't care what you are. Don't fuck this up," Sully said.

"No sweat, Sully. I ain't killed y'all yet."

The whimpering from the back seat intensified as Dempsey put the Humvee in reverse.

Forty-five minutes later, they were rolling through the gate at Camp Vance, which was adjacent to Bagram Air Base. The Humvees and MRAPs pulled up alongside the Base Defense Operations Center, and they dismounted. Sully stepped out of his Humvee onto the dirt and gravel ground, dust still swirling from the vehicles.

"Sully! On me," Rickets yelled as he headed for the door to the BDOC.

"Right behind, LT."

The two men, still grimy from days in the field patrolling around the base, stepped into the one-story building and walked a long corridor to the operations center. The hallway widened to large room filled with screens and desks. There was a skeleton staff on duty. Most of the camp's inhabitants had bugged out in teams and larger groups after the shooting started. The thought was that since nukes had already been used, there was nothing stopping someone from throwing one at them. So they dispersed as a contingency plan.

"Rickets! Sully! You guys good? No worse for wear? How's the platoon?"

The booming voice belonged to Colonel Jackson. He was a fireplug of a man with what he called "ice blond" white hair and a broad smile that didn't quite reach his eyes. Heavy is the head that wears the crown, he often said.

"Colonel, we're good. Men are good. Tired and hungry, but ready for whatever you need us for, sir," Rickets said. Sully had been in for fifteen or so years and had many combat tours here and in Iraq. He'd mentored and grown Rickets from fresh butter bar lieutenant into the competent and respected first lieutenant that the men of First Platoon looked up to now.

"Come over here to the plot," he said, referring to the large table that usually had maps of the surrounding area on it. As Sully walked over, he saw that the map wasn't of their area of operations but of the east coast of the United States.

"You boys are going home. First Platoon has the mission. We got an unencrypted sat phone call about an hour ago with mission orders from the Acting National Command Authority, whatever 'acting' means. Actually, I'll tell you. It means president and VP were in DC when it was hit. Those that could made their way over several days to Mount Weather here in the Blue Ridge Mountains west of DC. The only cabinet member that arrived was Secretary of Transportation Madison. They got justice to swear him in as president a couple of days ago."

"So, President Madison, sir?" Sully asked.

"Ha! Yep, President James Madison. Go figure. Anyway, they apparently had some visitors, and one was identified as Iran's chief spy or something. I don't know. It's some crazy shit. He was able to provide all kinds of information. They called all over, but either no one was answering or didn't have the assets to assist. We're the only ones that answered that can do the thing, lads."

"So what's the mission, sir?"

"Time is of the essence 'cause they, Russians or the Chicoms, probably listened in on that call. These three bridges right here—Point of Rocks, Brunswick, and Sandy Hook—cross the Potomac River, close to Harper's Ferry. Drop, secure, demo. Once you've completed that, and you will complete it, you will make your way to Mount Weather and attach your platoon to whatever command you can find."

"Question, sir. Why these bridges?" Rickets asked.

"Chinese are landing at Baltimore, if you can believe that shit. They're going to try to secure our bread baskets. The Shenandoah Valley being one of them. The bridges around DC were taken out in the nuke strike. These three bridges would provide them direct access to the valley, central Virginia, and, most importantly, Mount Weather."

"Sir, looking at the map, all they have to do is cross this railroad bridge at Harper's Ferry and go south a few clicks and cross back into Virginia. Also, this doesn't jibe, map-wise. We'd be funneling them into the northern part of the valley by dropping those bridges. What's the catch?"

"Sharp eyeballs, Lieutenant. The Navy Commander on the sat phone said the Marines from Lejeune was heading north into the Shenandoah. Dropping those bridges will funnel the Chicoms into II MEF and deny them the high ground of the foothills of the Blue Ridge, where Mount Weather is situated. There's a big bag of what-ifs, lads, but you concern yourself with those bridges and get to Mount Weather."

"So the EMP didn't knock out their vehicles, sir?" Sully asked.

"Plenty of tracks and trucks were left, actually. Based on the sat images we got from CentCom operating on the Blue Ridge in the Indian Ocean now, they're about two-thirds strength on everything but armor. A lot of their tanks are gone. That would be Second Tank Battalion. The Iron Horse. You can probably expect around forty to fifty M1s, along with artillery support. After you drop those bridges, the Chicoms will have to go around Harper's Ferry into the Valley and meet the II MEF. Copy?"

"Copy, sir," Rickets said.

"Colonel, how are we getting there? The Air Force bugged outta here days ago," Sully asked.

"The Hog," the colonel responded.

"Beg pardon, sir, but that plane is broke. Been sitting for a month waiting for parts, or so I heard."

"They've been working on that one engine for days in case we all had to bug out. Looks like you all get the pleasure instead of us. Oh, and you'll be taking a team of six engineers to do the demo. We'd send more, but only these six are jump qualified, so you make do. You secure the bridges. They drop 'em. Now, get going before we get hit here, and you're stuck or dead. Roger?"

"Roger that," they both said in unison.

"Godspeed, gentlemen. Give 'em hell."

Salutes and handshakes were exchanged, and they left the building.

It was just ninety minutes from being on the side of a mountain to Sully and the platoon plus six combat engineers getting strapped into the rear-facing seats of the upper deck passenger compartment of the Hog. The Hog was a particularly problematic C5A Galaxy transport aircraft. The largest type in the US Air Force. It could carry a single seventy-ton main battle tank in the cargo hold below them, but today the cargo hold was filled with pallets meticulously placed by the airmen and crew chief/load master to ensure that their weight didn't pull the aircraft out of balance. The engines were just spinning up, and the airplane vibrating, when the senior master sergeant, a wiry-framed, tattooed man named Russo, entered the cabin from the ladder in the rear with headphones and mic on. Sully supposed it was for comms with the cockpit and crew.

"Listen up! Strap in. Secure the gear you have with you. The rest of your gear, chutes, and equipment are on the pallets below. Once we're airborne and cruising, you can get up and move around. You need anything, let us know." He raised his voice, which was already booming for such a slight man, and continued, "Don't go wandering around my aircraft without me or one of my crew, and clean up after yourselves. You all smell like a bag of dicks. I don't know how I'm gonna get this stink outta here. Copy?"

"Copy, Chief," Lieutenant Rickets responded without looking up from the map in his lap.

"Sully, why's the stewardess yelling at us?" Corporal Dempsey's Louisiana drawl came from somewhere in the middle of the compartment, eliciting barks of laughter from the platoon.

"What was that?" the chief snapped.

"I got this, Chief. Corporal Dempsey, the stewardess wasn't yelling at us, just you. Now shut the fuck up," Sully said to more laughter as the chief put his hands to his headphones and then held up a hand for silence.

"Quiet! Listen up! Strap in quick. We're going wheels-up no-shit fast. The AWACS says we got an incoming missile strike!" the chief yelled.

All the banter ceased, and there was only the clicking of seat belts as the chief disappeared down the stairs and the giant aircraft began rolling with the engines roaring. Within sixty seconds, they were screaming down the runway. The Galaxy felt like she'd break apart, she was vibrating so badly. Sully had to force himself to relax his hands, which had a death grip on the armrests. The lights in the cabin dimmed, leaving only the two portholes on the exterior doors just in front of the tail section, but the sun had set by now so no light was coming in. The plane tilted up, and since they were all sitting backward, they leaned forward in their seats toward the rear of the plane. The sensation didn't stop. It felt like they were going straight up with the engine's nearly deafening howl.

A minute or so later, Sully saw an incredibly bright light come through the porthole windows on the two exterior doors, and the chief yelled, "Brace! Brace! Brace!"

Everyone held on tight to whatever they could find. Sully held his breath. He knew what that bright light was. Bagram just got nuked and they were probably gonna die. In the seat to his right, Corporal Dempsey was saying the Lord's Prayer very loudly and continually crossing himself. The plane lurched and they were all thrown forward since they were sitting facing the rear. The cabin erupted with curses and prayers from all his troopers. He looked to his right, and saw Lieutenant Ricketts sitting calmly. They locked eyes and Ricketts actually smiled at him. Jesus. Balls of steel.

The plane settled from extreme turbulence they'd just experienced and a voice from behind him called out.

"Sully! We gonna die?" It was Sanchez.

"Sanchez, Lieutenant Ricketts is sitting up here smiling at me. Calm down. We're either gonna be fine or we're already dead," he called back and Ricketts laughed.

TWELVE

He sat in his chair by the rusty radiator that was barely providing any warmth. This flat was acquired for him short term by his battalion executive officer, Major Budin. Budin was a good man and a better friend than Viktor Morozov deserved. He'd drifted away from what he used to be. A good father. A good Starshina. A company sergeant. He drank too much vodka. He set down the MP-443 Grach nine-millimeter Parabellum pistol on the small table next to the badly upholstered and stained chair. Unscrewing the top to his bottle of Stolichnaya with one hand and then pouring a generous amount of the clear liquid in his squat glass, he thought about how he'd come to be here.

It had been almost three years since his wife, his beloved Mina, had been killed. Murdered was the better word. They found her face down in the mud with her hands and feet bound. A single, small caliber bullet to the back of her head. He downed the vodka in one gulp and picked up the pistol, ejected the magazine, and set the pistol on the scuffed coffee table in front of him. One by one, he used his right thumb to eject each round onto the old table until all eighteen bullets lay in front of him. He then picked each one up and reloaded the magazine. He did this several more times between refilling his glass and downing more vodka. At some point, the tears began to stream down his face.

He wasn't there to save her. She'd gone to pick some items up from the store. His son, Valeri, had been with her father, Boris, for an extended stay where he lived in Karagandy, Kazakhstan. It was to be the last time he visited Boris. One last time. He and Mina didn't want their son to be around Boris and his business affairs. They knew what he did and what he was. Valeri was still impressionable for being fourteen then. Mina had told her father this was it. That conversation was tense, but Boris seemed to take it in stride. They weren't that close as it was. Mina had grown up in the middle of Boris's business, and since he wasn't going to change, she was taking matters into her own hands. Viktor had completely agreed.

He'd been a rising noncommissioned officer in the 31st Guards Air Assault Brigade. A beautiful wife and teenage son they both loved dearly. Now where was he? Mina was gone. Valeri was god-knows-where and hated him. He was relegated to guard duty and administrative security. Gone from his brother paratroopers, even though they still supported him. The knock on the door that evening and the voice yelling through it, he'd never forget. The police had arrived to tell him his wife had been found dead. They searched their flat in the small city of Ulyanovsk along the Volga River, where the 31st was based. They found a small-caliber pistol with one round missing in a closet and arrested him for Mina's murder. The knock on the door startled him, just like that night so long ago.

"Who is it?" he asked when he got to the door.

"Budin," was the response.

He opened the door for his former commander. "Come in, my friend." They shook hands as he shut the door. Major Ivan Budin was a very tall man at six foot, seven inches. He towered over Viktor, who was only five foot, eleven inches tall. Budin removed his Ushanka to reveal blond hair, high and tight. The Ushanka, or fuzzy Russian hat with earflaps tied up at the top, was ubiquitous in Russia. The rank of major was front and center.

"This is a shit place. I'm sorry I couldn't get you something better, but at such short notice and with everything else going on, it was challenging to get even this."

"It's fine for me, Ivan. I'm grateful for your help," Viktor replied and motioned to another glass and the vodka. Budin nodded, and they sat, Viktor in his chair with Budin across from him at the coffee table. He poured several fingers in each glass, and they clinked the glasses and gulped them down. Budin then pulled out an envelope and handed it to Viktor.

"These are your orders. It wasn't difficult to get the old man to sign off on them. He's happy to be rid of you. You're a serious pain in the ass, Viktor. First of all, it's been three years since she died. We know you didn't do it. It's why the brigade stuck by you. I'm sorry you got bounced. The charges didn't stick. Boris is a fucking monster. We all know this. We know what and who he is. The gun was planted. His men did it. He's an untouchable, Viktor. But, you got bounced all by yourself. You got your son taken from you yourself. Now this latest incident…"

"I know, God dammit!"

"You have to stop drinking. Getting drunk and hitting your son was the last straw with the old man. He thought that maybe you could come back to the Brigade from security service since there's a war on now, but you lost that once you hit Val. What were you thinking?"

"I had him for visitation from Boris for the weekend. The bastard is filling his head with lies about Mina and what happened. Regardless what the court finally decided, Val thinks I had something to do with it. He thinks he's a man now. We had words."

"You dumb bastard. Stop having words with Val. He's your son, and you love him, and he loves you. You just need to show him. Enough of this. It's for you and Val to sort out if you can even find him. Are you sure you want to go through with this? I have the information, but are you capable?" Budin gestured at the almost empty bottle of vodka.

"I'm capable of this, Budin. What do you have?"

"Okay. Your orders are as a liaison for the detachment we're sending in. We were going to go with a more risky plan for you, but this mission came in hot and for immediate action. They leave within the hour. I just arrived with them and took a car here to bring you back."

"I haven't jumped in three years, Ivan!"

"And you won't jump this time. The detachment will jump to take a bridge to secure it for the Chinese landing in Baltimore. The plane will then land to refuel at Dulles Airport west of Washington, DC. You will stay as liaison. What you do after that is up to you."

"Do you know where they are?" Viktor was inquiring about Val but assumed that he'd be with Boris by now.

"Well, there's the thing. Word travels, and I have friends in some places. Everyone's talking about everything very quietly. Seems it started with the International Space Station occupants landing in Kazakhstan. Got them to the hospital, no worse for the wear. Our cosmonaut used to work for Boris somehow. So odd. Anyway, Boris came and got them out, then when they landed in Saint Petersburg, they stole the plane from Boris, and your son stayed with them. They then were intercepted by our Combat Air Patrol, but the Finns shot down our fighters, and they escaped to Scotland and then on to just south of Dulles airport."

"How do you know this?" Viktor was sitting forward, listening intently now.

"Boris is well known in the FSB and was funneling heroin on his plane for the FSB to use for other things. They paid top dollar for him to transport it, but when it flew off to America, there was some big dustup. War, it seems, has many different facets to it. Making money is one of those facets. Now, they've told Boris to get their drugs back, and he's doing that. Boris's plane was tracked to America as well. FSB doesn't let people on their payroll move about without knowing where they are. I've heard Boris has an FSB agent with him currently. Her story is, we should say, extreme."

"Well, where is he, and what's her story?"

"I'll tell you in the car. I need to get you to the plane. You set to go?"

"Da!" Viktor holstered his pistol and headed for the door. Behind it on the floor was a small backpack, which he grabbed, along with his web vest with extra magazines for his AK-47, which he picked up last and slung around his back.

Fifteen minutes later, Budin pulled the car up to the gate and flashed his identification to the guard. The gate went up, and they sped through, heading toward a massive Ilyushin IL-76. Men in camouflage were walking in a line up the rear ramp under lights from inside the aircraft. The rest of the base was dark. Shagol Air Base was situated in the northwest corner of Chelyabinsk in central Russia. It would be a long flight, but he was close to his son now. He would find him. That was his only goal, he kept telling himself. *Don't focus on Boris. Focus on Val.* Budin had provided what location information he'd been able to get, and it was close enough. Budin stopped the car thirty yards from the plane, and they got out. The wind was fierce tonight, and it bit.

"There you go, my friend. Godspeed." Budin embraced him as a brother.

"I am grateful and can never repay your kindness for this, Ivan."

"Don't be stupid any more than you already have been. Get your son. Do what you must. Your brothers are waiting for you. Should be a good flight to catch up with them. They missed you." Budin waved at the officer by the ramp, and they waved back and gestured for Viktor to hurry up.

"Goodbye, my friend." With that, Viktor jogged to the plane. He was home with his men. At least for a time. He boarded just as the ramp was being raised. Between bear hugs and insults, he strapped into a seat, and the large transport rolled down the runway and into the air. A few minutes later, he unstrapped to hit the head. Walking toward the front of the plane in the large cargo hold, he stopped next to an exit door to look out on his home country, possibly for the last time, when the lights in the cargo bay flickered. The lights on the ground, however, all went dark. It was like they had never been. The ground was just…gone.

The intercom crackled.

"Attention! We've been hit with some kind of electromagnetic pulse. All the power on the ground that we can see from the cockpit has gone dark. This aircraft has been hardened against this type of pulse weapon. We're still flying and okay. We will continue to the mission objective. If you have vodka, now would be a good time to drink to Mother Russia," the pilot said.

Viktor's need to urinate had disappeared. Standing there staring out at a dark Russian landscape below him, he pulled a flask from his pant pocket and took a long pull.

THIRTEEN

Major Tang put the H6-K heavy bomber down on the mostly darkened runway at Northeast Wyoming Regional Airport on the outskirts of Gillette. Mostly darkened except for the portable LED lights the infantry had set up on either side of the runway for night operations. It was an easy mission. Drop their ordnance on several enemy positions and fortifications. The enemy was explained to him and his crew as ruthless counterinsurgents and the famed American militia that their Constitution spoke of. Regardless, they did their duty, their jobs, successfully. He taxied the aircraft over to a spot where the ground crewman gestured for him to go with flashlights.

Their night wasn't over. They'd get to relax for about an hour while the bomber was refueled and rearmed for their second mission. Then they could sleep awhile. He saw that Captain Liu's aircraft was already back, sitting to his left with a fuel truck between them. A large transport waited about a hundred yards away with its rear ramp down and men unloading what looked like cruise missiles or external fuel tanks, probably for his next mission. They had ordnance carts which he assumed came with the transport. One was heading toward Liu's aircraft while a second fully burdened cart descended the ramp. A helicopter was landing about a hundred yards away, and he stopped to watch.

"Hey, you have a cigarette?" he asked his wingman, who pulled a pack of Marlboro Lights from his flight suit breast pocket and offered him one, taking one for himself.

"You've never seen a helo before?" Liu asked in jest.

"I just like them. Well, I like to watch them. Not so much fly in them," he said as they stood in the cold, smoking. Then things got interesting. The doors on the helo opened, and quite a few soldiers exited. About half were in winter camouflage, and the rest, about a dozen, were in what he knew to be uniforms of State Security troops.

One of the Security squad, the leader, it looked like, ordered all but two of the white-clad soldiers to the terminal to wait for the transport. They were all armed except for two. One male, one female. They were surrounded by the rest. An SUV pulled up by the terminal behind him, followed by a covered truck. Both were Chinese-made. Must have come in on one of the transports. Several had. A woman got out of the driver's door and waved at the group. The officer in charge pointed to the SUV, and the man and woman walked toward it. Most of the security troops boarded the truck that was waiting with the Security SUV, while a few stayed with the officer and the two soldiers. Or were they prisoners?

As they neared Tang and Liu, the woman from the helo looked at the two bombers on either side of them and then over at Tang. He got an uneasy feeling just as the woman passed him, and that's when she spit at him. The warm, thick liquid hit his face. He didn't know how to react, but he took a step back and wiped at his face.

"You're a murderer of women and children. Civilians! Coward!" she screamed at him as the other white-clad soldier with her got between her and Tang and held her back. The male soldier whispered something to her. A captain, he could see now, who gave him a long, severe stare. The spitter was also a captain.

"Enough! The car is waiting," the officer said, and they all walked off.

"What the hell was that about?" Liu asked.

"The town you bombed was filled with children and civilians!" the spitter yelled over her shoulder as one of the guards pushed her toward the car.

"What is she talking about?" Tang said.

"Our mission was to hit military and militia outposts in support of commandos, Major. I wonder if those were the commandos?" Liu said.

Tang took a last drag on his cigarette and dropped it, smashing it out with his boot.

"I need coffee and to wash my face. Let's see what they have in the flight room they set up in the terminal for us, and find out what's going on here," Tang said, and they headed to where the SUV had just been parked. As they walked to the terminal doors, the ground crews where busy refueling the bombers and rearming them. There was a great deal of activity aside from these soldiers and security, and parked in the shadows was another of the Chinese-made SUVs.

How many of those things did they fly over here? he wondered, just as the pop of distant gunfire startled him. A high-pitched scream drifted across the tarmac and then silence.

Mei heard the last of the encounter in front of her vehicle as she rolled the window down. The SUV she sat in was one of three flown over from the mainland a few days ago. No one cared if she drove it. Not now. The minister, the Security Service people, the regular Army, and the infiltrators that helped them here in Gillette were too busy making plans now that communications had been lost with the High Command in China. Something had occurred, and it seemed that neither the regular Army nor the Ministry of Security could communicate any longer with their commanders in China. It could be they were on their own now. She had to act quickly.

Seeing Shan for the first time in months, even from a distance, warmed her. Then her captain was taken away again.

So close and yet so far from her.

She was still reeling from what the minister told her after his meetings with the colonel and then the major. For whatever reason, Shan had disobeyed his orders and then he tossed a man out of a helicopter. He was to be tried and executed in the morning by State Security along with the missile operator on his team. Apparently, she'd shot her commander. What was going on?

All Mei knew was she had to free him. But then what? They couldn't drive out of Gillette. There was nothing out there in this frozen wasteland.

As she watched the ground crews refuel and rearm the two bombers, she decided—it had to be the pilot. She'd do it like the Canadians had done it with her. Play to his emotions. It looked to her like he was a bit confused as to what they were doing here, from what she'd heard from this distance. Maybe.

But first, the soldiers.

Mei opened the door, and the cold hit her. The wind never stopped here. As she walked to the terminal, the wind blew waves of frozen snow in lines across the pavement this way and that. She reached the door and entered the dark terminal building, pulling the door closed behind her against the wind. It wasn't much warmer in here, but there was no wind. She looked around. Small LED lanterns gave the area a ghostly feel. To the right were the soldiers standing in a circle, talking. Still armed. Good. To the left, there were the aircrews. Eight men in all, but the pilot she was looking for was seated by himself, holding a steaming cup.

There was no one else around except for the ground crews working outside on the planes. She walked up to the soldiers first. None were really tall, but one was very muscular under his jacket and gear.

"Excuse me. Who's in charge of your group?" she asked the assembled men.

"I'm the team sergeant. What can I do for you? Who are you?" the muscular man responded.

"You can call me Mei. Perhaps your captain mentioned me? I'm his girlfriend. I'm also the assistant to the minister, who is now in charge of this region for the Party," she said. At the mention of her name and her explanation, they all smiled.

"Ah, Mei. Captain Chao doesn't really talk much about his personal life, but when he does, it is you he talks about. You know what happened, right?" the sergeant asked.

"I do. The minister explained it to me. He also said that Captain Chao and the other officer will be tried in the morning. It's a formality. They will be executed for murder."

Several of the men cursed. The sergeant just stared at her, then quietly said, "The captain is a good man. Fair. We are loyal to him. Party be damned. I think it was a mistake for them to let us keep our weapons. Tell us what you need." The sergeant smiled at her.

Relieved, Mei said, "How's your English?"

Major Tang sat holding the hot cup of coffee between his hands, more for the feel of the warm cup than the taste of the bitter liquid. His co-pilot and crew chatted about thirty feet away with Captain Liu and his crew by the coffee machine. It was electric and got its power from a portable generator that was running out a side door with a long extension cord. While he preferred the soothing flavor of tea to this bitter brew, the coffee here was plentiful, and would tide him over until he could return home.

He couldn't stop thinking about the woman spitting in his face and subconsciously rubbed at his cheeks for any remaining saliva. He watched the short woman with the big coat talking with the soldiers on the other side of the terminal. At one point, a couple of the soldiers turned and stared at him. That was slightly unnerving. A few seconds later, the woman turned and walked over to him.

"Do you mind if I sit? I have some questions for you," she asked.

"Who are you?" He was a bit taken aback and just wanted to be alone with his thoughts, but she seemed like she wouldn't take no for an answer.

"I'm Mei. I'm the personal assistant to the minister of this prefect. I heard that soldier yell at you. She seemed angry. Angry enough to spit in your face. What was that about?" this woman, Mei, asked directly.

"So the minister wants to know what happened? An investigation? So soon?" he asked, somewhat confused.

"No. No investigation. I want to know if you have heard yet about China?" she asked.

He was very confused now. *Why is she talking to me?*

"Okay, I haven't heard about China, and apparently, that angry soldier was under the impression that we bombed women and children on our last mission when we were told it was a military target. Can you explain that and then tell me about China? I have family back home. A wife and two-year-old son. Did something happen there?" Wary now, he wondered if she was State Security, and if something was going on with his family.

Ah, Mei thought. *Perfect.*

"This isn't about your family, directly. What we know is that the Americans and their allies have apparently struck back at us in the same way we struck them. All communications are down with the mainland. Do you know why we attacked the West, Major?"

"I follow my orders, not question them, Mei. We didn't really ask nor were told why. Do you know why? Did the US threaten China?"

"We attacked and invaded for land. Specifically, land to grow food. Our harvests are failing. America has ample farmland. The only problem with America is that it's full of Americans."

"Well, humans have been fighting over land since the beginning. I'm not necessarily concerned with that. But what about home?" he asked, turning fully to face her and leaning forward. She sensed that the hooks were digging a little deeper. It was a delicate game.

"We had plans in place to keep America and the West from doing the same to us. We hit their bomber bases. We blinded them with the EMP. They tried to launch ICBMs from just north of here, and we had anti-missile batteries in place and intercepted the ICBMs during launch. We also took out all their communications with their submarines. We thought we'd covered all the bases. Apparently, we did not. Our intelligence reports that a full nuclear strike was successful against Iran. There is still at least one submarine out there with the ability to communicate with what's left of American leaders. The fact that all communications are down from the mainland tells us they hit Asia with EMPs. We are alone, Major." Mei embellished the last parts, but from what she knew, it probably wasn't far off the truth.

"So they've killed the power in Asia? What about ground strikes?" he asked.

"If the West only has one sub, then they have access to a limited number of missiles. They've used some on Iran, then more for the EMP blast. If they were to attempt ground strikes, they would need to be selective. Where is your family?" Mei asked.

"My wife and son live with my parents on a small farm in Haitou at the north edge of Magong Bay. It's east of Hong Kong on the coast. No targets there of interest," he replied, and she saw him relax.

"You are totally correct. I believe they are safe. However, how long they will remain so is another story," Mei said, laying her trap.

"How so? Why are you telling me all this?" She noticed him tense up again. He was getting agitated.

Mei put on a patient expression. "The only way for us to be successful here in America is to rid it of its occupants. You didn't bomb a military target. You bombed a town full of civilians. The EMP knocked out power in the middle of winter. Most Americans won't survive the winter and early spring. Those that we needed gone sooner, like those living around the ports, we removed using nerve agents dispersed in the air. Millions are already dead. The rest will starve to death. The gunfire you heard when you entered this terminal was our Security forces executing more of Gillette's population. Bullets are something we have plenty of, for now. However, think about your family without power. There isn't an invading army there; however, there is danger."

"Oh, my God. Civilians? Are you sure?" he said, his face ashen. She knew she was close now.

"Major, this is total war in all its ugly, horrific nature. China is using everything in its arsenal here and you are going to be delivering some of it. I have it on good authority that most of your future missions won't be dropping bombs. You'll be dispersing chemical weapons. That's what they're loading on your aircraft right now. You'll confirm this in your mission briefing shortly. Do you want to continue to kill civilians, or do you want a chance at seeing your family again?" She tugged the hook deliberately hard. It was a risk, but she had no choice.

"Look, I want to see my family again. If I disobey orders, that won't happen. What are you asking of me? What can I do from here in the middle of nowhere?" He leaned back and stared, as if coming to grips with what he was going to be doing. He hadn't walked out to get security, so time to yank hard.

"Like I said, there is no communication with China any longer. We are an island here. Do you see the soldiers over there?" She nodded in that direction.

"Who are they?" He glanced and then his eyes locked back onto hers.

"They were an advance force. Their captain and another officer killed two others. An officer and a state security spy that had been placed in their midst. They had protected some of the civilians that you bombed. For that, the state security will execute them in the morning. Those soldiers and I are going to free those two officers, but then we need a means of escape from here." She put it down there, waiting for him to pick it up.

"Ah. You want a ride." He stared at her.

"Yes. I do. I also want to relieve them of your bombers and the nerve agent being loaded on them. And after we are safely away, we can find a way, a route, to get back home and to your family. Remember, we are alone now. Your command in China will never have any idea that you helped us. Who knows who will come out on top here? Better if you and we weren't here," she said, weaving the lies and letting them settle over him.

She could see him working out his choices. It took a few minutes. He got up and paced, sipping his coffee. She tried to speak at one point out of nervousness, but he held up a finger to quiet her. He stared into his coffee cup and then out at the bombers. She saw his shoulders drop as he watched the ground crews load the chemical weapons canisters on his aircraft.

Then, hushed, he said, "I can only take two. I need a co-pilot. There would be two empty seats. We could possibly squeeze one more in, but it will be tight, and they'd have to be small. I'm assuming that would be you? I could get us away, probably to the east. The further, the better. But look, we've just met, and you came to me. I could report you to the Ministry of State Security and be done with it." She could see he was thinking of how to do this, but was also ready for that last statement.

"Major, all I ask is that you sit through your next mission briefing, and if you want to report me after that, go ahead, but things are going to change around here either way. Pick your co-pilot quietly, whoever would be most willing to help. The soldiers and I will do the rest. We'll disable the other bomber as well. When is your next mission?" she asked, and he looked at his watch.

"Alright. I'll see what the briefing holds. I know who my co-pilot will be. We leave in ninety minutes after our briefing. Can you get them here by then?"

"I will have to, won't I? Major, we have more allies in this than it appears. They just need some help and a push. I am determined not to be on the wrong side of history in this. I sense that you also have a need to cleanse the red from your recent history. We can do this together. There is a difference between soldiers fighting a war honorably and following the Politburo and the Ministry of State Security blindly."

He nodded and walked away to join his crew. Mei also stood, turned, and looked toward Shan's team and the sergeant. They locked eyes, and she nodded to him as a covered truck pulled up outside. Their ride was here, but it wouldn't be going where the driver thought it would tonight.

FOURTEEN

Sully woke up stiff. Whatever uncomfortable seats the airlines used, the Air Force considered it a challenge. As he began to stir, he turned to find Corporal Dempsey's head on his shoulder with the Louisiana man's left arm draped on Sully's lap. Several glorious ideas ran through Sully's mind, but he lightly removed the arm to its owner's lap and push the corporal's head away. As he did, a line of saliva from Dempsey's mouth drooped to Sully's shoulder, where there was a large wet spot. He pushed harder, and the man and his sleep spit readjusted against the aircraft window. Didn't even wake up.

Looking to empty his bladder, Sully stood and stretched. Happy that he was unencumbered of all his kit, which was down in the massive cargo bay beneath them, he turned and headed forward to find the head. As he made his way down the aisle, a bunch of his troopers were gathered around one soldier with his tray down. They were in his way.

"What's goin' on here?" Sully asked, somewhat irritated 'cause he had to pee.

"Well, First Sergeant, since we nearly got our asses nuked comin' outta Bagram and the Hog here may not make it anyway, we figured —hot sauce competition. Trying out these bad boys on various MREs to see what kills the taste best," said the soldier in the seat.

"Well, what ya got? And don't tell me that Sriracha shit."

"So far, looks like this one here with no label is the winner," another soldier said.

"Bullshit! This yellow one, Claude's BBQ, is the shit, First Sergeant!" a squad sergeant said from across the aisle. Sully noticed another trooper sitting by the window with a half dozen little

Tabasco sauce bottles lined up on his tray, along with several jalapeno cheese spread packets.

"Whatchu got goin' on over there, Private?" Sully asked him.

"Winning, S'arnt. I'm a Tabasco fiend. These'll be like gold when their special sauces run out. Imma be rich. Also, got me some Army jalapeno cheese packets," the private said.

Sully nodded at his entrepreneurial spirit, then said, "Okay, make a hole. I gotta pee. Plus, y'all stink. Damn."

They parted, and Sully continued to the front of the passenger compartment where the six combat engineers attached to their platoon were sitting. Seats were empty and he pointed at them in an unspoken question, looking around.

"They were studying the pictures of the three bridges we're supposed to hit, First Sergeant. Went down to the cargo bay about an hour ago with the LT. Head's that way, First Sergeant," the corporal across from the empty seats told him, pointing towards the front of the compartment in answer to his second unasked question. Sully nodded to the trooper before continuing on. When he found the door to the head, he grabbed the handle.

"Occupied!" a voice said from inside.

Dammit, Sully thought and saw the stairs, more a ladder with a railing, and followed it down to the cargo bay, looking for relief. Once in the cargo bay, he took in just how massive it was. They said it could hold six full-size school buses, two abreast, three deep. It was bright from the LED lights along the bottom and top of the fuselage. There was a great deal of activity around the four pallets lined up down the center of the plane. Several airmen and the four combat engineers, three Army and one Marine, had unpacked a good deal of what looked like C-4 explosive bricks, along with other kinds of explosives in different shapes and coils of detonator cord. He knew what some of this was, but damn, did he have to pee.

"Chief, where's the head? The one up top is occupied," Sully yelled over to Chief Russo.

"Up the front ladder, you'll see it," Russo yelled back.

With a thanks, Sully walked toward the front of the cargo bay toward the nose of the aircraft and stopped and stared at what looked like one of those old Airstream campers. An antique. It was just sitting there. *What in the world is this shit?* he wondered as he climbed the ladder and passed through the compartment where the aircraft's load crew normally sat, empty but for two female airmen. He always fumbled with that one. Females, but Airmen. Both had their backs to him, talking over some computer screen.

"Either of you tell me where the head is?" Sully asked a bit curtly. The one that was standing came up to his shoulders, her dark hair pulled into a tight bun on the back of her head turned to him, and he realized his mistake.

"Ten-hut, Sergeant!" She wasn't an airman but a captain. She. Sully saluted.

"Beg pardon, Captain."

She returned his salute and stepped up to him. She glanced down at his name tape. "Sergeant Sullivan. Did I hear you and your troopers call my plane The Hog earlier?"

Sully hated this shit. He had to pee.

"Captain…" was all he got out.

"Or were you and your men calling me a hog?"

Shit.

"Think fast, Sergeant!"

"No, ma'am! We were referring to your splendid aircraft that sat for quite a long time on the tarmac at Bagram," Sully quickly explained. "With all due respect, ma'am, my troopers and I are usually very hungry, and we equate everything to food. We especially enjoy a good barbeque. Pork barbeque, ma'am. Since we didn't have any, we just pretended that your broke aircraft was a hog."

Damn, he'd just run out of steam…

The captain narrowed her eyes, then smirked. "Jesus Christ, Sergeant. That's some bullshit right there. I'm fucking with you. At ease."

"Yes, ma'am." Sully relaxed, trying hard not to roll his eyes.

"Two things, Sergeant. Chief Russo is sub-level with your engineers sorting out the payload. You should have passed them on your way here. Second, if you gotta use the head, this one is mine.

Yours is in the passenger compartment in the rear. I'm not gonna have you and your men urinating all over my seat. Copy?"

"Yes, ma'am." Sully turned to find the down ladder and ran right into another female officer coming out of the head, this one a major, God dammit! He sprang back to attention and saluted. She was tall and thin and looked him in the eyes. Hers were red like she had been crying, but he didn't have time to find out why.

"First Sergeant Sullivan. I'm Major Vincent. This is my co-pilot, Captain Peck." The major returned his salute. "At ease. I've spoken with your Lieutenant Ricketts about the drop and preparations for that. Chief Russo and his team are in the cargo bay with your engineers and LT currently. There is no rigging of demo on my plane, only inventory and repacking. This is my head." The major stepped past him and headed to the cockpit.

"Yes, ma'am. I've been familiarized with the rules regarding the head," Sully replied gruffly. Perhaps more gruffly than he'd meant to. Major Vincent stopped and turned to face him.

"First Sergeant, regardless of what you and your men are going to do after we drop you, if you come into contact with whoever the hell we're fighting, kill those motherfuckers for me, will you?" she said and entered the cockpit.

"Yes, ma'am."

Captain Peck leaned in to say, "The major's family and my husband were in San Diego when it got hit. Kick their asses, Sullivan."

"Roger that, Captain!"

Sully watched her join the major in the cockpit, then he got himself to the cargo bay. As he was walking by the trailer, Private Sanchez opened the door and came out, nearly bumping into him.

"Sorry, Sully!" Private Sanchez said, scooting by him. "Looking for the head? In there. Small but pretty nice. A VIP setup or something, according to the chief."

Sully heard laughing from the rear of the bay and held up a middle finger, which elicited more laughter. Sully entered the Airstream and a wall of stench hit him.

"Jesus H Christ, Sanchez, what the hell did you do in here?"

"Haven't taken a shit in three days, Sully. I feel better, though. MREs had me bound up."

"My God, Private—!" Sully found the lavatory, held his nose, and began to relieve himself. He leaned sideways a bit against the paneled wall and closed his eyes as he peed. *Well, that was fun*, he thought. After a long minute, he finished, cleaned up, and headed out to find the LT.

"What we got here, LT?" Sully asked as he walked up to the group working to move gear around.

"You find the head, First Sergeant?" Lieutenant Ricketts asked.

"Not before I ran into our pilot and co-pilot upstairs. Thanks for that, Chief." Sully eyed Russo sternly.

"Sorry, Sarge. Couldn't resist. It's the stewardess in me," Russo replied with a toothy smile.

"Okay, so here's the plan, Sully. We got three bridges, so we're gonna drop in three teams, each with two of these engineers here," Ricketts said, and one of the sappers raised his hand and waved while not looking up from his work.

"This is a lot of explosives, LT. Captain up top said no rigging this stuff. Why can't we do that? Would be quicker once we're down," Sully said.

"No rigging!" Russo barked. "There's like a shit-ton of voltage built up outside the plane up this high in the atmosphere. One spark and splat—" Russo stopped talking, put the other earmuff speaker on his ear, and looked to the front of the cargo bay, listening intently to whatever was being said into his headset.

"What?" Ricketts asked.

"Yes!" Russo yelled and pumped his fist in the air. "We just made contact with the battle group off West Africa that's gonna refuel us. Didn't know where they were, but they knew we were coming and found us. Once we refuel, we'll be good to go to target.

"This is how it'll go when we get there and start the drop. The ramp will open, pallets go out for bridge one, then the troopers out the left side rear door. Hot minute later, same thing for bridge two, except troopers go out right rear door. Then the same for bridge three, but alternate to the left door last. We'll get you all rigged up and settled a couple hours out and do safety checks and re-checks. Only got one shot at this."

"Roger that, Chief," the lieutenant said. "Sully, get the platoon together down here, and let's start planning this out. We got about six or seven hours, and I want everything wired tight, including all possible contingencies that we can come up with. We're gonna get into LGOP mode, Sully."

"Copy, LT. I'll get the men going." Sully turned and climbed the rear ladder to the passenger compartment but heard the conversation below.

"The hell is LGOP mode, LT?" Russo asked.

"Little Groups of Paratroopers, Chief. It's how we fight when we land. We may land all over the place, so you grab the men near you and form little groups."

"Oh yeah, I've heard of that. Then what?" Russo asked.

"Head toward the sound of gunfire, Chief," Ricketts said with a smile.

FIFTEEN

Major Tang, Captain Liu, and their crews sat in the operations center, which was just a second-floor conference room in the building that used to be Gillette City Hall. Tang listened to the colonel from the People's Republic Army Air Force walk them through their mission. There were no electric lights operating in the room. It was lit with several kerosene camping lamps, which provided enough light, although eerie in their dancing flames. A large map of the slice of the United States they were in was on the wall. It showed the front range of the Rocky Mountains from Montana in the north down to Arizona in the south.

"Does everyone understand? Any questions?" the colonel asked as he completed the briefing, walked to his seat but didn't sit. The man was sloppy with his uniform. Ruffled is what he'd call it. The colonel was balding with a pinched, aggravated face. Too much time in the Party will do that to you, it seemed. He looked around the room and then met Tang's stare.

"Your briefing didn't include any military targets, Colonel?" Major Tang stated. He wanted to see what was really going on here. Decisions needed to be made.

"Major, all missions being conducted are deemed military in nature, and many of the people that inhabit these areas support the American military. Therefore, Beijing has determined that these are military targets. Do you have an issue with this?"

Tang chose his next words carefully.

"Sir, we've invaded their country. I'd assume all of Americans are against us. That doesn't mean dropping nerve agent on families is called for or even legal," he said. It was his intent to come right to the line of insubordination, but not cross it, to get a reaction.

"Major… everyone here, actually… our orders come from High Command. They've deemed it reasonable to use all of the weapons at our disposal in order to prosecute this war as quickly as possible. There is no longer any 'legal' or 'illegal,' only war. Total war, gentlemen." The colonel leaned forward, his hands folded on the table, and stared at Tang.

"Do you have a problem with the orders that High Command have provided us, Major?" He sneered as he said it and a little spit flew from his mouth and landed on the table in front of Tang. He didn't move a muscle.

"I understand the mission, sir. There will be massive civilian casualties, though. Is Beijing not concerned about those?"

"As I just explained, Major, Beijing wants a quick end, so these are your orders. It's critical that we gain control of these areas eventually. The presence of civilians hampers that objective. Do you have a problem carrying out your orders?" the colonel asked, his voice rising.

Tang made his decision.

"No, sir."

"Good. Get some more coffee and thirty minutes' rest if you can. I know it's a heavy weight, but it's the only way to ensure our plans are fully successful. Good luck."

With that, they all rose from their seats and headed down the dark stairs and outside into the wind. The truck was waiting to take them all back to the airport a couple of miles north. Tang noticed an SUV parked outside the building. She was waiting for his answer. He turned to the seven men with him.

"Liu and I will be along directly. The rest of you take the truck back, and get ready. It's going to be a long night," Tang said as he saw Captain Liu tilt his head in confusion. Once their crews were on the truck and it pulled away, his wingman spoke.

"Okay, what's up? That was our ride."

"We have our own," Tang said, nodding at the waiting SUV. Then, in an undertone, asked, "How do you feel about this mission?"

Doubt crossed Liu's eyes. "I don't like it one bit, but what choice do we have?"

"Something took down all communications with Beijing and China. We are alone now. I know you're a good officer. Loyal. That said, you know our last mission was dropping our ordinance on several small towns. We killed civilians, Captain. I didn't become a pilot to kill civilians like our own families. I am going to save what is left of my honor. I won't be killing any more children, Liu." He let Liu digest what he'd just said.

His wingman pulled out a pack of Marlboro Lights from his flight jacket and lit one against the wind. Tang knew he was taking a chance, but his mind was set. He hoped he was right.

Liu sucked on his cigarette, then let out the smoke in a long, slow stream. "We'll be lined up against a wall and shot."

"By who? Clearly, the Americans or someone struck back at our homeland. There's only our forces here in theater, and they've got their hands full. I bet they're not even communicating from here to the East Coast. I'm willing to be my life on it. How long do you think they'll last here?"

"What about our families? They'll be shot, too."

"How will they know? No comms, remember."

"Okay, two things. I also don't want to have to carry the heavy weight, as the colonel put it, on my conscience any more than I need to, and you have to promise me we'll get back to our families. This whole thing is going sideways. But I'm in."

"Good. Thank you, my friend. Now, we have our ride here with a very interesting driver. Let's get in out of the wind, and she'll explain further, and I promise I'll do everything I can so that we'll see our families again."

Fifteen minutes later, Mei pulled up to one of the hangars on the far side of the airport after dropping Tang and Liu off at the terminal. Tang seemed to have convinced the other pilot, Liu, of the viability of her plan. The captain actually seemed rather eager and positive after she detailed it all out for him, and they told her about their mission and what their planes were carrying. There were two guards standing outside the hangar doors, but she noticed they weren't Ministry of State Security. She put the SUV in park but left the engine running to keep the heat going and got out. One of the guards gestured with his thumb over his shoulder to the door, and she entered. On the floor to her left were three State Security soldiers, face down with their hands bound behind them. They seemed to be unconscious.

"Beginning to think you weren't coming. That would have been awkward," the team sergeant said as she walked up. She looked around at all the gear and supplies stacked against the walls. It had all been flown in on transports over the last few days. His men, there were about a dozen of them, minus the two outside, were in various stages of preparation.

"I can imagine. Thanks for all this, Sergeant. Did you find what we need?" Mei asked.

"Yes, right where you said. My men will take the rifles and extra magazines to the school directly. We also found grenades and RPGs." The sergeant grinned like a kid in a candy shop.

"Good," Mei said with a relief. "I'll need a couple of your men to accompany me. Also, when this all goes off, be careful not to shoot at the bombers or any of the warehouses near the bombers. The bombers are loaded with pods filled with VX Nerve Agent."

At that, one of the soldiers looked at her as if a light bulb just popped on in his head and ran off to dig in his gear.

"Nerve gas? Shit. This is getting worse by the minute. Me and these two men will be coming with you," the sergeant said, and the two soldiers behind him nodded to her. "Let's go if we're going." The sergeant turned to the rest of his squad, who were busy around the hangar, slinging multiple AK-47s over their shoulders and getting ready to move. "Everyone staying behind, get to the school and recruit our new allies."

"Sergeant. Wait. I found these when we were procuring the weapons. There were a ton of them, so I took a couple dozen. May be helpful," said the one who'd run off. He handed each of them a small tube about the length of a human hand.

"What are these?" Mei asked.

The sergeant gestured at the man. "This is my team medic. In light of what you just told us about the nerve agent, these may indeed come in handy. They're antidote injectors to counteract the nerve agent if it comes to that."

The medic added, "Each injector contains three medicines that do something different, but together they'll save your life. Atropine, Pralidoxime, and Midazolam." He went back to his gear and got more injectors, and started handing them to the whole team.

Mei slid the injector tube into her inside jacket pocket as the sergeant pulled a pistol from his tactical vest. "You do know that this may end badly," she said.

"You're right, and if we get into trouble, you'll need this." He handed her the pistol. She took it and pulled the slide back just enough to see the chambered round, then released the slide and put it in her waistband.

"So, you know how to use that?" the sergeant asked.

"Your captain made sure of it," Mei responded with a smile.

"Good. Look, I'm not so worried about our regular troops. There's more of them here than state security. There's no love lost there. But, that said, the goal is to get you all out of here, just to be safe. We can handle the rest. We owe the captain that much. He's stood up for all of us in one way or another over the last couple of years," the sergeant explained.

"I can't thank you enough, Sergeant. This way," she said and led the three of them out to the warm SUV.

Mei dropped Tang and Liu off. The two bombers were fully fueled and ready for the mission. The large military transport plane was still sitting on the tarmac about fifty yards beyond the bombers with its ramp down. A crew was refueling it as well, but Tang didn't see any flight crew around. Either way, he needed coffee. Something strong. *This will be a long night,* he thought as they entered the terminal through the double glass doors. It was dimly lit inside and only slightly warmer than outside, but there was no God-forsaken wind in here.

He looked around and found his crews talking with the transport flight crew. They were all sitting in two rows of leather seats you found in any airport. The only other person in the terminal was a lone woman with long hair, sitting off by herself toward the back of the terminal. She sipped her cup, and while he couldn't tell in this light what she was looking at, it felt like she was staring at him. From inside his flight suit, the hair on his arms stood up.

"Hey. We're this way." Liu thumbed over his shoulder.

He looked at his wingman and nodded, and they walked to the group, which was disbanding as the transport crew began to leave. They headed deeper into the building. One of them mentioned sleep. Good. He and Liu met their crews in the middle of the terminal.

"Okay, listen up," Tang began. "There's been a change of plans. We've been delayed by a couple of hours. Go find a quiet place and rest up and be back here at two a.m.," he said, waiting for the questions and complaining, but there was nothing but nods and men happy to finally get some sleep. He and Liu had several explanations ready to go, but they weren't needed as their crews headed into the terminal in search of a warmer space to sleep.

Liu quirked an eyebrow at him and said, "Let's get one last coffee before this goes to hell." They stood staring out at the tarmac and their planes as they quietly sipped from their cups. Tang stared a long time at the long, gray pods that hung off each wing. They'd only be taking one plane. He wasn't going to leave the other one operational. His right hand moved down to the front of his flight suit, where his pistol was located secure in its holster. They were going to take his aircraft. Liu would to disable his own plane. Just before they boarded, when the rest were here, he'd make sure it wasn't operational by shooting the tires. They didn't have any replacements for those here.

"Come on, work to do," Liu undertoned, and they both braced against the cold as they headed out to their respective aircraft. Tang to prep his, Liu to disable the other.

He walked underneath his bomber and reached for the ladder that led up into the crew bay and cockpit. Across the lot, Liu was getting up into his too. Tang started climbing, but as he did, a shape caught his attention in the large, darkened window. The one nearest his plane. It was the woman he'd seen drinking something in the rear of the terminal minutes before. He paused in his climb, staring at her, and she looked back. She raised the cup to her lips again, then disappeared into the darkness, leaving him to the cold wind's bite.

At about the same time, Mei and the sergeant and his two men pulled up and parked outside the small police station and jail. She scanned the area as did the others. There was no one outside, which was good. No one wanted to stand guard in the wind, but she knew the guards were there.

"I haven't been inside, so I don't know the layout or how many guards there are," she said, looking at the front door to the two-story station.

"It's fine. Just walk in like you own the place. I know these State Security types. Fat, lazy, corrupt. We'll be right behind you to collect the prisoners to take them to the minister," the sergeant said with a half-smile.

"What if it doesn't work?" she said.

"We'll just shoot them," one of the men in the back seat said dryly.

"Just shoot them?"

"Quietly." The sergeant looked at his watch and the men in back laughed.

"Is it time?" she asked.

"It is. Going to get noisy all over the place. Let's go before it starts," he said.

As they exited the SUV, Mei put on her best Minister's Assistant face. She walked up to the single glass door and hesitated, holding her breath. Lights flicked on the other side, and that meant guards. A large hand rested on her shoulder and squeezed. She exhaled, pushed the door open, and walked into a lobby. There was a long counter in front of her with a gas lamp on one end. Cigarette smoke drifted, and five guards, who were neither fat nor lazy it seemed, all turned to stare. Two sat in chairs behind the counter. Two stood at the counter on her side, and one relaxed on a couch. All armed.

"It's late. What do you want?" the one on the couch said, his eyes measuring the three men that came into the lobby after her.

She froze.

"Speak, woman," one of the men behind the counter said, then chuckled.

She screamed in her own head, *Speak, woman!*

"We're here to take the two prisoners, the two captains that you're holding, to the minister. He'd like a word with them before their trial in the morning."

"Oh? And who are you?" the one on the couch asked, still watching the sergeant and his men behind her.

"I'm the minister's assistant. I've brought my own guards to escort them."

"I have no orders from my superiors to release those two. I'm afraid that won't be possible," said the couch-sitter. The two men behind the counter were now leaning forward. One guard took a long pull from his cigarette and dropped it on the floor, crushing it with his boot.

It was at this point that an explosion could be heard, along with gunfire, somewhat muted, but unmistakable. The five guards reacted as one, but they weren't quick enough. Mei felt herself yanked backwards and onto the floor like a sack of rice as fully automatic gunfire erupted in the small lobby. It was over in a matter of seconds, and she was now deaf and disoriented.

"Check them! With me!" the sergeant said as he pointed at each man. "Mei, you weren't shot! They didn't have time. Pull yourself together," he yelled as he and another man went through the door to the left of the counter. His words were muffled.

"Goddammit, I'm deaf!" Mei yelled.

"It'll go away soon. Get up and help me look for keys," one soldier said.

She looked at the carnage. All five guards were definitely dead. She made the mistake of looking at the one on the couch who didn't have a face any longer, and what food she had in her stomach found itself on the lobby floor. More gunfire from behind the door startled her to her feet as the commando finally found keys. Not on a guard, but hanging on a hook next to the door. He opened the door and yelled, then tossed the keys and let the door shut and walked past her to the glass door and looked out. Mei just stood in the middle of the lobby in shock.

The door to the rear opened, and four people came out. The sergeant first, then a woman, the other soldier, and finally Shan. Her captain wrapped his arms around her tightly, and they stood there silently for a moment.

"I'm assuming that this is some kind of rescue. I heard gunfire and explosions in the distance. I suppose he won't be needing this." Stooping, Captain Gao relieved one of the dead guards of his AK-47 and web gear with extra magazines.

"We have a plane with pilots waiting to get us out of here. We need to go quickly," Mei said to Chao.

"We'll explain everything in the car. Let's go," the sergeant said and slapped Chao on the back.

"Good to see you, too, Sergeant," Chao said with a half smile.

Mei took them on a circuitous route to the airport to avoid what was happening in town. They rode with the windows down and could hear quite a bit of gunfire and sporadic explosions in the distance. Captain Chao was next to her in the passenger seat with his AK oriented out the window. The sergeant and his two men were in the back seat, and Gao was in the very back in the cargo space, cussing at every bump.

"I don't like this plan of yours. It makes no sense. If you're right, and China has gone dark and we're on our own, we should stay and fight. I won't leave my team here to die, only for me to escape, even if it's with you, Mei," Chao said as he scanned out the window. Eyes watering from the wind.

"There are over eight thousand troops and infiltrators here, and many won't join us. The Americans here sound like they're fighting, but most probably aren't soldiers. We're just buying you time. We all owe you that much, Captain," the sergeant said from the backseat, and the other two commandos murmured agreement.

"We're not communists, Captain," one soldier said. "Many out there aren't either. Maybe we have a chance. Either way, you all must get out, if only to tell the world our glorious story." He slapped the other soldier on the leg, and they both nodded to each other.

"Also, Captain, you and Mei have a chance at a life after all this. Get somewhere safe. Have kids. Make your life and live it. Most of us only have elderly parents at home. We said goodbye already. Besides, someone has to keep an eyeball on Captain Gao, or she'll shoot more majors," the sergeant said.

"Or sergeants…" came the reply from the rear, and Chao snorted a laugh.

"Fair," the sergeant replied with a smirk as Mei pulled up behind the two bombers with the transport behind them to the left, ramp still open, and no one around that she could see. They all piled out of the vehicle, and the sergeant opened the tailgate so Gao could hop out. She took a couple of steps and went to one knee, scanning the tarmac with her AK. The two commandos did the same. There was movement under the bomber to the left, and Tang come down the ladder.

"Say your goodbyes, Shan. I'm going to check with the pilot," Mei said and jogged away.

"You have no choice, Captain. You are going. We are staying." The sergeant stuck out his hand, and Chao took it, and they embraced each other in a rough hug. Then Chao saluted his men, and they turned and ran off toward the continuing gunfire. He turned to see someone come down the ladder of the second bomber and start to walk toward Mei.

Crack!

The man dropped as the bullet, from somewhere, went through his head. Chao brought his rifle up, scanning for the target.

"Don't shoot near the plane! Nerve gas canisters!" Mei yelled to him. He saw her standing there under the wing of the bomber with a pistol raised toward the other plane. More shots rang out and the tires next to Mei partially popped and deflated at the same time.

Shit.

Chao saw the target now, stepping from behind the tires of the other plane, pistol raised toward Mei.

Nerve gas. Fuck!

He stepped sideways so the canister under the wing wasn't in his sights.

Bang, bang, bang!

The shots came from Chao's right. The sergeant and his men had returned. The target ducked in front of the wheels. He could see she looked like a woman, but his men couldn't.

"Cease fire!" he yelled as another shot rang out. He turned to see the pilot sprinting dead out to the transport plane, but Mei was down on the ground, grasping one of her shins. Gao came up and knelt in front of him and aimed her AK at the woman, who was now holding her side, but still pointing her weapon at Mei as the pilot ran past them.

"Get to the transport! She shot the plane's tires. It's done!" the pilot yelled and disappeared behind him. He watched Mei struggle to stand and face the other woman, then she looked over at Chao and tilted her head as the sergeant and his men approached from the other side of the bomber, stalking the woman. With a rumble, the engines on the transport spun up behind him.

"You're not going anywhere, Mei!" the woman shouted over the increasing whine of the engines.

"Neither are you!" Mei yelled back and, in one swift motion, raised her pistol and fired several rounds in quick succession.

Chao was frantic. He couldn't fire, but Mei could? Fuck! His men were almost behind her, but they couldn't shoot either because they might hit Mei.

"You missed," the woman said.

"Did I, Tori?" Mei said and smiled as the woman turned her head to see what was brushing against her head and face. Her eyes went wide when she saw the holes in the nerve agent canister spewing steaming wisps. She hesitated, which gave his men time to get a shot. Chao watched as the woman raised her pistol at Mei, but pitched sideways to the ground, still. It was Gao's shot that hit her in the side of the head.

Chao started forward to help Mei, but Gao grabbed his arm, and he stopped.

"We'll get her! Get on the transport!" his sergeant yelled over the full rage of the engines. Gao was pulling him back now as his men got to Mei and she collapsed. The sergeant picked her up, doll-like, and headed for Chao. But thirty yards out, he stumbled, dropping the love of his life to the ground. She was on her side, looking at him.

"Gas! They're gone! Come on or we'll all die!" Gao screamed behind him as Mei raised a shaky hand and waved him away.

"Mei!" He screamed even as his feet carried him backward to Gao's voice. He came back to the present, watching Mei die in front of him, as Gao began firing at something or someone on the other side of the bomber from the transport's ramp. He turned and ran up the ramp of the transport and hit the button to raise the ramp as the plane began to roll and bullets ricocheted around him. He stood watching Mei on the ground, further and further in the distance, as the ramp closed. He let out a primal scream.

"I need help up here, now!" the pilot yelled, and he and Gao raced to the cockpit. Gao jumped into the co-pilot's seat and followed the pilot's instructions.

Mei felt the chill cold of the ground seep through her clothes as she watched the transport roll away, picking up speed.

I love you, she thought. *My Shan. My captain. You're free. You're safe.* She knew what was happening to her. She heard coughing near her. *Sergeant. Men. Almost...* Then she was roughly rolled onto her back.

"Where is it? Where did you put it?" the sergeant was yelling at her as her head remained facing sideways. The plane was taking off. She watched it even as her vision narrowed to a single point. Only the plane was left, then it was gone.

SIXTEEN

West Virginia
An and Bao

It was going on 5 a.m. as An, Bao, and Dallas led by Frenchie, with Buford bringing up the rear, stepped back onto the asphalt road where multiple M1 and LAV husks sat, empty of life in the frozen air. They'd walked as quickly as a fairly inebriated Bao could go. He'd been drinking with that Chinese major. A lot. He was also still pretty emotional about his baby daughter and had to be hushed repeatedly on the long walk back to the LAV.

An was frustrated with two things. His brother's talking and the fact that the Chinesium radio was on the fritz. It was on, but he couldn't raise his team he'd left here. Could mean something bad, or it could mean theirs was dead. Either way, they proceeded with caution. Weapons at the ready as they approached their LAV. It was dark, but dawn would be coming soon in the small valley.

An glanced at Buford, who was scanning up the hills and down the road with his rifle's night vision optic. Everything looked the same. No movement that he could see in the moonlight.

"Gunny. No movement. Don't see the guys or anything here," Buford said in a whisper from a few feet away. Frenchie had wandered a bit, doing God knows what.

"Okay. Buford, go start up the LAV. Maybe that'll bring the guys down from wherever they are. Bao...?" His twin brother was heading over to his old LAV, completely ignoring him. An followed him to the open rear doors, knowing what his brother would find as Bao squatted there, looking into the open compartment. He stood next to his brother and put a hand on his shoulder.

"Look at these boys. What they did. I'm sorry, brothers. Sorry I couldn't do more. Save you..." Bao's voice broke, and his words trailed off as they both stared into the dark compartment where barely discernable bodies sat or lay on the floor. Several of them. An was grateful for the darkness. Bao wouldn't be able to see the char on the remains.

Their LAV's engine came to life just then.

"Alright, everyone, mount up. Bao, it's time to go," An said, then dropped his voice. "You'll see them again, but not yet."

Together the two brothers headed across the valley to the running LAV, but two headlights caught them in the open. He grabbed Bao and ran in a low crouch to the front of their LAV and took cover.

"Dallas, stay there behind the vehicle. Frenchie, let's go!" An yelled.

"On it." Buford had taken cover behind another vehicle and was lining up a shot on the now stationary vehicle about two hundred yards down the road.

"Wake up, you old bastard!" Captain Wu yelled and slapped the major across the face. The drunk was lying on the floor in the kitchen, bound and unconscious. When the major hadn't checked in, they went looking and found the Humvee with his dead driver out front. Wu had come straight here. He hadn't trusted that Vietnamese spy, and now he knew why. The major had told him he was a wealth of information and was off limits. Stupid.

"What?" the major slurred from the floor as he regained consciousness.

"What? That's all you have to say. Get him up," Wu said to the men with him. Two soldiers lifted him upright in the chair, and one cut him free of his bonds.

"Wu, is that you? That American tied me up."

"Welcome back, Major. Now, what happened? Precisely. What did you tell him in your drinking sessions?"

"There were other men with him. Don't question me, Captain! I was gaining intelligence. He's a Vietnamese spy and on our side."

"I doubt that very much, Major. Now what did you tell him?"

Wu's radio crackled to life. "Operations, Rover 2. We have multiple unidentified on foot moving—"

An was trying to figure out how he'd get Dallas to them when the passenger door of the Humvee opened, and a soldier stepped out, aiming his weapon in their direction. He was peeking around the vehicle, working it out, when fully automatic fire from up on the hill shattered the silence.

The Humvee's windshield was hit multiple times, and the soldier was thrown backward. The gunfire stopped after about thirty rounds impacted the vehicle.

"Friendlies! Friendlies!" a voice yelled from the right where the gunfire came from.

"Come down!" Buford yelled as he moved to the LAV, grabbing Dallas as he went, who was a bit stunned from the violence. They joined An and Bao at the rear of the vehicle.

"Get in, Dallas. Hurry up!" An yelled to the rest of the team, now running along the road, weaving in and out of the dead tracks and other vehicles. The three Marines got to the back of the LAV and piled in.

"Sorry, Gunny. Radio died. Batteries," the corporal said, somewhat out of breath from running.

"Where are your spare batteries?" An asked, agitated.

"In there." The corporal pointed to his pack in the back of the compartment.

"What the fuck! Get it and switch 'em out now," An said as he squeezed through to the commander's seat in the small turret. Another Marine took the other hatch while one of the other Marines secured the rear doors.

"Don't worry, Dallas. We're as good as home now," Bao said, trying to reassure the teenager who was looking around, a bit shell-shocked.

"Buford, turn this thing around and get us outta here!" An said into his microphone attached to his commander's helmet he'd just put on, and the LAV lurched forward and turned around on the shoulder of the road still lit by one headlight on the ruined Humvee. As they approached the light, An saw in their own headlights the driver with several gunshot wounds, clearly deceased. He raised his M-4 as they slowly passed the wreck. The other soldier was dragging himself down into the ditch on the other side of the road.

An squeezed his trigger.

Pop!

He stopped moving.

Suddenly, An yelled, "Where's Frenchie? Is he with us?"

"Not in here," a voice yelled back.

An turned around in his hatch and looked back down the road littered with dead vehicles and saw movement. Frenchie was moving toward them, arms full of plate carriers and ammunition.

Dumbass hillbilly hoarder, gonna get us killed, An thought.

"Frenchie! Hurry your ass up!"

That's when he heard the high-pitched whistle.

Captain Wu stood in the dark in the backyard staring in the direction of the gunfire, radio in his hand. He now knew where the American went, and apparently, the man had help with him. He didn't really care, but the fool major had been talking with him for days. Maybe he had learned something. Time to determine if he should care or not. Back in the kitchen, his commander was splashing water on his face from a water bottle.

"Major, apparently your American friend, the spy, wasn't a spy at all but was just trying to save his own ass. Now, I need to know whether his escape is going to have a negative outcome for us or not. Please tell me what you've told him when you thought he was on our side."

The major grabbed a kitchen towel from the oven and dried his face. He wobbled a little, still recovering. He looked at Wu, lit by a flashlight one of the soldiers held.

"I warned you, Captain, not to question me."

Wu's patience was at an end. "Major, I just lost two good men and one more in the form of your driver. I no longer care about rank, you drunken pig. I will ask one last time—" Wu drew his pistol, pointed it at the kitchen floor, and waited.

The major's eyes widened.

"You wouldn't dare!" he spat, and Wu raised the pistol and pointed it at the man's face. "Okay! In our discussions, I may have told him about the East Coast operations. Baltimore. I told him about our Baltimore operations."

"And?" Wu took a step forward.

"And… and about Mount Weather and the farmland in the Upper Shenandoah and Viginia and reinforcing Dulles Airport." The major looked down at the kitchen floor in disgrace.

"You bastard. Sergeant, I want B Company mounted up and ready to go in ten minutes. Get one of the fuel trucks ready to go as well. No telling how far we'll need to follow these Americans before we catch and kill them. We must clean up this mess before it spreads. Go now. I'll take care of the major. Leave me a vehicle."

The sergeant saluted, and the soldiers left through the front door. Wu holstered his pistol. He waited to speak until he heard the other vehicles out front drive away. He keyed his radio again.

"Operations, this is Wu. I want the mortars to pound the valley to the east. They already have it set up. Tell them to execute a three-minute barrage into that valley, over."

"This is Operations. Copy. Mortars will hit the valley to the east for three minutes. I will relay the order. Operations out."

Wu looked at the major and stared. He tried to straighten himself and puffed out his chest. Clearly trying to assert what authority or power he had left. Wu felt pity just then for the man.

"Captain, I'm still your commanding officer. I would appreciate your loyalty in this situation. You're a great asset to the Party and me. I need a shower and a fresh uniform. Then we can discuss your future."

"Of course, Major. It is my duty and pleasure to serve under you. We can forget all this. Shall we?" Wu stepped aside and motioned for the major to head out before him. The major smiled and walked past him, putting a hand on Wu's arm and squeezing it.

"Good man, Captain. Thank you," the major said and walked down the hall to the front door. He never made it. Wu's four-inch, People's Liberation Army-issued knife was inserted surgically into the side of the major's neck up to the hilt. Wu shoved the man toward the front door, where he collapsed, grabbing at his throat as blood spurted out in beats onto the floor. Wu watched until the drunk stopped moving, then bent down and wiped first one side of his knife and then the other on the corpse's pant leg and stepped over him and outside.

He took a deep, cold breath, then walked to the Humvee, contemplating just how far he'd need to go to fix this if the mortars didn't end it.

"Incoming!" An yelled. "Frenchie, cover!" The shriek of mortar rounds descending into the valley was horrifying, but then came the thunderous rounds impacting a couple of hundred yards toward the rear and walking right at them. He watched helplessly as the explosions chased Frenchie up the road to the LAV.

He didn't make it. One round detonated to the left of the road, next to the running Marine, tossing him and everything he was carrying off into the opposite ditch. A couple more rounds hit the road between Fletch and the LAV.

As the smoke and smell dissipated, An strained to see movement. There was none. Then he saw lights in the distance across the fields they'd just walked through. He stared—there was a flash from the lights, followed by a boom, and the dead LAV, a ways behind them, exploded.

"The hell! Tank in the field behind us. Buford, get us outta here as fast as you can get this thing to go!" he shouted.

The LAV lurched and rolled, picking up speed.

"Where's Frenchie, Sarge?" a voice from below yelled.

"Mortars. He didn't make it!" An yelled back. This was followed by cursing from below. "Look, guys, we're probably gonna have company on our ass, at least for a while. Let's get back to Frenchie's people at that gas station. That's our waypoint. Buford, you good for a while?"

"Roger that, boss," came the reply.

"God dammit," An said to himself as he slumped in his seat. He felt a hand grab his leg and squeeze a couple of times. He let out a long breath. At least they got Bao and Dallas. Now they just had to get back to Mount Weather and then home.

Ten minutes later, Captain Wu was in the little valley with a squad of his men. They had one Abrams and two LAVs. He stood in the middle of the pockmarked asphalt road and surveyed the area. There were a bunch of tanks and armored personnel carriers from the first battle on Christmas Eve. That seemed so long ago now. Up the road was a bullet-ridden Humvee and two of his men. They were dead. Killed by these Americans, whoever they were. They had come in the dark of night, quietly, specifically to retrieve the Vietnamese spy and his young friend. Dallas, the boy's name was. He suspected that these Americans weren't keen on leaving a man behind and came back for him, while the spy probably just played that part to survive. And now that spy had intelligence on Chinese operations on the East Coast and who knew what else. He had to silence them, but he had no idea where they were going.

"Captain! We have a live one! An American," one of his men yelled.

He stalked over to the ditch, where a medic was working on someone on the ground.

"How bad is he? Can he talk?" Wu asked his medic.

"He's alive. Looks like he's got shrapnel in his right leg, side, and the right side of his face and head. He's semi-conscious. You and you, help me move him out of this ditch. Bring up one of the LAVs so I can work on him in the back and get an IV started. That should stabilize him, at least," the medic said.

Two more of Wu's men came over, lifted the limp man, and began walking to the LAV as Wu waved to the driver to meet them. The wounded man was moaning and then let out a scream when one soldier stumbled in a mortar hole.

"Careful! I need him to talk," Wu said. Then he pulled the medic in close while they got the wounded man situated in the back of the LAV. "Look, I need him to be able to answer simple questions. I don't need him to survive. Do you understand me?"

"Yes, sir. I can probably get him coherent enough to talk, but his jaw and face on the right side are pretty bad. I don't know whether you'll understand him, but I'll do my best, sir."

"Good. Get it done. I'll be right here, so call when he's ready."

The medic ran over the LAV and began working on the man. His radio squawked just then.

"Captain Wu, Operations."

Shit. The general was probably up and aware now.

"Operations, this is Wu. Go."

"Captain, this is Command Actual. I was just briefed on the situation. Your orders are to find them, kill them, and return to base. This is a critical mission. Do not let them get away with everything that idiot major told them. Do not fail. Do you understand this order, Captain?"

"Yes, sir. I copy. I don't know how far we'll need to go. Can you send a fuel truck with escort to join us, sir? Also, all we have are these LAVs, which I will send ahead. They got one of the tractor-trailers running a couple of days ago. I'd like my Abrams track loaded on the trailer with my crew. We'll be slower, but I don't know what we'll run into out there. I'll wait here for them."

There was a minute of silence.

"Yes, Captain. That is fine. They will be on their way to your position in ten minutes. Get it done, Captain."

"Yes, sir! Out." Wu had quit smoking years ago but wanted a smoke now more than anything.

"Captain!" The medic's voice pulled him back to the LAV.

"Can he talk?" Wu asked as the medic met him outside the rear of the vehicle.

"He's conscious and aware. I pumped him full of painkillers to keep him from screaming, and the IV fluids will keep him stable. I also pushed something to keep him alert. You have a short window, Captain."

The medic stepped aside, and Wu climbed into the LAV. Switching to English, Wu began to work in his short window.

"Soldier, I am Captain Wu. We're going to take care of you," Wu said as he glanced the man over. Tall but lean. He had lacerations and a torn uniform down his right side. He was looking at Wu, eerie blue eyes wide. He seemed very alert, but Wu knew it was the meds.

"What is your name? Can you tell me that?" Wu couldn't make out the man's name on his uniform as it was half torn away.

"Frenchie," the dying man murmured. Although, with his facial wounds complicating his speech, it came out "Freshy."

"Okay. Freshy, I need for you to tell me where your comrades are heading. I won't lie to you, Freshy. I do need to know this. You can tell me, or we can go another route if you understand me," Wu said and stared at Freshy, who just laughed with some blood spilling out of what was left of his mouth. Wu pulled out a map and opened it. The map showed Kentucky, West Virginia, and the surrounding states. The wounded man looked at the map and then around at the others in the vehicle and at those standing outside the rear. Wu pulled out his knife and started digging in a wound on the man's leg with the point, which elicited a shriek from Freshy. Wu stopped and asked one of his men for a flashlight. Even though the sun was up, it still didn't quite provide enough light in the valley and specifically in the back of the dimly lit LAV. He handed the map to one of his men to hold up for Freshy to see while he shined the light onto the map.

"Come now, Freshy. You'll be taken back to the base hospital and cared for. Your own American doctors and nurses are still there. They're not happy about it, but they're there. Just point to where your friends heading, and I won't hurt you again. If you don't, I can promise that you will live quite a long time while I hurt you." The two stared at each as what seemed like forever passed while they sized each other up. Finally, Freshy turned away.

"Okay," Freshy said, turning back to look at the map. Using his left hand with a blood-covered middle finger extended, he traced a slow track across the map, still held up over his chest by a Chinese soldier. Wu watched him closely. The route seemed realistic. It was eastward on route 48 until he stopped. Wu watched Freshy hover his middle finger over a little three-way intersection in West Virginia. Wu saw a tear slide down Freshy's face from his left eye to his ear and an odd twist in the man's mangled mouth. Then the American stabbed the map with his middle finger leaving a red smudge on the map. Wu took the map and studied it. Satisfied, he handed the map back to his soldier.

"Thank you, Freshy. That wasn't so bad. You'll be taken care of now, as I promised. Move him outside," Wu ordered his men. He couldn't decide if the man's mouth was twisted in a grimace of pain or a smile. It wouldn't matter in a minute for Freshy.

SEVENTEEN

Baltimore, Maryland
Captain Zhou

His company of nine T-99 main battle tanks and three Type 92 Armored Fighting Vehicles sat in a line, engines running, on a road leading out of Baltimore harbor. It had taken a couple of days for the advance elements to secure the harbor and berths for the big container ships. Each ship looked like a normal, heavily loaded container ship with the ubiquitous containers stacked wide and high. However, these ships were not fully loaded with containers. Superstructures were built on the ships in port in China over the last couple of years to be able to load and transport military vehicles. Specifically, his T-99s and others. Containers were stacked all around the steel-reinforced infrastructure to make it appear normal.

Most of the actual troops were transported via cruise ships covertly commandeered by the military. Tens of thousands of troops in the cruise ships, and several divisions of armor, armored personnel carriers, artillery, and other vehicles and supplies in the container ships. They had unloaded his company this morning. The main elements were pushing ever deeper into Baltimore in all directions, backed up now by regular troops and creating a corridor west out of the city that a large force had used to exit the city earlier this morning on their way west. Captain Zhou could hear gunfire, sometimes a single shot, sometimes volleys of fire, from his commander's hatch, where he sat impatiently. His initial orders were to disembark and head to the jump-off point and hold to await further orders regarding which route he was to take his company.

They were sitting in an industrial area at the moment. It was much colder here than it was during the passage through the Panama Canal days prior. The limited time he was allowed up out of the hole they were in was beautiful. Here it was overcast, and a fierce wind blew in from the water. He hadn't seen the sun for days, and today was no exception. The sun was just coming up. Gray. The weather and this city.

His radio cracked to life.

"Dragon Six, Dragon Six, Warrior Actual. Do you copy?"

Zhou chuckled at the call sign his commanding general had given himself. The man had never been in combat, much like the rest of them. But this one had delusions of grandeur.

"Warrior Actual, Dragon Actual, go ahead," he replied.

"The latest intel and satellite imagery we just received is that the main bridges around Washington are too damaged by the nuclear strike to use. The bridges in Washington and the two beltway bridges are damaged. We had hoped that the American Legion Bridge, which is northwest of the city, was still usable. Unfortunately, it looks like it took the full force of the nuclear shock wave broadside. There is, however, a smaller bridge, Chain Bridge, closer to the city, which looks fully intact. Shielded by hills on the city side of the river and perpendicular to the shock wave. This is Route B on your map. The rest of the force will take Route C west once we make it out of this hellhole and follow the advance teams that left earlier. Whoever gets there first wins. Copy?"

Zhou always got irritated with his commander's lengthy radio traffic. All he had to say was "Route B," but the man loved to talk.

"Copy, Warrior. Same objective?"

"Affirmative, Dragon. We'll link up with you there. Also, for your situational awareness, we were receiving intel that the Americans may be trying to blow the bridges across the Potomac when we lost Command's signal. We're trying to reestablish communications, but in the meantime, this is the mission."

"Copy. Dragon Six out," Zhou replied. Comms issues happened all the time. He didn't worry about it and switched radio nets and gave the command to move out on the southern route, which his lead vehicle, an armored personnel carrier, already had loaded on the digital map. The same map he had up on his screen. After the first two vehicles began to roll, his driver put the fifty-one-ton main battle tank in gear and started to move.

The tanks and APCs in his column were all the latest technology, armor, and armaments his country had produced. Unlike his American adversaries, the T-99 had a 125mm smooth-bore main gun, as opposed to the American M1's 120mm gun. His tanks were also about twenty tons lighter and a bit faster than the M1. He had three APCs in his company, each carrying a crew of three plus nine soldiers to support his tanks.

They were riding buttoned up with their Nuclear, Biological, and Chemical protection system operating. At least until they got past Washington and into Northern Virginia. He hated riding with all hatches closed. It got hot in the tank. He got back on the radio and told the column to make the best speed, which was about forty-five to fifty miles per hour. He checked his optics for a view outside and saw that they were not on the main highway like they were supposed to be. Checking the map, he made their position in an area just south of Route 895, which would lead them to Route 95 shortly and down to the Chain Bridge and across the Potomac River into Virginia. The radio squawked.

"Dragon Six, Dragon 2. I think we missed the turn to the main road out. Going a bit further south to take the next entrance to the main. Copy?" The voice was one of his sergeants in the first vehicle, an APC.

"Copy, Dragon 2. Get us out of here quickly. This is an area we were told to steer clear of."

Dammit. How could you not follow a map at twenty miles an hour? he thought. Checking his optics again, he saw buildings on either side of the four-lane road they were on. They were three- to four-story structures interspersed with other shorter, one-story structures. Some appeared industrial, some were boarded up, and some looked like dwellings.

"Gunner, load HEAT. I don't like where we are."

"Roger, loading HEAT."

The acronym stood for High Explosive, Anti-Tank. It was really used for anything other than another tank. They had sabot rounds for those. Depleted uranium darts that melted armor when they hit and killed with their velocity and energy instead of explosives like the HEAT round.

Riding buttoned up with the NBC system running was only a contingency at this point. More than a week after the nuclear detonation in Washington would have brought the radiation levels from the fallout down to a manageable level, but they were taking no chances.

Zhou desperately wanted to test his and his team's training against the Americans, but there weren't supposed to be any forces between here and where they were going. The T-99 had a crew of three with an auto-loader as opposed to the M1, which had a crew of four. They didn't have an auto-loader, but the fourth crew member manually loaded each round into their gun. If their loader failed for whatever reason, he or the gunner could manually load their gun, but it was much slower. Zhou looked down and left as the auto-loader arm went to work loading the selected round from its rack in the rear of the turret, seated it on the runner behind the gun's breach, then smoothly pushed it into the tube. The gun's breach door closed and locked behind the round.

"HEAT up!" the gunner said. Several pings reverberated in the closed turret.

Just in time, Zhou thought.

Gunfire cracked, catching him by surprise.

"Where's that fire coming from? Sounds like from the right front," he said.

"Dragon Six, Dragon Two. We're taking fire from the tall buildings on the right side. Looks like one hundred and fifty meters ahead and from several floors and windows. Permission to return fire?"

"Roger. Return fire," he said and heard the machine gun on the APC up front spit rounds into the buildings before them as they approached. More rounds ricocheted off the turret.

"Enough of this. Gunner, slew right, elevate to second-story windows, right where my sight is resting."

"Roger, matched sights."

"Fire and load HEAT!"

The 125mm main gun kicked backward, expelling the base plate of the shell onto the floor of the turret, and the entire corner of the building disintegrated into dust and debris.

"HEAT up!" the gunner said.

They hadn't stopped moving, and they were picking up speed. No more pings. He wondered who he'd just killed. There weren't supposed to be American forces in the area. But they were briefed that firearms were everywhere here. He imagined that due to the lack of electricity and ability to move people and deliver food, a kind of warlord situation was building. Whose kingdom had they just rolled through? What other kingdoms would they encounter?

The briefings aboard the ship told them they'd encounter some resistance from the general population, but they'd be more concerned with feeding their families than fighting and would probably leave them alone. Zhou wondered about these things as the column finally took a circular ramp onto the main road south. Once they were on that road, it was fairly free of obstructions, and they sped up to around forty-five miles per hour.

The column had navigated barren streets just west of Washington, DC, proper and was overlooking the Potomac River. Their route then took them down a winding but picturesque switchback to the bridge below. He could see now why it was still standing when all other bridges near the city were damaged or destroyed. This narrow, two-lane bridge was sequestered below the ridges they'd just come down. The buildings at the top of the ridge, along with many of the homes, were rubble. There was still snow down in this valley of sorts, with the ridge on the city side protecting the bridge from the nuclear shock wave. They slowly rolled across Chain Bridge one vehicle at a time and, once on the Virginia side, made a right turn, which led them up into an area of what used to be large homes.

Zhou checked the NBC system monitor regularly. The radiation levels were normal up until they'd gotten within ten miles of Washington. The levels increased, but not by much. Then they got to the ridge on the city side. There it spiked to unsafe levels, then decreased a bit on the bridge. They were elevated again as they navigated this two-lane road. They had to slow several times to get around trees that had been blown across the road. He assumed by the shock wave. Through his optics, he could see homes with elaborately decorated fences and gates. *Opulence,* he thought. *Gone in a flash of fire and fury.* These homes were nothing more than burned-out husks. He wasn't prepared for what he observed in way of opulence further west.

The radiation sensors had reached normal levels again.

"Dragon Troop, Dragon Six Actual. Radiation is at normal levels. Secure from NBC. You can run open," he put out on the radio to the rest of the convoy. Then he opened his own hatch and stood up, his upper body above the turret. He grabbed the machine gun handle with his right hand to steady himself and scanned all the way around. Over the next ten minutes, he marveled at the size of the houses and the land they occupied. He checked the map. Great Falls was the area. The shock wave didn't reach out this far, and the fallout had apparently blown east of the city as there was none here. Then he was astounded by what looked to him to be a cowboy on a horse. To the right of the road, in the middle of a large, well-kept field, was a single, beautiful horse. The rider looked female from this distance. There was a rifle of some sort slung over her back. No threat. Not his mission anyway. He waved at the rider. She waved back. Surreal.

The loud ripping sound of a machine gun behind him broke his calm, and the rider and horse vanished in a mess of red spray into a heap on the ground.

"Cease fire! Cease fire, dammit! Who fired?"

The firing stopped at once.

"Dragon Six, Dragon Three. We saw a weapon. Determined it was a threat. Copy."

"All tracks, you are not to fire unless fired upon. I will determine if there is a threat or not if they aren't firing at you. Copy!" he yelled into the radio mic and received affirmatives from all tracks in response. He looked back at where the horse and rider had been standing. There was nothing but a red pile of flesh in the middle of the field as they rolled down the road until it was out of sight.

EIGHTEEN

Red Devils
Into the Breach

Sully stood next to Lieutenant Ricketts just in front of the four pallets of gear and explosives down the center line of the massive and brightly lit cargo bay. The rear clamshell doors were behind them as they faced the platoon. They were a quiet bunch at the moment, some men silently wondering why the hell they were about to jump out of a perfectly good airplane and some relishing the thought. Chief Russo and his loaders were double-checking the pallets, ensuring that they'd all go out the back when the time came with no hitches.

He looked to the red glowing jump caution light above each rear side door. They'd been on and red since the twenty-minute warning. Couple minutes until the ten-minute warning and "Get ready." That red light caused him no small amount of anxiety. Waiting for it to turn green was agony. He studied his men to keep the bile from rising in his throat. They'd been sitting like this for two hours now. Hurry up and wait, as usual. Airborne were a cautious bunch, though. Better to be all kitted up and double-checked rather than do it last minute and find issues. He looked down at Private Sanchez, sitting first in his stick, closest to the door on his right. Sanchez looked up and rubbed his eyes roughly.

"All right, Private?" Sully asked.

"First Sergeant, I'm still freaked by the parachute checker's log. It ain't right." Sanchez referred to the paper log on each parachute that was initialed by a parachute checker after each re-rig so the jumpers knew it was packed correctly.

"Private, I told you all not to worry about that. The checker is an expert. Just had an unfortunate name, is all," Sully said in an effort to soothe Sanchez.

"Not right, First Sergeant. Not fucking cool."

"Sanchez, the man can't help that his parents named him David Timothy Hastings. Relax."

"He shoulda just used first and last initial, First Sergeant. DTH is fucked up."

Sanchez was a tad nonlinear for Sully's liking. Stepping closer, he put a hand on the private's shoulder.

"Nut up, Sanchez. Airborne."

"Not fucking funny, Sergeant."

Ricketts's voice boomed, "First Platoon! Red Devils! Listen up. We're about to perform the first combat jump in a couple of decades. We're gonna land in three separate drop zones, secure those three bridges, and then drop 'em. First Sergeant Sullivan will take it at the ten-minute warning as Jump Master and jump last. I'm proud to lead you out the door. Airborne!"

"All the way!" came the collective response.

Crew Chief Russo looked at his watch and pressed one side of his headset hard against his ear. Sully stared at him, holding his breath. Russo looked up at Sully and held both hands out, ten fingers spread, signaling the ten-minute warning.

"First Platoon! Arrive!" Ricketts yelled, and the platoon yelled back.

"Violently!"

Ricketts pointed to Sully.

"Get ready!" Sully yelled, his stomach trying to climb out of his throat. Nerves were a bitch.

"Outboard personnel, stand up!" Sully yelled and gestured with both hands as he did so. It was immediately yelled back by the platoon as they all stood up. These procedures hadn't changed all that much since the 82nd dropped into Normandy during World War II.

"Hook up!" he shouted, using both index fingers in a hook motion. They returned the command, and as one, they all hooked their static line attached to their parachute to the anchor cable on either side of the cargo bay. Sully watched his men hook up. Each one's helmet straps so tight on their chins and cheeks that their skin was puffed out around the straps.

"Check static line!" It was returned in unison as all the paratroopers double-checked their static lines to ensure it was properly connected and not tangled in anything.

"Check equipment!"

The cadence continued as each man in his stick checked to ensure that all the gear he was carrying was properly secured to include the MAWC, or Modular Airborne Weapons Case, that each man had under his left arm strapped tightly to him. In it was each man's M-4 rifle or the several that carried M-249 squad automatic weapons or SAWs.

"Sound off for equipment check!"

Each man, beginning with the ones on both sides of the aircraft, slapped the man in front of him on the ass to let him know that his equipment was good to go. This repeated until the number-one jumper got his ass slapped.

Sully waited until both men in the number-one jumper position in each stick pointed to him, and both yelled, "All okay!" He glanced at his watch. 0700 hours.

At this point, Russo and his team went to work. The rear clam-shell doors opened, creating a deafening roar, while two airmen opened the doors on either side that Sully and his men would soon step out of into the icy morning air. Sully looked out the right side door, and off in the distance some miles, he could see the sprawling complex of Dulles International Airport. He'd never flown into Dulles before. The runways were empty except for what looked like a massive military cargo transport. Didn't look American.

The sun was just peaking over the horizon where Washington, DC, used to be. Sergeant Orlov was taking a leak next to the Pantsir Anti-Aircraft vehicle with a cigarette between his lips while looking around the tarmac at Dulles International Airport, just about four miles south of the snaking Potomac River. He couldn't tell the difference between the smoke and his frozen breath this morning. It was cold, but there was no wind. They had arrived a couple of days prior in an Antonov An-124 military transport, the Russian counterpart to the American C5 Galaxy.

They had two Pantsir Anti-Aircraft vehicles. Each had twelve surface-to-air missiles, which had a range of about eleven miles, and two thirty-millimeter auto-cannons, which were good out to about two and a half miles. They were loaded with tracer fragmentation rounds. His vehicle was situated in a grassy and somewhat snow-covered area off to the side of the western end of the cross runway. This runway was connected to the southern end of the two main runways running parallel to each other, north to south. He looked at his watch. 0700 hours.

Finished relieving himself, he turned to climb back into the fire control compartment by a side door behind the driver's cab up front. It wasn't as cold as his home in the Ural Mountains, but cold enough to want heat. As he climbed the foot and handholds on the side of the eight-wheeled vehicle, he could see from his elevated position most of the airport. Another Antonov had just landed, and Russian security forces held positions in armored vehicles around the massive tarmac. They weren't fully reinforced yet; however, there was a Guards Regiment with them that had secured the airport as a Forward Operating Base for follow-on forces. Some Chinese liaison troops were here as well, along with what was left of the Iranian commandos. He spat on the ground, took a last drag on his cigarette, and flicked the butt before entering the control compartment and shutting the door, smoke following him. The Iranians were worthless, he thought. They'd had their asses handed to them by a few American Marines and some civilians just west of where he sat. Completely failed in their mission.

The audible chirping from his fire control system focused his attention on the two large and very modern LCD monitors in front of him. The radar had picked up a new contact. It was close and low. Descending further still about two thousand feet altitude coming from the south, heading north just west of him. His radio squawked, and he picked up the receiver.

"Air Defense Two, Air Defense Two, Tower?" His commander's voice came through the speaker behind him in the bulkhead. He was sitting in the warm tower he'd taken position in for the three hundred sixty-degree visibility.

"Tower, Air Defense Two. Go ahead," Orlov responded. Air Defense One was on the other end of the airport.

"Do you have that contact to the southwest?"

"Da!"

"Tower has visual. American military heavy transport. Weapons free."

"Weapons free, copy," Orlov replied and hit a button on the keyboard in front of him. It was all automated from there. He heard the turret motor behind him on top of the truck begin to spin the weapons attached to it. He leaned back, grabbed another cigarette from the pack in his breast pocket, lit it, and took a long drag. He blew the smoke up above the monitors and waited.

Sully had stood in each door, gotten his ground bearings, checked to ensure there wasn't anything outside the door that was an obstruction, and come back inside to the middle. They were close.

"Someone has a radar lock on us!" Russo yelled to Sully and Ricketts. Sully looked back out on Dulles as they passed the western tip of the airport flying south to north toward the Potomac River and their drop zone. His eyes caught a smoke trail at the end of the long cross runway.

"Missiles!" he shouted. He could do nothing, but the aircraft began a sharp descent, which concerned him greatly because they were already under two thousand feet altitude. He turned his head to glance out the open rear doors. A line of flares and big clouds of chaff—little sheets of metal—were being deployed from both wings behind the massive plane. The missile took the bait and trailed away from its target. Sully heard an explosion, but couldn't see it. He looked back out the right door at Dulles just behind them now, and the same tiny speck began belching smoke, and he saw the rounds.

Shit!

The tracer rounds tore through the fuselage where the Airstream was sitting, shredding the VIP lounge and tearing holes throughout the aircraft, but well forward of his men. Out the right door, he could see black smoke and flames licking the door opening as the pilot jinked and jerked the behemoth around the sky. Someone roughly grabbed his arm and pulled him around. It was Russo.

"We're fucked! Captain says you all go at once, first drop zone. She won't be able to get you safely to the others. One-minute warning. If we make it," Russo yelled in his face, Ricketts standing next to him, taking in the situation. Sully went to work, determined to get his men out before bad things happened. He caught sight of Corporal Dempsey at the end of the left stick. Motherfucker was actually smiling at him.

"Stand by!" Sully yelled. "We're all going out at drop zone one!"

It was so loud with the wind and damage to the aircraft, he had each man repeat it to the man behind him until he got a return thumbs-up from each man in each stick. Just like that, the red caution light over each door turned green. Sully had Russo grab the static lines from the other side as he did on his side. Not optimal. It was what it was.

"Go!" he yelled to Sanchez just as another airman released the pallets, and all four pallets of explosives and other gear rolled out the back, each one's static line pulled taut on the anchor wire, yanking the parachutes out. Sully was grabbing static lines and gathering them in his right hand as his troopers went through the door. Then it was just him and Russo.

"Give 'em hell!" Russo yelled and saluted Sully. He returned it and rotated into the door. The flames from the engine were right fucking there. He stepped out, and the buffeting air caught him. He stuck his feet out straight together, arms across his chest as he felt the tug of the static line yank his chute free. Looking down, he was shocked at how low he was.

Sort this out quick, he thought, going through the motions that he'd done on dozens of jumps prior.

He looked up at his chute, which was fully deployed.

Check.

His lines were crossed.

Shit.

While he worked to uncross and free the lines, he saw in his peripheral vision a line of troopers already landing in the open fields running up to the Potomac River, which was now coming into view. That wasn't good.

Don't land in the fucking water, Sully! he thought. He was running out of room and time when he caught sight of the plane he'd just left, trailing flames and smoke. Going down.

"Major, inside starboard engine is done and on fire. Suppression systems inoperable and we've taken rounds in the cockpit behind us. There's something wrong with my legs. I think I caught some of that," Captain Peck said stoically. They had taken a ton of rounds. Virtually every warning light and alarm was on. Russo's voice came through both their headsets.

"Empty bay! Jump successful!"

"Captain, controls are near unresponsive. Are you bleeding?"

"I can't tell, Major. I think I'm probably done shortly. Starting to feel lightheaded here."

"Okay, hang on just a bit, if you can. Do you see any place to land out your side? Nothing over here but trees, not that it'll do any good. Landing gear is fucked. Troops are out, but DZ two and three missed. That won't work for them."

"I see nothing over here, Major," the captain said weakly.

"Hard left turn together. Follow the river. Decrease altitude."

"Water landing will be bad, Major," Peck said as they turned the mortally wounded plane.

"Captain, we can take out that third bridge for them. We've got nothing here," the major said without any emotion at all.

"Fuck it! It's been my pleasure serving with you, Major. Let's line it up. What about the crew?"

"No time. War is hell. Full throttle together, Captain."

They both reached for the throttles and pushed slowly all the way forward.

"The pleasure is mine, Captain."

Sully had just enough time to watch from over five miles away as the C5 Galaxy hit the furthest bridge upstream, center span, going clean through it, creating a fireball that rose hundreds of feet into the air, before he came swinging down into the trees just next to the river. As he dropped into the top of the bare winter trees, a branch smacked him on the left side of his face, nearly getting caught on his helmet as he passed. Searing pain blinded him as he jerked to a stop. He swung around and banged full-on into the tree that held his chute fast.

Gasping for breath, he looked around with his left eye shut. Right eye was fine. Left eye was probably fine too. He just didn't want to open it yet with the pain in his cheek where the branch had caught him. He heard the thuds of running feet.

"Sully, you a'ight?" Of course it was Corporal Dempsey.

"Think so. Branch hit my face. Tangled up and stuck."

He heard other troopers running over. The crunch of leaves and frozen snow drifted up to him.

"You got time to just hang out, First Sergeant?" That voice belonged to their medic, Sergeant Lars Hagen, a Viking of a man. Scandinavian ancestry.

"Doc, First Sergeant Sullivan forgot that landing in trees ain't optimal," Corporal Dempsey said.

"Y'all done? Quit fucking about. Corporal, climb your Cajun ass up here and cut me out. I'll hold on to the trunk while you do that. Can't do both." He was short on patience and on time.

After more troopers arrived loaded with quips about trees, Dempsey used a couple men to stand on, then climbed up far enough, a knife between his teeth, to where Sully was. He had rotated toward the trunk now and had a solid hold of the tree, which was about as thick as the doc. Dempsey grappled up to Sully and took a look at the lines.

"Howdy, bossman. Pretty good gash you got there. Chicks dig that shit. Also, not Cajun."

"Just cut the lines, for fuck's sake."

Dempsey made quick work of the lines and freed him. Sully hung on to the tree, arms and legs wrapped around it, and began shuffling down to the ground, where the doc took a look at his face.

"Sitrep? Everyone okay?" Sully asked while Doc cleaned and bandaged his cheek. He opened his left eye. Worked fine.

"We good, First Sergeant!" Sanchez said. He hadn't seen the private run up. "Good news is we're all here. Bad news is we're all here. Second bridge is two miles west. We gonna have to hump all that shit over there. Third bridge is even farther."

"Third bridge is down. Saw it as I was landing. Air Force put their wounded plane center-span and went clean through. Focus on this bridge for now. Where's the LT?"

"He's with the sappers and rest of the platoon rigging all the demo and gear for humping," Sanchez replied.

Doc finished up on his cheek.

"Okay. I'm gonna go meet up with the LT and give him the situation. You all get to the bridge and secure it. Wait for us if there's bad guys. Shouldn't be here, but never know. Go!"

After fifteen minutes or so, the whole platoon plus the six sappers were together, minus the team with Dempsey and Sanchez he sent to secure the bridge. Ricketts was the last to arrive with a couple men, all humping large packs, including the LT. They set the packs down, and the LT gathered everyone.

"Sent a team to the bridge, LT," Sully said. "It's not far. Airforce put their plane into the third bridge for us. Suppose they couldn't land it. Was pretty jacked up from the anti-aircraft fire."

Lieutenant Ricketts shook his head. "Fuckin' heroes right there. Let's not waste their sacrifice. We gotta get all this gear to the first bridge. Then we'll split up and do the job. First Sergeant, let's figure out where we are exactly and then plot the quickest course on the map."

"LT, right on the other side of these trees is the main road that goes to the bridge. Bridge is right there," Sully said, pointing northwest.

"Copy, Sully. But I've had to take a shit since we landed. Fucking with me. Take the platoon to the bridge. I'll be right there," Ricketts said and walked a few yards further into the woods and found a large tree to lean back against while he took care of his business.

Shit happens, Sully thought and out loud said, "You all heard the LT! Let's pack up and hump our asses to the road and make a right to the bridge where the corporal should have it secured. Squeeze it quick, LT. We'll see you there."

It took them about twenty minutes to get to the road and then on to the bridge. Point of Rocks. Sully took stock of the situation after he dropped the pack and walked out to the end of the bridge. It was empty as far as he could see to the other side of the Potomac River and to where the road curved and disappeared into Maryland. Sanchez came running across the bridge. Was about a hundred yards across the water below but continued on the Virginia side over the sloping banks for another twenty-five to thirty yards to where the bridge met the road.

"Sully, we left a two-man team on the other side as an observation post. The corporal is scouting for a good overwatch for the 249," Sanchez said just as Dempsey emerged from the trees behind them on the Virginia side.

"Hey, Sully, there's a good rock formation just down here that we can set up that machine gun at. Overlooks the water, even with the bridge, and can see the whole other side. Good field of fire," the corporal reported.

"Copy that. Get it set up," Sully said just as Lieutenant Ricketts came jogging up.

"Sitrep?" he asked.

"You all good now, LT?"

"Nature called, I answered, Sergeant. We good here?"

"Yessir. Was just about to get half the platoon on their way to the second bridge. Gonna take 'em an hour to hump it."

The three sappers that were detailed to this bridge were climbing around on the outside of the girders just over the water and pointing out good spots and problem areas to each other. That's when they heard it.

"Quiet! Engine. There." Sully pointed back to the Virginia side and upriver. There was a side road that headed that way. The rest of the platoon, which was getting ready to either march or dig in, all took cover where they could and covered the road with their weapons. Sully saw it first and walked back to where the side road met the main road at the mouth of the bridge. Ricketts followed him as the vehicle approached. Sully held up his right hand. The vehicle was a Ford flatbed pickup truck that had to be at least forty years old. Black smoke belched from its tailpipe. The truck pulled to a stop in front of Sully and Ricketts, its windows down. The bed was piled with hay bales that rocked and swayed when the truck stopped.

"Hope y'all are Americans. My buddy, Joe, said you were. I trust him. He was a Marine. Thought I'd come see what you were up to. So, what are you up to?" the driver asked.

Sully took him in. He was middle-aged, and his red-blond hair was close cut on the sides but longer and brushed back on top. Bit of a receding hairline.

"Call me Sully. 82nd Airborne. This is Lieutenant Ricketts. Who're you?" Sully reached his hand up to the window, and the man shook it firmly and then Ricketts's.

"I'm John Gearheart. I've got a farm up the road a ways, and up the hill behind me is my land. We've been watching y'all since you landed. Even watched you take a dump," John said with the smile.

"Binoculars?" Ricketts asked.

"Rifle scope. Joe's got a good vantage up on the hill. Covers the whole bend of the river here."

"Well, John, our mission is to blow this bridge and the next two up river. Airforce took care the third one. Don't mind if we drop your bridges, do you?" Ricketts said.

"Yeah, we watched the C-5 flame into the last bridge before Harper's Ferry and the railroad bridge over the other river where they join. Why you wanna drop these bridges?"

"'Cause there are several divisions of Chinese Armor that landed at Baltimore and are headed this way. We assume to get into Virginia and take Mount Weather."

"In that case, how can I help?" John asked.

Sully looked back at the platoon and all the gear. "You can give us a lift to the next bridge up river."

"Done! You'll need to knock all the hay off the back. I can't help you. Got horrible back issues. Screws in my shoulders and vertebrae. Hopped up on painkillers, which are now running low. I'm a handsome man but pretty useless otherwise," John smiled.

While Ricketts got the men to knocking the hay bales off the truck, Sully had another question.

"Could one of my snipers set up shop with your buddy on the hill? He's got a good spotter with him as well."

"Absolutely! Joe could use some company. He's itching for a fight, actually. Just have them walk that way, and you'll find him. He's watching us."

"Roger that," Sully turned and yelled for the sniper team that was staying here to head up the hill and find Joe, the Marine.

"Hey, how's your truck still running?" Sully wondered.

"It's an old farm truck. No computers or chips in it. Started right up when everything else died."

"So some stuff works. That's good to know. Thanks for your help, John."

Couple of minutes later, when all the hay was stacked on the road and packs were piled up close to the truck's cab, twenty paratroopers crammed into the truck bed with one in the cab with John. It was a tight fit, but better than humping it. While they were all packing up on the truck, Sully hadn't really paid attention to the sappers on the bridge. He turned around when John drove off up the road with half his platoon to see the sappers walking toward him, unrolling a wire as they approached.

"Y'all better back up and get cover. Gonna get loud in a minute," one sapper yelled to Sully.

"Shit. That was quick. Get cover! Gonna get loud!" Sully yelled to the rest of the platoon as he found a tree to stand behind. He looked out onto the bridge and saw two lines of shaped charges with four charges per line. They were laid out across the road in two sets on the span the sappers had decided was the one they wanted.

"Fire in the hole!" someone called, and Sully opened his mouth and covered his ears as a series of explosions ripped open the bridge deck concrete. Blast concussions rippled across his very soul.

"Motherfucker!" he said aloud but might as well have mouthed the words, the blast was so loud. Out by the river, the bridge was a wreck of rubble. Smoke rose and drifted downriver.

Smoke on the water, he thought, the guitar riffs playing in his head. Sanchez came over with the LT.

"Is that it, Sully?" Sanchez asked.

"Private, that's just the beginning," Sully responded.

Ricketts started to bark orders. "Okay, time to work! First squad, get across the bridge and relieve the OP. Secure that side. I want the CP over there in the shade by those rocks. Sully, see what the sappers need from us and detail it out. I'll get the rest of the men into fighting positions. It's quiet now. Maybe we stay lucky."

"Hopefully, sir. On it," Sully said and some men started hauling packs of C-4, det cord, and duct tape out onto the bridge. Engineers said on the plane that this part should only take like ninety minutes to two hours. Less if they don't hit snags. Pretty straightforward to hear them talk about what needed to be done. Just cuttin' steel. Cratering charges took care of the other stuff.

"First Sergeant, you want coffee? I want coffee. Who's on coffee duty?" Ricketts said and pulled a bag of Black Rifle out of his pants pocket and tossed it to Sully.

"Dempsey's got the burner and pot, LT," Sully responded as he caught the black bag.

"Good. Let's get the good stuff while we can," Ricketts said and walked away to sort the other men. Sully turned to Dempsey who had heard and was getting the burner and pot out of his ruck.

"Here, Corporal," Sully tossed the black bag to Dempsey, who caught it and turned, with one smooth motion, and tossed the black bag into the river. Dempsey smiled like a mad man.

Sully just mouthed "what the fuck?" as Dempsey pulled from his own pants pocket a black bag of Stocking Mill Wig Splitter and held it up for Sully to see.

Sully threw up his hands. "Jesus Fucking Christ!"

NINETEEN

The lights came on, and Tavis could see the light through his eyelids. He didn't open them. His head pounded as he attempted to remember the prior evening. The US president had launched nuclear missiles and then invited him, Pasha, Gale, and Joey, along with a couple of his cabinet, if it could be called that, for a drink. President Madison had one Scotch and then excused himself. Joey followed the president's lead, leaving the rest of them to it. That was a mistake, apparently.

"Get up! Up! Bunch of asshats. Up!" Tavis recognized Joey's voice. She sounded bloody pissed. He opened his eyes and looked around the room from where he lay.

Boots still on. Not a good sign.

Turning his head, he saw Joey kick the bunk next to his, where Gale was trying his best to rise out of it.

"Okay, we're up. Not so loud, please, honey," Gale said, unfortunately.

"You know, when the president of what's left of the United States invites you for a drink, has one, and leaves, that means you leave as well. It doesn't mean the four of you drink all his liquor!" Her voice got quieter as she spoke, which was unsettling.

Four?

He turned his head the other way to see the Acting Director of Central Intelligence the next bunk over, sitting with his head in his hands, rubbing his face. Two legs appeared next to his head as Tavis tried to sit up.

"Excuse, Sheepherder," Pasha's deep voice rumbled down to him.

"Just don't kick my head." He grabbed one of Pasha's legs and pulled himself to his feet, a bit unsteadily. He looked around and realized they were in a barracks sort of thing with lines of bunks, tops, and bottoms down either side, footlockers at the end of each set. A sudden flashback to his SBS days hit him, and then he was back to the present, where a very serious-looking Joey Washington appeared in his face.

"Damn, Tee, you smell like a whiskey barrel. Y'all have ten minutes to shower, shit, and shave and make your way to the operations center. We got shit to do. Bouncer, Duck, and the Chief are up and waiting. I know you think we're done here, but we're not. We can't go back to the kids yet. They don't have an extra vehicle to use, and the helo is going the opposite direction shortly. With you two idiots in it." Tavis realized just then that she wasn't wearing her Lieutenant Commander insignia. In place of it was a single star on each shoulder.

"Aye, aye, General," Tavis said.

She glared hard. "Does it look like I'm in the Army, Air Force, or Marines?"

He was confused for a second, still foggy. Damn, his head hurt.

"What?" he managed.

"It's Rear Admiral Lower Half. Navy. You Scottish twit. Dammit, but y'all are some dumbasses. You're lucky the helo pilots needed to sleep, or you'd be in the air already." She stared at him, then at Gale and Pasha, who were now standing or trying to. Jack still hadn't gotten up.

"Look, Joey… er, Admiral, I'll apologize to the president for drinking his liquor, okay?"

Her eyes narrowed at his feeble apology. "Ten. Minutes." She turned, giving Gale a death glare, and headed for the doors. "Check out your handiwork after you've made yourselves presentable." She slammed the door and was gone.

They all looked at each other and, as one, followed her out the doors. There, in front of the building, rather part of the building now, was one of the golf cart–type vehicles they used to get around this small underground city. It was well and truly smashed into the side of the building at its driver's side front corner. Pieces of headlight lay on the ground. They all just stood there, staring.

"Well, I suppose 'Acting Director of Central Intelligence' was good while it lasted. See you guys in a few," Jack said and walked off.

"You think Jack is his real name?" Gale asked when he was out of earshot.

"Pretty coincidental if it is. I say no," Tavis responded.

"Explain," Pasha said, looking confused.

"No time. She'll have our asses if we're late," Gale said with a smirk and led them back into the barracks to get cleaned up.

"Honestly, I think she's gonna have them either way," Tavis said and slapped Gale on the back as they went through the doors.

Well beyond ten minutes later, Tavis, Gale, and Pasha entered the operations center and made their way to the glass-enclosed conference room, where Tavis saw the rest gathered. They entered through the heavy metal door and, realizing there were no more seats, stood awkwardly next to the door. They were the only ones standing. Around the table were seated the president, Joey, Spenkmeier, Jack, Bouncer, Duck, the chief, and several others in uniform.

"You're late," the president said, staring at the three.

"Sorry, Mr. President," Gale responded.

"Y'all have fun last night?" Madison asked.

"About that—" Tavis started.

"Joey, continue with your briefing," the president said, ignoring him.

"Yes, sir. What we've been able to pull together overnight into an overall battle picture is that Chinese armored and mechanized divisions would have landed at Baltimore by now with the intent of occupying the Shenandoah Valley and this bunker. Based on Javad's information, the Chinese need to take and hold our food-growing regions. But we don't think that matters any longer, due to our EMP strikes over Russia and China. They're as screwed as we are. We don't believe the Chicom forces here now know this fully. How could they? So they'll continue with their mission. It's what I'd do absent comms and with orders in hand."

"So, what can we do about those Chicom forces?" the president asked.

"Well, we can't do anything here. We need help. The only help that's a possibility is the Marine Expeditionary Force from Lejeune. They're not there any longer, as we've discussed. We think they're moving north. They wouldn't stay near the coast, and Bouncer and Duck have told us that they didn't see them when they flew up here over central North Carolina and Virginia. That leaves western North Carolina and Virginia. Route 81. Our plan is to send the helo south to locate them if possible and apprise them of the situation."

"Approved. When can you all leave?" he asked Bouncer.

"We're fueled and ready to go. Now," Bouncer replied.

"You're going to need more eyes," Joey said. "Tavis and Pasha here will be going with you. Gale, you're staying here to help sort out any intel we receive. Copy?" She looked at the three men standing by the door.

"Roger that, ma'am," Tavis responded. "Any word on the Airborne and the bridges across the Potomac yet?"

"Ah, I almost forgot. Spotters up top this morning saw what they think was a C-5 Galaxy drop paratroopers well north of us. That should be them. They've also heard rumbles from that direction, so it looks like that part of our plan is working, hopefully," Joey explained.

"What about our families? It's been nearly two days. My niece, Nina and Val, Tavis's family, and your daughter, Layla. They're waiting for us to return. Gone too long as it is," Pasha said.

"Pasha, I think they're okay," Joey answered. "I'm worried as well, but there's no way to get back until the helo returns with you all. Besides, they have Alice, Ahmed, Lou, and the Marines to take care of them. They're probably having fun right now. Once the Marines are here, hopefully, we can all get back to them. Soon, my friend," Joey said, trying to reassure the big Russian.

"Okay, you all get going and bring our reinforcements. Good luck, gentlemen," the president said.

Everyone got up and left the room one by one except for the president. He sat, rubbing his eyes. Joey grabbed Gale's jacket sleeve as she passed, pulling him with her, but Tavis didn't move. She eyed him angrily, but it was too late.

"Mr. President, I take full responsibility for last night. Blowing off steam, as it were. Apologies," Tavis said.

Madison looked up at him and smiled. "Shit, I got a good laugh out of it. It's the Admiral there you need to worry about."

Tavis smiled then and Joey tugged at his arm to no effect.

"I have to ask, sir..." Tavis started.

Joey tilted her head and stared up at him.

"Go ahead," Madison said, leaning forward.

"You know, DC has only been razed when a James Madison was president. Must weigh heavy on you, aye?" Tavis said and he could feel Joey's fury burning next to him. Madison stared at him for a second before responding with a smile.

"First of all, Sergeant, I wasn't president when they nuked DC. That came afterward. And secondly, the first President Madison didn't incinerate his enemies' capitals in return."

They left Madison alone in the conference room and followed the others to the stairs topside. The rotors were already spinning up on the helo. Duck and the chief were onboard. Bouncer was waiting for them at the entrance to the stairs when they came out into the early morning sunlight.

"Everything good to go, Bouncer?" Tavis asked.

"Ready. We've got enough range to get well down 81 before bingo. If they're on the road or near it, we'll find them, ma'am," Bouncer said and crisply saluted Joey. She returned the salute, and Bouncer headed for the helo.

"Okay, you two. Take care of each other and keep the shenanigans to a minimum." She hugged them both and Gale did the same, but in a more gruff dude-bro way.

"We'll be back with the kids and family as soon as you get back!" Gale yelled to Pasha as the rotors were up to speed and loud.

Pasha gave a thumbs-up, and he and Tavis ran over to the helo with heads ducked and climbed in the open side door and slid it shut. He put his arm around his wife's back and she snaked her arm around his waist. Gale hoped that he was forgiven now as they watched the helo slowly rise from the ground and tilt to head out into a valley and follow a line of hills south toward route 81.

"I hope Layla is safe," Joey said and squeezed Gale's waist.

"I'm sure they're all fine. Sorry about last night. Things got out of hand," Gale said.

"Should have known better than to leave you with a Russian and Scotsman, specifically those two. Look!" Joey pointed out in the distance toward their neighborhood and Dulles Airport beyond that, not that they could see that far, but in the air there was a tiny speck.

"I don't have binoculars, but that looks like a big plane," she said. "Going north over into Maryland. Can't tell what or who's it is from here. Our Airborne already dropped, didn't they? Maybe they sent two planes…"

It disappeared into the intermittent cloud banks that dotted the bright morning sky.

"Anyway, I'm sure all the kids are having fun with the Marines teaching them shooting and doing what chores Lou and Mimi have for them. We'll see them soon. Nothing down there to bother them anymore."

They turned and went back down the stairs to sort out what intel was coming in, if any.

TWENTY

Sergeant Nelson had been up and about the cul-de-sac for a while, checking Alice and cleaning what needed to be cleaned and now playing with these speakers. He loved productive mornings, but he was starting to think about how they were all going to make it through the rest of this winter. They'd have to really start planning and make full contact with the rest of the neighborhood around them soon.

Mama had the coffee going already and that goodness fueled his efforts. It also smelled like she was fixing up some breakfast tacos over the fire. It was a long while since the helicopter showed up and then taken the commander and her husband, Gale, with the old man to Mount Weather. Hadn't heard a peep from them since. Kids were getting a bit anxious about that too. The last two days had been warmer than the prior week. All the snow had melted away and the ground softened enough for grave digging. They all helped, including some of the neighbors from the wider area. They picked a nice spot just behind Lou's house. He knew their names now. Bibi, who had just died from a heart attack. Donneker; Dennis; Eric and Ana, the two Russian spies who were Alex's parents; and finally Robert. Lou was stoic about it all, though you could tell he was heartbroken. The rest of the bodies, Iranian and Russian commandos, were moved away from the houses through the woods closer to the main road. They'd burn them soon. No burying those.

He and Jones were focusing on their important work now while he thought about things. Well, it was important to them. They had mounted the two large speakers from Lou's family room to the top rear of the tank's turret, just above the ammunition compartment. Once happy with that, they ran power to the tank's electrical system. Jones was an electrical genius with this stuff. He had a plan to wire the speakers for power and then connect the speaker wires to the dead spy's operational iPhone by using an iPhone USB cord, but unwiring the end that had the USB connector on it to get to the bare wires. The iPhone wouldn't run the speakers, but the tank's electrical system would be able to.

"That spy had a huge music library on this phone, man," Nelson said as Jones was working on the wires.

"I know, right? Can't wait to hear music again," Jones responded. Inside the turret, their loader, Stewie, was doing a PMCS, ensuring there was as close to a full combat load as possible. Fletch, their driver, was asleep in his compartment to stay out of the cold.

"Okay, S'arnt, PMCS is done. The Fifty and both 7.62s have mostly full combat loads. That won't last long if things get spicy. However, we're pretty good on main gun ammo. We got twenty-one sabot rounds, ten HEAT rounds, two MPAT, and two cannister rounds, which were like the old grapeshot rounds for personnel, for a total of thirty-five rounds. Should be able to handle whatever with that. Hopefully."

"Roger that, Stewie. All we need now is to refuel. Once Jones here gets the tunes working, we need to hit that gas station on the other side of the main road a ways and siphon from the tanks, if there's any left. Could do with a little patrol over there anyway. See what's what and make friends," Nelson said. Just then the speakers came to life and Nelson recognized "Bring Tha Noize" by Anthrax and Public Enemy.

"Fuck yeah!" Nelson looked over to the driver's hatch where the voice came from and saw Fletch's hand sticking out, raising the horns.

"Nice!" Sergeant Simmons was walking over with a steaming mug of coffee in one hand, his M-4 cradled to his plate carrier with his extra mags with the other.

"I'm gonna have to search for better tunes," Jones said.

"Hey, Sergeant, we're all set with PMCS. Need fuel, though. Only have about half a tank left. Gonna patrol over the other side of the main road. Gas station over there and see who's around and what they're about. Good with you?" Nelson said.

"Good with me. Head on swivel," Simmons responded when Alex and Layla walked up.

"What does PMCS mean?" Layla asked.

"Preventative maintenance checks and services, ma'am," Nelson replied.

"It's fancy tanker words for make sure my ride still runs and has bullets," Simmons said with a half smile.

That's when they heard a sort of ripping sound.

"What does that sound like?" Simmons asked Nelson from where he was standing next to Alice. "Sounds like it's coming from Dulles."

"Could be a Gatling gun from the rate of fire," Nelson replied.

Then they saw a plane trailing smoke a couple miles away headed north.

"The fuck is that?" Fletch asked, sticking his head out of the driver's hatch and pointing to what the others were looking at.

"Looks like one of ours. C-5. Wherever they're going, I don't think they're gonna make it. Anyone got binoculars?" Lou said as he walked up to the group while the plane got smaller in the distance. Nelson grabbed the tank glasses and tossed them to Lou who put them to his eyes. After a second, they had the plane in view and focus.

"Guys, I think they're gonna drop Airborne. I can see a side door open by the tail and the rear ramp looks like it's opening. I see movement in the door. They're gonna drop somewhere." He handed the binoculars back up to Nelson.

"Oorah, Airborne," Simmons said, watching the damaged behemoth disappear.

"Can we go with you? Sick of just sitting around with my thoughts. I want to ride on Alice," Alex asked Nelson.

"That's a negative, Alex. You kids will be staying close until the others get back. We still don't know who's out there and that is a perfect example," Lou said, pointing at the distant plane. Alex just looked at the ground, turned around and walked over to her house and sat on the stoop.

"There's only so much shooting practice and chores and moving supplies we can do. Even the radio has gone pretty quiet the last couple of days. Just intermittent stuff, Lou. I'm okay with that, but I'm worried about Alex. She needs something to take her mind off of things," Layla said and went to join Alex, looking dejected.

"It's hard on 'em, Lou. But, you're right they need to stick close. I'll see if Mama can find some things to keep them busy," Simmons said.

"Hey, someone take this little Marine. She just shat in the tank again. And save some of those tacos Mama is whipping up over there for us." Stewie was holding Chewie in both hands leaning over the side of the turret while still in his hatch.

"I'll take her. She just feels comfortable pooping in front of Marines, is all." Lou stretched up to take the little wriggling furball from Stewie and set her on the asphalt where she immediately ran over and attacked Simmons's boot strings.

"Ferocious," Simmons said, looking down at the yorkie with one fang, her short tail vibrating.

"Yeah, Sergeant! Save some for us. I been dreaming about tacos for two weeks now," Fletch said from his hole in the front of the Abrams.

"Alright, we're gonna peace out and get gas. Back shortly," Nelson said as Fletch spun up the massive turbine engine to a high-pitched whine. Nelson, Jones, and Stewie disappeared into Alice's turret, but not before Jones duct-taped the back of the iPhone and stuck it securely on top of the turret between the loader's and commander's hatches where they could fiddle with the music. The phone was fully charged from the tank's electrical system and the speakers were powered by the same; it even played through the crew's headsets. Fletch started rolling the tank while a Taylor Swift song began to play, and Nelson familiarized himself with the commander's setup. It had been a while since he'd commanded an Abrams. Rusty.

"What kinda white shit is this?" Jones said over comms.

"It's an eclectic mix, Sergeant," Nelson said with a smile. He loved Taylor's music. Especially this one.

"We...eee! Are never, ever, everrr...getting back together!" He, Stewie, and Fletch belted it out, throwing their hands up on the "Eee."

"Sarge! There's good shit on that phone. I seen it. I better hear some of it soon," Jones said, shaking his head.

"Hey, Jones, you need to calm down. You don't want any bad blood."

"Y'all can eat a bag of dicks," Jones said flatly.

"Fletch, take us out to the main road, and let's cross the overpass to the east toward that gas station."

"Copy. I like me some Tay-Tay," Fletch replied as Jones tried to kick him through the little bulkhead door that separated Fletch from the turret basket.

"How'd I get stuck with three pasty white dudes in the middle of world war three, playing cracka-ass music?"

"Luck. That's the word you're looking for." Stewie reached over to massage Jones's shoulder.

"I will shoot you," Jones said, and Stewie cackled with pleasure at hitting just the right nerve.

"Okay, roll out, Fletch," Nelson said, and the tank rumbled to the end of the street.

They made their way through several neighborhood streets out to the ridge road and across the overpass. Nelson looked to his right down onto the main road. There were several cars there in various states of destruction from the Iranian commandos shooting them up over a week ago. They hadn't gotten the bodies from those cars, he realized. They deserved a burial as well. He put it on his mental checklist for later.

Looking to his left, the main road curved to the right after the wedge of high rock on either side they carved out for the road when they built it.

Good choke point, he thought.

Fletch turned right at the next street after the bridge, and they wound down through the neighborhood and into some residential streets closest to the main road.

"Man, comin' from the country, I couldn't imagine living in a house this close to others or backing to that big road there," Stewie remarked from the loader's hatch.

They were heading east, the cul-de-sac now hidden behind trees. The gas station was on this side past the overpass east of the cul-de-sac. There were many football fields of distance between the two bridges. He couldn't feel each tread pad as they rolled, but they rumbled and the jet engine whined loudly. That and "Sweet Home Alabama" blasting brought people out to see what was going on. Then a group walked right into the middle of the street and one man held up his hand.

"Stop here, Fletch. Shut her down. I wanna chat with these people for a sec," Nelson said.

The tank came to a stop and Nelson scanned left and right. There were houses tightly situated next to each other with mature trees in all the yards. Many were evergreens, so his view of the main road was partially obstructed, but he could still see a sliver of the road between the houses on his right. He reached over and hit pause on the iPhone and it went silent on the street. Nelson removed his tanker helmet and set it on the turret next to him.

"Was that you all making all that racket across the road a week or so ago?" the man in the road said. "I'm Chris. Who are you all?"

Nelson surveyed the group and Chris in particular. A slightly heavyset, middle-aged man with dark, but graying hair. He wasn't carrying a weapon that Nelson could see, but several of the group had rifles of varying sorts. None of them seemed to be a threat. They lived here after all, and Chris had a smile on his face.

"Sergeant Nelson, US Marines. What's your situation here? Sorry we haven't been by sooner; many of us were down with the flu the past week. I'm sure you heard our firefight across the road a week or so ago."

"No flu here, but we did have a run-in with some soldiers, looked to be Middle Eastern. Same ones you all encountered, I suppose," Chris said.

"Affirmative. Iranian commandos. Had quite the firefight with them. They lost. Took casualties. You?"

"Yeah, several. But most of us are armed. A couple got hit and passed. Had one elderly gent up the street die on Christmas Eve. Pacemaker stopped working when the power died. He died with it. We've just been busy building our supplies. Some were already prepped, others weren't. We had teams take turns liberating food and medicine from the grocery store and pharmacy about a mile that way." He pointed east.

"That's where the gas station is. We're going to fill up Alice here. We should stay in contact on the regular. Strength in numbers. Also, we got a medic and a doctor over there if you all are in need of medical. Although, we haven't seen the doctor in a bit. Probably pretty busy."

"I like that idea. Be nice to have Marines and a tank to help, if needed. We don't need medical currently, but will eventually. Thanks for the offer," Chris said and moved his group out of the road.

"No problem. We'll check on y'all regularly." Nelson leaned over and hit play on the iPhone. "Bad Company" by Five Finger Death Punch started up.

How apropos, he thought and reached for his helmet, when another man yelled down from one of the second-story windows of the house between them and the road.

"Tanks on the road! Going west fast. I counted twelve. Not American. Red flag on the turrets."

"Shit. Chris, get all your people out of these houses and away from the road," Nelson yelled and put his helmet on. "Fletch, spin her up and let's go see."

"S'arnt, you're not really gonna take on twelve tanks?"

"Only thing to the west is Mount Weather. We got people there. No choice. What's in the tube?" he yelled at Stewie, his adrenaline up.

"HEAT is combat carry," was Stewie's response, referring to running with a live round in the main gun tube, ready to fire.

"Fletch, get us to the eastern overpass. Here's what we're gonna do," Nelson said and explained what he wanted.

"Holy shit," Jones replied.

TWENTY-ONE

Tavis was thankful that Pasha was in the back with him this time. He didn't like the man behind any controls of a thing he was riding in. The sun was well up as Bouncer took the helo south, down the front line of the Blue Ridge Mountains. Couldn't really call them mountains, they were more like tall hills. The way they sloped down into the farmland to the east reminded him somewhat of Scotland as he looked out. Doors were open and the air was freaking cold, but he'd manage. On his right, Pasha sat beside him, his AK-47 between his knees, muzzle resting on the floor, while the chief sat facing them both.

A few minutes later, Bouncer banked the Knighthawk to the right, taking them through a pass and over a highway. They followed it awhile until he banked left and out into the wider Shenandoah Valley. Tavis shifted in his seat to face out the open door, his FAL cradled in his elbow. He scanned for any signs of the Marine Expeditionary Force, or anything at all really. There was no movement, although smoke rose from some chimneys in the valley below.

"Hey, guys. Route 81 is coming up. We'll follow that south until we find them or hit bingo," Bouncer said over the crew's net, which was connected to his helmet.

"Can you go lower?" Tavis asked.

"Yep. We'll cruise at 500 feet. I'll slow down a bit as well. Keep sharp eyes."

"Roger that. Also, I'm going to assume that if these guys hear a helo, which they probably haven't heard in a couple weeks, they'll get our attention," Tavis responded, nearly yelling into the mic.

"Makes sense. Although, you know, they could have gone in any direction. We're just guessing here. They could be in Tennessee or Georgia by now, laying low."

"He has point," Pasha said, waving out the door in a gesture of anywhere.

"Have some faith. They have to be down here somewhere."

"Why you so sure?" the chief asked.

"'Cause if they're not, we're all fooked," Tavis said, focusing on the roads and small towns below them.

They continued south, following Route 81 below. Nothing moved. Dead vehicles littered the highway and connecting roads. The helicopter was flying with rising mountains on either side as if they were in a chute. A few minutes later, the mountain on the left abruptly ended in a high peak and the valley once again widened up, and before them sprawled a large town.

"We're coming up on Harrisonburg. Eyes sharp," Duck said from the co-pilot's seat. They flew over homes and businesses and what looked like a football stadium.

"That's James Madison University down there. We'll keep going south toward the other university towns. Blacksburg and Radford," Bouncer announced.

Tavis was focused out to the left and the path before them. He was getting frustrated and a bit worried when he glanced behind them and saw red smoke rising from a field in the distance.

"Yo! Red smoke at our 7 o'clock!" he said excitedly and pointed below.

Bouncer banked the helo to the left and decreased altitude toward the red smoke. As they got closer, Tavis saw quite a few soldiers step out from their cover and concealment in tree lines and hedgerows in what made up the borders of a large farm, with a house and barn in one corner of a field. One soldier walked out and flung his arms wide to direct Bouncer where to land. As the helo touched down, no bounce, Tavis stepped onto the field, followed by Pasha, as Bouncer and Duck shut the engine down. The soldier met Tavis between the helo and the farmhouse.

"Who are you?" the soldier asked directly. Tavis scanned the soldier's insignia and uniform.

Oops, he thought. Not a soldier.

"Sergeant Tavis Kinley, formerly of Her Majesty's Special Boat Service. We're looking for the US Marines from Camp Lejeune. Would that be you lads?"

The gunnery sergeant in front of him narrowed his eyes. "Affirmative, Sergeant. Where you from?"

Tavis turned to Pasha and backhanded him in the chest. "I told ya we'd find 'em, ya big doubter!"

"Da!" Pasha winced at the playful hit. He was still recovering from being shot.

"Ah, sorry, Pasha. Anyway, need to see your commander right quick, if you would take us," Tavis said.

"Again, where are you from?"

"Oh, sorry, we've got intel and orders from your president. We've just come from Mount Weather, where your government is currently."

"No shit?" the gunny replied, stunned.

"No shit, Sergeant. Time's a-wastin'."

With a nod, the gunny said, "Follow me."

Tavis, Pasha, and the helo crew who'd now joined them, all followed the Marine to the farmhouse. As they walked, Tavis smelled wood burning and as they got closer, food. Bacon to be specific. They entered the old farmhouse at the kitchen door, and once they were all inside, a deep voice in a very southern drawl called out from the next room.

"Gunny! Who've you brought me? Bring our visitors in here!"

They all followed the Marine into what was the dining room. It was very old farmhouse with a large wooden table. There was another Marine sitting at the head of the table at the other end of the room. He didn't look up. He was eating a plate of something Tavis couldn't make out.

"General, these men say they're from Mount Weather and are looking specifically for us."

"Thank you, Gunny. That'll be all. Gentlemen, care to join me for some coffee and this brilliant blueberry pie?" he said without getting up from his chair, or looking at them.

"Love to, General! Gentlemen?" Tavis replied and gestured for them all to sit at the other chairs around the table. Once they were seated, the general slid the pie down the table.

"Y'all can get your own coffee from the kitchen. The farmer was very generous with that and his wife made this fabulous blueberry pie. I'm Lieutenant General Joel Kobayashi, Commander of Second Marine Expeditionary Force from Lejeune," the general said. He'd stopped eating and was staring at Tavis now. Tavis was a little surprised, as the voice and Southern drawl did not fit what sat at the end of the table. The general, of Japanese decent, was in his fifties with dark, close-cropped hair and a serious-looking scar running from his ear down to his uniform collar.

"Kobayashi? As in Maru? I love *Star Trek*, General! But I thought ya couldn't stay in civilian homes. That whole Revolution and Constitution thing," Tavis said, and Pasha just closed his eyes and shook his head.

"That's clever. Never heard that before. You make me raff. Also, I slept in my track last night," the general said flatly and then went silent, staring at Tavis.

No one touched the pie or got coffee.

"Right," Tavis said, hurrying past the awkward silence he'd created. "So, we've been looking for you, General. Hoping you were out here. We're out of Mount Weather, where what's left of the US Government is bunkered. President Madison requests that you get there, like now."

"President Madison?" The general leaned forward.

"Most of the government was killed when Washington was destroyed in a nuclear strike with twenty-three other targets on Christmas Eve, leaving the Secretary of Transportation, James Madison, next in line for the presidency. Meanwhile, we've hit back at Russia and China with atmospheric EMP detonations and nuclear strikes on Moscow, Beijing, and their command bunkers. We are all now playing on the same field. Almost," Tavis explained.

The general leaned back in his chair and whistled a low whistle and then slapped his right hand on the table. "This is good news, gentlemen. We need to discuss some things now, like what our new president's battle plans are and how I can fit my Marines into it, but I have a feeling since you came looking for me, you have an answer for me. I have to tell you, after our figurative march north to here, me and my Marines have seen some things that could only be described as out of the worst parts of the Bible. Some of the towns and cities we went through and around are gone and in a gruesome way, guys. These bastards have well and truly fucked up my country and we're all out for blood."

"General, we're here to provide targets for just that purpose," Tavis said.

After about thirty minutes of intense and detailed discussion and pouring over a large map that the gunny had brought in and laid on the table at the general's request, Tavis had relayed all the intel he had. From his brother on the MV *Shark* off the coast with the two submarines to the Airborne operation from Afghanistan that they were pinning their hopes on and finally to the new president and the intel they had from the Iranian spy chief.

"General, can I ask how you moved the whole MEF from Lejeune up here?" Bouncer asked. "From what we were told by two old Marines at the airfield there where we refueled, you took as many family members as you could as well. But the EMP knocked most vehicles out. What's your strength? There's several divisions of Chinese armor, mechanized, and infantry you're going to face off with."

Kobayashi sat back and scratched at the old scar on his face, looking weary now despite the excellent pie.

"It was an effort. We were at two-thirds strength to begin with due to the holidays. Luckily, a lot of our trucks and tracks were either older and mechanical-only, so they weren't affected, or in the case of LAVs and Tanks, they were hardened and buttoned up. What was left, well, we have a lot of mechanically inclined Marines. We only have one full battalion of Abrams; that's fourteen tanks. We have many more LAVs and were able to tow thirty or so Howitzers. That's not much, knowing what we're up against. The good news is that we have hundreds of Javelins and Humvees armed with TOW missiles to bring to the fight.

"The trucks were able to move my Marines and their families along with ammunition for everything. We stacked shit on every vehicle we have and we got here. This is where we'll leave the families and form up into the game plan I have in my head." The general took a drink from his coffee cup and looked around the table at them all.

"So you have a plan, then?" Tavis asked.

"Well, it's not a great plan, but the element of surprise is ours, I do believe. Wish we had air support, but alas, we couldn't fix that shit. Now, son, you said the USS *Virginia* is out there off the coast with your brother's boat, right?"

"Aye, correct."

"Well, last I heard, some of those subs had vertical launch tubes stacked with Tomahawk cruise missiles. Are you in contact with them? This is what I want, right here—" he said, pointing out several spots on the large map.

Tavis shook his head. "I…didn't even consider that."

"General." Kobayashi grinned and tapped his temple.

"It's hit or miss, General. But, aye, eventually we connect," Tavis responded.

"Good. Sergeant Kinley, tell President Madison we're coming. Late afternoon action. But I've got shit to do, so get outta here. I'll see you on the other side." The general stood and shook their hands.

As they headed out through the kitchen, leaving the general to his plan, Tavis heard Kobayashi call out his name.

"Sir?" Tavis said

"I also don't believe in no-win scenarios," the general said, not looking up from the map. Tavis barked a laugh and left.

TWENTY-TWO

Moira sat on the cold concrete floor of the basement with the little girl, Carly, on her lap, brushing her hair. Light poured in from the window above them, warming the gloomy basement with midday sun. Her daughter, Meg, sat next to her with Carly's younger brother, Stevie, and together they flipped through a picture book. The little boy had a death grip on a small, round plushy that looked like a panda. It had little red stains on it. She ignored those. He seemed happy to have the toy in his chubby little hands.

Boom!

Moira tickled the little girl's sides as they both jumped a bit. Carly giggled and waited for the next one. She was making a game of it, so Carly wouldn't be scared of the noise when the tank fired its main gun and they heard the subsequent explosions.

When they'd heard the thundering noises, Mimi had ushered them all into the nearest house. She wasn't to be trifled with, that one. And it was certainly a merry crew down here. Mimi sat on the stairs, holding the nameless little newborn girl and singing quietly, while the baby's mother, Brook, took the opportunity to rest awhile in the corner. Moira remembered those days well. Sleep whenever and wherever you could. Susan, the veterinarian, was upstairs keeping watch at the front door. Moira was the last to descend to the basement.

She was amused by the teenagers. They sat in a group—her twin boys too—in the middle of the room. Teens would be teens and they gather in packs. She tried to recall their names and places in this new reality. There was Layla, who she knew already as the daughter of Joey and Gale. They'd spoken before this all had happened on the phone when their loved ones were on the International Space Station. Then there was Sara, whose grandmother, Bibi, had just passed away. Poor girl. She was resting her head on Layla's shoulder now as the teens talked. She had the little Yorkie, Chewbacca, sleeping in her lap and was stroking her fur. They were mostly asking questions of Valerie, or Val and Nina, who were Russian. She knew Nina as well, as the niece of Pasha. Her English was broken, but Val's was good. The poor girl seemed to be holding up well, even though she'd just lost her mother a week before.

What she wasn't happy about were the two rifles standing up against the wall near them. Her kids had never used firearms. One, because they lived in Britain. But also she wouldn't hear of it, even if Tavis had wanted to take them on base when he was still in the Special Boat Service. Yet here they were, in the hands of mere children. Layla even had a pistol holstered under her jacket. *What's the world coming to?* she wondered. The only one missing was Alex. She had run off to her house to retrieve the pug. She continued to brush Carly's hair and listen to the teenagers talking quietly.

"So, how'd you get the shiner?" Duncan asked Val, whose black eye was nearly healed up with only a slight yellow spot left.

"I was in a fight with my father. We had words. He was drunk. Is first time it came to blows," Val responded.

"Your dad punched you?" Dougal asked.

"Da. I pushed him. I got punched."

"Was this a regular occurrence?" Layla cut in.

Val shrugged. "Nyet. He drinks because he misses my mother, who died several years ago. They blamed him, but he was proven innocent. Then he started drinking and got kicked out of his military unit. I stayed a lot with my grandfather, my mother's father, Boris. He and my father don't like each other."

"Well, he can't get to you here, so that's good," Layla said reassuringly.

"You misunderstand. I actually wish he were here now. We would fight, yell at each other. But, he's really a good man and a good father to me. My grandfather is also very good to me, but not a good man. He doesn't think I know what he does, but I do. He's a drug smuggler and criminal. I think he's got friends in the FSB. The

Russian state security service. Like your CIA. My father is honestly a good person, just drinks too much." Val was getting agitated.

"So that's whose plane my mom stole, with your dad?" Layla was putting two and two together now and looked over at the twins.

"Aye! I suppose that's right," Duncan said.

"What about you, Nina? Are you doing okay?" Layla asked the quiet girl. She was about the same age as the rest of them, but hadn't said two words the whole time they were down here in the basement.

"Da. Am okay, but miss… how do you say?" Nina tilted her head toward Moira.

"Mother? Oh, I'm so sorry about your mom," Layla said. Sara sat up straight and wiped the tears from her eyes and put an arm around Nina who was sitting to her right. The two girls cried softly together for Bibi and Nina's mom, Galina, who'd been killed when they were attacked on the way here.

Boom! They all jumped a little at the next main gun round being fired. Carly giggled as Moira squeezed her chubby sides.

"That sounded closer. They're getting closer," Brook said as she pushed herself up in the corner.

"Did you sleep at all?" Mimi asked her daughter-in-law.

"Not really, but just closing my eyes was good, even with the noises out there. How's she doing?" Brook said, referring to the little bundle in Mimi's arms.

"Sleeping like all's right in the world."

"What about you, Layla? How are you doing?" Val asked, probably to keep the group's scrutiny off himself, Moira supposed.

Layla thought about it. "I'm okay. It was nice to have my mom and dad back together for a hot minute. And now… honestly, it's just like they were back in space, with our parents and Pasha flying off to Mount Weather. Hopefully, they'll be back soon. Maybe they'll bring some help for whatever's going on outside."

As if on cue—*boom!*—another round fired and another giggle fit from Carly.

"Where the heck is Alex?" Layla said.

"She went after the pug, sweetie. Lou went after her. They'll be fine," Moira said, resting back against the concrete wall and closing her eyes.

"You okay, Mum?" Meg asked her in a whisper.

"Aye, girl. I am, however, gonna kill your father when he gets back," Moira responded without opening her eyes.

"Excellent," Meg said with a grin.

Boom!

More giggles.

TWENTY-THREE

It was late morning on the Potomac. Sully was watching the engineers and some of his men as they finished duct-taping blocks of C-4 to the steel structure that rose above the road on the bridge. The wind had picked up, and the guys were moving more slowly and deliberately as they climbed on the girders and hung to the sides of the bridge. Lots of duct tape applied. While one engineer told them where to place the charges, the other two sappers ran det cord from one charge to the next. As they'd explained, the charges would be daisy-chained together and the charging wire run to the plunger box well behind where he stood. When they pressed the button on the plunger box, the charges would go off, one at a time, quick, cutting the steel and dropping the bridge.

That wire had been rolled out to the underside of the bridge on this side of the river where the det cord from both sides of the bridge connected. He took a deep breath. Everything was going smoothly so far.

If those sappers can get the underside wired quick, we'll be on our way. His face throbbed, though. *Fucking tree.* He walked over to the small observation post where Sanchez and Dempsey were pointing down at the river, chatting and drinking coffee.

"Lookit, I didn't know they be livin' up in these parts," Dempsey said with mild excitement. Sanchez stood up to see.

"No shit! Look at those little guys."

"What we looking at, gents?" Sully asked as he approached.

"Otters, Sarge. Down there. Playin' in the water," Sanchez responded. Sully walked to the edge of the drop-off and peered over the rocks that gave the OP cover and sure enough, otters. Three of them, just goofin' off.

"Y'all know, they called 'river wolves.' Own the river. Eat errthing," Dempsey said in his Louisiana drawl.

"River wolves, huh?" Sully said. "Quiet! Listen," he ordered. He heard an aircraft. He ran back out onto the road to get a better look. He glanced up the river and saw nothing, then looked downriver and there it was.

"Sanchez! Binoculars!" Sanchez tossed his set over to Sully who raised them to his eyes moving them around to acquire the aircraft. Took a second, but he saw it.

"Shit! LT!" Sully yelled and walked toward the bridge where Ricketts was watching the engineers.

"What you got, Sergeant?" Ricketts responded as Sully got close and handed him the binoculars and pointed east in the sky.

"We've got company. That's Russian. Transport. Low. Coming upriver on the opposite side." Ricketts was tracking with the glass. "I've got canopies! Paratroopers. Russian." He handed the binoculars back to Sully, frowning.

"What you wanna do, LT?" Sully asked.

"Pull in First Squad to this side of the river. They're here for this bridge. Only thing it could be."

A series of explosions sent shock waves down the river from the direction of the other bridge.

"Well, looks like this is the only bridge in question now, and we'll get Third Squad back soon, just in time. Gonna get spicy. Sanchez! Tell First Squad to get back here now!" Sully yelled over his shoulder.

"Roger, Sarge!"

"And get status on Third Squad and the other bridge. If it's done, tell them to get the fuck back here quick!"

"Sully, First Squad is on their way, but be advised there's a white pickup truck with friendlies coming in before them," Sanchez reported.

"Okay, well, things are getting interesting. Tell them to hurry up, we're having company!" Sully yelled to Sanchez as he and Ricketts watched the Russian transport continue to fly west out of sight, leaving behind a long string of drifting airborne troops in its wake.

"How far you think they'll land?" Ricketts asked.

"Looks close. Maybe a mile. Maybe less for some of them. I can make them out with my eyes now, so they can see us. Those few right there are close. They'll land on the road parallel to the river, just on the other side behind all those trees," Sully said as he watched them descend.

A white pickup truck came speeding around the corner on the other side of the river and down onto the bridge.

"We're going to have contact directly! How close are we to finished?" Ricketts yelled to the engineers who were under the bridge now as Sully walked out into the road and held up his hand, Dempsey on his right, M-4 pointed at the truck, finger straight out, not on the trigger, but ready. The truck slowed and dipped down and rocked as it went over the cratered pavement, then came to a stop, windows down and two men in camouflage uniforms in the truck bed in the rear. Sully walked quick to the driver's side.

"Who are you all? Nice truck. How's it running after all this?" He counted four men in the truck plus the two in the bed. Those two climbed over the sides and onto the debris-littered pavement. The one that jumped out near Sully landed on a piece of concrete debris and buckled, collapsing on the ground in a fit of expletives.

"Ya alright there?" Sully asked as the man hopped back to his feet. Sully did a double-take. Were those crocs on his feet, and cargo shorts? Sully smirked.

"Yep, fucking rubble," the man said, brushing dust from his shorts.

"Howdy!" the driver called out, then went on to answer Sully. "I had it parked in the bottom of an underground parking garage. Long story. The four of us in here are SEALs. On our way to Mount Weather from Fort Detrick. Had some business there to keep that stuff from the Chicoms. Picked these two up walking down the road south of Frederick, Maryland. Hey, you know you got Russian paratroopers landing right behind us and a whole column of Chinese armor and mech about ten minutes out, right?"

"What the hell!" Ricketts spat and turned back to the engineers. "Y'all better be ready to drop this thing in two minutes!"

The two men from the back of the truck had joined them. Dempsey was still keeping watch, although his M-4 was pointed at the ground now.

Sully looked the one dude from the bed up and down. He had a multicam heavy jacket on, but was wearing cargo shorts and sporting what looked like his dad's Remington 12-gauge pump shotgun with a bandolier of shells draped across his chest. He checked the man's belt and sure enough, there was a Colt 1911 .45 caliber pistol in its holster. That and crocs over thick wool socks with duct tape all over and nearly made him laugh out loud. He supposed the duct tape was to keep them from flying off.

"What?" the man said.

"Just admiring your kit," Sully replied flatly.

"Yeah, well, was all I had handy when things went to shit."

"An' you two are?"

"We're from Frederick. Home on Christmas leave. Cav Scouts out of Fort Hood. My friend here is Ryan and I'm Picorrello."

"Well, welcome to the shitshow," Sully said.

"Where you want us?" Picorrello asked.

"First, let's settle your name. I won't remember it. You're just Pickle now. Join the OP over there. You can watch the otters with them."

"All good. I go by Pickle anyway. Drill instructors pick that shit up quick," Pickle replied.

Crack!

The shot came from up on the hill. Then "RPG!" drifted down, yelled by someone up there. Looking across the river, Sully spotted several Russian paratroopers moving in the bushes by the bank. One had fallen nearly into the river, dead from the hill sniper. The one next to him raised a rocket launcher and fired. Sully and the rest scattered and dove, flattening themselves as the missile streaked from the far bank and detonated in the white pickup truck just as it was starting to roll forward.

Then Sully's recon squad came running up on the bridge, initiating a firefight. As he watched from his position on his stomach, two men at a time stopped, turned, and let loose with their M-4s.

Dempsey and Sanchez had the machine gun in their position lighting up the far side of the river where the RPG had come from and more shots cracked from the hill behind them.

Sully rose to one knee and surveyed the formerly nice pickup truck. The passenger compartment was destroyed and the seats were on fire. All the windows were blown out and the roof was wrenched up. The seats, he realized, weren't really on fire. But the four Navy SEALs were. He almost called for a medic, but he knew there was no one alive in there.

"Shit!" Sanchez yelled as Dempsey loaded another belt of ammo into their Squad Automatic Weapon, the gun battle at a momentary lull. Sanchez pulled a Marlboro Light from his pants pocket and lit it, taking a deep breath and blowing the smoke out, before inserting it between Dempsey's lips while he was loading the gun.

Sully looked around. "Everyone alright? Check your guys!" he yelled as Pickle and Ryan walked over and First Squad ran by. Sully grabbed the squad sergeant by the arm. "We're gonna get hit again. Get your guys some good cover on the left side of the bridge and kill anything over there that moves."

"On it, Sarge! Let's spread out down here," the squad sergeant yelled at his squad, who were breathing heavy but not injured.

"Jesus Christ! What happy horseshit we get into here?" the newcomer Ryan asked.

"Yeah, we're gonna blow this fucking bridge," Sully informed him. "You're with us now. Support the OP there with Sanchez and Dempsey. Pickle, see if the good corporal will let you borrow his M-4 while he's on that SAW. Not gonna do shit with that shotgun here."

"Copy," Pickle said and turned to jog to the OP in his taped-up crocs and Ryan behind him. Lieutenant Ricketts climbed the bank next to the bridge. He'd gone down to make sure the engineers were okay and still doing engineer shit underneath it. He joined Sully as Doc walked up.

"Everyone's good to go, bossman. Cuts and bruises mostly from First Squad," Sergeant Hagen said, the scene otherwise quiet. Too quiet.

"Well, so much for the SEALs," Ricketts said offhandedly. "Fuck, that truck is bad. Won't get that out of my head ever. Engineers got it all wrapped up under the bridge, ready to blow it," he continued as a rocket-propelled grenade came streaking from the other side of the river and hit under the bridge where Ricketts had just been. They all dropped to the ground as his men spread out beside the bridge opened up.

"Truck's coming back with the rest of the platoon, LT!" Sanchez yelled and pointed to the road that followed the river upstream, a bit higher on the hill, about halfway to where the snipers were set up.

"Shit!" Sully said as Ricketts got up and ran to where the driver, John, and the men on the back of the flatbed could see him and started waving at them, then motioned with his hands to the ground.

"Get off the truck!" Ricketts yelled but it was too late. Two rocket-propelled grenades shot out of the trees from the other side of the river, and a machine gun opened up. They watched in horror as one projectile hit the truck and the other got close enough. The truck erupted in a fireball, then started rolling downhill toward the river.

"Cover!" someone from First Squad yelled, and the whole riverbank on their side thundered with gunfire.

"Doc! Get up there and see how bad it is. Do what you can," Ricketts said as he aimed his M-4 across the river into the trees, pulling the trigger as fast as he could, adding his own rounds to the volume of outgoing.

Sully grabbed the LT by his plate carrier and tugged. He barked over the gunfire, "LT, you get your ass over in the OP where you can see if the engineers are okay and have some cover! I'll coordinate this."

Ricketts nodded and jogged away, leaving Sully, who stepped over to the pickup truck on the bridge and took a knee in front of it, looking at the shiny, silver grill, knowing the four SEALs were still smoldering inside. He could smell it. *Damn.* He glanced up the river then down the river. Then up on the hill where Doc looked like he was at work on one of his boys, and there were others helping. The volume of fire had lessened.

"Cease fire! Cease fire!" he yelled. The gunfire trickled to silence, and there was none from the other side. For now. He grabbed a water bottle from his plate carrier and chugged it, suddenly consumed with thirst. Wiping his mouth and rubbing his face, he had a bad feeling there was worse coming, from what the SEALs had told him, this being the only bridge standing and all.

"Welp," he said to himself, waiting. He tilted his head, listening intently. He thought he heard music.

TWENTY-FOUR

Zhou was sitting half out of the commander's hatch in his T-99 Main Battle Tank. They were doing about forty miles per hour. His track just passed three burned-out vehicles in the grass median between the east- and westbound lanes. There were two lanes going each way. This was about where their intel said Iranian commandos would be. He hadn't seen anything resembling that, but maybe they'd hit those vehicles and moved. One of his T-92 armored personnel carriers had point and was about twenty meters in front of his track. The rest of the column followed in line. They weren't expecting any American forces between crossing the Potomac and Mount Weather, so they weren't employing a bounding overwatch on their route. But as he looked back at his column, he spotted a line of heaps—bodies—laid out along the road. Were those the Iranians? A nervous feeling grew in his stomach.

There were two T-99s behind him, then another APC. The same order to the back. Three tanks with an APC in front of each set of tanks with a T-99 a rear guard. The last T-99 had just gone under the overpass behind him, and the APC in front of him was about to go under another overpass. The last tank's gun was pointing left.

"Warrior Three, Warrior Actual. You're rear guard. Your gun should be scanning behind the column, not to the sides," Zhou said, a bit agitated. The column was spread out too much for his liking as well, taking up about a thousand meters on this straightaway. That's when he saw the tank, an American Abrams, peek out from the north side of the overpass behind him. He tried to warn the column, but Warrior Three was talking.

"Copy, Warrior Actual. Swinging gun to rear."

"Lou, Ahmed! There are tanks on the main road. Chinese. Nelson just radioed to warn us," Simmons yelled at the two men in front of Lou's house as he ran toward them holding his chinesium radio over his head.

"How many?" Ahmed asked, picking up his AK-47.

"Does it matter? We can't fight tanks," Lou said.

"Nelson said twelve. Three armored personnel carriers. That means soldiers," Simmons responded as he got to the Humvee and opened the rear hatch. He grabbed the one LAW they had. The light anti-tank weapon was shoulder-fired, like a bazooka, but just one shot and done. The two corporals ran up.

"What's up, Sergeant?" one asked.

"We're going into the woods by the main road. Tanks. Nelson's gonna engage."

"Tanks? No one said anything about tanks!" the other one complained, and they all ran between the houses into the woods, with Lou and Ahmed bringing up the rear.

"Hey! What's going on, Lou?" Alex yelled from her front porch. She was standing there with Layla, Sara, Val, Nina, and the Kinley kids.

"You all stay put! I mean it!" Lou yelled back and disappeared between the houses.

They had inched Alice out onto the overpass, just by the last of the trees. Nelson lined up the 50-cal remotely from his controls onto the furthest two vehicles. A T-99 and a T-92 APC at the front of the column.

"Fire!" Nelson yelled into his mic while at the same time depressing the trigger for the 50-cal above him. The main gun kicked, and the rear tank that was swinging its turret toward them exploded with the HEAT round to the engine compartment, just as Nelson walked rounds over the T-99 and onto the APC.

"Load sabot! Walk it up the column! Kill those motherfuckers!" he ordered.

Captain Zhou screamed into his helmet mic. Once Warrior Three stopped talking, he was able to get a couple of words out before rounds began striking his tank, and he dropped into the turret for cover.

"Warrior Three! Do you read me?" Zhou yelled into the mic.

"Warrior Three is hit. American M1 on the overpass!" another tank commander said on the net.

"Gunner, traverse right! Tank on the bridge. M1. Fire when you have it." Zhou changed to the team net. "All tracks, M1 Abrams on bridge to our rear. Destroy it!" Zhou said as two more loud explosions rocked the column.

Shit!

"Sabot up!" Stewie yelled, letting Jones know that a sabot round was in the tube. Jones didn't even acknowledge, but fired at the next tank closest to them. *Kill the biggest guns closest to you first.* That's what Nelson had ordered him to do while Nelson engaged the APCs with the 50-cal. He could just hear the music playing up top, "Can't Stop This" by Thousand Foot Krutch, when Nelson's voice boomed in his headset.

"Popping smoke. Fletch, reverse us now!"

He hit the smoke grenade trigger, and smoke grenades shot out of their tubes on either side of the tank's turret as Fletch rolled them backward. The front of the tank jerked suddenly to the left as they reversed.

"We just took a round up front. Can't tell damage," Fletch yelled in Nelson's ears. "We're still rolli—"

Another round slammed into the turret next to the commander's hatch.

"Shit! We gettin' hit. Haul it, Fletch!" Nelson yelled as the tank quickly backed up and out of sight of the Chinese tanks that were now hunting for them. While they rolled back toward the side road with the houses, he opened his hatch to check for damage. Standing now, he scanned the turret and front quickly.

"Good news, bad news. We're still operational. Bad news is the 50-cal is gone along with half my sights. Gun's just not there anymore. Right front fender is all chewed up. If we hadn't moved, that round would've hit center. Spin it, Fletch! Head to the other overpass the way we came."

The tank slowed and spun around so they could go forward. Fletch floored it up the road with the houses. Nelson used the commander's override to traverse the turret and main gun to the left as they moved, hoping to get a shot through the houses as "Monkey Business" by Skid Row started pumping through the speakers, which were, by some miracle, still working.

"That's barely good news, S'arnt! We're gonna fucking die," Stewie said.

"God's on our side, Stewie. He won't let us die," Nelson replied.

"Ah, Jesus Christ!"

"He's on our side too! God loves Marines and Skid Row!" Nelson said, and the sun shone through the clouds as they headed back up the street.

Zhou ordered his driver to turn left across the grass median and move toward the rear of the column on the eastbound lanes. As they did that, he surveyed his column through his commander's optics. The APC in front of him was burning. The machine gun rounds must have cut right through its thinner armor. Coming around to the front of his tank, he saw three plumes of smoke where there used to be T-99s. In twenty seconds, one M1 had killed a third of his force.

"White-skinned pigs! Sons of whores!" Zhou hollered as he looked through his sights. Smoke obscured the overpass, and he couldn't tell if the M1 was still there. He changed freqs on his radio to all.

"Warrior Eleven and Twelve, get under that rear overpass for cover and dismount. All tanks, time to hunt these sons-of-whores down."

"The M1 backed up," another tank commander said on the net. "It's on the north side of the road. Possibly around the houses."

"The two tracks to the rear, on me. I'm going up the ramp to the overpass and going after the M1."

Zhou's driver was going fast now. About forty-five to fifty miles per hour when they started up the ramp to the overpass. Two other tanks fell in behind him. The other three operational tracks stayed on the road, slowly maneuvering with their guns pointed toward the north side of the road, in and out of the smoke smothering the road between the overpasses.

Simmons and the other two Marines, Carrington and Walker, along with Ahmed and Lou, approached the last trees before the road. They were close to the easternmost overpass, nearly to where they'd moved the bodies of the Iranians. The bodies were beginning to stink with decay. If they got out of this, they needed to burn them. They stood dead-still behind trees as three Chinese tanks rumbled up the off-ramp, made a left turn, and headed away. Once the tanks had passed, Lou peeked out from behind his cover.

"Sergeant. Two APCs under the bridge. We can help with those, I think. Between the LAW and Carrington's grenade launcher, we've got a chance," he said.

"Roger that. Walker, set the LAW up on the APC facing our position. Carrington, that other APC is facing away from us. Rear doors are open. Think you can get one in there?" Simmons asked.

"Hell yeah! Got four grenade rounds left," Carrington replied as Walker aimed the LAW at the other APC.

"Hit 'em!" Simmons said.

The LAW anti-tank missile burst from the tube and streaked to its target. It hit the APC right where the turret attached to the body and punched through into the vehicle. No explosion on the front, but screams and smoke exited the rear where the doors must have been open.

Then *bloop!* went a grenade from the launcher, followed by an explosion within the body of the other APC. The grenade had gone through the open doors and done its work. Lou stared at the carnage —until rounds started peppering trees near him.

"They're shooting back now. Someone's still alive. More grenades!" Simmons yelled, and there were two more *bloops!* followed by explosions under the bridge.

The shooting stopped.

Now they waited. For what, he didn't know, but then he heard music from across the road.

"If you have a shot, you kill those fuckers. Copy?" Nelson said to Jones.

"Copy!" Jones replied.

They were going fast for the M1. About forty miles per hour. Jones was sweating profusely. It was hot in the turret, but this was nerves. The houses passed his sight one by one, from right to left. These people had a lot of trees in their yards, which obscured the road beyond to some extent. Three houses, now four houses. The fifth passed in his sight, and there was an opening and the road.

Tank!

He laid the crosshairs on the turret and pulled the trigger on his joystick. The gun kicked backward, and he could just see the impact before the sixth house obscured his line of sight.

To his left, he knew that Stewie had hit the knee button, which opened the ammunition compartment, and in one smooth motion, grabbed another sabot round, flipped it around, laid it on the gun breach, and pushed it all the way to stop with his fist. The gun breach slammed closed just as Stewie pulled his hand away.

"Sabot up!" Stewie yelled.

The whole process took six seconds. Maybe less.

"Haul ass, Fletch," Nelson said. "Get us to that curve in the road. Houses on the right side of the street will conceal us."

Just a little further, then the curve, and two left turns to the overpass road. Nelson spun the turret with the commander's override to the rear just as they were starting the right curve. Through his optics, he saw all the way to the bottom of the street, and there was a T-99 just completing its turn onto the street. The tank was momentarily obscured by the smoke of the main gun firing.

A second later, a loud thud vibrated the turret.

"The fuck was that?" Jones said.

"Did a round just bounce off the turret?" Stewie asked.

"Looks like… Jones!" Nelson yelled.

"Got it," Jones replied and laid the sight on the lead tank. There were now two, with a second one coming into view. The main gun rocked back again, ejecting the spent sabot baseplate to the floor of the turret while Stewie went back to work reloading.

Zhou's T-99 turned left onto the neighborhood street and started to pick up speed when his gunner's voice popped into his ears.

"Tank! Dead ahead!"

"Fire, dammit!" Zhou yelled at his gunner, and the gun kicked backward, ejecting the shell's baseplate, and the autoloader went to work. He tracked the sabot round to its target and watched in frustration as the round hit the top of the angled part of the turret and ricocheted straight up into the air. Then in horror as the M1's main gun fired. A second later, there was an explosion, but he was still alive.

"Warrior Six, Warrior Eight took a direct hit. They're gone. Coming around now to your rear."

"Copy, Eight. On my six. We're going to kill these bastards if it takes all our tracks!" Zhou yelled into the mic. "Driver! Max speed. Follow that tank. Go!"

The T-99 sped up to fifty miles per hour.

"Tracks still out on the road, orient toward the western overpass," Zhou commanded. "We're following the American tank now. They will likely try to cross it."

Ahmed and the others were still in the tree line, watching and listening. The Chinese APCs and dismounted soldiers were dead or dying. That threat was gone. However, the three Chinese tanks were still sitting out on the main road. He was trying to come up with some way to deal with them when the middle tank exploded after a sharp boom. He flinched. More startled than affected by the shock wave. The tank's turret flew into the air and landed upside down next to the burning husk.

"The Marines are putting up a good fight, but it's too many to one. Isn't there anything we can do to help?" Ahmed asked Lou and Simmons.

"Not yet. If I'm right, the M1 is gonna come flying over that overpass, and it'll be a slugfest," Simmons said.

"How you figure that?" Lou asked.

"You see all their turrets turn at the same time toward the overpass? Those other tanks are chasing Alice out of the houses. They're getting ready to hit 'em," Simmons replied.

"Well, we can try to distract them," Lou said flatly.

"With fucking what?" Walker asked.

Lou studied the scene. "Small arms won't defeat them, but it may take their focus off the bridge."

"I've got one grenade left. I can hit the closer tank," Carrington said.

"Okay, let's do it," Simmons agreed. "Get ready. Focus all your fire on the turret of the closer tank. Fire when I fire. Then get ready to scatter."

Carrington loaded his last grenade into the tube attached below his M-4's barrel and aimed it so the grenade would arc in the air and down onto the tank's turret. They all leveled their weapons at the tank.

Simmons fired. They all fired.

Bloop! The last grenade left its tube and, a second later, exploded right on the turret. They kept firing until the turret began to swing toward them.

"Fucking run!" Simmons yelled, and they scattered as quickly as they could before the tank engaged.

"Fletch, when we make the left onto the overpass road, get Alice going as fast as she'll go. Jones, traverse left. There should be two tanks out there and two APCs. As soon as you have 'em, kill the biggest guns first. Don't stop for anything, Fletch. Got it?" Nelson was in the zone now and wired tight.

"Oo-fucking-rah! We should get the fuck outta here, S'arnt," Stewie complained.

"We can't," Nelson said. "We're engaged. They were going for Mount Weather. We're here. We got the duty. Just do your job, and we'll all be good to go. We've already killed five of their tanks!"

"So it's still, like, four to one, Sergeant! Those odds ain't great."

"Stew! Shut the fuck up! I'm trying to drive here," Fletch yelled, and Stewie stopped complaining as Fletch turned left onto the overpass road and picked up speed. Jones swung the turret from the rear to facing left and depressed the gun's angle as they'd be above their targets. Nelson looked through his one working optic on his commander's hatch at the bridge coming up fast. There were concrete barriers on either side of the overpass, like Jersey barriers.

"Okay, pucker time," Nelson said as they came out onto the overpass. He saw it the same time Jones fired.

"Tank!" Nelson yelled.

Boom!

The main gun rocked backward, and Stewie replaced the spent shell with another sabot. Then Nelson scanned with his remaining working optic to the right of the tank they'd just killed, and there was another one. He used the commander's override to slave the main gun to his sight til Jones could shoot it.

"Tank to the right! You got it, Jones?" Nelson yelled as he traversed the turret and main gun onto the second tank.

"Got it! Three hundred fifty meters!" Jones yelled and pulled the trigger just as their target fired its main gun at them.

Ahmed ran through the woods away from the traversing tank turret. Its co-axial machine gun peppered the tree line as it swung around, and then it exploded. The machine gun fire ceased. He stopped behind a tree just on the edge of the woods and peeked around it. There was another Chinese tank with its gun pointed at the bridge, and it seemed to be moving with the M1 crossing the bridge. He held his breath. Both tanks fired their main guns nearly simultaneously. The bridge barrier disintegrated as the Chinese round hit the concrete barrier and showered the M1 with concrete debris and dust, which turned the M1 a grayish white and left chunks of concrete on the hull and turret, large enough that he could pick the pieces out at this distance.

"Holy shit!" Simmons said. Ahmed hadn't even noticed the Marine sergeant behind the next tree about five yards away.

"Yeah, that other tank is dead. Not on fire, but look at the tube," Lou said from another tree. Ahmed looked at the last Chinese tank, and the main gun was drooping at an odd angle. Ahmed looked around at this small battlefield, and it triggered long-dormant memories of the City of Blood back in the Iran/Iraq war. He counted six dead tanks, most of them on fire or belching smoke, and three APCs, all dead. Then there was the column of smoke on the other side of the easternmost overpass. Were there more? He didn't know. Three had gone over to that side, but there was only one column of smoke.

"Come on. We have to get everyone into basements. Marines are on our side of the road. Badies will follow," Lou said, and they all took off through the woods and between Lou's house and Mama's house.

Ahmed scanned the cul-de-sac and street and yelled, "Everyone into basements! Now! Wherever you are!" His booming voice fell on an empty space. He saw no one until Susan, the vet, appear at Floyd's front door, which had been open.

"We're all in here except for Alex. She went searching for the pug," Susan yelled back to him.

Then the ground beneath his boots vibrated. Ahmed turned to look at the entrance to the street just as Alice appeared and began to rumble down the street. He could tell she'd taken several hits, at least.

"I'll get Alex!" Lou ran across the street to Alex's house and disappeared through the front door, shouting her name. Ahmed took cover behind the corner of Mimi's house. It sounded like the other Marines were on the other side of the house, and Simmons appeared next to him again. The man was quiet as a ghost.

"Fletch! Turn right and get behind that house on the right," Nelson ordered. "With luck, they'll turn in to follow, and we can get behind them. The house on the left is concealing us now."

He couldn't see shit out of the one sight, so Nelson opened his hatch and popped up to get a better view—just as the house they were going to hide behind took a hit. The round came from the bridge. The sabot round made no real explosion, as it was basically just a depleted uranium dart meant to slice through armor. Staying on the asphalt and then up onto the yard of the corner house, Nelson tried to use the commander's override to slave the turret to the right, but it didn't move.

Another sabot round crashed right through the far side of the house, spewing debris and bringing all kinds of shit with it as it melted on its way out the other side, which is where they were now.

"Jones, what's up with the turret? You have power?" he yelled, panic creeping into his voice.

"Shit! Hydraulics are down. That hit on the bridge must have killed it. Still got power. Fuses are good. Definitely the hydraulics. Switching to gas sight and manual hand cranks. This gonna suck, I think," Jones replied.

"Well, this is just fuckin' great," Stewie complained.

"Stew, shut the fuck up!" Fletch said over the headset.

"I"m just saying, shit's gonna ruin my fuckin' paint job, is all."

"Stewie, open the ammo compartment and lock it open, just in case we lose power. Now, here's the plan," Nelson started and explained what he wanted.

❋❋❋

Zhou's tank was just turning left onto the overpass road. His other tank was twenty meters behind him and followed. Through his commander's sights, he surveyed the scene from right to left. The bridge, which they were fast approaching, looked like it had taken hits. Concrete debris littered the road. Beyond that, there was no sign of the M1. He traversed the turret, and his sights showed him the destruction of his platoon. He already knew it was bad. No one but the tank behind him was on the platoon net. They were all dead.

"Warrior 6, Warrior 4, shouldn't we disengage and continue the mission?"

The tank commander to his rear was probably right, but he ignored him. He would finish this. The American bastards would pay. His tank sped across the bridge. This road was elevated above most everything else around, as it was on a ridge. To the left before him, was a subdivision, then more trees, and a parallel road lower than this one that led to many more houses. The two roads were separated by trees and open fields that gently sloped down to the houses. The tank behind him fired their main gun just as Zhou caught a fleeting glimpse of the M1 turning into the neighborhood nearest the road. The American tank disappeared. The buildings closest to him obscured them as the round from his wingman went through one house, just missing the mark.

"You missed Warrior 4. I see where they went. Follow my track. They're in those houses," Zhou ordered. Now that they were over the bridge, he saw that there were places where they could cross the sloping ground to the left.

"Driver! Take us left and down to the lower road and those houses where you see a good spot to do so," he said.

"Yes, sir!" The tank started moving left and sloping downward, and soon they were on the lower road and quickly approaching the left turn into the neighborhood where those American whores' sons were hiding.

"Alex! Where are you?" Lou said as he ran through the open front door.

"Trying to find Christopher! Help me find him!" the girl yelled from upstairs.

"Alex, he'll be okay. Probably hiding under a bed. We have to get to the basement. Now!" Lou was frantic. He knew what was coming, but Alex didn't.

He was running back to the foyer and starting to climb the stairs as a wrenching, ripping sound took the step he was on out from under him. It just dropped away, and the whole staircase jerked aside. He clung to the handrail. A loud *boom* followed the ripping, and a cloud dust and debris covered him. He looked left into the living room just as the first-floor ceiling caved in, and he heard a scream.

Shit.

A tank round must have taken out floor joists and supports.

"Alex! Where are you?" Lou found some footing on the wrecked stairs and strained to pull himself over to the front door and stable flooring. He called her name again.

"Lou! Here…"

Through all the dust and crap in the air, he saw Alex, powdered white, next to a bed that a second before had been upstairs. She was covered in dust and bits of rubble. The AK-47 that she had been given by the Marines was slung tight across her back. Surreal. Thankfully, the roof hadn't come down on top of her… and him.

He scrambled over to her and reached out to her. "Take my hand, Alex! Are you hurt?"

"I don't thing so. Well, my leg hurts. Gouged it." Lou felt her tiny hand in his and they gripped each other's hand tight as Lou pulled Alex to him on the stable part of the living room.

There was smoke creeping up from the basement. That round had to have been a sabot. Must have melted as it went through and the bits of molten metal were starting fires.

"Lou, Christopher was under this bed. I was reaching for him when the floor jerked. He's under here somewhere," Alex said, pointing back at the bed.

Lou crawled over to it and reached in between the rubble and the bed frame, searching with his hand until it hit fur. He gripped and pulled. Christopher was soft and limp and he handed the dog to Alex so he could guide them out through the smoke-filled, debris-strewn wreckage of a home.

"Go, Fletch!" Nelson yelled into the mic and Alice jerked forward and rolled around the back side of the wrecked house. Jones was furiously spinning the crank wheel to traverse the turret while cranking the elevation wheel for the main gun tube so it was level to the ground. As Alice came around the house, Nelson saw the second tank was right in front of them, from his vantage point with his head sticking out of his hatch. It was rolling into the cul-de-sac, its main gun pointed down the street.

"Jones! Tank! Point blank! Kill it!" Nelson yelled. Jones kept spinning the gear to move the turret and main gun to the right, following the T-99. He was looking through the gas-powered sight. He laid the center of the sight on the center of the Chinese tank's turret and pulled the trigger on the joystick. Nothing happened.

"Gunner! Fire, God dammit!" Nelson dropped back down to see what the issue was just as Jones realized that the joystick trigger wasn't working because of all the failures and reached over to a manual T stick they called the master blaster, grabbed it, and twisted. The main gun rocked backward and the circular base of the spent shell popped out and landed on the floor with the rest, like so many tuna can tops. The shells were designed to burn up when fired, so only the base was left.

Stewie automatically reloaded another sabot round. "Sabot up!" he yelled.

Nelson stuck his head back up just in time to watch the turret of the T-99 blow away from its body. It was like watching in slow motion. The turret flipped forward over its gun and landed upside down in front of the tank's body. He looked to his right as Fletch kept rolling, turning to the right, over the lawn and curb onto the asphalt next to the upside-down turret.

"Go, Fletch!" Nelson yelled. The last tank was right there, perpendicular to them, showing their side, but neither Alice's gun or the T-99's was on target yet. Theirs was traversing faster. Fletch closed the distance to the T-99 just in time. The nearly seventy-ton M1 slammed into the side of the T-99, which weighed about ten tons less, at thirty miles per hour.

As Lou pulled Alex, who held Christopher limp in her arms, out onto the lawn, a deafening boom thundered. The concussion knocked them both to the ground, followed by a horrific explosion. Lou looked up, wiping mud and grass from his face, and saw a Chinese tank in the middle of the road, its gun swinging around toward him and Alex. Out of the corner of his sight, as he was trying to clear his vision from the concussion, Alice came screaming down the road and rammed the T-99 broadside so hard, it lifted the Chinese tank up on the far track. Lou stood and scanned the street. One tank was dead and these two were sword-fighting with their main guns. Neither tank could get their gun past the other's turret. It was like watching a giant toy death match, but the Abrams had the other one broadside, its right tread already up on the curb, so the Abrams had weight and leverage.

Then he heard a sob. Alex was bent down, hovering over Christopher, stroking the pug's head, crying "no" over and over. Lou could tell his little buddy was gone. There was no movement. His brown eyes were open and staring off into the distance and his tongue was limp, hanging out of his mouth.

"You motherfuckers!" Lou found himself yelling. He walked over and grabbed Alex by the shoulders and lifted her up to her feet and crushed the small girl in a fierce hug.

"We can't leave him, Lou!" Alex pleaded into Lou's chest.

"We'll get him, girl. But first…"

A loud screeching noise made him release Alex and turn in time to see the M1 pushing the T-99's right track up off the ground so far that it tipped all the way over to rest on the left side of its body.

"Like a fucking turtle. You're mine now," Lou said and stalked toward the tank. Alex raced ahead of him, her AK-47 in her small hands and screaming Russian profanities. He was about to yell at her to go back, when Ahmed loomed from behind the flipped T-99 and grabbed her up in his arms and, taking the AK from her, carried her toward Lou. She continued to scream in Russian. Simmons and the rest of the Marines came running up as Alice slowly rolled backward from its kill.

"Take care of her, Ahmed. Give me the rifle," Lou said loudly. His hearing was shot and everything sounded like it was in a tunnel, but muffled, including the music still coming out of the speakers that used to be his and Robert's on top of the tank. "OOO-WA-AH-AH-AH" just started Disturbed's "Down with the Sickness."

How appropriate, he thought.

Ahmed held the AK out to him and he took it. Removing the magazine, Lou reached over and racked the bolt back. There hadn't been a round chambered.

Good girl.

Reinserting the magazine securely, he reached under the rifle in front of the mag and released the bolt, which snapped forward, chambering a round. He walked around the T-99 to the top of the turret where the hatches were.

"I'm going to count to three. When I reach three, all of you will be out here with me or I'm going to have our tank blow a hole through the bottom of your tank and out through the top of the turret!" Lou yelled.

No response.

"One!"

The hatches opened and Lou and the Marines covered them quickly. There were three. The driver's hatch, the loader's, and the commander's. There was much screaming and orders to get out and on the ground by the Marines.

"Secure that music, Sergeant!" Simmons yelled at Sergeant Nelson half visible in his hatch. He reached over and tapped the screen, and in the silence, everyone stared at the three Chinese tankers lined up on their knees in front of Lou semi-circled by Marines. Lou pushed the little pug and Robert to the back of his mind now. There was work to do. He looked around. Ahmed was now carrying Alex down the street behind him to where Mimi and the rest of his neighbors were exiting Floyd's house and staring as a group at him and the carnage all around. He turned back to the task at hand.

"You! Speak English?" The question was directed at the officer that came out of the commander's hatch.

"Yes, but I won't tell you anything," the officer defiantly declared. He had a cut on his forehead that was bleeding into his left eye which didn't stop him from glaring at Lou.

Lou looked at the other two. "Do you two speak English?" He pointed at each of them with the AK. They both looked at their commander and nodded.

Good, Lou thought. *Not here, though.*

"Get them up and move them to the other side of the tank," Lou ordered the Marines. They did so as Lou walked in a wider circle around to the other side and the Marines lined the three Chinese soldiers up on their knees again. He glanced over to where Christopher's little body lay in the grass, still. The rage returned and he stalked over to stare down at the commander.

"What are your orders? Where were you going?" Lou asked flatly.

"I can't tell you any information except my name, rank, and…" He trailed off as Lou reached the end of the rifle barrel to touch the man's nose. The other two soldiers stared and one of them turned his head away as if to shield his face from what he knew would spray onto it.

"Lou, a word," Sergeant Simmons said behind him. He turned and glared at Simmons.

"What is it, Sergeant?"

"I know where you're going with this, but we're Marines, and they are our prisoners. We can't go there."

"Sergeant, we're in a world without rules now. These aren't your prisoners. They're mine. I need to know where they were going. There may be more on the way. We need this information. I'm going to get it. You and your men are relieved. Go see to the women and children," Lou and Simmons locked eyes for a few seconds, then Simmons broke contact.

"Corpsman! Go see what you can do for Alex and check the rest of them. Get them back in the house. The rest of you with me. We need ammo and weapons from the Chinese tracks and check for any still alive. Move!"

As the Marines moved out, Lou turned back to the kneeling soldiers.

"You killed my dog." Lou pointed to Christopher's body, then raised the rifle again. "What were your orders?" he asked quietly.

The commander puffed out his chest and squared his shoulders. "I can't tell—"

Boom! The round went through the commander's left eye socket and ended with much of what was inside his head splattering the bottom of the tank. The other two soldiers flinched away and one went prone on the ground, belly first with his hands over his head.

"Holy shit!" Lou heard from behind him, forgetting the tank and Marines in it. Ignoring them, he reached down and grabbed the soldier by his collar and put him back on his knees.

"Now, what were your orders?" he said. "I promise you, once you tell me, you will be free to go. We have no place to keep you and don't want you here."

The two soldiers looked at each other.

"Orders!" Lou screamed in their faces.

One soldier turned to see what was left of their commander's brain sliding down the under side of their former tank.

"We meet with the… division at bridge," he said, haltingly.

"Bridge? How did you get here? Where are you from?"

"Baltimore. Our tanks come across small bridge in Washington. Rest of division on other side of river."

"Okay. What bridge were you going to and are there any more behind you on this side of the river?"

"Called Rock Point. I think. None behind us. Advance. We are advance."

"Point of Rocks? What is this division's objective?" Lou got real close to the man's face.

"Yes! Point of Rocks, is it? Main objective is Mountain Weather and secure Shenandoah Valley. Like song!" The man smiled and was now very talkative.

"Shit. Yes, like song," Lou said, thinking. That plane they saw earlier this morning was going that way. Airborne drop to take the bridge? Or drop it. Wasn't the only bridge, though. Lou's mind raced. The plane was taking fire from the direction of Dulles Airport, just miles away.

"Do you know Dulles Airport?"

"Yes! Is close, I think," the smiling man responded.

Lou pointed off to the southeast.

"Yes. It's that way. Chinese are there. Or Russians. Or both. You are free to go there. If I see you again, I'll kill you both. Now run," Lou said while still pointing. Both men jumped to their feet and started to run in the direction Lou was pointing. He watched them run up the street and around the corner and out of sight.

"Nelson! Get down here!" Lou yelled as he walked to the Abrams, turbine engine still whining. Nelson climbed down from Alice, and Fletch and Stewie watched from their hatches.

"Damn, Lou. Got your inner John Wick on. I'm here for it. Whatchu thinkin'?" Nelson said.

"Did you hear all that?"

Nelson nodded.

"Good. Here's what we're gonna do. And by we, I mean you. I think that C-5 we saw earlier this morning was an Airborne drop on the bridges across the Potomac. Dude said a whole division, I think more, are gonna try to cross the river on one or more of those bridges and then try to take, or take out, Mount Weather. That's bad enough, but we got people at Mount Weather. Those Airborne brothers gonna need some help."

"Lou, I don't know the area, we're short on gas, and I got bits falling off my tank," Nelson said, throwing a thumb over his shoulder at Alice. She was running but all busted up. Stewie was tossing pieces of concrete from the bridge off the turret, and his machine gun on the hatch was a total loss. Looked like it took the force from a round. The left front skirt and armor were all bent and hanging.

"Okay, I have a paper map of the area. There is a gas station on your way. I need you to go there. Then I need you to get to Mount Weather and warn them what's coming. While I get the map, I want you to use Alice and push this Chinese tank back over. I'd like my own tank," Lou finished with a smile, then jogged back to his house on the pipestem.

Nelson climbed back up on Alice. "Okay, guys, listen up. Once Lou gets us a map, we're gonna go save some Army guys on a bridge."

"Can we turn the music back on?" Fletch asked.

"This is gonna go great," Stewie muttered and lit a smoke.

TWENTY-FIVE

Fletch had just gotten Alice off the ramp in Leesburg, Virginia, onto Route 15 North that would take them to Point of Rocks and the bridge over the Potomac River. It was twenty minutes since they left the 'hood, and Nelson was waiting for the inevitable thrown track. They'd been lucky so far with the one break found when they were in the cul-de-sac. While they hadn't found any other trouble spots, it would come. "Wild Child" by the Black Keys was blasting through the speakers that were miraculously still working on the back of the turret. With all the hits or near hits they took, he was amazed.

"Jones, how's the targeting system? You close?" he asked in his mic over the music.

"Some of it's fucking shot, I think. Replacing the last of the fuses, and maybe that'll work, I don't know yet, dammit."

"Hey, I don't want to alarm anyone, but we're kinda running on fumes here. How far's that gas, S'arnt?" Fletch said.

"It's like four miles ahead, just before we get to the bridge. We gonna make it, Fletch?"

"Fuck if I know, S'arnt. Gonna be a close thing."

"Back in business, gents! Fuck yes!" Jones yelled as the turret began to traverse fast, and the main gun elevated and leveled.

"Noice!" Stewie said.

"Hey, Stewie, can I switch with you for a few? Also, hork me a smoke, man," Jones asked as the opening guitar from "More Than a Feeling" by Boston began playing. Jones and Stewie switched spots, and Jones popped up out of the hatch and took a deep breath of the cold January air.

"You know hork doesn't mean give, right, man? You don't even smoke," Stewie said.

"It means both, and that shit was fucking intense, dawg. Imma smoke one now. What was it, Sergeant, eleven to one or twelve to one? And we still alive! Damn," Jones said.

"Something like that, Jones. Y'all are the best damn crew I've ever seen. Imma put all of you in for medals and shit. Honored to roll with you," Nelson said.

"Oorah, S'arnt. Don't want a medal, though," Fletch said over the team net.

"Whatchu want, Fletch?"

"Fuckin' tacos, man. Tacos."

"Hells yes! Let's save these lads and get back to Mama's tacos," Stewie said enthusiastically as Jones inhaled deeply from the cigarette and let the smoke billow around his head as they rolled up Route 15 at thirty-five to forty miles per hour. He put the smoke to his mouth again, hand trembling from the fading adrenaline. Fletch was weaving in and out of dead vehicles on the winding, two-lane road.

"Hey, Stew, I tell you about my homie on Thanksgiving?" Fletch asked as he weaved one way, then the other around the cars.

"What about him?"

"So, dude got one of those newfangled grills from Traeger, I think. Connects to your WiFi and shit. Well, he's up on Thanksgiving getting ready to throw that turkey on the grill, and it's got this LED screen on the front, and he goes to hit ignite, and the shit says, *currently updating software, please wait.*"

Stewie started laughing.

"Bro was legit agitated. Threw that shit out on Twitter, and shit started trending. Who buys a grill that needs a software update?"

They were all laughing now.

"Dude, that's a hard pass from me. Only charcoal or wood for the smoker. Old-school is best school. Bet homie ain't grillin' nothin' now," Stewie said, waving his hands around at everything.

"My man never heard the end of it. I miss Twitter, y'all," Fletch said as they came up a hill, and there was the gas station on the right where the road curved to the left. "Stayin' Alive" by the Bee Gees came over the speakers.

"Here we go, Fletch. Pull in near the fuel tank access holes. Stewie, grab the siphon, and let's get ready to get gas!" Nelson said as he reached over and hit the pause button on the iPhone still duct-tapped to the top of the turret. The Bee Gees disappeared, and silence returned except for the the turbine's whine.

"Fuckin' oorah," Jones said, taking a last draw on the smoke and flicking the butt behind him as Fletch stopped Alice near the fuel tank access covers.

"The fuck is that? Stewie, hand me my M-4," Jones said as his rifle appeared before him, and he grabbed it and brought it up.

"Y'all get us fueled. Me and Jones will see what this is," Nelson said as they all dismounted. He and Jones walked toward the convenience store attached to the gas station. There were some dead cars there, but their focus was on a tall, white male with a shaggy, gray beard, wearing jeans and a flannel shirt with one of those puffy jackets with no sleeves. He was standing next to a shopping cart filled with odds and ends, one hand gripping the cart.

"Hey, buddy," Nelson said loudly as they walked toward the man. M-4s at low ready.

"Hi! You are the last thing we expected to see here. Where you going?" the man said as a second man stepped out of the gas station convenience store. He was of a short and somewhat effeminate build.

"Bob, you'll never guess what I found. Gas station bleu cheese!" the second man said and then stopped, holding a cellophane-wrapped block of bleu cheese, staring at Nelson and Jones, who had raised their M-4s at him, then over to the massive Abrams behind them.

"What are y'all doing around here?" Nelson asked, lowering his M-4 slightly, staring at the two men over his rifle optic.

"Well, for starters, we're hungry and thought the store might have some food left after being picked over. We're from out of town and got stuck here at a friend's place. We're all our foraging for food and supplies. What are you all here for? I guess you're going that way to the fighting?" the man said and pointed in the direction they were heading. Bob was his name, Nelson assumed, since the other one had called him that.

"Fighting? Where?" Jones asked.

"Um, that way. Down by the river. We went over that bridge with our friends who we're staying with before Christmas. Point of Rocks, I think," the bleu cheese man said. Nelson didn't catch his name.

"Do you know who's down there?" Nelson asked.

"No, but we assume Americans since we saw a bunch of paratroopers jump out of a burning plane earlier this morning. I don't know who they're shooting at or who's shooting at them. Been going on for a while now, although it's quiet at the moment," Bob explained.

As if on cue, gunfire and explosions broke the silence, drifting up from the direction of the bridge.

"Stewie, how we doin'?" Nelson yelled, head turned to the distant battle.

"About half a tank, but it's running out now, Sarge! Thing was low anyway."

"Okay, secure it all, and let's move. It'll have to do. We gotta go to work. Mount up!" Nelson yelled again.

"You guys should get going that way," Jones told Bob and Bleu Cheese Man and pointed the way they had come.

"Y'all kick their asses, whoever they are. Good luck!" Bob yelled to Nelson and Jones as they jogged back to the tank and climbed up. When everyone was in their hatches, Nelson pulled out the map that Lou had given him to orient himself and studied it quick.

"Okay, look, the road goes down that way and curves right to the bridge. I think we can do better if we cover this mile or so through these fields down to the river where we'll have a better view of the whole situation, be able to cover the bridge and put fire on the opposite bank. Y'all good?" Nelson said.

"Sounds like a fine plan, S'arnt!" Fletch responded and fired up Alice and moved her through a paddock-type fence next to the gas station and into the fields Nelson was talking about and down toward the river. Nelson reached over and perused the playlist and selected one, hitting play. "Party in the USA" by Miley Cyrus started to blast out of the speakers and through their headsets.

Nelson sang along. "I hopped off the plane at LAX—"

"God dammit!" Jones said.

"Come on, Jones, this the best song ever to yeet some motherfuckers to," Stewie said, laughing.

"Knock it off. Y'all hydrate now. We don't know what we're getting into," Nelson said and took a long pull from a water bottle. The rest did the same as Alice dug tracks through the fields toward the river. As they got close to the bottom of the field, the far side of the steel and concrete bridge came into view.

"Jones, traverse left until you see the bridge. Button up!"

Alice's turret swiveled left and they all shut their hatches.

"Tank on the bridge and two more on the other side!" Jones yelled.

"Those are T-99s. Chinese! The hell are they doing here? Fuck, that first one is moving out of sight, blocked by those trees. Jones, kill those other two!" Nelson yelled into his mic. "So I put my hands up! They're playing my song—" And the song did play on.

"Sabot up!" Stewie yelled.

TWENTY-SIX

Point of Rocks Bridge
Red Devils

Ricketts looked around from behind the rocks. Sully was yelling at the engineers under the bridge from in front of the destroyed truck, but there was no answer. Sporadic fire from the opposite side of the river was returned violently by his guys to the left of the bridge, and the frequent single crack of his sniper on the hill with that Joe guy. Doc was doing the Lord's work on the hill, but it didn't look good from his position. He looked behind him and followed the wire from under the bridge to the detonator box that was about thirty feet away next to a large tree. The engineers' silence wasn't good.

He froze. *No…* He was out of engineers. He'd done some training with the EOD guys a while back. He was coming to the realization that it would be him when Pickle yelled.

"Tanks! Other side, on the road!"

Ricketts turned and stared for a moment in sheer terror. Three Chinese T-99 tanks were rolling down the road in a "V" formation, with one in front and two behind and abreast of each other. It was now, or they all died.

"Sully! Tanks! Get to the detonator! NOW!" Ricketts screamed.

"It's not set, LT. Something's fucked up," said Ryan.

"Y'all Cav Scouts? It's shitty, but I need you two to cover me, come on!" Ricketts said and ran down the embankment and disappeared under the bridge, not waiting for the other two.

"Fuck! Let's go!" Pickle yelled, and they both sprinted after Ricketts and ended up under the bridge where the LT was looking at two dangling wires, one from one side and the other from the side they'd just come from. He looked down and saw his bag of Black Rifle coffee floating in the water.

"I told you it was fucked up!" Ryan yelled as bullets ricocheted off the rocks below them and the steel girders above them.

"Suppressing fire that way. Let me work," Ricketts said, and Pickle and Ryan both turned and fired into the trees on the other side.

"Sanchez! Cover fire!" Pickle yelled up the bank, and the machine gun started barking. Ricketts had both wires from each side in each hand, and he tried with all his strength to stretch them to meet. He got them to touch, but not enough to twist them together.

Sully was waiting for a lull in the incoming fire to make his run to the detonator box, hearing the LT and other yelling at each other under the bridge. When it came, he took off as fast as he could run, turning his head just in time to see a massive Chinese tank halfway across the bridge fire its main gun into the wrecked pickup truck he was just hiding behind. The resulting explosion literally tossed him to the detonator box. He shook his head and looked around from the ground where he landed and saw the box just feet away. He scrambled to it, thanking God that there was slack in the wire that ran from it to where the LT was. Grabbing it, he did a slide into home plate behind the large tree and did a quick check to ensure the wire was still attached. He armed it.

"Lieutenant! Ready to blow it!" he yelled as loud as he could, but it sounded muffled. His ears were definitely shot. He looked around the tree. All his men were engaged sporadically. One of the tanks across the river fired its main gun, and he followed the barrel's elevation to the hill to his left and behind where the snipers were, and that precise spot erupted and flung pieces of rocks and dirt over the whole hill, even down to the street to his left.

Fuck! This is not doable. No bueno, he thought.

It was now or never. The first Chinese tank was pushing the pickup, engulfed in flames again, out of its way. It was right on top of the LT now, who was under the bridge.

"Come on, LT! What's the holdup?" Pickle yelled over his shoulder, still firing his borrowed M-4 into the trees and brush on the opposite side of the river. The return fire had dwindled.

"I can't get the two wires close enough to tie off, but I can get them to touch!" Ricketts said.

Ryan and Pickle looked at each other and knew.

"No sacrifice, no victory!" Pickle yelled.

"The old Witwicky motto, right, Sergeant?" Ryan said with a grim smile. There was a boom and explosion above them on the bridge, and dirt and rust from the girders made a cloud around them. Then Ricketts heard the rumble on the bridge above them, and the whole thing vibrated with it. There was a distant boom just then and an explosion on the far side of the bridge. Ricketts didn't know what it was and had no time.

"Fuck it," Ricketts said to himself. "SULLY!" he screamed.

"GO!" Sully yelled back.

"BLOW IT!" Ricketts was straining with every last bit of strength he had to keep the wires touching.

"WHAT?" came the reply.

Sully was staring at the tank at the end of the bridge, straining to hear Ricketts. He couldn't blow it with them down there, but they were out of time. There was a lull in gunfire, and he listened, still as death.

"DO IT! DO IT! DO IT!" came his lieutenant's voice. He got as small as he could behind the tree and pushed the button.

Sully watched in horror as the demolitions went off under the bridge first and then in rapid succession up both sides of the steel bridge supports that held it up, literally cutting the steel beams clean through. The smoke cleared seconds later on a strong, cold breeze blowing from upstream. His mouth fell open as the Chinese tank was still there, on an intact bridge. Then in a split second, it was gone. That section of the bridge, along with the tank, disappeared into the river below with a ripping and squealing of metal. It was done, but at the cost of the lieutenant and the Cav Scouts and what was probably more of his men than he could bear to think about.

Then he saw the burning tank on the other side of the bridge just as the one next to it exploded. What the hell was going on? Then his hearing cleared more, and he heard machine gun fire in the distance. 7.62 caliber. It was tearing up the far bank.

Okay, now or never.

"Devils, to me! We are leaving!" Sully yelled at the top of his lungs, and he watched as the squad down by the river scrambled up to his level as Corporal Dempsey fired the last of his machine gun ammunition, and he and Sanchez grabbed it and ran to join him. He saw Doc coming down the road that led up the hill above the retreating squad leading what was left of that team. It wasn't many.

"Doc! What about our snipers?" Sully yelled, hopeful, but Doc just shook his head.

"This is it, Sergeant. I could only do so much. They were caught in the open on the hill and that truck." Doc turned and pointed to where the flatbed truck was burning, where it had hit a tree, keeping it from falling into the river, but it was fully engulfed in flames. Sully hadn't even noticed it until now.

"Shit. Okay, let's get back up this road and out of range! Move!" Sully yelled one last time. A minute later, what was left of his platoon was up the road and out of sight of the river, the bridge, and the far bank, and he called a stop to get a sense of the carnage. As the men and walking wounded all dropped where they were, completely exhausted, most chugging water and passing bottles to those that were out, Sully counted. Out of three squads and the engineers totaling about forty-some men, he had fourteen left here with him. Doc was checking each one, seemingly not fazed nor wounded at all, dispensing bandages and painkillers where needed and telling them to drink more water. All the water they could drink.

Sully sat on the ground, looking at each man. Dempsey and Sanchez were oddly silent. None of the engineers made it. The Cav

Scouts, Ryan and Pickle, were with the lieutenant, whom Sully killed dropping the bridge. He was thinking about that when he heard music again. What was that? Coming from up the road, he felt the rumble first. Armor.

"Tank coming from up the road! Get ready!" Sully said to the men around him, and they all spread out in hasty positions. The rumble got louder from up the road and around a tight curve. Then he made it out. "Heavy Is the Head" by the Zac Brown Band. He stood up and walked to the middle of the road, M-4 aimed straight in front of him.

"Y'all keep cover," he said as a pretty torn up Abrams Main Battle Tank churned around the curve with two men riding high out of the turret's hatches, music loud now. He lowered his weapon and raised a hand as the tank slowed to a stop. The commander reached over and touched something on the turret, and the music died.

"United States Marine Corps at your cervix! I'm Sergeant Nelson. Who y'all?" Nelson said.

"Eighty-Second Airborne. Good to see you," Sully said softly.

"Crayon-Eaters are here," Dempsey flatly said in his Louisiana drawl.

"More like at your prostate, am I right?" Sanchez said and elbowed Dempsey.

"Shut up!" Sully barked.

"What y'all doin'?" Sergeant Nelson asked.

"Just dropping bridges. Three of them. Had Air Force help with the third one upriver. We blew two. I take it that was you guys hitting those tanks?"

"It was. Happy to help. That musta been you all in the C-5 burning in earlier this morning. We saw you from where we were. This all of you?"

"All that's left," Sully replied. "Had a full platoon this morning. Could use a ride. Where y'all come from? Single tank out here all alone. Looks beat to shit. Y'all seen action?"

"Sorry to hear that. We're from just over yonder, by way of Fort Knox. Yeah, we destroyed a Chinese armor unit earlier this morning. I hear there are a couple of Chinese armored and mechanized divisions across the river. Now I suppose they'll have to go around. Probably not done yet. Where to?"

"Gotta get to Mount Weather. Think it's fairly close."

"Yeah, we know where it is. Get your men and wounded up on top, and we'll go direct," Nelson said as Sully got his men up off the ground and onto the Abrams. Once they were all up, Sully looked back down the road and took a deep breath. He turned and grabbed Sanchez's outstretched hand, and climbed up all the way to the top of the turret. The tank did a 180 pivot in the road and started back up the hill. Sully thought the tank looked like a momma possum with all her little possums riding on top of her. He sat between two big speakers somehow fastened to the turret and lowered his head and closed his eyes, listing names in his mind.

TWENTY-SEVEN

Tavis sat near the helo on the pad, watching the clouds move in. It was getting overcast and smelled like snow. It had been about four hours since they landed back on the mountain after meeting with the general. He'd passed on the plan as it was. President Madison was thrilled they'd found the Marines but not too happy about the plan. They were pushing the Chinese right to the bridge west of the mountain. It was close. They had no idea if the Airborne had made it or not, nor yet if they'd dropped the bridges. So many unknowns.

He'd been calling his brother, Tanner, on the satellite phone at the top and bottom of each hour. He'd also texted him via the sat phone as well. "CALL ME ASAP" was the message. Nothing yet. He was beginning to worry that something had happened to them when he heard the door to the bowels of the mountain slam shut. He turned to see Joey hobbling toward him on her crutches.

"Anything yet?" she asked as she plopped down beside him, laying her crutches next to her.

"Not a peep."

"They're all worried about everything, but specifically the Airborne," she said.

"I wouldn't worry about them. They got it done."

"How are you so sure?"

"'Cause we'd be dead or captured by now if they hadn't," he said with a smile. She backhand-slapped him on the bicep.

"You don't know that, Tav. Chinese tanks could be at the gate any moment."

"Well, then we become gophers and bunker in and wait."

"Trapped gophers," Joey replied.

"The fook is that?" Tavis said and pointed past Joey to the road that led to the main gate, just as the door to the stairs burst open and a bunch of people ran out, mostly medical staff, with Gale, Pasha, and Jack. He helped Joey up, and they stood and stared at the M1 Abrams rolling toward them with a dozen or so soldiers on top of it. The sound of 50 Cent's "In da Club" died away as the tank slowed to a stop on the helo pad, and men hopped down all around it as the engine went silent. One of the soldiers jumped down and met the group of them, Joey and Tavis joining the rest.

"I'm Sergeant Sullivan. You can call me Sully. Eighty-Second Airborne. We're the Red Devils, formerly stationed at Bagram Airbase in Afghanistan. When there was a Bagram Airbase," he said and shook all the outstretched hands.

"Sergeant, I'm Admiral Joey Washington. The bridges? And what do you mean about Bagram?" she asked, stepping forward right in front of Sully, putting a hand on his shoulder, looking up at him.

"All three have been destroyed and are impassable, ma'am. Bagram was hit by a nuke shortly after we took off. My men need medical attention. Can you swing that?"

"Jesus! I think we can take real good care of you all," she said as Gale walked up to the tank and stared at the turret where Alex had painted the skeletal fairy. It was Alice and the Marines. Tavis and Pasha joined him.

"Howdy, y'all!" Nelson said from the commander's hatch.

Tavis squinted a bit and cocked his head to the right. "How the hell are you with these guys, Sergeant?"

"Well, you see, there were these Chinese Commie tanks coming down the main road, and we saw 'em. Thought maybe they were heading here—"

"Chinese? How many?" Tavis asked.

"Between us and the other Marines blooping grenades at the dismounted Commies, I counted nine tanks and three APCs or thereabouts," Nelson said.

"Wait, in the cul-de-sac? Is everyone okay? What about Layla? The others?" Gale was leaning on the wrecked front skirt of the Abrams covering the front and sides of the tank's treads as he peppered Nelson with questions.

"Everyone's okay. They're safe."

"You left. How do you know more didn't show up?" Joey asked.

"Lou interrogated their commander. They were the only ones on this side of the river."

"This is new," Pasha said as he crouched down to survey the damage to the metal skirt that was pushed in nearly to the treads.

"Yeah, we got into a sword fight with the last Chinese tank after it destroyed Alex's house. Had to ram it. Pushed it over on its side," Stewie said with a smile from the loader's hatch.

"What?!" Joey yelled.

"Oh, yeah! They put a round into the house, trying to hit us. Killed that poor little pug," Stewie continued and crossed himself.

"Then Lou went all John Wick on their commander," Nelson said, "and got the info from the crew about the bridges across the Potomac. So we figured the C-5 we saw earlier this morning could have been an Airborne drop to take or destroy the bridges. We headed out to help if we could. Got there just in time."

"You sure everyone's alright, Sergeant? Anything else you need to tell us?" Gale said without any emotion.

"My niece? Other kids?" Pasha was now standing.

"Yeah, guys, everyone's good. Like I said."

"Well, you keep bringing up worse things, one after another. For fook's sake, we all have family there," Tavis said.

"Oh, sorry. Yeah, the hood is safe and secure. No more bad guys," Nelson said.

Joey shook her head and started barking orders.

"Sergeant, you get your crew inside. Get some coffee and food. You're not done here. Gale, Pasha, go find the helo crew and tell them to get ready to go. I think some of us need to get home now. Tav—"

Just then, the satellite phone in Tavis's hand started a high-pitched chirping. He pressed the button with the green phone symbol on it and raised it to his ear.

"Tanner?"

"Aye, Tav. Can you hear me?"

"Loud and clear with a little delay."

"Sorry we had to stay silent. More Russians about."

"Listen, you need to tell USS *Virginia* that the president has authorized a fire mission for his Tomahawks."

"Copy. Will try. Hit or miss. I'm ready to copy."

"Okay, I will verbally tell you and text as a backup. Copy?" Tavis asked.

"Roger. Go ahead," Tanner replied, and Tavis loudly and slowly passed on the targets the general gave him.

"I copy good," Tanner repeated them back to confirm.

"Affirmative! As soon as you can, Tanner! Out."

"Roger that. Out." Tavis lowered his hand from his ear. He hadn't realized he had been yelling into the phone to make sure his brother could hear him. He turned around, and everyone was staring at him.

"We good, Tav?" Joey asked.

"We good, Admiral."

"Well, why is everyone just standing around? Go get the helo crew, Gale. Tav, you come with me," Joey said and then saw the tankers still sitting in their hatches. "You all come with me too. Let's go!"

With that, they all rushed to the stairs and headed down into the mountain.

About fifteen minutes later, they were all in the conference room with President Madison. It was a motley crew. The paratroopers were all there, even the wounded ones. There was the smell of gunfight residue in the room. Joey assumed it was from the paratroopers and the tank crew. She looked at the president, who nodded at her.

"Okay, listen up. Here's the plan now that we have a tank and some soldiers." She pointed to a large map of the mountain laid out on the table that she was leaning on.

"We're relying on those Tomahawk missiles from the USS *Virginia* to come in, but we don't know when they'll hit if they do. The Marine Expeditionary Force is pushing up the valley, and they're going to pin the Chinese, if they can, against the river and destroy them. Sergeant Nelson?"

"Ma'am?" Nelson stood on the other side of the table.

"Route 7 goes over the mountain up from the east, down the west side, and over this four-lane, two-span bridge here. I want you and Alice, with the Airborne, to position yourselves with a good vantage point on the bridge, but up as far as you can and cover that bridge. How's your ammo situation?"

"Roger that. Between last week and the rounds expended today, we've got just under a combat load left."

"In English, Sergeant."

"We've got about twenty main gun rounds. Half sabot and some HEAT or high-explosive. Got plenty of co-ax."

"If they start coming across the bridge, how long do you think you can hold them off?"

"Well, if we can hit the first couple or three, we may be able to block their way. If we run out of main gun ammo, I suppose we could throw snowballs at 'em," Nelson said with a smirk.

"Sergeant, just keep them at the bridge. Hopefully, the Marine force that's coming will do the rest."

"None shall pass, Admiral," Nelson replied.

"Good. Mr. President, in light of what these guys told us about our neighborhood and families, I want the helo to take Gale, Pasha, and Tavis back to them. Now. Having the helo doesn't do us any good here. General Kobayashi's Marines and the Tomahawks are the key," she explained.

"Approved, Admiral. Get your people home, but I need you here," Madison said.

Joey looked at the rest of them.

"Get outta here. Sergeant Sullivan, can you and your men support our tank here on the mountain?" she asked as the helo crew left to get the aircraft ready.

"We're a tad light on ammo, ma'am."

"We've got ammo in the weapons room. I'll take you there," said an Air Force major standing against the wall behind the president.

Joey nodded. "Good, get to it."

"Ma'am, we'll do what we can. I left my platoon commander and the majority of my boys at Point of Rocks Bridge," Sully said.

"Sergeant, when this is over, if we're still here, I'll personally come with you to get them," President Madison said.

"Thank you, Mr. President. That means a lot. Oh, congrats on the promotion," Sully said dryly, and they shook hands.

"Appreciate that, Sergeant. It's a shitty job."

"I get it," Sully said.

"I, too, would like to see my family again," came a raspy voice from the doorway as Doctor Rahimi wheeled Javad into the room, an IV bag suspended above his head.

"Ah, our Iranian spymaster is alive. How is he, Doctor?" Madison asked as she wheeled Javad to the table. Everyone that was getting ready to leave stopped at the old man's entrance.

"He did surprisingly well, Mr. President. Most of his wounds were superficial. The one that would have killed him was the shrapnel in his upper back. We were able to remove that and patch him up. Either the shrapnel or the infection would have done him in, but we've got both taken care of now," Rahimi said.

"Mr. President, I would suggest that even though Javad here pretty much started this whole thing, it would have occurred anyway, and the intel he passed us over the years as well as the information on the current situation warrant some leniency," the acting CIA director said.

Madison nodded.

"I was thinking the same thing," the president said and turned to an aide who handed him a folder, which he opened and pulled a piece of paper out of, and laid it on the table. He took a pen from his shirt pocket and signed it at the bottom.

"We have a copy here, but this is for you. Full pardon, just in case anyone ever wants to find and prosecute you, if we have a country in the future." Madison handed the sheet of paper on presidential letterhead to Javad.

He took it and read the whole page.

"There's also the part at the bottom which conveys United States citizenship to you, your daughter, Sara, and your friend, Ahmed."

"I'd clap for you, Javad, but you did help start World War Three, so…" Joey said.

"I understand completely. Can I go with you back to my family?" Javad asked.

"I'm afraid no one is going anywhere for a while yet. Chopper's broke," Bouncer said as he came back into the room.

"Define broke," Tavis said.

"Senior Chief found a hydraulic leak. Hard to get to. He and Duck are working on it now. An hour or two, they think. We should be able to get it fixed and have you all back just before dark."

"We can give you a ride," Nelson offered.

"Negative, Sergeant. You all have a job to do, so you best get to it and get in position," Joey said.

"Sorry, y'all. Shit breaks." Bouncer shrugged.

"I can help with helo. Let's go up," Pasha said, and they left.

Javad reached out a hand to Madison, who took it. "Thank you, Mr. President. I am grateful for your generosity and mercy. You could have easily had me shot."

"If I had wanted to do that, I wouldn't have let my medical team fix you up. Also, don't thank me, thank the CIA director."

Javad turned to Jack, and they nodded to each other.

"Okay, everyone happy now? Let's get going. Y'all go up to the helicopter. I want you gone as soon as it's fixed," Joey said.

"Joey, try not to worry. I'll be with Layla soon. You stay safe in here," Gale said and wrapped his wife in his arms while the rest left the room, Tavis wheeling Javad.

"Don't worry about me. I don't have a fighter jet to do anything with. It's all on them," Joey whispered in Gale's ear.

"As soon as this thing is done, you get home." He kissed her and turned and left her with the map and the empty room.

Then President Madison came back in.

"I wanted to give you two a moment alone," he said.

Joey rubbed her forehead. "What a shitshow this whole thing is. I leave my daughter at home, and a whole battalion of Chinese tanks wreck the neighborhood…"

"We'd be in deep shit right now if those Marines hadn't done what they did. But you're right. It seems like we're hanging on by luck and the blessings of Christ himself," Madison quipped.

"There certainly are a lot of devils dancing around us, sir."

"Well, you're kinda right, Joey. It's like a pride of lions. A group of devils is called a dance." He smiled.

"A dance of devils? Is that what that's called?"

"The fuck if I know. I just made it up, Admiral," Madison said and walked out of the room laughing.

TWENTY-EIGHT

An stretched as much as he could in his hatch. They'd pushed hard with only one stop to refuel, but they were getting short on gas. There would be a welcome stop at the gas station with Wrench and the 'billies. They could get out and walk off the kinks and refuel for the rest of trip. Short sprint to Mount Weather and then home.

He glanced over at his brother sitting in the gunner's hatch. Bao was fast asleep. Hopefully, he'd slept off the hangover. He was pretty lit when they found him, and seeing all his boys again, dead in their vehicles this morning, didn't do anything good. Bao startled awake just then and looked down, then disappeared into the troop compartment below them. An looked at his watch. 1530 hours. Getting on late afternoon. Couple hours til dark. They were lucky to have gotten this far without any mishaps, breakdowns, or fucking clowns. Dallas climbed up into the gunner's hatch.

"I hope it's alright that I ride up here awhile. Need air," the teenager said and winced against the cold that smacked him in the face.

"You get used to it after your face goes numb. How you doing otherwise?" An asked.

"I'm okay. Thinking about my dad. Hope my mom's alright."

An digested this before responding. He and Bao had just lost their dad as well. He wanted to tread carefully.

"Your mom's well, Dallas. She helped patch up my guys with my medic until a doc arrived from the other side of the neighborhood. Did you get along with your stepfather?"

"He was an ass most of the time, especially at the end of their marriage. He didn't treat my mom well. Hated him for that. Why do you ask? He back around, trying to get back together with my mom?"

"He did come around. Was sketchy at first. Your mom filled us in. Didn't know how you felt about him, but want to let you know he was stand-up at the end. Got killed trying to help your mom and the neighbors," An explained as Dallas stared straight ahead.

"Well, I have no love lost with that guy. I suppose he did good before he died. I'll leave my thoughts at that. Just want to get home and see my mom. Is Layla okay? Do you know her?"

"Bro, Layla is better than okay. She's worried about you. Her and your mom were insistent that we find you. She helped at the end of a fight with Iranian commandos in Lou and Robert's basement. Shot their leader. She's a strong young lady, Dallas. She's a keeper, dude." An reached over and squeezed the young man's shoulder.

They rounded a bend in the road, and about a hundred yards ahead were two cars blocking the road. The driver slowed to a stop.

"Get below, Dallas. Gunner, get up here!" An ordered, and there was a flurry of activity as Dallas was replaced by the LAV's gunner. A lone man with an AK-47 walked out into the road just in front of the cars. An held up a hand in a friendly gesture.

"I've got him, Gunny," the gunner said over vehicle comms. An watched the 20mm cannon slightly lower as the gunner depressed the angle. The man waved them in.

"Don't let your guard down, Gunner. Watch for others." An breathed deeply. He hoped these were the same 'billies as before. They were certainly close enough. The station should be just up the road a bit. The driver moved the LAV forward to stop next to the man. An recognized him as the same man from the tree line on their way to Knox.

"Quick trip. Successful, I hope?" the man said to An.

"It was very. Anything we need to know? Any contact with anyone?" An asked.

"Nope. Been quiet. We've got our roadblocks up now, though. You expecting any followers?"

"It's a distinct possibility. We've got intel about a Chinese invasion at Baltimore. They know we know. Y'all should be prepared if anyone's behind us," An explained.

"We'll keep a eyeball on it. Y'all can go on up to the station. I'll let 'em know you're coming," the man pulled a can with a large cone on it off his chest rig and held it high, and pressed the button twice. It was an air horn. Two loud blasts echoed through the trees.

"Two is for friendlies?" An asked.

"Yep. One long one is for the bad thing." Some more men came out of the woods and rolled one of the cars backward to let the LAV through. "They'll be waiting for you."

"Thanks, and good luck," An said as the LAV rolled through the roadblock and down the road. A minute later, they stopped again. This time their path was blocked, permanently, it looked like. There were a half-dozen large trees felled across the road. Totally impassable, even for armor. The gas station sat off to the left past the trees, where he saw the old Marine, Wrench, and the A-10 pilot, Voodoo, sitting in chairs watching them. Some more men appeared seemingly out of nowhere and started pulling on a rope which was tied to a smaller tree just to his left. That log raised up just enough for the LAV to get through and around the roadblock. They drove the LAV right up to the station where Voodoo stood to meet them.

"Y'all can get out and stretch for a few while we get topped off," An said down his hatch. The back doors of the LAV opened, and everyone piled out. An climbed down and hopped to the ground in front of Voodoo.

"It's good to see y'all again," An said and shook the pilot's hand and nodded to Wrench.

"What's the word?" Voodoo asked.

"We got my brother and our neighbor's kid. But we may have followers 'cause we have intel. Big Chinese landing in Baltimore. Objectives are Mount Weather and the Shenandoah Valley. Breadbasket of the east coast or something. On our way to Mount Weather, then home. Maybe you have some targets for your Hog now."

Voodoo frowned. "What's the makeup of the Chinese? You have that?"

"Armored and mechanized divisions."

"I suppose it's time to do some work. Let me get up there and see what I see. Thanks for this, Gunny. Been feeling a bit useless here but got to watch the boys build this roadblock, and they improvised some surprises for bad guys along the road before the trees," the pilot explained, and Wrench got up from his seat and came over.

"Now, you don't worry about us," he said. "You just go do what you do and give those Chinese fuckers the business. We'll deal with any followers. I got a score to settle anyway. Get your gas, Gunny, and get going. Pilot, to your plane."

Just as he finished speaking, a long, single blast from the air horn sounded through the trees.

"Shit! I can help here," Voodoo said, looking at Wrench.

"We got this one. You go get the Chinese tanks and come back. We'll break out the shine," Wrench said. Voodoo nodded and took off running up the hill. An turned to yell at his men to fuel up, but they were already doing it.

He turned back to the old man. "I can't thank you enough. Give 'em hell, Wrench."

Gunfire echoed through the trees from the first roadblock.

"Go! We got it. Godspeed."

They shook hands, and An turned and climbed back up on the LAV and down into his hatch as he heard the whine of a jet engine over the hill. A minute later, they were rolling east, away from what surely would be a score settled.

Wrench watched the LAV disappear down the road, then turned and walked into the gas station. A few seconds later, he emerged with his old M1 Garand. He walked out into the middle of the road and loaded one clip of ammo, pushing down hard with his grizzled old thumb until the bolt locked forward. He looked around and only just realized, in the late afternoon light, that it had begun snowing. In the distance, over the hill, he heard the A-10 Warthog take off down that road away from him. Sporadic gunfire reached him from up the road, and he waited.

"Ready, boys!" he yelled with all he had, and a cacophony of whoops, hollers, and oorahs echoed from the trees.

The first vehicle, an LAV, appeared, its 20mm cannon traversing to the tree line on its right, then more vehicles appeared behind it. Some Humvees and two more LAVs at the rear. He smiled as they rolled right up to the felled trees in the road and stopped.

It was on him now. He raised the M1, aimed at the first LAV, and pulled the trigger repeatedly until he heard his old friend... *PING*.

The turret traversed to him and settled.

Got your attention, Commie.

The first round hit him in the right arm, and he was spun around, dropping the rifle. As he lay there, he heard the improvised explosive devices they'd planted along the road go off, one after the other, and then gunfire popped from the trees. He was taken back, as he died, to his brothers in Korea.

I'll be there in a minute, boys. But first...

"Welcome to hell, motherfuckers!"

TWENTY-NINE

Natasha Petrova, colonel in the FSB and the Russian president's primary liaison officer, who coordinated Russia's part in the commencement of hostilities on the West, sat in a plush, beige leather seat. The large executive jet flying somewhere over the Mid-Atlantic states of what were the United States of America had every amenity. Certainly, she'd never see this opulence at home. She was a long way from there. A week ago, she was sitting in an operations center bunker in the Ural Mountains with the Russian president.

She hadn't been asleep for a while now. However, her eyes were closed. She was mentally taking inventory. Her primary weapon was her Vektor 9mm Parabellum pistol with an eighteen-round magazine in a shoulder holster with two extra magazines on the opposite side and two more attached to her belt. She also carried two knives, both Kizlyar six-and-a-half-inch blades. One on her belt and one in her right boot. One was given to her by her husband, Ivan, years ago. The other given to her by the Russian president as a memento for her recent efforts. She could kill equally efficiently and effectively with knife or pistol. As an FSB officer as well as the wife of a Spetsnaz officer, she'd been training for years in the Russian martial art, Systema. Hands were just as good, but she preferred to fight smarter, not harder. She also had a small, thin pen light that she carried in her jacket pocket. Never knew when you'd need a flashlight.

Boris the Wolf had been sitting across from her for some time. She could feel his eyes upon her, but she refused to acknowledge him before she was ready. Agitated was too soft a word to describe her feelings for him and his inept crew. She'd used her last leverage over him to get out of Russia and on this plane. Her goal was to get to her daughter, Alexandra, in Virginia. This coincided with Boris's goal of retrieving his other aircraft with what Boris called his retirement. His retirement was a massive amount of heroin in that aircraft's cargo bay. The plane had been stolen. Lucky for her, not for Boris. However, the closer they got to their goals, the less leverage she had over Boris.

Fine, she sighed to herself.

"Are we there yet, Boris?" she asked in English, opening her eyes. The older man sat comfortably in the leather seat across from her, staring at a piece of paper he held in his lap. She had insisted on speaking in English so she could dust hers off, even though hers was much better than his.

"Close, Natasha, close," Boris replied with a smile.

"About time. Our little layover in Gander was a stupid mistake, Boris," she snapped. Her irritation couldn't be held in check, even though she tried. Making Boris angry wasn't going to be helpful.

"Would you have rather landed in Atlantic Ocean, my little spy?"

Natasha sat up and leaned forward, her icy blue eyes piercing his pedantic demeanor. She tucked a wisp of long, blonde hair behind her ear.

"I would have rather you employed competent crew that didn't run out of fuel, necessitating the need to land at Gander Air Force Base in Canada instead of making it all the way to our destination. We barely landed safely in Gander in a blizzard and then had to wait a week for the snow to melt enough to refuel and take off again. A fucking week, Boris. Sleeping in an airport lounge and fucking shoveling snow and eating out of vending machines. We haven't had food for two days. Anything could have occurred in that week, Boris. I have no contact with my husband nor any Russian forces in the area or in Russia. You operate your little enterprise under the protection of and with the permission of the FSB and, more importantly, me." Natasha was whispering in Boris's face now. Her business with him wasn't for his men to hear, and he had made it plain to her that she was to keep her position and role here to herself. They were cat and mouse. Who was which depended only on the timing.

"Da, da. It was an unfortunate delay. One stop more. Then we go to this address." Boris held up the piece of paper with the neat handwriting on it. He'd done this several times to taunt her. He was a bastard that way. She hid her irritation with Boris in the fact that she'd known for years where her daughter lived, and she had a map of the areas roads and the neighborhood fully memorized. He truly was a stupid bastard.

"Yes. Unfortunate. You've said before that is where Commander Washington lives. The same street where my daughter lives. Remember, Boris, our deal is done once we're back in Russia with my daughter and husband. Hopefully, he's gotten to her," she thought aloud.

"What about her current parents? We haven't spoken about them."

"They will be welcome to come home with us or stay. They've done nothing but provide my daughter a good life. I have no issue with them. I just want my daughter back if she'll have me. If she'll forgive me."

"From my understanding, little spy, you had no choice in matter. Now that war has begun, surely the bosses won't mind."

"You'd be surprised at what the bosses mind or don't, Boris. What of your grandson, though? Shouldn't we get him first? He should be with them at that address, yes?" She changed the subject from Alexandra quickly. Perhaps he'd change his mind and go to the address first.

"In good time. I know he's safe with Pasha. Although, it will cost him dearly for taking my grandson," Boris trailed off, looking out the window.

Natasha knew from the telling of the story repeatedly that Val, his grandson, could have gone with Boris but stayed on the plane with Pasha and the rest. She'd get as far away from this angry little Russian mafia boss as she could as well. The pilot's voice came over the intercom in Russian.

"We're approaching the coordinates, sir."

"Land if possible!" Boris yelled to the cockpit. "You stay aboard, little spy."

Natasha nodded and looked out the window as they landed in what seemed to be the middle of nowhere. The remnants of snow held to the edges of the runway as the wheels touched it. The plane slowed and came to a stop, and turned fully around. Out the window, Natasha saw the remains of what once had been a very expensive executive jet, now sitting a burned-out corpse on the ground in the afternoon light. The door opened, and Boris yelled commands as his men poured over the wreckage.

"Mikhail, find it! Look for bodies!"

Natasha watched Boris as he stood stock-still, waiting for his men to sift through what was a plane. Minutes later, Boris's second-in-command, Mikhail, approached Boris and spoke to him through his bushy, black mustache, and Boris flew into a rage. She didn't hear the words, but she heard his deep, guttural scream. Within a minute, they were all back onboard and readying for takeoff. He sat in front of her again and leaned his head back, eyes closed.

"I'm sorry, Boris," she softly said, imagining the remains of the dead grandson they'd found.

A barely audible laugh emanated from the old man across from her.

"Oh, little spy, there are no bodies. Val is alive. My retirement, however, burned to the wind. For that, there are… consequences," Boris swore to the ceiling of the cabin as the aircraft took off to their final destination, only thirty miles away.

THIRTY

Voodoo's Last Stand

Captain Wu sat in the left front seat of the up-armored Humvee, watching the snow hit the nearly vertical windshield in the gray, late afternoon light. He listened to the radio in his left hand while he took a drag of the cigarette with his right. He'd found a pack in a pocket of one of the dead Americans lying in the valley back at Fort Knox, waiting for the fuel truck and tractor-trailer with his Abrams on it. If he was going to start smoking again, this was the time.

The Humvee was in front, with the fuel truck following about thirty meters behind him. The semi hauling his M-1 brought up the rear. His crew rode in the tank, and he had told them to be ready to fight at any moment. He didn't know what they'd find out here in the Appalachian Mountains. There were many dangers here in the United States, but all the briefings he'd been part of warned of this region. So far, there was nothing. Some roadblocks back near population centers, but they'd dealt with them quickly and violently. Perhaps the briefings were wrong.

His team should have made it to the point on the map that the American, Freshy, had pointed to. He was impatient and sucked on the cigarette again, blowing smoke that hit the windshield and dispersed.

"Captain Wu, advance team. Do you copy?" His radio came alive, finally.

"Advance, Wu. Go ahead," he replied.

"We've reached Baker. There's a gas station off to our left and a road that leads left over a hill. There are large trees lying across the road, blocking our way. Hold one."

"Copy, Advance. Any contact?"

"Captain, there is one man standing in the road on the far side of the downed trees with a rifle." The voice on the radio sounded way too relaxed.

"Advance. It's an ambush!" Wu could see it in his mind. Tree lines on both sides of the road with the road blocked. Shit.

"Captain, Ambush! We are fighting through it. Both sides of the roa—" The transmission ended.

"Stop here. We'll dismount the tank and go support," Wu said to the driver. The vehicle stopped, and Wu got out and ran back to the semi. After a couple of minutes, they'd backed the massive M-1 off the trailer, and Wu was in the commander's hatch again.

"Driver, let's go. Fast!"

The tank rolled forward and around the semi and passed the fuel truck to the Humvee. The driver was standing next to it with his rifle.

"What about us? What do we do?" the driver yelled up to Wu.

"Go back to Fort Knox. We'll find our way alone," Wu yelled back and left the small convoy in the road to their own devices.

Voodoo pulled back on the stick, and the A-10 Warthog slowly lifted off the bumpy, two-lane West Virginia back road. The fallow fields on either side fell away. The Warthog could land and take off from most surfaces, but this was perfect. As he climbed into the low, gray clouds that were starting to drop their snow, he banked right. East toward Virginia and Maryland. It would be a quick sprint across the Shenandoah Valley, with the Shenandoah River on the other side separating West Virginia from Virginia, where the first of the Blue Ridge Mountains rose up. He had a full load of fuel, so whatever he got into, he had enough to get back.

The Marines said there was a whole damn Chinese army out there somewhere coming in from Baltimore. The thought boggled his mind.

How did we screw this up so badly?

He increased power and dropped down under the clouds as he came out of the Appalachian Mountains on the west side of the valley, where it became fairly flat with farmland. His plan, as he thought it through, was to follow the Shenandoah River north, where it joined with the Potomac River at Harper's Ferry. Then he'd follow the Potomac aways and pop up into Maryland until he found the Chinese. Shouldn't be hard to find if there were as many as they said there were. He'd do what damage he could, but it wouldn't be more than a bloody nose with just one A-10. The good thing, he thought, was that they wouldn't be expecting anything from the air. So maybe they'd be sloppy and bunch up. He'd be looking for Command and Control vehicles or big groups.

Just up ahead, the front range of the Blue Ridge appeared. He got ready to drop, and bank left to follow the water north. Decreasing speed a bit, he banked hard left and was rewarded with a view of the Shenandoah River of "Country Roads" fame. Leveling out a couple of hundred feet over the river, he laughed to himself and said aloud, "Just like Beggar's Canyon back home."

He twisted and turned, following the river to Harper's Ferry, where he banked hard right to follow the Potomac and was immediately presented with a bridge with the center span missing and the wreckage of what looked like a large aircraft in the water. He flew over that and found the next bridge with one span next to the right bank gone. What the hell was going on here? Then it clicked. If the Chinese were on the Maryland side, someone was trying to keep them there. He banked left, then right, following a bend in the river, and Point of Rocks bridge was in front of him. He'd crossed it many times. He saw one section in the water with a tank on it. There were two tanks on the Maryland side. They were destroyed. As he flew over the wrecked bridge, he banked the A-10 slightly to the left so he could get a better look at them. They were not American Abrams. Had to be Chinese.

So they were about. They had tried crossing here but hit resistance, but from who? There were other bridges across the Shenandoah south of here. He knew that Mount Weather, that very public undisclosed location, was under one of the mountains that he had passed. Well, he didn't have the ordinance to drop a bridge, but he could misbehave.

He throttled up and screamed downriver, staying as low as he dared, just in case they had anti-aircraft radar running. After a minute, he banked left into Maryland just west of Sugarloaf Mountain and followed it north, and banked left again, heading back west. Voodoo figured if the Chinese were going around Harper's Ferry now, they'd be convoying on Route 340. There was one ridge in front of him running north/south with Route 15 parallel to it. Route 340 would be on the other side. He saw nothing moving on the ground here, which led him to believe they were all over the ridge. Time to do Voodoo shit. He increased airspeed and hugged the ridge up and over, dropping down to the farmland on the other side.

As he dropped below the cloud cover, thanking God that it wasn't snowing here yet, he saw them. Off in the distance was Route 340, the major east/west highway in this area. On it sat tanks. Lots of tanks. But that wasn't what concerned him.

Flying west were six helicopters. Not American. Attack type.

He prioritized threats and got his attack plan. He banked hard left, then leveled, then banked hard right. This put him on the helicopters' left side, and they were lined up abreast heading west. He smiled and increased altitude so that he could see all six from slightly above them as he came in. He lined up the A-10 on the first helo and squeezed the trigger on the joystick as he pulled back on it.

The 30mm Gatling gun that the Warthog was built around spun and spit, vibrating the airframe. The first three helicopters disintegrated, one after another. It was a three- or four-second burst. He jinked right as he screamed past the other three on their six. He did a full turn coming in behind them and selected his AIM-9 Sidewinder missiles. He had three under his left wing on one pylon. As he came about, the three Chinese attack helicopters were just reacting and starting to dive toward the ground. He let one missile after another go in two-second intervals. They were heat-seeking, so there was nothing more for him to do but bank away and line up on the highway, but he was able to watch the missiles track in. The Sidewinder was developed to take out fast-moving fighter aircraft.

The much slower helos were no match, especially since they were the only three heat sources in the air. Each missile found its heat source in two-second intervals. That would wake up the ground troops.

He lined up on the highway heading west. The same direction all the tanks and armored personnel carriers were driving. There were at least two miles of armored vehicles coming into his sights. Off in the distance was solid white. The snow was coming in. He had to work fast.

Thud. Thud.

"Shit!" He was taking fire.

Work faster, he thought.

He was basically sitting a titanium bathtub of armor. They'd have to do better than that.

He pushed his joystick forward a tad and lined up his sights on the line of tanks, and squeezed the trigger for a count of three. He repeated this process down the highway. The further he got, the more the tanks started to move left and right, but not enough. As he flew his Death Cross down the highway, he spotted a bunch of vehicles and APCs in a group off to the right in a field. Five or six of them. He made a mental note and continued down the highway until his Gatling gun was empty.

Banking hard right, he completed a large and low loop coming in on what he assumed was a Command and Control group of vehicles. He selected one of his two AGM-65 Maverick missiles. He lined up his Heads-Up Display sight and confirmed the Maverick was locked on the center of the group and fired. The missile dropped from the pylon, its engine lit off, and it streaked away as Voodoo banked left. Heading back east toward the rear of the Chinese convoy, where he assumed would be more vehicles of the soft variety. More humans, less armor.

He looked back over his left should and was rewarded with a massive explosion where his Maverick hit dead center of the command vehicles. Turning back to business, the vehicles did switch from tanks to APCs and Humvee-like vehicles ahead. He had six 500-lb dumb bombs, which he dropped down the highway as he went, then switched to his 2.75-inch unguided rockets and fired all nineteen in quick succession. He had one Maverick left, and he was done.

As he jinked left and right to avoid the small and large arms fire coming up at him, he spotted his target. There was a Sheetz gas station up the highway with a line of vehicles siphoning fuel from the underground tanks. He was surprised there was any left, but that station was well away from anything, alone at an intersection. He counted more than a dozen vehicles parked, waiting their turn as he sped by.

He performed another low loop and came back in, putting his Heads-Up Display sight on the pavement with all its covers to the underground fuel tanks removed. These vehicles were smart and were starting to move. The missile showed lock and he fired. It was only a mile or so out, so it happened quick. He turned hard, but craned his neck to see the resulting blast. The Maverick must have hit perfectly cause it seemed the entire gas station went up in a fireball. He went to full power and headed northeast and climbed away from the carnage and any retribution they thought to send up.

A short time later he dropped from the clouds and found his lonely little road. Just past it, in the distance, over the small hill, there was black smoke. As he landed on the bumpy road and taxied up to the hill where he had started from, he thought his kin must have had some fun with the Chinese chasing those Marines. He taxied to the right just before the hill and the Warthog came to a rest. Voodoo was physically and mentally exhausted. He raised the canopy, removed his helmet, and took a deep breath, letting the snow hit his face.

Then a thought came to him. He had downed six helicopters today. Did helos count? Fuck it, they did today. He was an ace!

He unstrapped and turned his head to the left to see the large, menacing form of an M-1 Abrams tank coming to a rest at the top of the little hill. Its main gun wasn't trained on his aircraft yet, but then he recalled those Marines and what they'd said. He stared at the tank. It just sat there. Then its turret started swinging that main gun to him. Dread crept in on him, but he forced it down and scrambled to get out of the cockpit. He looked up in his struggle to get out and the main gun had settled on him.

"Fuck it!" he screamed and pulled his 1911 from its holster and aimed at the tank, and squeezed the trigger.

When Wu and his tank finally got to Baker, what he found wasn't optimal. His entire advance element was destroyed. Some of his men lay on the road. They were obviously dead. As he scanned through the commander's optics in his hatch, he saw that two of his vehicles had been thrown off to the side of the road. Blasted there by something, probably improvised explosive devices placed on the other side of the road. A clear ambush. He saw the trees in the road blocking it and him. He didn't think his tank would be able to get over that and he wasn't willing to try only to get stuck. He doubted that whoever did this had the ability to kill his tank, but they could disable it. Whoever it was, they were gone or hiding in the woods. He had his orders.

"Driver, forward slowly. Let's see if there's a way."

The tank rolled toward the roadblock of trees.

"Stop!" Wu said as they reached the roadblock. He traversed his commander's optics to the left and down. It was snowing and had been for a while here and that revealed the ghost. There on the ground was a well-worn track. Not vehicle tracks, but a single line of people had been through, or gone back and forth. Between the felled trees and the tree line there was a pathway. He could see it dipped a bit off the road before it came back up. Wheeled vehicles couldn't pass it, but a tank could.

"Driver, turn left and go forward very slowly between the tree line and trees on the road," Wu ordered and the driver did just that. The tank dipped down at first, but the tracks caught the other side of the dip and clawed at the muddy snow until they were through it.

"Gunner, traverse and look for targets. Driver, take us up over this hill. I want to check it before we move on."

The tank's turret turned right and the tank mounted the hill.

"Driver, stop!"

The tank settled at the top of the hill. Wu looked through his optics. Puzzled at first, he then smiled.

"Gunner, traverse left. Aircraft on the ground. Load HEAT!" Wu ordered as he stared at what appeared to be one of the Americans most feared aircraft by ground troops. The A-10 Warthog. The pilot was still in the cockpit, staring at his tank, but started to quickly get out once his turret began turning.

"HEAT already loaded!" yelled the loader.

"Aircraft on ground. Acquired. Ready to shoot!" the gunner said. Wu savored the moment as he watched the pilot pull a pistol from a holster and began firing at his tank.

How ironic, Wu thought as he admired the tank killer through his sights.

"Fire!"

The main gun recoiled into the turret, expelling the base plate of the HEAT round and the hit was instantaneous at such close range. The round hit right under the cockpit and the pilot and plane were gone.

"Driver, turn us around and get us back on that road. Go as fast as this tank will move. They can't be that far ahead."

Settling into his seat, Wu barked a laugh, and the tank hit the road again in pursuit of his quarry.

THIRTY-ONE

They'd been on the west side of the mountain, if you could call it that, for about an hour. Sully stood in the middle of the east-bound lanes of Route 7, the four-lane highway that snaked over the mountain east-west. As he stood, facing west out into the Shenandoah Valley, or at least this little part of it, he studied the terrain and features. As the road came over the west side, it sidewindered before flattening out to cross a short, but fairly wide, two-span bridge across the Shenandoah River, and then it went straight out into the valley. The Chinese would be coming from the north on the other side, so to his right. The Marines, if they showed up, would come from his left or the south on the other side. They would converge right here at this bridge. Jesus, he hated bridges now.

There was still a lot of snow on the ground up here, but just in patches in the valley farmland, and it had just started snowing again. He and his men, only a squad now instead of the platoon they'd started out with in Afghanistan just two days prior, had been busy building fighting positions. They'd gotten full ammo loadouts from the complex's weapons room, so there was that. Wouldn't do much if the Chinese armor got up here, though. Their only chance was for the Marines and their Abrams to stop them on the bridge and build a roadblock with dead Chinese tanks.

"Well, we have the high ground at least," Sergeant Nelson said as he approached from behind. Sully turned as Nelson stopped next to him, cigarette hanging from the side of his mouth and his M-4 slung to his chest over his extra magazines. He looked just past Nelson to where the tank, Alice they called it, sat. It was covered with tree branches now and waited on the right shoulder of the west-bound lanes. They were up above the right curve, so its turret and main gun were traversed to the right a bit. It would be hard to see from below.

"High ground and surprise. You're gonna need to stack them up on that bridge. If they get up here, my men are dug in on both sides and in the middle grassy partition." He pointed them out to Nelson.

"I hope they have ear protection. Y'all are in front of us. Gun is loud."

"We do. Our fallback positions are ready as they can be. By yours up around the bend where it flattens a bit," Sully said.

"Hey, I'm sorry about your men. We'd have been there earlier if we'd known earlier. It was all happenstance anyway," Nelson said.

Sully stared out over the river and bridge and into the valley. Large snowflakes brushed his face. He exhaled and his breath froze and floated away to mingle with Nelson's cigarette smoke.

"You didn't know, but you came when you did and saved what's left of us. I suppose you Marines are good for something after all," Sully said and turned and slapped Nelson on his shoulder and started walking back up the hill to his position.

"The fuck is that?" Nelson pointed across the river to the road on the other side. Sully turned back and they both strained to see through the falling snow and gray overcast light.

"That… is an LAV," Nelson said after a few seconds.

"The Marines showed up."

Nelson smiled, then said, "I'll be damned! Those aren't the Marines we're waiting for. Well, they are, but different. Maybe. That would be crazy."

"Well, whoever they are, they're coming fast," Sully said and turned and yelled to his men. "We've got company! Look alive!" Sully and Nelson ran back to the tank.

"Jones! Track that LAV coming up and cover us if they aren't friendly!" Nelson yelled up to Jones who was sitting in the commander's hatch.

"On it!" Jones replied and the turret started to traverse and the main gun tracked the LAV as it crossed the bridge and made the curve. It started to slow when it saw the paratroopers in the road. There were several now out of their fighting positions with their weapons trained on the approaching vehicle. Nelson strode across the grassy median and into the east-bound lanes and held up his hand.

The LAV slowed to a stop a few yards from Nelson who was smiling now. Sully joined him.

"Welcome back, Gunny! Can I have my LAV back now?" Nelson yelled up to An.

"The hell are you doing here, Sergeant? I'll trade you for my tank," Gunnery Sergeant An Nguyen yelled back and pointed to Alice behind them.

"Deal. Why don't y'all dismount here and I'll fill you in real quick," Nelson said and An climbed down. The rear doors opened and the occupants piled out. Sully watched all this, slightly confused.

"Sergeant Nelson, this is my twin brother, Gunnery Sergeant Bao Nguyen. Nelson here's been taking care of Alice for me while I was retrieving you," An said to his brother and he looked over at Alice.

An's smile faded. "What the fuck did y'all do to my tank?" he shouted, pointing at the crushed front skirt and the damaged fifty caliber on top and the scorch marks from main round hits that ricocheted off during the tank battle in the hood.

Nelson shrugged. "We had a little tussle with some Chinese tanks on the main road next to your neighborhood. It's a long story and we don't have time now, but one thing led to another and we killed nine tanks and three APCs and then went to Point of Rocks bridge over the Potomac and got there just in time to save these here Airborne guys who came all the way from Afghanistan to drop the bridges." Nelson turned to Sully. "Sergeant Sullivan, this is my commander, Gunny Nguyen."

Everyone shook hands.

"Well, shit. Y'all been busy," Bao said.

"Yeah, it's been a day," Sully replied.

"Oh, hey, we also found Dallas, the vet's son. Come over here, Dallas!" An said and waved the tall teenager over to the group.

"Dallas! Good to see you, my man. Your mom's been extremely worried about you. Layla as well," Nelson said.

"Are they okay? How far is it to home?" Dallas asked.

"They're fine, an' you'll get there," Nelson said and continued, "So look, there's a shindig about to happen here. I'm gonna make a command decision. Gunny, Alice is yours. I'm gonna take your brother and Dallas back up to the complex. There's a helo that's gonna take some folks back to the neighborhood once they've fixed some hydraulics or something. Should be almost done by now. Then I'm gonna bring my LAV back here. We need the gun."

"I'm good with that," An said.

"The hell I am," Bao hotly replied. "I'm not leaving you here to fight while I go home safe."

"We should let the admiral make that call then. It's not up for discussion here. Bao, Dallas, hop in. Wait..." Nelson looked around at the rest of his returning guys that got out of the LAV.

"Yeah, we lost Frenchie, Sergeant. We took some mortar rounds leaving Knox, and he was in the open," An said.

Sully was quietly amazed. They came all the way from Knox in an LAV. He supposed they'd had a long day too.

"Well, shit. You two. Get in. Let's get to the complex. The rest of y'all stay here and augment these troopers. I'll be back quick," Nelson said.

An and Bao bear-hugged each other.

"I'm not happy about this. We'll see what this admiral has to say," Bao said.

"Brook and your little one need you at home," An replied. "She's not gonna name her unless you get back to them. So, move it. I'll be along."

Twenty minutes later, Sully and An were taking turns with the binoculars watching the bridge and valley. Stewie had Motorhead's cover of "Sympathy for the Devil" driving through the Alice's speakers. The snow was coming in waves now. Heavy one minute, then it'd fade a bit, then heavy again. It was sticking fast to the road.

"Well, Gunny, all we need is a bank full of gold now," Sully said without taking the binoculars from his eyes.

"What?"

"We got a tank and a bridge. *Kelly's Heroes*, man," Sully replied and then pointed to the road on the far side of the bridge.

"Yep. Looks like a Humvee to me," An said

"Humvee's coming up!" Sully yelled out.

"If these are the Marines that are coming to save us, I hope they brought more. At least the Humvee has a TOW launcher," An said flatly as the vehicle sped up the highway to their position, where it slowed to a stop in front of the two sergeants, just as the song changed to "Gonna Make You Sweat" by C+C Music Factory. The passenger door opened, and a Marine got out. Sully saw the lieutenant bars, but he was more interested in the anti-tank guided missile launcher on top of the vehicle. The TOW was guided by wire to its target. It was within range of the bridge from here.

"Y'all having a rave up here? I'm Lieutenant—" As he took a step forward with his hand out, the step was bit too long, and his foot slipped forward on the gathering snow and ice, and down he went in the splits.

"God dammit!" the lieutenant barked.

An stepped cautiously forward and held out his hand to the red-cheeked, baby-faced Marine officer who looked like he was drowning in all his gear. "Here, Lieutenant."

The fallen Marine took An's hand and was lifted effortlessly to his feet. Three other Marines were now out of the Humvee, and Sully noticed one roll his eyes.

"Let's try that again, Lieutenant. I'm First Sergeant Sullivan, and this is Gunnery Sergeant Nguyen, who just picked you up from the ground," Sully said.

"Thanks, Gunny. Slippery here. Second Lieutenant Lars Gunderson."

They all shook hands.

"With a name like that, snow should be your expertise, Lieutenant," Sully remarked.

"Sergeant, the LT here is the forward observer for the MEF's artillery. He's one of the best I've seen. That's why we're here. High ground," one of the Marines from the Humvee interjected. Probably to save his LT from further embarrassment.

"Is that so? Well, we have the high ground for sure, but how you gonna adjust fire without a radio?" Sully asked.

"We've got four working radios in the whole force," the lieutenant replied, interjecting himself back into the conversation. "One is with the artillery, one is with General Kobayashi, and one is here in the Humvee. The last one is with our Recon team out in the valley."

"Did you say, General Kobayashi?" An asked.

"That's right."

Nodding, An said, "I've met the general. Was back a ways, before all this. He's a good combat leader. This party is looking up."

"Does this mean that this is a no-win scenario then?" Sully asked as the LAV appeared over the hill behind him. They all turned as it pulled to a stop next in the middle of the road but behind the tank, and the rear doors opened.

"Looks like y'all got more company. I brought the boss," Nelson said to the group from the top of the LAV as Sully watched as the admiral on crutches awkwardly exited the LAV just as House of Pain's "Jump Around" started playing. The music was loud, but they could talk normally and hear each other.

"Where's Gunny?" Admiral Washington demanded.

"Here, ma'am."

"I put your brother and Dallas on the helicopter going back home. He tried to argue with me. He lost. Who're you?" The admiral stared at the lieutenant.

"Lieutenant Gunderson, ma'am. The general sent me up here to direct and adjust our artillery fire. I'm the forward observer," the LT explained quickly.

"I tried to tell her it's not safe out here on the mountain for her, but she insisted on seeing the situation for herself," Nelson said as he dismounted from the LAV.

"Admiral, he's right. It's not safe out here. You don't even have a weapon," Sully said.

"That's quite the promotion… Ma'am," An said with a half smile.

Unfazed by both scolding and praise, the admiral said, "Yeah, I'm the Chairman of the Joint Chiefs of Staff now or something, Gunny. Sully, the only weapon I fight with is an F-18 Hornet. You got one around?"

"No, ma'am. However, I would suggest we fill you in, and then you return to the complex," Sully pressed.

"That's fine, Sergeant. The quicker we can get through this alive, the quicker I can hand off this new title to General Kobayashi. I've got a feeling I was promoted to this role by President Madison more to the fact that he was pissed off at the other general down there in the bunker and not because of diversity and equity, Gunny."

"Ma'am, I have zero doubt that you're in charge for a reason, and that reason is that you've gotten us this far. Orders?" An replied.

Washington looked at Gunderson. "Lieutenant, get yourself a good vantage point and set up. I'm assuming you've got a radio."

Lars nodded. "I do. One of four. The general has one, artillery, and Recon team."

"Good. You Marines…" She turned to the Humvee and stared at the TOW launcher. "This thing work? You got ammo for it?"

"It does, and we do. Got two missiles loaded now and four more in the back," the Marine that spoke earlier said.

"I want you to set up where First Sergeant Sullivan tells you to. He's got command of the defense here. Where are the rest of the Marines, Lieutenant?"

"Ma'am, the tank battalion is arrayed a few miles out into the valley. We've got more Humvees and LAVs with TOWs and teams with Javelins and AT4s in interlocking fighting positions. We're assuming the Chinese are going for the bridge here. We're gonna make sure they do. The tank battalion will ensure the mechanized troops won't get flanked. It's pretty hairy for us here, but we're gonna make them pay for it.

"The general is nine to ten miles southwest of our position on the far side of the river with his command element. The artillery is set up near there as well. If all goes as planned, the Chinese will either be dead, in the river, or both, when we're done," the Marine explained.

"Yeah, if? I would have thought you'd bring more of force with you up here. We're pretty much relying on the Chinese not knowing we're here and the USS *Virginia*. This is gonna be tight, but I have confidence in you guys," she said as "Little Miss Can't Be Wrong" by the Spin Doctors started blaring from the tank's speakers.

"I'll take that song as a good omen, ma'am," Sully said, and the admiral raised her eyebrows and nodded.

"The general needs all his assets in the valley down there, ma'am. We're it," the Marine continued.

"What's that over the river?" one of the Marines said and pointed out over the river. They all turned and saw it.

"That's a drone! Of course they have a drone. Nelson, get the admiral back to the complex and get back here. Now!" An yelled as the first artillery came screaming in and hit in the trees above them, and through it, Sully heard, "Little Miss, Little Miss, Little Miss can't be wrong—!" blaring from the tank.

General Kobayashi stood on the putting green, next to the clubhouse of the Blue Ridge Shadows Golf Club. His command and operations teams were working inside the clubhouse. They had a fire going in the fireplace and he could smell the wood smoke out here. He loved the smell of wood smoke. He needed to be away from the noise inside to be alone with his thoughts and chain-smoke cigarettes. There were now seven butts on the ground scattered around the green as he paced in the falling snow that was just starting to cover the ground.

He paced and watched his artillery units working like little ants in and around their gun emplacements scattered around the golf course. They'd been able to get twenty-eight of the newer M777 Howitzers here. Most of the ammunition were the normal high-explosive 155mm rounds. Although they did have a few that were equipped to fire the much longer-range rocket-assisted projectiles. Those meant he could reach out and touch these Commie bastards at forty miles instead of only fifteen. He was going to introduce the Chinese to the King of Battle as the artillery was known.

It was an okay plan, he thought. His subordinates inside all thought it was a great plan. It was okay. Not great. Not bad, but not great. He wanted to bloody the Chinese so badly in the first minutes that they didn't want to try again. If they kept pushing and made a slog of it, who knows who'd come out on top. It was extremely risky to have all his mechanized troops out there without air cover. He'd had to adjust and didn't like it, but it's what he had and he was going to make the Chinese wish they were dead. Just before they became so. He wasn't married and had no kids. These Marines were his family, and many of his family would die today. He pushed that away for later and pulled his pack of Marlboro Lights from his pants pocket, and lit another one.

"General! Radio traffic from Recon!" his ops chief, a stiff and unhumorous major, yelled from the clubhouse door. He just stared at the man, cigarette hanging from his lips.

"Well? Come out here an tell me what it is, Major," he replied, squinting through cigarette smoke. "Snow won't bite."

The major bowed his head against the lightly falling snow and jogged the twenty yards to where the general stood, followed by a sergeant with a notepad in case the general wanted to send traffic back.

"Recon radioed in. We've got Chinese tanks coming down from the north," the major said, and Kobayashi looked at him for a minute.

"Okay. What I want you to do is put your best men together in hunter/killer teams armed with RPGs. Have them dig holes fifty meters apart and wait for the Chinese tanks to approach, then attack them in force."

"General?" The major was confused, but the sergeant quirked a smile and locked eyes with the general, which entertained Kobayashi, so he turned around and waved his arms at the golf course.

"And I want some anti-aircraft here!" he yelled.

"General, I..."

"Major, I believe the general is quoting *Red Dawn* again," the sergeant explained flatly as dull thuds echoed down the valley from the north.

"Listen! Is that artillery?" Kobayashi asked with his back still to the two men.

"Sounds like," the major replied.

"Are the Chinese hitting our positions with artillery right now? Or are they hitting Mount Weather with artillery?" he nearly yelled in anger.

"Well, it's not ours, so yeah," the major said.

Turning round, Kobayashi walked up to the major and exhaled smoke.

"Major, find it. Kill it. Rapidly. I want you to turn all their terrain into chaos. Take those assholes to pound town. Go, go, go, go," he said and shooed them back toward the clubhouse. Once they were gone, he turned back to the sound of the distant thunder and looked up at the sky.

"There goes my plan. Fuck it," he said aloud and walked back inside, flicking the cigarette butt out into the snow.

THIRTY-TWO

Dulles International Airport
Viktor and Natasha

Nearly eleven hours after leaving Chelyabinsk, just before the whole country went dark, the massive Ilyushin IL-76 was approaching the drop zone. Viktor and his old comrades discussed during the flight whether the aircraft would actually make it all the way, as the drop zone was at the far edge of the plane's ferry range with no payload. They crossed their fingers and prayed to whatever gods might listen that, with only a platoon of paratroopers and the gear and ammunition they carried with them, it would be enough. Apparently, someone had listened, since the aircraft had been descending for some time now, and the crew chief was yelling at them to get ready.

Viktor wasn't jumping with his friends. Of course he knew their mission. To land, seize, and secure one bridge over the Potomac River for the Chinese armored and mechanized divisions that had landed at Baltimore. By chance, military intelligence had intercepted a satellite phone call from American leadership at one of their underground complexes that had survived to their base in Afghanistan. They were sending Airborne troops to destroy three bridges, one of them the target of his comrades. Viktor, however, would be staying with the aircraft as it landed at Dulles Airport to refuel. He would not be returning to Russia with the plane or wherever it was going to go.

He was confused at first on the long flight why the paratroopers were coming all the way from Russia if they had already taken Dulles Airport. However, his friends had pieced together, via rumor and intelligence, that the Russians and Chinese who had taken the airport were engaged somewhere south of Dulles against US Marines that came north from their base at Quantico. The Marines had marched on foot with few vehicles to transport heavier weapons and ammunition. It was a slog, they'd heard. The Russians at Dulles had no units free to secure the bridge, even though it was only a thirty-minute drive north. The overall plan all relied on the Chinese moving inland from Baltimore to take Mount Weather and the valley to the west of that. Then, when they linked up, they could finish off the Americans in the south.

Red lights in the cargo hold came on, creating a hellish glow down the lines of paratroopers. Viktor sat near the front of the plane as his former platoon stood, hooked up, and then, when the green light replaced the red, filed out the doors on either side of the cargo bay. With a pang, he wished he were going with them, but then remembered why he was here. Val.

The crew closed and secured the doors and some semblance of warmth, and his hearing, returned. Soon they were landing at Dulles. The plane taxied to a stop, and the crew chief lowered the ramp, and cold air once again enveloped Viktor. He walked down the ramp onto the tarmac, looking fully like the Russian paratrooper he was. White-splashed green camouflage uniform. Sergeant insignia visible under his webbed harness. Carrying six extra magazines for his AK-47. He donned his cold weather cap but kept his earflaps tied up. He walked a ways toward the rows of gate buildings where many useless commercial aircraft sat.

There was a hustle and bustle to the activity here. Another transport was off-loading more Russian troops outfitted in winter gear, more white than his. He recognized their makeup and insignia. Siberian troops. Eastern District. Good. They'd need reinforcements, from what he'd heard on the flight. He wondered how his platoon was getting on, but those concerns faded fast as he made his way further into the activity and found a quiet corner to set up and begin his watch. He had decided not to check in as he was instructed to do. They'd put him with the next unit going to fight the Americans. There was no time for that bullshit. He needed a vehicle.

It had taken some doing, some back and forth, but they'd finally been granted approval to land at Dulles. However, that came only after Natasha had personally gotten on the radio and flexed her FSB credentials. Now she waited, watching the snowy ground come up quick as Boris's executive jet landed at Dulles. It had been a fast trip from the small strip where they'd found Boris's heroin shipment burned to cinders. They came to a stop near empty aircraft and empty buildings that would have been full of travelers just a week or so before. A modern ghost town now.

"You remember what the story is, my little spy, yes?" Boris asked her as he stood. Their next step was to report to the operations center and explain what they were doing here in a war zone to the commanding officer. They would need to procede with care.

"Boris, it's my story," she replied flatly. "However, just so you keep your expectations in check, I will remind you that we are in a Forward Operating Base. It is unlikely that they will have an extra vehicle for our use."

"Da, but you will explain to them our urgency. Is win-win. I want, but you need. Is in your best interest to convince," Boris said as he was walking towards the cabin door that his main bodyguard, Mikhail, held open. She sighed and rose to follow Boris and his men out into the late afternoon cold. Something about how Boris said that last part solidified in her the decision to part ways with Boris and his men here, if at all possible. Boris was her ride, nothing more. She was here. She had work to do.

They walked as a group, somewhat spread out, to what the man on the radio told them was the operations center. As they walked, she let herself drop to the back of the group so she could scan the field without notice. There was much activity near the buildings, but she quickly caught sight of a vehicle off by itself near the end of the runway they'd just landed on. Anti-aircraft. Pantsir. Three crew members.

Interesting, she thought, and filed the observation away as they arrived at the door to the operations center. Boris and his men entered while she took a look around closer to the buildings. Nothing but a lone sergeant standing at the corner of the next building, smoking a cigarette. She stopped short of the door. That face. The rank matched. His manner. He was watching the field.

"Natasha! Come," Boris said, holding the door for her. She snapped out of her shock and went inside.

Once inside, they were greeted by a short, grizzled Russian general who had walked over to them from a set of tables covered with maps. She glanced around. Light came in through the window on the door, but the large room was lit by lamps run by the generator outside. About two dozen men and women worked busily at tables filled with radio equipment and laptop computers.

"Who are you? Why are you here?" the general asked pointedly without introducing himself. She didn't recognize him, but that didn't matter. There were many generals she didn't know.

"General, I am Colonel Natasha Petrova, FSB. This is my team. Thank you for allowing us to land and refuel. We understand it may seem odd for us to be here, but there are FSB agents west of here that we need to retrieve. Quickly. Any support you could provide to us would be portrayed glowingly in my report when I return with these agents. We need a truck, if possible."

It was a solid cover story, one not far from the truth.

But the general wasn't buying it. "Well, Ms. FSB Colonel, I have a great many problems currently, including loss of all communications with anyone in Russia or anywhere, and now you're one of them. I don't have any trucks for you and your team, and I certainly couldn't care less about some bullshit report. Glowing or not. I'm fighting a war here. Did you know that there were supposed to be no American forces anywhere near this airport? Fucking US Marines walked, on their god-dammed feet, from Quantico to a few miles south of here. In the fucking winter! And you want a truck?" The general's voice climbed higher and higher as he spoke.

"Indeed we do need a truck. General. This mission was approved by the head of FSB and the president. It's critical we retrieve these agents. Will you help us?" She gave no ground. Knew his type. She just had to outlast him without being taken outside and shot. The general looked her team up and down. His eyes lingered on Boris.

"Fucking FSB. Fucking KGB. All the same. Only trucks I have left ten minutes ago to take more troops to the front with the Americans. You can have one when they return. I will need it back when you're finished getting your agents. Get out." With that, he walked back to his maps, yelling something at the soldiers around the tables, who looked over at them, some shaking their heads. She led them out the door quickly. They grouped up outside.

"Okay, so we'll have a truck. A few miles, he said. We probably have thirty minutes to wait or so," she told Boris.

"I suggest we wait in the plane. Warmth is needed," Boris said.

"That's a good idea, but I need a bathroom first. I will be along shortly," Natasha said and went to look for a bathroom on a route that would avoid the general. And Boris. Most doors along the first floor of this long, rectangular, two-story building were locked, but she finally found one that opened at the opposite end from the operations center. As she entered, she glanced back to make sure that Boris and his men were not following her but had headed toward the plane. They were indeed at the plane. The space she walked into was similar to the ops center at the other end, but it was empty. She scanned around while holding the door open for light, and there on the far side was the sign for restrooms.

She let the door shut behind her and pulled her small pen light from her jacket pocket, and turned it on. It provided enough light to do what she came to do, which was to relieve herself and consider this loss of comms with Russia. That changed the equation.

She finished her business and walked back into the larger space. There was a hallway that led around the end of the building, which she followed, pen light flicking one way, then the other. She wondered what had become of all the passengers that had been here on Christmas Eve when the lights went out as she came around to the other side of the building. It was identical to the other side, with a door to the outside.

Perfect.

Now for the tricky part.

Viktor had been lurking around the terminal buildings for hours, trying to stay well out of the way and wait for his chance. And so he'd noticed the executive jet landing. Its occupants disembarked and entered the operations center. They didn't pay him any notice, but he saw them.

Boris was here. His rage rose to a point where he almost didn't care about getting to his son and ending Boris right then. Almost. If that bastard was here without Val, then his son was still out there. Good.

He'd watched them reboard the jet and then turned his attention back to the Pantsir anti-aircraft vehicle some three hundred yards away near the end of the runway. He'd watched them for a while now. Crew of three. He was still working out his plan when he heard footsteps behind him.

"Viktor?" a female voice asked. He turned to face a pretty blonde woman. He couldn't make out her age, but she was the woman he'd seen with Boris. He relaxed, and took a last drag from his cigarette and dropped it to the ground, crushing it with his boot. Completely aware that she'd stayed just out of sight of the jet.

"Who are you? And why are you hiding from your friends?" Viktor replied with his own questions.

In true Russian fashion, not one emotion played across her face. "They're not friends. They were a necessary evil and my ride to get here. I believe we have common interests, Viktor. I know your son, Valerie, is near here. West a bit."

Victor's mind raced as she spoke his son's name, but likewise kept his demeanor controlled.

"Okay, what's going on? What is this?" he asked the woman, while noting that back at the Pantsir, two of the three crew members were walking across the field, probably to get food. It was dinnertime or close to it.

"My name is Natasha Petrova, colonel in the FSB. My daughter, Alexandra, is with the same people as your son right now. I'm not associated with Boris the Wolf any more than that he was my transportation from Russia here. I need another ride to where my daughter is. I can do it myself, but if we work together, we'll have a better chance of reaching both our children. We don't have much time." She tilted her head toward the two soldiers from the vehicle that were nearly walking by them now to one of the other buildings.

"So, you're the FSB agent I was told about before I flew here. FSB doesn't like it when their drugs go missing, do they?" Viktor said flatly.

Natasha tilted her head. "Your information is correct. If you know that, then you know I'm not lying about my daughter. Whoever gave you this information is well connected. Those two crewmen that just passed us won't be gone for long."

"They are very well connected, Colonel." They both smiled at his mention of her rank, and he continued, "Did you fly in directly from Russia? Are the lights still out?"

"What? Lights out?"

"As we took off from Chelyabinsk, there was some sort of EMP, and all the lights went out on the ground. Our plane experienced some issues, but we made it. I figured the Americans hit Russia in retaliation."

"I've been sitting in Gander for days and days with Boris and his goons. Had to land to refuel or crash and were immediately snowed in. Just made it here today, but the Russian general mentioned a loss of communications with his operations command in Russia."

"Well, it would seem that may be confirmation for me that the Americans hit Russia. This has an effect on the landscape, Natasha. Shall we go get our kids?"

"Da. I'll walk on your right, so those in the jet can't get a good look at me. They'll just think it's the next shift walking out. They're not very bright." They started a brisk but leisurely walk in the failing light. They did not look around. Viktor lit another cigarette, took a long pull, and exhaled a smokey stream.

"We'll have to deal with the last crewman. I'll do it," he said.

"I can do it more quietly." She reached into her jacket to her belt and drew one of the two Kizlyar knives as they approached the

Pantsir. She walked out in front of Viktor before he could say anything. The large, eight-wheeled vehicle was oriented away from them and slightly to the right, which was perfect. The driver's door and the left-side radar operator's door wouldn't be visible to the rest of the eyes behind them if they were watching.

Viktor followed her around the left side. It was tall with the missiles and two auto-cannons on top, so they were hidden. This could go sideways if the last crew member was in the driver's seat instead of in the radar compartment behind the cab... a mirror was there. There should always be someone in the windowless compartment attached to the missile launcher and guns behind the cab. He stopped just behind her and pressed himself against the side of the running, slightly vibrating vehicle, and turned his head to the right to watch and be ready to jump in if she couldn't handle whoever was inside.

Natasha took a breath and exhaled as she put her boot on the riser that ran under the radar compartment door. There wasn't a mirror or windows there, so she was still hidden from whoever was inside. She slipped through the door and snaked in, leaning left so the knife in her right hand could have more freedom of movement, to find the soldier in front of an array of screens and keyboards asleep. Even the door opening hadn't woken him. She sunk the blade into his neck as far as it would go in one smooth, violent motion.

The soldier jerked awake, grabbing at his neck as she withdrew the knife and plunged it in again through his fingers, batting away his flinging arm as she did so. Warm blood shot out of the hole in his neck, bathing her face, and she twisted the knife in his neck against his futile struggling. Soon the deed was done. She was quick, vicious, and absolutely businesslike.

"Can you drive this thing?" she asked Viktor as she stepped down, pulling the corpse after her to thud on the snow-covered ground, still except for the blood flowing from his neck. Viktor looked at the name on the uniform and the insignia.

"Poor Sergeant Orlov," he said. "Yes, I can drive it. I'll have to find the controls for the ground stabilizers, too." In its firing position, the large vehicle had four vertical steel stabilizer rods that descended hydraulically to the ground with flat feet to keep the vehicle from rocking when firing.

"Good. Let's go. Get in and give me your rifle." She climbed up into the cab and across to the passenger seat, looking in the back just to be certain there wasn't any other crew back there in the tight space behind the seats.

Viktor pulled himself up into the driver's seat as he handed her his AK-47 and shut the door. It took a moment for him to familiarize himself with the workings in the cab. There was an up/down switch on the console, which he assumed was for the stabilizers. He pressed up and heard a whining sound and then silence. He looked out the window into the mirror, and sure enough, that did the trick.

"There. We need to get on that little service road over to the right. You see it? It will lead to the perimeter road and the major highway beyond. Don't stop for anything or anyone," she said, leaning forward and looking back out through the passenger door window. "Hurry. The other crewmen look like they're on their way back."

Viktor stepped on the clutch and scraped the gearshift into first gear, and let out the clutch, giving it gas. They started to roll, and then he was into second and then third gear, heading toward the service road.

"What are they doing?" he asked.

"They're back by the jet. Just standing there and staring at their truck leaving."

"Perfect. How do you know about these roads?"

"I've studied the maps for this area for some time. It's all here." She looked over at him and tapped her forehead with a bloody finger.

"Okay, so, how far are we going? Where are they?" he asked, looking over at her calm, blood-spattered face.

"After we get on the highway, maybe ten minutes. Close." She checked the rifle to ensure it was on safe, then set it, butt down, by her feet, and held it steady between her knees as she wiped both sides of her knife on her pant leg before resheathing it.

Out of the corner of his eye, Viktor watched her lean her head back and take a deep breath.

"You alright?" he asked.

She looked over at him and smiled. "Why wouldn't I be? Drive faster. Do you have food?"

Boris had been sitting with his eyes closed in the warmth of his aircraft for what seemed like forever, but it was only twenty minutes or so. He was alone with his rage, but you wouldn't know it from looking at him. He kept his seething anger battened down. Millions of dollars of his drugs were ashes. He would visit a very Russian vengeance on his old friend, Pasha. Him and those with him. Boris didn't care about loss of comms with Russia. He had other operations in the global South he could continue.

He fiddled with the piece of paper in his hands with the address on it. They were so close. Mere miles. Yet he waited. His pilot had shown him a digital map in the cockpit of where the address was in relation to them. So close. The route was burned into his mind's eye. He didn't even need the piece of paper any longer, but he fiddled. They'd been in this plane too long. The half-dozen men in the seats behind him, along with those outside, had begun to stink many days before. It was nearly unbearable. There were cold showers of a sort they set up when at the terminal in Gander, but they couldn't do anything about their clothes.

"Boris."

He opened his eyes and found his man, Mikhail, standing next to his seat, looking down at him. His right-hand man, stocky and capable. Under that heavy coat was an array of weapons and ammunition fixed on his belt and a webbed harness. The man's AK-47 slung tight to his chest.

"What?"

"The general is outside. Wants to speak with you."

"Interesting. Let's go see what the general wants." He rose and followed Mikhail to the aircraft's door and down the few stairs to the tarmac. Snow had begun to fall while he was waiting. It was not sticking to the ground yet. The same short and grizzled man stood alone, staring at him. Boris walked over to him. He looked like someone had stolen his favorite toy.

"General. What can I do for you?" he asked cordially as he noticed several soldiers standing at a distance out of earshot, facing away from them. Guards.

"We have a problem. Your little FSB agent killed some of my men and made off with one of my anti-aircraft vehicles. What do you know about this?" The general was so angry there was spittle at the corner of his mouth as he spoke.

Natasha, what have you done? he thought.

"General, my apologies for your men. She and I had an agreement. It seems that she's disappointed us both. How can I help?" Boris asked as a truck pulled up in front of the jet. It was a Russian cargo truck, also used for troop transport.

"I want my Pantsir anti-aircraft truck back. You were going to the same place, yes? Well, go get it for me, and while there, you can take care of any business you need to. Just bring it back. I need it! Here is the truck." With that, the general stalked back across the tarmac with his detail.

"We are in business, as they say, Mikhail. Get the men ready, and let's get going. I want to be back and airborne as soon as we can be," Boris said to Mikhail as they returned to the plane. Mikhail went in first and roused his men, and they all began to sort through gear and changing into different coats or jackets, shedding their dark security detail outer wear for Russian winter camouflage military jackets. When they finished strapping on various web gear or armor plate carriers with extra magazines in pouches, they filed out of the plane. Each man had an AK-47.

Boris watched his men climb into the back of the truck. It had metal struts erected over the back area, over which was strapped a covering tarp. Once in, Mikhail lifted the tailgate and secured it, then turned to Boris.

"Mikhail, you drive. I will show you the way."

They got in, and his security chief started the engine, threw it into gear, and rolled out across the airport's expansive field until it hit the runway apron that led to a gate, which was guarded, but the guards waved them through.

"Well, Natasha, you've certainly earned your place with Pasha when I find you both," Boris said as he stared out the window as the truck gained speed.

THIRTY-THREE

The Neighborhood
Layla Washington

Standing in Lou's front yard, Layla shivered in the cold. It had been an hour since they'd buried Christopher. Lou had dug the hole with Alex near a tree on the pipestem. Sara leaned on her as they stood over the tiny grave, and Alex sat on the cold ground next to the pug's resting place with the little Yorkie, Chewbacca. They both missed their friend. It was nearly dark, and snow was again falling, but it came in waves. Heavy for a few minutes, then barely anything, but it was sticking. Mama was in her garage cooking something over the fire pit with the smoke rolling up to the slanted tarp they'd erected to catch it and send it out. Whatever it was, it smelled good.

Ahmed and Susan sat in folding chairs next to Mama in the garage, talking quietly. Lou was with Moira and Brook and their daughters, Maighen and the yet-to-be-named baby girl. The little ones were with them inside Lou's house by the fire. He'd said he needed tiny human time after burying Christopher. Nina was in the woods. She said she wanted to explore and be by herself. The snowy woods reminded her of home and her mother, Galina, who'd been killed the week before. She was having a rough time of it, and Layla decided it was best to let her have some alone time.

The teenage boys, Val and the Kinley twins, were with Sergeant Simmons and the Marines in the cul-de-sac, climbing all over the Chinese tank and one of the Chinese troop carriers. The back doors were open. They called it an APC, whatever that was. It hadn't been damaged in the fighting. It was the only thing not damaged in the fighting, she thought as she looked across the activity to Alex's house, which was partially collapsed. Well, except for the Marine's Humvee, which was parked at the top of the street.

The pistol was still on her hip, and the heavy AK-47 was slung across her back. She thought about the weight of it as she watched

Sergeant Simmons and one of his young Marines. *"Young,"* she thought. She was younger than that Marine!

"Say what again, Lance Corporal?" she heard Simmons exclaim from thirty feet away.

"The charging handle just broke, Sarge," the corporal said, handing his M-4 rifle to the sergeant so he could inspect it.

"Son. My brother in Christ, how in the Alabama fuck do you break a charging handle?" Simmons looked at the rifle in one large hand and the snapped-off charging handle in the other.

"I was cleaning it—"

"With what? A hammer? Corporal, I'm gonna call you Ricky from now on."

"Ricky, Sergeant?"

"Yeah, Ricky Retardo."

Layla watched the exchange, nearly laughing out loud.

"I don't feel retarded, S'arnt," the corporal said.

"That's a burden for the rest of us, Corporal," Simmons replied, just as a vehicle with guns and missiles on top of it turned the corner at the entrance to their street and stopped abruptly. Its headlights bright in the twilight. The Marines spread out in front of it, aiming their weapons at it as they yelled. All except the corporal who was now frantically looking around for another rifle while drawing his pistol.

"Go get Lou, Layla! Stay inside, girls!" Ahmed bellowed at her from Mama's driveway as he ran with his rifle into the court toward the commotion.

"On it!" Layla yelled back, running to Lou's front door, Sara behind her, but Alex was up and walking over to the Chinese tank.

Dammit, Alex, she thought.

"Lou, there's a military truck here. Ahmed said to get you!" she said as she ran through the front door and into the foyer of Lou's house. Lou handed the little newborn baby girl back to Brook and rose from the couch, grabbing his rifle as he hurried past the girls.

"Stay here," Lou said and left. Layla did not stay there, though. She followed Lou out the door. There she saw the headlights of what appeared to be a Russian vehicle of some sort. She'd never seen anything like it before. She ran across the cul-de-sac, following Lou to where Ahmed stood.

"Just rolled in and stopped. Marines have it in hand," Ahmed said and looked back to where he'd run from to ensure Susan and Mama were still there out of the way. The two women were standing just outside the garage, watching. Layla watched as Simmons and the Marines surrounded the truck as both front doors opened. Two sets of hands were quickly stuck up and out of the openings while the Marines yelled at them to get out and keep their hands up. They did so as the Marines moved the two people, a man and a woman, to the front of the vehicle, where they were all lit up by the truck's headlights.

"Nana!" Layla heard a voice behind him from near the Chinese tank yell out.

"That means 'Dad' in Russian, but whose dad?" Lou said. They all turned to see who yelled as Val ran past him.

"Val!" The man seemed surprised and embraced Val as he pushed past two Marines. Layla saw Lou studying the woman as this was happening and was watching her as well. She was smiling and looked around as if searching for something or someone. Her eyes settled on the destroyed house where Alex and her parents, the Russian spies, had lived.

"What's going on here? Who are you?" Lou said as he stepped into the direct light of the headlights and held up a hand to Simmons, who told his Marines to relax.

"I am Natasha Petrova, formerly a colonel of the FSB. This is Viktor Morozov, formerly a sergeant in the Russian Airborne. We've come a long way. Who are you?"

"I'm Lou. This is Ahmed. That's Sergeant Simmons, and these are his Marines. You look like you're looking for someone and it seems he already found someone," Lou said, gesturing at Val and Viktor as Layla took it all in.

"I'm Valerie's father." The man reached out a hand, and Lou shook it. "I flew in earlier today to Dulles and found Natasha there. We realized we were going to the same place, so we stole this truck, and here we are. We came to find our kids." Then he turned to Val and held the teenager's face in both hands, and kissed his forehead.

"Are you okay?" Viktor asked his son.

"I'm fine, Nana. You came to find me. I left Dedushka and came here with the astronauts and Pasha. Dedushka was good to me, but he's not a good person," Val said to his dad.

"What does that mean, Lou?" Layla asked.

"You were supposed to stay inside. It means 'grandfather' in Russian. Stay close to me," Lou said.

"I know, Val. I know. Explain astronauts to me," Viktor said.

"It's a long story and one that we'll tell you in due course," Lou said. "First, I want to know why Natasha is here. You said kids, Viktor. Plural. The only Russians around here used to live in that house. They were killed in fighting on Christmas."

Natasha grabbed Lou's arm. "The girl? Alexandra?"

"She's okay. With the other kids in my house. What's this about?" Lou asked her, and the blonde woman's face smoothed back to an icy calm.

"Alexandra is my daughter. My husband and I were forced to give her up so the FSB could send a family here as deep undercover operatives long ago," she explained, and something clicked in Layla's brain.

"Those parents were Eric and Ana then. There was someone else here a week ago asking about Alex. A Russian Spetsnaz," Lou said.

"Yes! My husband. Is he with her?"

Layla saw a glimmer of hope in the woman's eyes and knew Lou was about to crush it. The snow had started to fall harder again, and it stuck to her hair. She had what looked like smeared blood on her neck and chin, like it was wiped off, but not all the way. She figured that story would wait. FSB colonel and smeared blood. This was a hard woman, but everyone has a weakness.

"Natasha, Alex is safe, but I'm afraid your husband was killed the day after the fighting when he took one of our friends hostage," Lou said and Layla saw that hope vanish.

Natasha bowed her head. Layla saw the hard woman break in front of her. She knew that Lou was in much the same mental state after losing Robert and Christopher. Lou hugged the woman, and she melted into his shoulder and sobbed. Ahmed tapped his shoulder. Layla's happiness for Val turned into confusion and then sadness for Alex.

Could this really her real mother? she wondered.

Ahmed tapped Lou's shoulder again.

"We should get everyone in out of the cold and snow. I'm freezing," the Iranian said, when Layla heard a helicopter's beat and looked up to see navigation lights about a mile or more away. It came in fast, descending to hover above them.

Simmons walked out to the open space between the Pantsir at the top of the street and the Chinese tank and APC near the cul-de-sac and waved the helo down to sit in the middle of what was becoming a quite crowded little neighborhood. They all moved away from the landing helicopter.

Layla glanced back at Lou's house, all the kids and women were out on the front lawn now, including Sara. Everyone bathed in the headlights' glow. Layla looked around for Alex. This was going to be quite the shock for her. A silver lining, but she was already fairly broken, emotionally and mentally. She worried how Alex would take it, knowing she still had a mom.

As the rotors slowed, the side doors of the helo opened on both sides, and six men got out. One was helped out by two others, and they were lit up by the truck lights, and then everyone started running and calling out names. Layla was the first one there and ran up to Dallas, ingoring her father, and threw herself at him in a hug.

"What about me?" Gale said, standing with his arms out to his sides.

"Hi, Dad! Dallas is back!" Layla squealed happily.

"Yeah, I know. We brought him. You're welcome."

Lou laughed and slapped Gale on the back. "Her boyfriend's back. You don't rate, Gale." Her father shook his head and waited as others were reunited. Sara met her father, Javad, and they held each other in the falling snow as Ahmed joined them. Susan found her son, Dallas, which freed Layla up to hug a now happy Gale, but she kept an eye on Dallas, now with his mom. She couldn't believe he was here.

"Are you okay, Dallas?" Susan asked her son and held his face in both hands and brushed back his hair from his forehead, looking at him intently.

"I'm fine. The sergeant helped me." After a few seconds, he continued, "Mom, Dad died," Dallas said, and he broke at that point and couldn't say more. Susan hugged her son as Sergeant Bao Nguyen stepped close to them. Layla felt her eyes well up with tears.

"Ma'am, your son saved me," Bao said quietly. "I was wounded and happened to seek refuge in the house he was occupying. He bandaged me up, but I needed further medical attention, so he played along with a ridiculous idea I had, and we survived. Together. Dallas, I'm forever in your debt. You've got a good young man here."

Before he could say more, Brook walked up behind him and put a hand lightly on his shoulder. He turned around, and the sergeant and his wife said nothing to each other as they were finally reunited. He wrapped his arms around his wife and crushed her in his embrace.

"Honey, not so tight. You'll squish her," Layla heard her say softly. The sergeant apparently hadn't realized she was holding a tightly swaddled, little bundle.

"I didn't think I'd ever see you again. Sorry," he said as Brook handed him his daughter, and he took her gently and moved part of the blanket away from the little face that looked up at him, and the Marine gunnery sergeant began to cry softly. Layla was now fully sobbing. It was all too much. The losses and the reunions.

"Oh, honey, you're here now. You came back to us."

"An told me you wouldn't name her until he brought me back," he said, stroking the little baby's face with one finger.

"I want to name her Alice," Brook said.

"Alice? Why Alice?"

"It's a long story, but I like it, and it's appropriate," she responded. He smiled and leaned over and kissed her for a long moment. Layla suddenly felt awkward standing so close to this reunion.

"Alice, it is," he said and kissed his daughter on the forehead.

Layla smiled, thinking, *She named the baby after a tank. Appropriate indeed.* Now she was giggling as well as crying! She stepped away from one family reunion only to nearly get knocked over by another one.

Moira and Maighen ran up to Tavis. As he hugged his daughter, Moira yelled, "You fookin' left us here with Chinese tanks attacking us, and we had to hide in a basement. We coulda been kilt!" She was furious and shocked him with an open-handed smack across his red-bearded face. Not a lot, but enough to make her point. Then she kissed him as his twin sons sauntered over cautiously, not wanted to get caught in their mother's anger. Layla took a couple of steps back too.

"I'm here, love. I don't know I deserved that, but fair enough. You are still alive!" he chided his wife while rubbing his face and feigning injury.

"I'm sorry. Did it hurt?" she said quietly with their faces so close their frozen breath intermingled.

"Aye. A bit."

"Good."

"Da! We got a tank," Dougal said, and Duncan slapped his dad on the shoulder.

"I can see that, boys. Had some little excitement, didn't ya?" He stepped back from Moira as she raised her hand again, only partially joking.

"Come on, Da, we'll show you the tank and tell you what happened," Duncan said to his father, and Layla watched as the teenaged twins excitedly dragged Tavis to the Chinese tank, jabbering a mile a minute with his wife and daughter in tow. Layla looked at the tank. There was Alex. Her head just sticking out of one of the hatches in the turret of the tank.

"Layla, where is Nina?"

Suddenly the large Russian was at her elbow, asking for his niece. She hadn't even seen him walk up to her.

"Oh, Pasha! Scared me. Last I saw, she went for a walk in the woods to explore a bit. Should be back by now," Layla explained and pointed to the woods beyond the pipestem where Lou's house was.

"It's dark," Pasha said and walked away from the happy group toward the pipestem. Even the Marines were standing with the helicopter crew, chatting and smoking. Layla felt safe again for the first time in a while. Her dad put his arm around her shoulder and squeezed.

"Layla, I'm sorry I wasn't here," Gale said to her.

"It was pretty intense, but we were safe in the basement. The Marines took care of us. Where's Mom?"

"Your mother is helping the new president at Mount Weather right now. She's safe in the mountain. We'll see her soon."

Layla heard his words, but knew that within the last week or so, nothing had been safe. She hoped he was right.

"Nina! Nina!" Pasha was yelling his niece's name. Calling for her. Then others began to call her too.

"Go find her!" Simmons ordered his Marines, and they started to call out and walk toward the spaces between the houses.

"Uncle Pasha!" a female voice screamed from the other direction.

Pasha ran back to the group, shouting, "Nina!"

"She's here with me, Pasha." Headlights on another vehicle came on just then. It was well behind the truck with the guns and missiles on top. It had come in on the road connecting to the rest of the larger neighborhood, and no one had noticed it in the commotion. The truck was perpendicular to the street. Layla saw several men now silhouetted in the headlights, one of which was holding Nina before him with a gun to her head.

"Boris!" Pasha yelled.

"Yes, Pasha. Boris the Wolf is here," the man gripping Nina said.

THIRTY-FOUR

Battle of the Shenandoah

Sully stalked across the median of the four-lane road. The admiral was now in the LAV but not really happy about it. Rounds were still coming down on the higher elevations above them. They'd start walking them down soon. They were up the mountain a bit, so there was still some light on the west slope facing the valley. The snow had ceased its onslaught, and he could see a fair way out, but those rounds—they were problematic.

"Lieutenant! What the fuck are you doing? Do we or do we not have our own guns to fix this?" he yelled as he approached Gunderson and the Humvee.

"Sergeant, there's another forward observer north of our position out in the valley. They're calling counterbattery fire," the lieutenant replied, somewhat irritated.

"Well, tell 'em to hurry up, or we're gonna get fucking killed here."

There was a lull in the incoming rounds, and in the distance, booms drifted up from the south.

"That's them, Sergeant. Should deal with it," Gunderson said as another round landed just up the hill from them but on the road about fifty yards away. The shock wave hit them, peppering asphalt grit on the Humvee's hood. The lieutenant dropped to his knees and covered his head as Sully stood there, watching him.

"Goddammit, Lieutenant! Get up!" Sully yelled that.

The lieutenant waited. That was the only round that hit. He held up a hand and stood as he listened to the radio traffic in his headset.

"They're firing for effect now. I think we're good," the lieutenant said. "Forward Observer says rounds are on target."

"Good." Sully turned and yelled, "Sanchez! Dempsey! Get that machine gun set up in that rocky outcropping up the hill a bit." He looked around at the other men, some in their positions trying to be as small as they could, but he saw one Marine with a sniper rifle kneeling close to the tank.

"You! What's your name?" He pointed at the dark-skinned Marine.

"Sergeant Buford," he replied.

"Buford, you good with that rifle?

"Yup."

"Good, you go with Sanchez and Dempsey over there and get yourself up in one of those trees or a high vantage so you can cover the river and bridge. Got night vision?"

"Copy and yep," Buford replied and jogged off to follow the two paratroopers off the road and up the hill.

"Sullivan! Tank on the road heading this way. He's way out there still. Got him on thermal. It looks like an American!" An yelled to Sully from the commander's hatch on the Abrams. Sully could see the Abram's turret slowly traversing, tracking this new target.

Wu was sitting in the commander's hatch of his Abrams as the tank sped down the eastbound lanes of the four-lane divided highway. He was frustrated. He was sure he'd be able to see his quarry at some point across the valley they'd just crossed, but no luck so far. They were approaching what his map said was the Shenandoah River. A bridge would take them over it and up this small mountain looming in front of them. His gunner was traversing the turret right and left, looking for targets, and keeping awake. The tank rode softly and smoothly even though they were pushing its maximum speed. It was sort of rhythmic, and he struggled to keep his eyes open. The mountain in front of them was just visible in the twilight, hitting it from behind them.

"Tank! Ten o'clock! Four hundred meters!" his gunner yelled, snapping him out of his stupor. He slid down to look through his commander's sights to verify, and when he did, his blood ran cold.

"Confirm tank! Loader, load sabot!" he ordered.

"Captain, there are now three tanks in my sights. They're Chinese Type-99! Those are ours!" his gunner said with excitement.

"We're in an American tank, dammit! They don't know we're friendly!" Wu yelled as the first two Chinese tanks rolling across a field to their left both fired. In the horrifying few seconds it took the rounds to travel, Wu had just enough time to curse.

"Sullivan!" Sully turned to see the gunny in the tank waving at him. He jogged over, and the gunny pointed to the tank's rear and held up an imaginary phone. Ah. The soldier phone. He walked behind the tank, boots crunching slush and snow, and grabbed the handset for dismounted infantry.

"What's up?" Sully said. The metal phone was freezing cold on his ear.

"We just saw an Abrams on the road coming to the bridge get hit twice and killed. I think I know who that was, and it wasn't an American. Long story. That means Chinese tanks are near."

"Okay, I'll let the guys know action is imminent."

"Hey, tell the TOW guys to use their rounds first. It's unfortunate, but they're gonna get knocked out before us. Use 'em while we can. They can't see us here with these tall trees next to us and the trees on the other side of the river. Only when they get out onto the main road and onto the bridge will we be visible. And them to us," An said.

"Copy." Sully put the phone back in its cradle. At least the artillery had stopped falling. He ran to the Humvee with the TOW missiles on top, and the busy Marines all stopped what they were doing to focus on Sully.

"Okay, listen up. Chinese tanks are coming. I want you all to hit those tanks only when they get out onto the bridge. The mission is to block that bridge with dead tanks. Copy?"

"Roger that, S'arnt!" one said, and the rest nodded.

"Fire as fast as you can once they're on the bridge, and when you're out of missiles, find a hole and get ready to hold what you have."

"Against tanks?" one asked.

"That's why we have her." Sully thumbed over his shoulder at Alice.

"A'ight, then," the Marine said stoically as a shot rang out, and one of Sully's men a bit further down the hill cried out.

"I'm hit!" the paratrooper screamed, and they all ducked.

"Medic! Get to that man," Sully yelled, and the large Scandinavian medic, Sergeant Hagen, sprinted from his position down to where the wounded man was.

"Buford! Sniper down by the river somewhere! Find him!" Sully yelled up the side of the hill where Sanchez, Dempsey, and Buford had made their perch. Buford was now up in a tree. Sully could barely make him out with the light failing now.

Crack!

"Got him!" Buford's voice came down from the hill. "Sergeant, I've got a whole shit-load of Chinese armor coming up the road and through the fields now. Gonna get sporty!"

"Don't fire yet! Let the trap spring!" Gunderson yelled to Sully, who was straining his eyes to see the Chinese tanks approaching the bridge, just as dozens of missiles sprang from concealed positions all along the opposite, south side of the main road and further to the north on the far side of the Chinese tanks. It was mostly dark now so the missiles presented quite a show.

Sully couldn't tell exactly, but there had to be a couple of dozen Chinese tanks out there. Who knew how many more were behind them? *Well, this sucks*, he thought, as Javelin anti-tank missiles began to hit the tanks from above and smaller LAW anti-tank missiles slammed into the tanks from the sides. In just seconds, bright explosions and fire illuminated the road and fields across the river, revealing more than a dozen tanks burning. It lit up the situation perfectly.

"Sullivan! You better get up here!" Buford yelled from up the hill. Sully humped down the small dip off the side of the road and up the hill through the trees. Snow made the going difficult, and he hadn't realized how far up they'd gone to position themselves. It was a ways. After falling and slipping for a long minute, he was there by the large rocks that Sanchez and Dempsey had set up their machine gun on. Buford was up the large tree just behind him.

"Look out there, Sergeant," Buford called, and Sully gazed across the fields and hedges that made up this part of the massive valley. Tanks and armored personnel carriers burned all over it. He could hear more explosions coming from further north. It was all lit up with the fire.

"Well, shit," Sully muttered. Moving fast in and between the dozens of burning Chinese vehicles were even more Chinese tanks. But they were indeed moving or being pushed toward the river. He could see it all from up here.

"How many you think, S'arnt?" Dempsey asked.

"That's at least a brigade's worth of armor. I suspect more behind," Sully said as a Chinese Type-99 tank appeared in the field next to the road and bridge. It came out of the tall tree line next to the river.

"TOW Team! Your first target is coming up on the bridge!" he yelled down as the tank pivot-turned onto the road and started rolling out onto the bridge. This was going to get close. The tank was halfway across the bridge, and Sully started to yell again when a flash from the road below him provided the acknowledgment he wanted. The wire-guided TOW missile shot from its launcher, lighting up the Humvee, and streaked down to the bridge, hitting the tank right where the turret met the hull just to the right of the driver's hatch. The resulting explosion blew the two hatches on top of the turret off, and it rolled to a stop, burning.

"Fuck yes! Homies killin' it!" Sanchez exclaimed.

"More tanks behind that one," Sully said, pointing.

"They're gonna have to kill a lot of tanks to block that bridge, Sully," Dempsey said. "It's pretty fuckin' wide."

Gunfire erupted from the far side of the river. None hit up where they were but sprayed across the road further down. Clear muzzle flashes reflected off the water.

"Sanchez, light 'em up," Sully said, and Sanchez fired the machine gun in arcs across the far bank as more tanks appeared on the road, lit up by their burning comrades in the first tank. These picked the other span to cross, but there were a lot of them now. Sully counted four when another TOW streaked down the mountain, killing another tank on the other span. He saw now what Dempsey was saying. They'd killed two, one on each span of the bridge, but there was plenty of room on each side of both burning tanks to drive around. That's just what the others were doing as another TOW hit another tank, knocking a tread off but not killing it. That tank returned fire, hitting the Humvee, causing a large explosion.

"Fuck!" Sully said as a round from Alice hit that same tank and destroyed it spectacularly.

Then several tanks on the bridge eased themselves around their burning comrades, and a couple fired. One round hit near Alice, and the other one winged the LAV in its rear side, ricocheting off into the woods. The LAV returned fire with its 20mm cannon. Most rounds did no damage as they hit their targets, but hopefully, it was causing them to panic a bit. Maybe.

Alice's main gun roared again and another Chinese tank erupted in flames. To Sully, from his elevated position, it looked like the southern span of the bridge was blocked by burning tanks. It was the northern span, on his right, that was fairly open and they were starting to exploit it.

"Cherry Pie" by Warrant drifted through the battle's thunder, and Alice's main gun expelled another round into another tank on the bridge. Sully could do nothing. Sanchez was suppressing Chinese fire on the other side of the river. Buford's rifle cracked with a quick cadence. His men, yes they were all his men now, Marines and Airborne, were in it and coming out with the short fucking stick. If they lost Alice, they were done.

Sully glanced over to their tank and she was backing up quickly, firing as she went. He looked back to the bridge and his heart sank. There were two Chinese tanks across it now. There was a single passable bit of bridge left and they were coming through it. Alice was fighting the two already across. Trading rounds in the chaos.

"They're coming up!" he heard Buford yell above him.

"I see it!" Sully said, his heart in his throat.

"Keep backing up, Fletch! Slowly now. The angle is nearly there," An said as the tank rolled backward to get a shot at the tank coming up the hill. There it was. Jones fired the main gun and An was rewarded with a hit.

"We got six rounds left—three sabot, three HEAT!" Stewie said.

"There's too many of them, and they're coming through that gap on the near side of the bridge. We're gonna have to get in there, guys. Driver, forward fast now! All the way down and plug that hole. It's the only way. Gunner, target tanks on this side of the bridge as we go around that right curve, then traverse right and fire at will!" An ordered.

"This is gonna suck," Stewie said.

Sully was about give the order to fall back when he saw Alice barrelling past their position going down the hill, speakers blaring "Jerry Was a Race Car Driver" by Primus. The tank fired as it rolled. Sully was dumbstruck. They were going to plug the gap.

"Out of ammo!" Sanchez yelled.

"Looks like the Marines and their tank are going to save our asses again," Sully said and pointed down the hill where Alice was engaged now with a third tank that had gotten across the river, but they were hiding behind another burning Chinese tank, playing peek-a-boo. But there were just too many on the bridge.

That's when something shiny reflected the light from all the fires, streaked in low over the river, and hit the north span of the bridge. *BOOM!* A massive fireball blossomed, almost too bright to see.

"The fuck was that?!" Dempsey said.

"Navy's here, boys!" Buford yelled down from his tree. "There's another one!"

A second Tomahawk missile, fired from out in the Atlantic by the USS *Virginia*, hit the north span again a bit more on their side of the river. Two more came in after that, hitting what was left of the north span and digging into the south span. Sully watched as the entire section furthest from their side disappeared into the river. Burning tanks falling with it.

But Alice was still trading rounds with a lone Chinese tank on Sully's side of the river. The Chinese tank fired, and Alice's butt was sticking out a bit too far from the cover of the dead tank she was hiding behind. The round hit the back of her turret, exploding on the armor and destroying the speakers. The music died, but Alice rolled forward out of cover. Her turret traversed quick and fired. The Chinese tank exploded, adding fuel and flames to the other raging fires around it.

Sully surveyed the situation as an explosion to his left knocked him down and he almost rolled down the hill. He shook his head. His ears were ringing. Gaining his footing again, he looked across the river. There was a mass of Chinese armor in the field and on the road on the other side of the bridge. They couldn't get across but they could still kill his men. Or, kill more of them. He looked at the road and saw the lieutenant standing behind the LAV and he started to run down the hill. It took him less than a minute to reach Gunderson, but in that time more rounds from the Chinese armor hit the hill and the road below him.

"Lieutenant!" Sully yelled as he got to the LAV just as a large explosion hit in the middle of the Chinese armor. Gunderson ignored Sully.

"Fire for effect!" he yelled into the radio then looked up at Sully. The lieutenant had blood running from his left ear and multiple lacerations on his face and neck, but smiled at Sully.

"What are you smiling for? We need artillery!" Sully yelled.

Gunderson only smiled wider as artillery rounds whistled in. The barrage lasted for several minutes as Sully and Gunderson watched in morbid fascination. And then Sully realized that the admiral was here, standing next to him on her crutches.

"Well, that was fun. Nothing like being in a big bullet magnet," the admiral said as the artillery barrage stopped. She was standing awkwardly, supporting herself with her crutches, dangling one leg in a half-cast. Her curly brown hair was loose and in disarray. They were illuminated, even at this distance, by the fires on what was left of the bridge and the remnants of the Chinese armor on the other side.

"What?" Gunderson said.

"I said, that was fun!"

"Admiral, we should get you back to the complex and let them know what's going on," Sully said. "The lieutenant is probably pretty deaf at the moment. He could probably use some medical attention. And my men—"

"Sergeant, you can call me Joey. Until a week ago, I was floating in outer space. We're not gonna be all formal here," she said, as they watched Alice roll up the hill and halt next to the LAV. Then the screams of the wounded began.

THIRTY-FIVE

Boris the Wolf

It was full dark now in the cul-de-sac. Boris stood in front of the truck at the top of the street. The girl, Nina, struggled some, but not much. He had her by the hair in one hand with his Makarov 9mm pistol pointed at her head in the other hand. All of these traitors were out in front of him.

"Pasha! Where is my airplane? It has my shipment in it. I want it back. In return, I'll give you your niece," Boris lied. He wanted to toy with them. See if they lied to him or not.

"Boris, you don't have to do this. Your plane is safe with its shipment just south of here," Pasha said in reply.

Ah, poor Pasha.

"Oh, I know where it is. I was there. You burned it to the ground along with my drugs!" Boris yelled back. He was breathing heavily now, knowing what would happen next. He turned his head to look at the truck and his men array in and around it. The flap facing his enemies was open now, revealing two machine guns at the ready.

"You don't have to do this, Boris! Take me. We didn't burn it. It was on fire when we landed. It wasn't our fault," Pasha yelled back.

"You betrayed me, Pasha! You took what was mine after I helped you and your friends." Boris searched the others in front of him and found his grandson.

"Val! You come to me now," he ordered.

"No, Boris, I don't think so!" Viktor yelled back, stepping in front of his son as the others around him began to slowly move to the cover of the APC.

"Ah! My precious son-in-law has returned. Perfect!"

"I won't go with you," his grandson said, which Boris ignored.

"Where are your two astronaut friends, Pasha?" Boris continued.

"Joey isn't here, but I am," Tavis said and walked around the tank. Boris watched him carefully. He also saw two figures climbing on the tank, one on top and one on the front. Then they disappeared from view. Another two figures, women they looked like, ran from the tank to the other armored vehicle in front of him and disappeared.

"Ah, Tavis Kinley. We also have business to finish."

"If it's payback you want, you take me and Pasha. Leave the rest alone and let the girl go."

Boris listened to the Scotsman talk. Others were moving in front of him. They were twenty to thirty meters away, fading in and out of the shadows of the headlights that reflected off the helicopter.

Enough of this.

"I will take what is owed, Pasha! You remember why they call me the Wolf, yes?" Boris yelled. He pulled the trigger of the pistol that was against the girl's temple. She dropped to the ground as he released her hair at the same time as a round hit him in arm. He heard screaming and more muffled shots. Even as he moved, he saw Natasha firing her suppressed pistol at him, the rest of her rounds missing.

His men opened up with the two machine guns, scattering all in front of him as he stepped over the dead girl's body. He was grabbed by one of his men and rushed to cover in front of a Humvee, while another of his men fired his AK-47 on full automatic down the street.

"What do we do?" Alex screamed in the cramped turret. Duncan and Dougal were in there with her. One twin in the turret and the other in the driver's seat.

"Dougal, can you hear me?" Duncan yelled.

"Aye!" came the reply.

"Do you remember what the Marines showed us? Do you remember how to start—"

The tank's engine roared to life.

"Got it, Duncan! What now? I can see through these sights!" Dougal yelled. It was muffled from up front, but Duncan and Alex heard him.

"WE'VE GOT A TANK!" Duncan yelled and Alex laughed for the first time in days.

Lou and Ahmed saw the man shoot Nina and reacted at the same time, grabbing everyone around them and pushing them quickly to the armored personnel carrier and into the back and relative safety. As they went, Lou saw one of the helo pilots go down and there were also Marines down. They weren't alone in the back.

"Who are those fuckers? He shot that girl in the head, man! Brook, cover the baby's ears!" Bao said as machine gun rounds ricochetted off the APC's armor. Lou saw Brook toward the front of the APC, huddled with her little girl, her hands over the baby's ears. Javad was here with Sara. Dallas with Susan, who also had those little kids, the boy and girl.

"I don't know! Where's everyone else? Gale? Layla? Tavis and his wife and kids? We have to go out there!" Lou yelled. The machine gun fire was constant, but rounds were no longer hitting the APC.

"Ahmed, my friend, you certainly chose an odd little neighborhood," Javad said as Lou grabbed Ahmed's arm.

"Big man! You stay with them. Keep them safe. You! Gunny! With me! Out and to the right. We'll still have cover there," Lou said, and Bao nodded and flicked the selector on his M-4 from safe to fire, and followed Lou out into the chaos. What they found left Lou speechless.

From the cover of the front of the APC, Layla was firing her AK steadily at the truck with the machine guns, and Gale was right there next to her, firing a pistol in the same direction. Huddled on the ground next to the APC was Moira and her daughter, who was screaming. Lou pulled Bao around the other side of the APC, where the back doors were still open, and peeked around.

The remaining helo crew and Natasha were pinned down in front of the anti-aircraft vehicle. Lou found his targets next to the Humvee, and fired several rounds, with Bao beside him joining in. The machine gun fire stopped, and he quickly stuck his head out and let out an involuntary laugh in the midst of the remaining gunfire.

The Chinese tank was rolling into the machine gun truck. He watched as first the tank's main gun went through the side of the truck and then the front of the tank hit the truck's side, violently and at full speed. It was no match. The truck tipped over as the tank's treads caught the side of the truck and climbed up and over it with a satisfying crunch.

Several men had jumped from the truck's bed and were cut down by him and Bao, along with continuous gunfire from Layla and Gale. Men screamed from under the tank and then—silence.

Rounds suddenly struck the APC's door next to his head, and he ducked back, pulling Bao with him.

"Boris! We have to go. Get in the Humvee. It's armored. Truck is gone," Boris heard one of the two men with him say. The other one was providing cover fire. Boris complied and he and the man who spoke crawled in the passenger door. His man was in first and climbed over to the driver's seat and slapped around for the engine start button and finally found it. Boris was in the passenger seat and slammed the door shut. The rear passenger door opened and the other man was about to get in.

"Mikhail! Mikhail! Come! We're leaving!" Boris heard the man call to his loyal second-in-command. He strained to see out the driver's side window and there was Mikhail standing in the street, taking off his heavy jacket, shouting, "Go, my brothers! Get Boris to the plane! I will finish this!"

His man got in the back of the Humvee and pulled the armored door shut. The man in the driver's seat put the vehicle in gear and they sped up the street and away from the tank and the crushed truck.

"God dammit!" Boris yelled. Then he felt pain in his arm and reached up to feel what it was. His hand came away with blood on it.

"You've been hit, Boris!" the driver said as he sped down the road and took several turns to get to the main four-lane, divided highway in the direction of the airport.

"I'm okay. It's just a scratch. That bitch shot me. Get to the airport and the plane. We are going home," Boris said and punched the dash with his bloody hand in a fury.

Tavis stood in the remaining truck's headlights. He was pointing his FAL rifle at the last remaining goon. The man dropped his AK and removed his jacket, revealing a webbed vest with AK magazines. He stared at Tavis, then pointed.

"Just you and me, Scotsman."

"Aye!" Tavis replied, looking past the man to Nina's lifeless body. He dropped his rifle and put his hand on the hilt of his Kukri the man had pointed at.

"I win, I walk."

"You're Mikhail, right? Boris's right-hand man?"

"Da."

"Deal."

"No!" Tavis heard his wife's voice behind him while the large Chinese tank approached, turning behind Mikhail. He could only assume that his boys were in there. A sense of pride washed over him and he bent his knees, right arm out, left hand ensuring the Kukri was loose in its scabbard. Mikhail pulled a large machete from its upside-down scabbard on his web vest and wasted no time, striking first with a yell. The machete came down as Mikhail closed the distance quicker than Tavis had anticipated.

In one smooth motion, he drew the Kukri. It was backward in his hand, blade toward the incoming machete. There were two little notches in the Kukri's blade near the handle at the bottom of the blade. They were sword-breaking notches, meant to catch Japanese swords in World War II. They worked just as well on machetes. The blades met with a spark and the machete's blade slid down and into the first notch.

Tavis violently twisted his wrist and the notch locked the other's blade into it and it twisted easily from Mikhail's hand. The blade flew to the ground. Mikhail was startled for a second, but tried to grab Tavis with his other hand. Tavis withdrew his Kukri hand and quickly repeated the same motion he'd just done to disarm the man. This time, even as the man's hand reached his face to poke him in the eye with a thumb, his Kukri blade struck diagonally from one side of Mikhail's face and up to the other, splitting the man's screaming mouth and nose open with a spray of warm blood.

Tavis stepped sideways, flipping the Kukri around in his hand and coming down and through the man's arm that was attached, for the moment, to the hand that grabbed Tavis's beard. The arm was severed cleanly at the forearm, and both the hand and Mikhail fell to the ground. The man's screams of agony went unnoticed by Tavis, who flicked the Kukri with a twist of his wrist, watching the blood on it fly from the blade. He resheathed it, its job done.

Meanwhile that leviathan of a Chinese tank was coming at him and not stopping and he heard one of his sons yelling, "Brakes! Where's the bloody brakes?!"

Tavis ran toward the oncoming tank and jumped up onto the front, landing on his stomach, and hooked a hand into the open driver's hatch. He pulled himself to the opening. His son, Dougal, was frantically trying to stop the inexorably rolling tank.

"Just push the engine start button that you used to start it!" Tavis yelled.

Relieved, Dougal reached over and pushed the button. The tank's engine died and it slowed to a stop. Tavis tussled his son's hair.

"Good job, buddy," he said and slid from the front of the tank and walked around the side to look for Pasha. There, underneath the tank's tread, was what was left of Mikhail. The tank had run him over midsection. His upper torso and head were visible. His legs crushed.

"Aye! When you all get out, get down on the other side!" Tavis yelled to the boys and Alex, who had just popped up out of one of the turret hatches and yelled, "That was awesome!"

Then he saw Pasha. His friend had picked up his niece and was walking in circles in the lights from the anti-aircraft vehicle. The snow had started falling heavy again, giving the scene a ghostly appearance. He approached slowly and put his arm around the Russian.

"I could not protect her. I could not protect her mother. I have nothing. I am nothing," Pasha said, droning on in his sorrow.

"You need to put her down and I will help you dig her grave. There is nothing more to do. We did all we could."

"I cannot put her down. Ground is cold. She will be cold. I have to keep her warm," Pasha said quietly.

Tavis's eyes welled and he put his hands on Pasha's shoulders, now standing in front of him, and squeezed gently.

"She's no longer here, brother. She's with her mother and safe now. Safe from all of this."

"We do this now. Her grave," Pasha said and looked at Tavis. His eyes were empty, deeply empty.

Behind them, someone screamed. Tavis turned to see that his wife and daughter had discovered Mikhail under the tread.

"Get away from there!" Tavis yelled and they quickly went back behind the APC, but others came out. Gale and Lou and the big Iranian—he forgot his name. "Others." Tavis's head was swirling, so he focused on the one thing he knew: *Do the next needful thing.*

"I need shovels. To dig a resting place for this gentle soul," Tavis said to all of them and they just stood there looking at him. "NOW!" he yelled a bit more angry than he'd wanted, but he felt for his friend.

"Come on, Ahmed, the shovels are in my garage," Lou said. The two jogged off to get them.

"We can put her next to Christopher, the pug. She liked him and they'll be together," Layla said with tears running down her face as she walked up to Pasha as someone yelled, "MEDIC!"

Tavis stayed with Pasha as the rest ran to the wounded.

After having to yell at the guards manning the airport's gate, Boris and his two remaining men pulled up to his plane at Dulles Airport. His pilot met him at the bottom of the stairs that led into the cabin.

"We are refueled and ready to take off, Boris," the pilot said as Boris exited the Humvee.

"Good. Get us out of here. Just get us up. I will tell you where when we're up," Boris growled and climbed the stairs followed by his men, then the pilot, who raised the stairs and secured the door. Boris found his seat and waved away medical attention from one of his men. He poured himself a vodka and downed it. Poured another and let it sit as the plane began to roll down the runway.

"Poor Pasha. There is always a price for disloyalty. There must be payment. Now you live with it," Boris said under his breath. He felt the plane rise into the air and bank gently to the right.

Three of them had dug the grave in short order, Gale thought. Simmons and Ahmed had done the lion's share. It was one of the most difficult things he'd ever done. As he dug, he thought what he would do if this had been Layla. None of them had dry eyes when they'd finished. Susan and Moira had taken care of Nina's body. They wrapped her tight in bedsheets and laid her next to where Christopher was buried. Pasha knelt over her, lightly touching her wrapped face and whispering something.

Gale stood there, leaning on his shovel; Layla leaning on him. He put an arm around her. She shouldn't have had to grow up so quickly and violently like this. They'd get Joey back and never be apart again. This was his vow.

It had all gone so quick. Only thirty minutes or so ago, there was a firefight right here in his cul-de-sac. Again.

The snow had stopped and it was silent. That's when he heard the sound of a jet in the distance.

"That has to be his plane!" It was Natasha that had been helping with one of the wounded Marines up the street by the helicopter. Pasha's head snapped up at that and he stood and turned.

"The Pantsir!" the newcomer, Viktor, yelled and sprinted to the truck with the guns and missiles on top of it. Natasha met him there. It took a second for Gale to figure out what was going on as Pasha left his niece and ran to the vehicle. Gale found himself running with him. By the time he got there, Viktor had started the truck's engine and Natasha was in the rear compartment. Pasha got there just before he did and he found more confusion. Mostly on his part because they were all yelling at each other in Russian.

"English please! What's going on?" Gale demanded.

"That is Boris's aircraft," Natasha replied. "We're trying to figure out how to shoot the bastard out of the sky. Now, quiet!"

Gale stepped back from the three Russians and looked up. The plane was close and low, but climbing. He could tell because the plane's running lights were on. It was only a mile or so away and banking slightly. It was going from left to right in the sky, so its banking kept it close. He heard a whining sound and turned. The guns and missiles on top of the truck were quickly turning with a flat radar dish. It swiveled swiftly towards the aircraft and he heard more yelling.

"Auto! Auto! That button!" Viktor yelled at Natasha. Pasha stepped away and joined Gale watching the plane as it passed them.

"Yes! Lock!" Natasha exclaimed.

Gale held his breath for what seemed like minutes, but it was only two seconds until one missile, then another, leaped off their rails and shot into the sky.

"This button. Manual. Do it!" Viktor said and she must have, because a deafening ripping sound made him jump and cover his ears. He watched tracers burst into the sky following the plane until there were several sparks up there, just as one missile seemed to close with and stop right underneath the plane. Then it exploded.

The other missile followed its twin into the fireball and added to the carnage, making for a brilliant, fiery display.

Natasha and Viktor joined them in the street and yelled what he could only assume were Russian curses at the flaming plane falling to the ground.

Gale turned to Pasha and said, "He's dead in a bunch of pieces, Pasha."

The big Russian stared at the falling wreckage until it was out of sight.

"Boris the Wolf. There is always a price, and payment must be made," Pasha said and walked back to where his niece lay.

THIRTY-SIX

Aftermath

The sun was rising over Mount Weather. The snow storm had passed in the wee hours of the morning. Joey stood on the helicopter pad, leaning on one of her crutches, looking out over the rolling eastern hills. She adjusted her weight, her booted foot crunching the icy snow. To her left was the LAV facing away from her. The rear doors were open. Lieutenant Gunderson was fast asleep in a chair. His radio on his lap, headset on his head. Alice was next to the LAV. There were more tanks, LAVs, and Humvees arrayed in defensive positions further down the access road.

She'd been out here for a couple of hours now. Watched Gunnery Sergeant Nguyen and his tank crew transfer main gun rounds from other tanks to Alice an hour earlier. They'd all been down inside the complex moving the wounded into the infirmary and getting food and coffee for the others that weren't wounded. Those men were back out here now with their vehicles. She'd been wondering all morning why the helicopter hadn't returned. Cigarette smoke filled her nose, reminding her she wasn't alone. She looked at the four men with her. They were all smoking. She'd never seen a United States president smoke. Likely many had, just not standing next to her. The CIA director, Sergeant Sullivan, and An were all puffing away with the president, blowing their smoke out in front of them to mingle with her own frozen breath.

"You know, I was thinking, we're all alive right now and there's not Chinese crawling all over my mountain because some astronauts escaped a crippled space station and a Scotsman had a sat phone. Paratroopers from Afghanistan came across the world and took out bridges, and a single tank saved us all. I need a fucking drink," President Madison said dryly.

Jack pulled an already opened, slim bottle of MacCallan 12 out of his jacket pocket and handed it to the president.

"Don't forget about that Marine Expeditionary Force from Lejeune that we pinned all our hopes on but didn't know where the hell they were," Jack said.

Madison took the bottle, uncorked it, and took a short pull from it directly, then handed it to Sully who took a drink and gave it to An.

"Yeah, I went all the way to Fort Knox and got back just in time before the whole valley got blowed up," An said and took a drink and handed it to Joey.

"You couldn't write this shit in a Clancy novel," the president said.

"Excuse me, Mr. President—my name is Jack, and I'm the CIA Director," Jack said. Joey was mid-drink and nearly choked to death.

"Where is the fucking general?" the president asked after he recovered.

"Gunderson said he had to backtrack from north of here to a bridge to the south and come in the back way. Apparently, they pushed the Chinese forces way back," Sully responded.

"Ask and ye shall receive. The devil comes dancing in," Jack said, pointing at several Humvees coming up the access road. They all turned and waited, passing the bottle around again. Three Humvees pulled up and Madison raised his hand in greeting. They stopped next to the group and a short Marine in full battle gear got out of the first Humvee. He walked around the vehicle and stopped in front of the group.

"I'm looking for President Madison. General Kobayashi, Marine Expeditionary Force," the man said, a large scar tracing across his Japanese features.

"President James Madison, General Kobayashi. Great to see you here. Want a drink?" Madison said, stepping forward to shake the general's hand. Joey held out the bottle of Scotch, and the general took it.

"Looks like this is gonna be a nice little party. I love MacCallan," the general said in a deep Southern drawl and took a drink. Joey found his accent surprising but oddly comforting. They spent a few minutes on introductions and explaining where everyone had come from to pull all this off.

"That's some crazy shit," Kobayashi said.

"Yeah, it's true," Joey said.

"Weren't you in space a little over a week ago?" the general asked.

"I was, but I'd like to get back to my family now. Just out there about twenty miles," Joey said and pointed out over the rolling hills.

"Admiral, I think I've found your relief. General, you're now my Chairman of the Joint Chiefs and, well, of everything. Please relieve the admiral," the president said.

"You are relieved. Also, this is what I want. We hear there's some Marines that fucking walked from Quantico and engaged whoever, Chinese or Russians, that are occupying Dulles Airport and the surrounds. We've established lines up north and there are units with armor and artillery moving south of here to clear them out. I've brought another few units with me. They're setting up positions below the mountain here." He looked around. "Who do the Abrams and LAV belong to?"

"That would be me, sir. Gunnery Sergeant Nguyen." They shook hands. "Me and my Marines—" An pointed over to the tank where his crew, Buford and Nelson along with Dempsey and Sanchez, were standing in a group, smoking and watching them. Dempsey waved at them.

"You defended this mountain and piled them up on the bridge with that crew?" the general said and held up the bottle to the other group in congratulations.

"Sir, we had Sergeant Sullivan's men and your Lieutenant Gunderson calling fire, helping us. But to answer your question, yes," An said.

The general hadn't given the bottle back to anyone and took another long drink from it.

"Well, damn," he said. "Tell you what, why don't you and your men escort the admiral home to her family as advance recon for my units that will start that way tomorrow. It'll take my Southern force some time to get across the state anyway. You, you're not Marine Corps. Who are you?" the general asked Sully.

"First Sergeant Sullivan, sir. You can call me Sully."

"Ah, now I'm putting it together. Your boys dropped in on those bridges from Bagram."

"Correct, sir."

"Fuck me," he said and took another drink from the bottle, this time handing it to Sully.

"General, would you join me inside please? We've got things to discuss. Joey, I can't thank you enough. You, your husband and that Scottish astronaut of yours saved our asses. Indebted to you. Pass my regards to them," Madison said.

"Get her home, guys. Sully, you and your boys go with them," the general said.

"Yessir!" An replied and he and Sully saluted and left the group to wake up and round up their people in the vehicles.

As Joey started to walk away with An and Sully, she heard the general say, "Mr. President, your name is a good omen."

"Ha! Yours as well, General. No-win scenario, indeed," Madison said.

Tavis was up early with everyone else. There was work to do in the cul-de-sac after the prior night's firefight. Gruesome work. He, Simmons, and Bao had moved the Chinese tank and went about the nasty task of putting the large pieces of Mikhail on a couple of bedsheets, then scraped the middle, squishy remnants off the asphalt street and in with the rest of him. While they were cleaning that up, Tavis looked around at the other activity. Bouncer and the chief were working on something on the helo's engine. They said it was minor, but nothing on a helo was minor.

The smell of meat cooking and some sort of Mexican aromas were coming from the fire pit on Mama's driveway. Brook was there with her, holding Alice, the baby girl. Layla and Sara were setting up plastic plates and utensils on a folding table near them. Breakfast was coming. He didn't know if he'd be able to eat after scraping Mikhail off the ground, but he'd try. His wife, daughter, and boys were still asleep in Lou's house by the fire.

Viktor had been moving the bodies of Boris's goons with all the now-frozen Iranians and Russians into Alex's partially collapsed house. The Marines that weren't wounded or dead had helped him, along with Lou and Ahmed. They'd left Alex's parents—or now that he knew the story, her adopted parents—where they lay. Also Donneker, Susan's ex-husband. Dennis was there, Gale's former boss. Duck, the helo's co-pilot, and several Marines. Bibi had also been brought out. They'd bury them all later that day. A lot of digging. Many lost. He was thankful to God that his family, with all they'd been through, were all okay and safe now.

He glanced over to where the remaining lay between the houses. Alex was there on her knees with Natasha next to her. They were talking quietly. He couldn't hear them. The girl had been through quite a bit. He hoped she'd be alright as he watched the two. Alex leaned sideways and rested her head on Natasha's arm and the older woman cradled her as she cried, stroking her blonde hair and kissing her head.

"Bao! My son, come over and eat. Breakfast is ready," Mama yelled from her driveway.

"Feed the others first, Mama," Bao replied.

"Don't talk back to your mama! Get over here. I have you back safe with Brook and Alice. You eat now!" she scolded the Gunny.

Tavis laughed. "Go get your food, man. We'll take care of this. Don't talk back to your mother," Tavis ribbed him as Lou approached from Alex's house.

"Oh, breakfast! All the bodies are in the house. Can we get one of your Marines to use that tank to push the rest of the walls into a pile in the middle? We'll douse it with gasoline," Lou said to Simmons.

"For sure, Lou. I'll do it myself and then toss a Willie Pete in there," Simmons said, referring to a white phosphorous incendiary grenade.

"Just wait for all of us to eat breakfast first. Burning bodies will spoil appetites," Tavis said.

"Roger that," Simmons replied and went to the tank and squeezed his large frame through the driver's hatch. The tank's engine came to life and Simmons went about his task. Tavis and Lou carried the bundle of Mikhail over to Alex's house and tossed it into a hole in the floor where they'd dumped the other bodies, then jumped out of the way as Simmons toppled the last wall on top of the hole. They walked back over to the smell of food. Tavis saw Javad was there and was refusing a plate of food from Mama.

"No! You take it. Build your strength," Mama said. No one argued with Mama. Javad took the plate and bowed his head in thanks. Ahmed stood next to Javad, who gestured around the cul-de-sac.

"I am the cause of all of this. Humbled by your generosity," the older man said.

"Let it go, my friend. We are safe now. As you said before, it would have happened anyway, and you sending us here saved us from death in Iran," Ahmed said to Javad.

"Yeah, you're an American citizen now, with Ahmed here and your daughter. All is well," Tavis said.

"Javad, what you actually did was save us all by your actions," Gale put in. "Yes, you were part of planning the attack, but you also tried to warn us. You're good in my book."

"Sara, Layla, take these plates for the wounded Marines in Lou's house and wake up those kids. Tell Moira there's food," Mama ordered.

"Yes, ma'am," Layla replied and they each took two plates of food and went to Lou's house next door.

In all of this work and smells of food, Tavis had forgotten about Pasha. He followed the girls over to Lou's house with his eyes and found him. He was sitting in a folding chair next to his niece's grave with his head down. Tavis grabbed a plate of Mexican food. They still had a good deal of frozen meat and vegetables stored outside in coolers packed with ice and snow. Should last a good while, but then they'd have to get into the large stash of freeze-dried food and MREs from the neighbor's basement. Floyd was his name, he remembered, as he approached Pasha.

Just then his family burst through Lou's front door, along with his wife. Layla and Sara came out behind them with the two little ones, Carly and her younger brother, Stevie. He was about to hand Pasha the plate when Carly walked up to him and tapped him on the arm.

"Uncle Pasha, you can have this back. It will make you happy." Carly put the little, round plushy panda in Pasha's upturned hand as he looked up. He wrapped the little girl up in his arms and squeezed the plushy. Tavis noticed there was dark brown dried blood on the plushy that Pasha held so tightly.

"Thank you, little one. It does make me happy." He let her go and she kissed his cheek and ran over to Mama who had set a chair for her at the folding table.

"Pasha, eat," Tavis ordered his friend. The little Yorkie, Chewie, sat at Pasha's feet, looking up at his plate of food. Her short tail vibrated and he gave her some meat.

"Da. Thank you, my friend. I think she will rest at peace here in this little spot."

"She will. Pasha, we have one more thing we need to do and I need your help. I had contact with my brother, Tanner, an hour ago on the sat phone. As soon as Bouncer and the chief finish whatever they're doing to the helo, we need to go get him. He wants off his boat. His chief engineer is Russian and wants to go home to his family. Tanner's family is here. Duck is dead. Bouncer needs a co-pilot and while you weren't my first choice, it's just a lack of options," Tavis explained to his friend with a toothy smile.

Pasha thought about it, then smiled too. "Da. I will go."

"Hey, Tavis. Helo's fixed. Ready when you are." Bouncer and the chief were walking up Mama's driveway to get some food.

"Roger that!" Tavis said as Moira turned to stare at her husband.

"What does he mean, Tavis Kinley?" Moira asked pointedly.

"She may actually kill you this time," Pasha said as a large main battle tank turned onto the street followed by an LAV. They rolled into the cul-de-sac and stopped, and everyone gathered at the end of Mama's driveway to meet them as they dismounted and piled out of the LAV's rear doors. Gale and Layla ran up to Joey to welcome her, and Tavis joined them.

"What the hell happened here, Gale?" Joey said, looking around. There was a crushed truck and spent ammo casings all over the place. Another tank and APC along with the Pantsir truck.

"We had a party, Joey. It's over now. Gale can fill you in," Tavis said as An and his tank crew beelined toward the smell of food.

"Jonesy! Tacos!" Fletch yelled.

"Yes! I guess there are tacos in the apocalypse," Jones replied.

There were other soldiers here as well, Tavis saw. Not Marines. He walked over to the one who looked like he was in charge.

"I'm Tavis Kinley, who're you all?"

"Sergeant Sullivan. Call me Sully. This is what's left of my platoon from Bagram, which doesn't exist anymore. Are those tacos?" Sully said.

"Indeed. Wow, Bagram's gone, huh? Help yourself, Sully," Tavis said.

"Yeah, thanks. We took off just before the Russians nuked it," Sully said and waved his men up the driveway, where Mama was ushering them into a line, and they were doing what she said. Alex and Natasha walked up to the group, followed by Viktor and Val.

"I'm glad you're back, Mrs. Washington. This is my mom, Natasha," Alex said to Joey with a smile.

"What? I thought—?" Joey started.

"We've got time, babe," Gale said and Layla gave Alex a tight hug.

"Tavis, the four of us, all here by different ways and for different reasons, find ourselves without a home and a bit out of place," Viktor said, interrupting the hugging and chatting.

"You all are now part of our family here. You're welcome for as long as you want to stay, which is for a long while, I hope. There will be a lot of work to do to get back on our feet and whatever we have to do to survive now. This is your place now if you want it to be," Gale said to them.

"We do," Viktor said simultaneously with Val.

"I wouldn't be anywhere else but here with Alex. I'm not going anywhere," Natasha said and put an arm around Alex and squeezed her. Alex smiled for the first time in a long time, Gale noticed.

"Gale, I have been relieved of duty. Replaced by General Kobayashi. I'm home for good," Joey said and Gale kissed her and Layla piled into them.

Tavis felt a full happiness watching all this. Everyone was here and safe, with the obvious exceptions and sadness that would go along with that, but he had one more thing to do. He turned and came face-to-face with his wife.

"What da fook do you think you're doin'? Pasha just informed me what you're up to. You can't leave us again," she said.

He'd dreaded this.

An hour later, Tavis was sitting in the back of the helo with the chief while Bouncer lifted off. Pasha was in the co-pilot's seat. The bloody, plushy panda was secure by the instrument panel in front of him. It had taken a long conversation with a lot of yelling, most of it by his wife, to convince her that he had to go. He needed to retrieve his brother and whoever else wanted to come back with them.

"Moira is big mad at you, yes?" Pasha said over the comms.

"Aye, big mad."

"Relax, you are still alive. Is win-win," Pasha said, and the chief laughed.

Tavis looked out the window. Everyone, including his kids and Moira, were standing below waving. He waved back. Bouncer turned the helo and gained altitude and hovered. Tavis watched as Simmons tossed his grenade into the pile of rubble and wood that used to be Alex's home. It went up violently. At least they wouldn't have to deal with the decaying bodies of the bad guys. He was glad he wouldn't be there to dig the graves for the rest. He'd done too much of that over his life already.

THIRTY-SEVEN

Nearly two and a half hours later, the chief shook Tavis awake. He grabbed his FAL rifle and sat up straight and looked around. Getting his bearings, he took a deep breath and rubbed his bearded face.

"Easy, man. You good?" the chief asked.

"Aye. Good to go. Dreams," he said.

"Roger that. We're five minutes out." Tavis looked into the cockpit and Pasha had the controls. He thought better of slinging pilot insults at his friend since they were about to land.

"Copy. I hope Alfred and Owen are still there," Tavis said.

A couple of minutes later they landed at the same spot they had before and Tavis was rewarded with waves from the two old and grizzled Marines.

"Hey, Tavis. That transport plane wasn't there before. 10 o'clock," Bouncer said. He looked out his window as the rotors slowed and sure enough, there was a Chinese transport on the tarmac about two hundred yards from them. He opened the door and hopped out with his rifle, ducking as he moved around the front of the helo and walked toward Al and Owen, who were standing next to the same table they'd been sitting at days before.

"Whose Chinese transport is that over there, guys?" Tavis yelled. As he approached, a man in a flight suit and a short woman in battle fatigues stepped out of the hanger they had their table set up in front of. Al and Owen weren't armed.

Tavis quickly raised his rifle. "Who're they?"

"Easy does it! They're okay. New arrivals. Got here last night," Al said with his hands up, motioning Tavis to lower his rifle. He did, mostly. But he stayed focused on the new people.

"You! Come out here. Who are you?" Tavis ordered.

The two walked into the sunlight. There was no snow here and it was a mild temperature with a breeze from the ocean. The short woman spoke first.

"My name is Gao. This is Tang. He is the pilot of that transport. My captain is in the hanger sleeping off his hangover," she said and Tavis saw that they were both armed with pistols, but holstered. What was going on here?

"Yeah, they got here last night," Owen said. "Had a tense few minutes with them until we came to the mutual conclusion that they weren't real Commies and we decided to welcome them with beers. Might as well drink and swap stories. Told them you may be coming back this way at some point. So they decided to stay. Don't have enough fuel in the truck for the tanks on that thing, anyway. Enough to fill yours, though."

Then the other Chinese soldier stepped out of the hanger with an AK-47 in one hand.

"I am Captain Chao. Formerly of the Army of the People's Republic of China," the man said.

"Formerly?" Tavis asked as Pasha joined him.

"Yes. We stand apart. Also, we are not Communists. Just soldiers," Chao said.

"I'm not a soldier. I'm a pilot," Tang added.

"Correct. He's a pilot," Gao said.

Tavis looked over the three. The captain was a serious sort. Tang was of slight build and looked fairly harmless. Gao on the other hand had a scowl on her face. Had it the whole time.

"Okay, Al, Owen, can you work with the chief to refuel the helo? We're headed back out to the ship to pick up my brother."

"Sure thing. Y'all don't start any wars while we're at it, you hear me?" Al said to the group.

"I wouldn't dare even say anything amiss to Sunshine here," Tavis said and smiled, gesturing at Gao, and she frowned even more if that was possible.

"What does 'sunshine' mean?" she asked.

"It means that you've been staring daggers at me since I walked up. Sunshine is the opposite of that. It's a joke," Tavis explained.

"Oh. Ha," she replied without smiling. They spent the next ten to fifteen minutes sharing their stories while the helo was refueled.

"So, the three of you are looking to get back to China then?" Tavis asked after they relayed where they'd come from and what they'd seen.

"We obviously can't fly with no fuel. Or, easily obtained fuel. You're going out to a ship? I sailed with my father on his fishing trawler before the Air Force took me," Tang said.

"My family is near Tang's. What about it, Captain?" Gao said.

"Fine. I'll get my gear," Chao said and walked back into the hangar.

"They killed his woman," Gao explained quietly. "The Chinese Ministry of Security killed her. She was supposed to come with us."

"Aye. You're with us then. The deal is we land on the ship. You three stay, and we leave with whoever wants to come," Tavis said.

"Agreed. It's not perfect. Nothing is now, but it's our best current chance of getting home," Tang replied.

A few minutes later, Bouncer yelled from the helo, "Fueled and ready to go!"

"Get your things and get aboard. Al, Owen, thank you again. You'll see us back here in a few hours, probably on our way back," Tavis said, and they all shook hands and were back on the helo and lifting off. It was more crowded now with the three newcomers. Two facing rear and three facing forward. Tavis had given Bouncer and Pasha his brother's approximate location. They were about two hundred miles out and southeast of Lejeune, little over an hour. He closed his eyes again but didn't sleep.

A long while later, Tavis opened his eyes as the helicopter dipped suddenly. He sat up and leaned forward.

"What was that?" he said into his mic.

"I'm having slushiness in the collective," Pasha said.

"You mean sluggishness? Shit," Tavis replied.

"Is okay. Ship in front of us."

"Motherfucker!" the chief said.

"Looks like our patch didn't hold, Chief!" Bouncer said. "I've got controls."

Pasha let go of his sticks.

"If you crash us, Pasha, my wife will kill you."

"Yes, my friend, she is only thing I'm scared of. We will not crash," he said.

"I don't know. We might," Bouncer said as he brought the helo in next to the ship and paced it, then slid the helo to the left and hovered over the deck. Tavis held his breath and closed his eyes. The helo, in true form, bounced on the deck and then settled. They quickly cut the engines, and Tavis waited for the rotors to stop.

"For fook's sake! Now what? Can we fly again?" he asked, looking at the chief.

"I don't know. I'll need some time and see what the engineer has on board," the chief said. Tavis shook his head and opened the door and exited with everyone else, just happy to not be in the water. His brother, Tanner, came walking up to him with a cigar in his mouth and gave him a bear hug.

"That looked sketchy, Tav," Tanner said.

"Aye, had a bit of a skirmish back in the 'hood, and the helo took a round in the upper parts there. They fixed it. Until it wasn't fixed a few minutes ago. Can your engineer work with the chief and the pilot to see what can be done?"

"Of course. We'll get it worked out. How's the family?" he asked as he waved his engineer over, who was on deck to watch the helo land.

"They're good. They all asked after you, except Moira. I've left her with the kids one too many times. If I don't get back in one piece, she's gonna kill me."

"Well, let's let them work, and you and I can have a smoke. Who did you bring here?" Tanner tilted his head at the three odd passengers.

"Captain Chao, Tang, Gao, this is my brother, Tanner. He's the skipper of the boat. MV *Shark*. We picked these three up in Lejeune. They are not Commies." Tavis smiled, and Gao squinted at him.

"Good to meet you, Tanner." Chao shook the skipper's hand. "We are not Commies. We are only looking to get closer to home. China."

"Ah. Okay, well, if we can get this helo fixed up, I'm going with them, you all can stay with the boat. Engineer's staying as well. He'll be glad of the extra hands." Tanner handed Tavis a cigar and lit it for him, and they left the captain, Tang, and Gao and walked to the starboard railing. Rain misted from a steel-gray sky.

"Are our friends still down there?" Tavis asked, puffing on the cigar.

"Aye, they're about. Blackstone surfaced his periscope about thirty minutes ago and sent me a message via Morse code. They're tracking multiple surface contacts well north of our position. We've been getting intermittent ham radio broadcasts out of Florida and from around the Gulf of Mexico. Looks like it's no longer an American body of water. The Cubans and Venezuelans are up in there asserting themselves, and the Mexicans are around as well, but it's unknown whose side they're on," Tanner explained.

"Well, without the American Navy, others will step in to fill the void," Tavis said. Pasha joined them then and put a hand on Tavis's shoulder.

"I have good news, bad news," Pasha said.

"Well, out with it," Tavis said.

"Good news is we are alive. Bad news, we almost weren't. Hydraulics are complete failure. The repair they made held us to here, then it broke wide open. Bouncer says we won't make it back to land if we try a quick fix. They need specific parts. Can't fly. What do we do now?" Pasha said. Tavis turned and looked out at the ocean. The cold, gray Atlantic. He flicked the cigar over the rail and rubbed his eyes.

"That's not optimal," Tanner said.

"Clearly not!" Tavis shouted.

"Look, we've also been hearing some chatter to the south of us. It's a ways, but there seems to be a flotilla of ships south. Didn't mention it 'cause didn't think it was relevant since we were leaving. We should go south. We can't go north due to the heavy Russian naval presence. Europe is a darkened mess. South is our course," Tanner said.

"Well, you're the captain," Tavis said.

"I am. Look, little brother, sometimes the correct choice is the hard one. We have the armored personnel carriers. We can find a port."

"A port where, Tanner? We can't go north. Africa? Brazil? Where?" Tavis was losing it.

"We go around. Left or right doesn't matter, same thing," Pasha said.

"What do you mean left or right?" Tavis asked.

"He's right, Tav. We go around. It'll be a long way, but it's doable. We go north; we get sunk. But don't forget, we've got friends below," Tanner said.

"Okay, fine. Left or right what?"

"Which Cape, of course—Horn or Good Hope? Tip of Chile or South Africa?" Tanner said and pulled a flask from his jacket pocket and handed it to his brother who took it and tipped it up.

"Bloody 'ell! We go south. We'll make that decision if and when we get there."

The End of the Middle.

ACKNOWLEDGEMENTS

I want to thank the many people that helped me with my stupid questions as I wrote *A Dance of Devils*. I will miss some here and I'm sorry for that. It's the price I pay for taking so long to write it as over time, I've forgotten a lot of my questions and who I asked them to.

First and foremost, I am honored that all of these men gave me their time and knowledge and I'm deeply grateful to each of them, as well as to the ones that I've missed. I'm also thankful for the absolute truckload of shenanigans on the Twitter (X) timeline from many who are not mentioned here, but are immortalized in this novel in one way or the other. Forever.

CPT Eric Bohlen (former 82 Airborne) – Eric was my muse of sorts. He was the inspiration for my paratroopers. He complained there was no Airborne in Mongol Moon, so I got that idea in my head and here we are. He kept me honest with my Airborne scenes.

Pickle – Yeah, that's all you get. Pickle makes some amazing hot sauce about as frequently as I write books and he knows something about tanks and armored personnel carriers cause he's regularly in one. Helped me sort out some scenes properly.

MAJ Shawn Morris – Shawn was instrumental in ensuring that my armor scenes were plausible and technically accurate. He helped me breathe life into Alice. I feel that he loves her just as much as I do. Maybe more.

MAJ F. Davis – The good Major was my first choice when I had a conundrum with one scene regarding night vision. I was stuck there and couldn't move forward. He completely sorted out my questions with enthusiasm and actually gave me options to go with regarding what was possible. Was perfect.

MSgt Shane Kelly – When I needed to know about what would carry my Airborne (above) to their dropzone, Shane was my first ping. I needed to really understand the interior workings of a C5 Galaxy and he came through for me in spades.

J. Copenhaver LT,SC,USN – I had some pretty interesting (for me) questions about submarines, sonar, and needed to plug some plot holes and my man provided me with the answers that allowed me to pick and choose what I could do plausibly.

Dale Stark, Lt. Colonel (Ret) – When you need Brrrrrrt! in the book, who's brains are better to pick. Dale was gracious to take the time to get on the phone and talk about what was possible and realistic for the A10 with what I had in mind. I got the idea from Ukraine and the fictional "Ghost of Kiev" coupled with Dale's daily Warthog Good Morning pics on Twitter (X). I'm honored to immortalize an A10 with Dale's help.

Terry Schappert – Last, but certainly not least. Terry has been gracious with his time on the phone with Mongol Moon feedback and supporting me on the Twitter (X) timeline as well. There was no one else on my list to bring narration life to the Mongol Moon world than Terry with his sultry voice.

ABOUT THE AUTHOR

Mark Sibley is a corporate crisis manager and war gamer. He's developed and facilitated over a hundred war games for various organizations over the years and managed as many real-world crises for those organizations. This experience, along with a life-long dream of writing a novel, provided him fertile ground for pulling together all the aspects of this story and developing them into what became Mongol Moon. If you tell a war gamer that a particular bad thing can't happen, that war gamer will come up with a plausible scenario to prove you wrong...eventually/.

He is a life-long Virginian and lives in the Commonwealth with his wife, three kids, and current pack of female terriers, two Boston Terriers, Izzy (the Alpha) and Dobby (the one without a brain), and the ever-ferocious Chewie the Wookie, a five-pound Yorkshire Terrier with one fang. At any given time, there is also a foster dog at the house, rounding out their pack.

You can follow him on Twitter **@mnsibley**

* 9 7 9 8 8 8 9 2 2 0 5 1 0 *